P9-DOB-904

WITHDRAWN

As I step out into the sand, I look up at Nova Vita, huge and bloody red in the sky.

The planets arc out from the star in various crescent shapes—watery Nibiru is the closest, followed by little Deva and dusty Pax. Far off in the opposite direction is frozen and war-ravaged Titan, dwarfed in the Gaian sky though it's at least three times the size of Gaia in reality. I'm one of the few people in the whole system who can boast of having been to each of them, and a few dozen times at that—with the exception of Pax, which we visited on one especially illegal trip that required us to wear full antiradiation space suits. Yet every time I look up from a planet's surface, I get a pang of longing to explore that vast emptiness between them.

I'm torn from my thoughts by someone clearing their throat. I turn toward my mother, standing a few paces away with both hands in the air. I raise my eyebrows at the strange pose and the furious expression on her face.

"What...?" I cut off, finally noticing what she's seen. A dozen armed and white-uniformed Gaian officers are circling the ship, with more still trickling out from behind *Fortuna*, where they must have been waiting for us to exit. Most of them have their hands on their weapons, and all of them are now staring at me.

I sigh and put my hands up.

NOV 2019

WITHDRAWN

FORTUNA

The Nova Vita Protocol:
Book One

KRISTYN MERBETH

Mount Laurel Library
100 Walt Whitman Avenue
Mount Laurel, NJ 08054-9539
856-234-7319
www.mountlaurellibrary.org

orbit

www.orbitbooks.net

This book is a work of fiction. Names, characters, places, and incidents are the product of the author's imagination or are used fictitiously. Any resemblance to actual events, locales, or persons, living or dead, is coincidental.

Copyright © 2019 by Kristyn Merbeth
Excerpt from *A Big Ship at the Edge of the Universe* copyright © 2018 by Alex White
Excerpt from *Adrift* copyright © 2018 by Rob Boffard

Author photograph by SunStreet Photo
Cover design by Lisa Marie Pompilio
Cover art by Arcangel and Shutterstock
Cover copyright © 2019 by Hachette Book Group, Inc.

Hachette Book Group supports the right to free expression and the value of copyright. The purpose of copyright is to encourage writers and artists to produce the creative works that enrich our culture.

The scanning, uploading, and distribution of this book without permission is a theft of the author's intellectual property. If you would like permission to use material from the book (other than for review purposes), please contact permissions@hbgusa.com. Thank you for your support of the author's rights.

Orbit
Hachette Book Group
1290 Avenue of the Americas
New York, NY 10104
orbitbooks.net

First Edition: November 2019

Orbit is an imprint of Hachette Book Group.
The Orbit name and logo are trademarks of Little, Brown Book Group Limited.

The publisher is not responsible for websites (or their content) that are not owned by the publisher.

The Hachette Speakers Bureau provides a wide range of authors for speaking events. To find out more, go to www.hachettespeakersbureau.com or call (866) 376-6591.

Library of Congress Cataloging-in-Publication Data
Names: Merbeth, K. S., author.
Title: Fortuna / Kristyn Merbeth.
Description: First edition. | New York : Orbit, 2019 | Series: The nova vita protocol ; book 1
Identifiers: LCCN 2019015305 | ISBN 9780316453998 (trade pbk.) | ISBN 9780316454001 (ebook) | ISBN 9780316453981 (library ebook) | ISBN 9781549100000 (downloadable audio book)
Subjects: LCSH: Smugglers—Fiction. | Outer space—Fiction. | GSAFD: Science fiction
Classification: LCC PS3613.E67 F67 2019 | DDC 813/.6—dc23
LC record available at https://lccn.loc.gov/2019015305

ISBNs: 978-0-316-45399-8 (trade paperback), 978-0-316-45400-1 (ebook)

Printed in the United States of America

LSC-C

10 9 8 7 6 5 4 3 2 1

For my brothers, Todd and Lucas

CHAPTER ONE

Fortuna

Scorpia

Fortuna's cockpit smells like sweat and whiskey, and loose screws rattle with every thump of music. I'm sprawled in the pilot's chair, legs stretched out and boots resting atop the control panel forming a half circle around me. A bottle of whiskey dangles from one of my hands; the other taps out the song's beat on the control wheel.

Normally, this is my favorite place to be: in my chair, behind the wheel, staring out at open space and its endless possibilities. I'm a daughter of the stars, after all. But I've been in the cockpit for nearly eight hours now, urging this ship as fast as she can go to make sure we unload our cargo on time, and my body is starting to ache from it. Scrappy little *Fortuna* is my home, the only one I've ever known, but she wasn't built for comfort. She was built to take a beating.

My shift at the wheel wasn't so bad for the first six hours, but once the others went to bed, I had to shut the door leading to the rest of the ship, and the cockpit soon grew cramped and hot. No way around it, though. I need the music to stay awake, and my family needs the quiet to sleep. Someone needs to be coherent enough to throw on a smile and lie their ass off to customs when we get there, and it's not gonna be me.

I yawn, pushing sweaty, dark hair out of my face. Envy stings me as I think of my younger siblings, snug in bed, but recedes as I remember they're actually strapped into the launch chairs in their respective rooms, with gooey mouth-guards shoved between their teeth and cottony plugs stuffed up their ears. I don't know how they manage to sleep with all that, but it's necessary in case of a rough descent, the likelihood of which is rising with every sip of whiskey I take. *Fortuna*'s autopilot can land the ship on its own, but it tends to lurch and scrape and thud its way there, with little regard for the comfort of its occupants or whether or not they hurl up their dinner when they arrive. Some pilot finesse makes things run more smoothly.

Given that, I'd normally avoid too much hard liquor while at the wheel. But as soon as Gaia came into sight, anxiety blossomed in my gut. Now, the planet fills my view out the front panel and dread sloshes in my stomach. It's a beautiful place, I'll admit that. Vast stretches of water dotted with land masses, wispy clouds drifting across, like a damn painting or something. Historians say that after centuries of searching for humanity's new home, the original settlers wept with joy at the first glimpse of Gaia. I, on the other hand, always go straight for the bottle strapped to the bottom of my chair.

Beautiful Gaia. Rich in alien tech and bad memories. Ever since Corvus abandoned us to fight in his useless war, even the good ones from my childhood have turned bitter.

"Damn," I mutter, and take another sip. I've once again broken the rule I invented in the early hours of my boredom. Every time I think of my older brother, that's another drink. It's a tough rule when my memories of Gaia are so deeply entwined with memories of him.

I was seven when we left Gaia. It's been twenty years since we were grounded there. And after a brief stop on Deva, where Lyre was born, we spent another six years on Nibiru, while she and the twins were still too young to live on the ship. Those were better years, when we spent our days playing and fishing in the endless ocean and our nights sleeping in a pile on our single mattress. Yet even then I could never shake my anxiety that Momma wouldn't come back one day, and I'd be stranded again. I never felt safe like I did on *Fortuna*, never stopped waiting for someone to notice I didn't belong. The days on Gaia wouldn't loosen their hold on me.

And every time I see the planet, it all rushes back to the surface. Memories of Corvus's smile; of digging through trash for food; of playing tag with him in the narrow streets of Levian, the capital city; of huge alien statues staring down at me with their faceless visages.

Memories of Momma wearing hooded Gaian finery to blend in on the crowded street and saying, *"It's just a game, Scorpia,"* as she showed me the best way to slip my hands into someone's pocket without them noticing. When she taught me my first con, dressing me up like a little lost Gaian child, she said, *"It's like telling a joke, but you're the only one who knows the punchline."* Guess Momma didn't anticipate that once I started, I wouldn't be able to stop thinking that way. Or maybe she didn't think I'd live long enough for it to matter. I probably wouldn't have, if Corvus hadn't been around to get me out of trouble. Corvus, who was never any good at lying, so he went to school while I learned to be a criminal.

"Damn." I sip again. Through the viewing panel, Gaia looms closer.

As I wipe my mouth, I glance over the expanse of screens and gauges and lights all around me, tracking the radar, fuel tank, and various systems. The numbers are blurry, but the lights are all the soothing red of Nova Vita, which means everything is running fine. Good enough for me. I take another swig, and choke on it as the ship shudders.

It's not a particularly menacing rumble, yet the hairs on the back of my neck stand straight up. I let my boots thud to the metal floor one after another, dragged by the ship's artificial gravity, and frown at the panels. Nothing on the radar. It could be some debris too small to pick up, a cough in the machinery...or a cloaked ship. It's rare for us to have company out here, when interplanetary trade and travel have all but ground to a halt due to the tense relations between planets. Rarer still near Gaia, whose border laws are tightest of all. But it could be those pirate bastards on the *Red Baron* hounding us again. If they picked up cloaking tech, we're in trouble. Not for the first time, I wish *Fortuna* was outfitted with weaponry for self-defense—but of course, weapons on ships are illegal, and we'd never be able to land anywhere in the system if we had them. With current laws, the planets are wary enough about ships without the added threat of weapons on them.

Indicators are all a solid red. There's not so much as a blip out of place. Still, my skin prickles. *Fortuna* is saying something. I slap the button to shut off the music, tilt my head to one side, and listen to the silence.

The next rumble shakes the whole craft.

The bridge goes dark. Every screen and every light disappears. My sharp intake of breath echoes in the darkness.

"*Fortuna?*" I ask, as if the ship will answer. I clutch tighter to the whiskey with one hand and the wheel with the other as my muddled brain tries to work out what else to do. I've dealt with my fair share of malfunctions, but I've never seen the ship go dark like this.

The lights blink back online. A relieved laugh bubbles out of me, but cuts off as I realize all of my screens are crackling with static.

I smack a few buttons, producing no effect, and turn from one end of the control panel to the other. My eyes find the system indicators on the far right. Life support and the engine are still lit red, signaling that they're online and functioning. But navigation is the shockingly unnatural green of system failure. Radar is green. Autopilot is green.

The ship has everything she needs to keep flying, but not what she needs to land.

"Aw, shit." Judging by the fact that we haven't been blasted or boarded yet, this isn't the *Red Baron* or any other outside interference. It's an internal malfunction. I flash back to my sister Lyre begging for new engine parts on Deva, and curse under my breath. Our little engineer is usually too cautious for her own good, but it seems she was right this time.

I take a final sip from my bottle, cap it, and tuck it between my boots. Once it's secure, I reach toward the neon-green emergency alarm button on the left side of the control panel. At the last moment, I stop short.

Hitting that button will send alarms screaming and green lights flaring through the ship, cutting through my family's earplugs and waking them from their strapped-in-for-landing slumber. My ever-scowling mother will be here in less than a minute, barking orders, taking control. And at the first sniff of whiskey in the cockpit, she'll relieve me from my duty and send me to bed.

Fortuna will stay in orbit until everything's at 100 percent and I've passed a BAC test…which means we'll miss the drop-off on Gaia *and* the side job I hoped to pull off beforehand.

And I'll be the family screwup. Again. One step further from ever amounting to more than that, or ever prying my future out of Momma's iron grip. One step further from *Fortuna* belonging to me. I can already hear her usual speech: *"You're the oldest now. You can't keep doing this shit."*

Plus, this side job is important. There's not much profit in it, but I can use all the credits I can get after I blew most of my last earnings on Deva. I can't deny I'm looking forward to seeing the pretty face of my favorite client, too.

And, of course, I want to see Momma's expression when I tell her I pulled off a job on my own. I know that she was grooming Corvus to be in charge one day—Corvus, who was always so obedient and ready to follow in her footsteps—but he's been gone for three years now, fighting in the war on his home-planet. We all have to accept that he's not coming back. Instead, Momma's stuck with me.

This deal I set up is the perfect chance to prove that's not such a terrible thing. And once the ship falls to me, I'll finally have a place in the universe that's all my own. A home that nobody can kick me out of. I'll get to make my own decisions, be in charge of my own life. I'll keep my family together and make things better for all of us, like Corvus always promised he would before he abandoned us.

But if we don't make it in time, this will just be one more disappointment on the list.

I sit back in my seat, running my tongue over my teeth. I'll have to land the ship as planned. Even if it's bumpy, and even if Momma smells the whiskey on me once we land, she can't give me too much shit if I get us planet-side intact and on time.

It's a damn nice thought...but it's been a long time since I landed the ship without autopilot. And, lest the blurry vision and stink of whiskey in the cockpit aren't enough to remind me, I'm drunk enough that I could get jail time for flying a simple hovercraft on most planets. There's no law out here to punish me for operating a spacecraft under the influence, but down there the law of gravity waits, ready to deal swift and deadly judgment if I fuck this up.

"So don't fuck it up," I tell myself. I suck in a slow breath, blow it out through my nose, and hit the button to connect to Gaian air control. Static crackles through the speakers, followed by a booming robotic voice. I wince, hastily lowering the volume.

"You have reached Gaian customs. State your registration number and purpose. Do not enter Gaian airspace without confirmation or you will be destroyed."

I know the automatic Gaian "greeting" by heart, and I also know it's not bullshit. As a kid, I saw many unregistered ships shot out of the sky before they got close to landing. The locals would cheer like it was some grand fireworks show. I always felt bad for the poor souls. If they were entering Gaian airspace illegally, they had to be desperate. Using the opportunity to pick some Gaian pockets felt a little like justice.

"This is pilot Scorpia Kaiser of merchant vessel *Fortuna*," I say into the mic, working hard to keep my words from slurring into one another. "Registration number…" I run a finger down a list etched on one of my side panels, and blink until the numbers come into focus. Of course, the Gaian registry is the longest number of them all. Damn Gaians and their regulations. "Two-dash-zero-two-one-eight-eight-dash-one-zero-three-six," I say. "Registered to Captain Auriga Kaiser, Gaian citizen. We're delivering freeze-dried produce from Deva."

It's not the whole truth, but it's not a lie, either. If customs agents peek into our cargo crates, they'll find neat packages of fruits and vegetables dried and sealed for space travel. The good shit is well hidden. We're professionals, after all.

"Checking registration," the robotic voice says. There's a pause, followed by a click. "Checking landing schedule." Another pause, click. "Ship two-dash-zero-two-one-eight-eight-dash-one-zero-three-six, you are cleared for entry. Noncitizens are not permitted to travel beyond the landing zone. Entry elsewhere will be considered a hostile act. Welcome to Gaia."

"Yeah, I'm feeling real welcome," I mutter, severing the radio connection. But the recording has provided a good reminder of what's at stake here. If I crash, we all die. If I land so much as an inch outside the legal landing zone, same shit. I roll my shoulders back and slip the safety belts across my chest, clicking them into place and yanking the straps tight. "Okay, *Fortuna*," I say. "Hope you're ready for this. It's gonna be a rough landing."

I fish in my pocket for the gooey lump of my mouth-guard, chomp down, and shove the control wheel forward.

CHAPTER TWO

Family

Corvus

Monitor the radar. Check the armory. Count the supplies. Three weeks in this outpost, and I've started every morning with the same routine. Three weeks in the middle of nowhere, with no orders other than to hold this position and keep an eye out for anything unusual. We haven't had so much as a glimpse of the enemy. General Altair must have stationed us here for a reason, but my patience is wearing thin, both with the situation and my stir-crazy team. Our skills are put to waste as lookouts. Not a day has gone by without them reminding me of that fact and pestering me for news. I swear, these soldiers can be worse than my little siblings were.

Given that, this time alone would normally be a blessing. Titans have infuriatingly little regard for personal space or privacy, and over these three years I've learned to snatch moments of solitude when I can. That's why I've gotten into the habit of waking up an hour before the rest of my team to fulfill duties like these, rather than passing the chores on to them.

But lately, my thoughts weigh heavily on me, and now I have nothing to distract me from them. My hands stay busy as I run through the morning routine, but my mind wanders, barely aware of the gray walls around me or the dim lights overhead or my breath fogging in the air. My cold fingers punch in the passcodes to enter each doorway without pausing to think about it. Everything is the same as every other morning, and it all fades into background noise. But this time I pause, running my fingers over the brand on the inside of my right wrist, those eight numbers and squiggly lines they marked on me when I entered the service. Now, my mandatory years are over. But no matter where I go, the war will always be a part of me. What if this is where I belong?

Perhaps this was Altair's intent all along: to give me time to think. He knows I have a choice to make. Merely a few weeks ago, I thought it was already made. After we lost Uwe to a bomb on our last mission, with the image of the explosion waiting every time I closed my eyes, I sent a message to my family without a moment's hesitation. All these years, I never thought anything could convince me to stay here and keep fighting in this awful war. I believed it was the desire to leave that kept me moving. It was memories of my family that gave me the resolve to do terrible things, anything necessary to survive. My only goal after enlisting was to live long enough to return to them, and protect my siblings like I always swore I would.

When it was just the two of us on Gaia, Scorpia was always the one to take care of me, to lie and steal and do all the things I couldn't do. I was never any good at it, so instead Momma paid for some fake papers to get me into a Gaian school, calling it an investment in the family's future.

Once we went to Nibiru, where Scorpia couldn't shake her bad habits and found an even worse one in a bottle, I took that mantle upon myself. I looked after the little ones, tried to keep

Scorpia from drowning in her vices, did my best to soothe Momma's anger by being the perfect son she wanted me to be. Scorpia and I would huddle by Nibiru's ocean, or later in the ship's cargo bay, and whisper about our dreams for the future. We would talk about all of us having a say in the family business rather than being threatened into following orders. No more risky jobs, no more Primus technology, no more weapons. *"When I'm in charge, we can be whoever we want to be,"* I would always say.

But that was before. Before I became attached to this place and its people. Before I believed that I could do something good for this system rather than returning to my family to smuggle drugs and other contraband. Altair's offer changed everything. I've climbed rapidly through the ranks here, guided by the general's hand—and now, he wants more for me. He wants me to work directly under him, learn from him, take his place as a general one day. I wouldn't be another pawn in this war . . . I would be one of the people running it, shaping a better future for my people. Just like I always dreamed of doing for my family, but on a much grander scale. Here, I could make a difference.

The door to the supply room bangs open and startles me from my thoughts. A stocky blond woman, our latest recruit after we lost Uwe, stands in the doorway. Her face flushes as she sees me. Three years on Titan, and it still shocks me how their skin is commonly pale enough to show emotion in a surge of startling color. The system has a wide range of skin tones, but this is the one planet where the majority of people are fair enough for my own tawny coloring to stand out.

I clear my throat and turn to face her, straightening my posture so that I stand—just barely—taller than her. My height is yet another reminder that I may be Titan by birth but not by blood. Elsewhere in the system I stand above the average, but not here.

"Sergeant Kaiser, I'm sorry. I didn't mean to intrude. Everyone's looking for you, and it's—they sent me," she says, the words coming out in a jumble. She's still new enough to be nervous around me, and new enough that it takes me a few moments to remember her name. I would feel bad about it, but I've seen far too many new faces come and go.

"Ivennie," I say, remembering. Ivennie Smirnova. "I've told you, Corvus is fine."

"Yes, sir, Corvus, sir," she says. Her face turns a deeper shade of red, which I didn't think was possible. I suppress a sigh. It always takes recruits a while to accept that they're part of a team now and don't need to follow the same rigidity as during training. Our army has a strict hierarchy, and we're always expected to show deference to superiors, but within a team, things are different. We're encouraged to be close. Intimate, even.

So I lay a hand on Ivennie's shoulder. The act still feels odd to me after all these years, too familiar given we've only known each other for a few weeks. But the new recruit leans into my hand despite her earlier anxiety, relief crossing her face. All of the Titans complain about being touch-starved after basic training.

"You don't need to be so formal with me. Here, we're"—the next words stick in my throat, as they always do, but I finish the phrase I learned from the general—"a family."

She stares up at me with wide eyes. I can't bring myself to force a smile, but I give her an encouraging nod. *Family.* That's what we're supposed to say, anyway. Altair taught me that physical touch is so deeply ingrained in Titan culture that they don't bother trying to stamp it out in the military. He said it's good for them to feel that closeness, when many of them have lost their blood relations to the war. But I suspect he knows the truth: that nobody would fight as long or as hard as we do without something to care about, even if that something is a lie.

I step past the still-blushing new recruit into the dim underground hallway. As much as I've tried to make myself believe it these last few years, and as much as I've grown to care about them, I've always known deep down that my team could never truly be family. I already have one waiting for me—a family bound together by blood.

Titans, who often grow up in large, blended families with multiple sets of parents to fill in any gaps left by the war, don't place much value in blood. But I wasn't raised as a Titan. I still remember the time I dared to ask about who my father was at dinner, and the taste of copper in my mouth after Momma hit me—one of the few times she raised a hand against me. My siblings were just as shocked as I was. *"You have no fathers,"* she told us in the silence, using that tone of hers that brooked no argument. *"Forget about them. Forget your birth-planets, too. The blood you share is the only thing that matters. No one outside this room is ever going to accept any of you, so you need to look out for each other."*

I shake off the memory. The past has been haunting me far too often these days, and the distraction could get me killed out here.

"Take me to the others," I tell Ivennie. She rushes to obey, leading me to the stairwell. This outpost was built to house a much larger unit than ours if necessary, and it takes a while to traverse the stairs. I can feel Ivennie's eyes on me as we walk, practically hear the questions on her tongue.

We haven't spent much time together, just the two of us, since she arrived. Moments of one-on-one time, like solitude, are rare here. Our team is expected to spend every moment together: eating, training, showering, sleeping. We're expected to share everything. *Privacy leads to secrets, secrets to jealousy, and jealousy is a disease of the soul*, a common Titan saying goes. I try to respect Titan customs, I truly do, but some I can't bring myself to follow. Just as Momma always told me, no matter how hard I try, I'll never truly be a Titan.

Though I suspect I've been avoiding Ivennie for other reasons, as well. Knowing I may be leaving soon makes me loath to add another name to the list of people I care about here. Especially so with Uwe's loss still so fresh. The rest of my team has been hesitant to welcome the rookie as well.

The shock of Uwe's death lingers in all of us. Before that, it had been over three months since we lost someone. We had fallen into a rhythm, a strong team dynamic, and now everyone is struggling once again to figure out where they fit, trying to adjust themselves around the missing piece my off-worlder customs leave.

We shouldn't have lost Uwe. It was a stupid, senseless death. I've replayed the day a thousand times over, running through all the ways I could've prevented it.

We were in Niivya, a border town freshly liberated from the enemy. Drunk on victory, newly armed with information Daniil had extracted from a captured Isolationist sergeant. The townspeople were eager to celebrate with us. Feeding us, filling our mugs when they were empty. Putting us at ease.

Everyone but me was very intoxicated when word arrived that a child had fallen into a sewer. I should have gone alone. But I couldn't carry both a child and a light in the darkness of the sewers, and so someone needed to come with me. Since Uwe lost the hand of cards, it fell to him. He was drunk—staggering, singing drunk. He nearly fell on his face when we dropped down into the sewers to look for her.

When we found the child, she wasn't injured at all. Instead, she was clutching an explosive device in her hands. When Uwe raised the light, she ran at us.

I had a gun. I should have used it. But she was a child, and in her face I saw Scorpia, Lyre, Andromeda. I froze. Drunk though he was, Uwe still reacted before I did, and his first thought was to shield me from the worst of the blast. He tackled me to the ground with his armored body on top of mine. My only injury was a gash on my cheek where my face hit the concrete floor. There wasn't enough left of Uwe for a proper funeral. When I emerged from that tunnel, covered in the remains of both my teammate and a little girl, I was ready to leave Titan, despite the love that I've gained for both the planet and its people. I sent the message to my family the next day, when I was still so sure, before Altair made his offer and the doubt set in.

But Ivennie doesn't know any of that, and none of it is her fault. She's a quick learner with exceptionally high potential, perhaps even for leadership, according to Altair's recommendation. I should be doing a better job of teaching her how a team operates. If there's one thing I can do for the others before I leave them behind, I should at least give them the ability to rely on each other.

I clear my throat and lower my hand as I realize I'm touching the scar on my cheek. It would have been an easy thing for Titan doctors to fix, but I asked to keep it as a reminder. My eyes shift to Ivennie, who immediately glances away as if she hadn't been staring.

"You can ask, if you want," I tell her. "I'll answer any questions you have. I know you must have heard plenty of rumors." A sergeant who was raised off-world is no small thing on Titan. I know the things they say about me, both good and bad.

No doubt Ivennie would have asked the others about me already, if they weren't as reluctant to accept her as I am. She hesitates for barely a moment before she gives in to curiosity.

"Is it true you're an off-worlder?"

"No. I'm a Titan. I was born here." The response is automatic. Confusion creases her forehead, and after a moment, I relent. "But, yes, I've spent most of my life off-world, though I've always been Titan at heart. I returned when duty called me." A mouthful of lies. When I was growing up, Momma always reminded me that blood

15

came first. The last thing she said to me was *"You're a Kaiser, not a Titan. Don't forget that."* But the truth would not serve me well here.

"So before coming here, you lived . . . where?"

"I lived on a ship. But I grew up mostly on Gaia, then a few years on Nibiru."

"Ah. Gaia." Some of her confusion clears up. "So that's why you're"—she fumbles for a word—"abstinent?"

They always ask about that.

"I'm not. It's just different for me."

It's clear she doesn't understand, but this is an issue I'm not eager to provide more explanation about. I've tried it with Titans, many times, but our attitudes are too deeply ingrained, and too different. Maybe it is the years in Gaia's conservative culture affecting me more than I like to think. Or maybe it was one too many lectures from Momma about avoiding unplanned children on any of the planets. With those concerns, she was always more strict with Pol and I than with our sisters, even after she gave us all birth control shots from Gaia, where they're mandatory.

Either way, I've never been able to make myself comfortable with Titans' extraordinarily casual attitude toward sex. I don't judge them for their own dalliances—though constantly being woken up in the middle of the night drove me to demand having my own room, despite it being against Titan custom—but the lifestyle doesn't suit me.

I tried during basic training, when my loneliness was a raw wound I was constantly trying to sew shut. It didn't work. And here, where I'm in charge of these people, tasked with ordering them to fight and die as I see fit, attachment is too dangerous. I know I wouldn't be able to be objective. If only knowing was enough to keep my heart from wanting.

The conversation ends as we travel higher in the stairwell,

drawing close enough to the cafeteria that the voices of my team bounce off the walls around us. The sound of their laughter and easy chatter makes my guilt heavier with every step. Ivennie is still barely more than a stranger, but the others have been with me for a long time. *Secrets lead to jealousy*...and I haven't told them of the upcoming end to my service, or the message I sent to my family, or the possibility this could be my last mission. Though I've never been able to view them as my kin, my team has always seen me as a part of their family. No matter what choice I make, I'll be leaving someone behind.

CHAPTER THREE

A Warm Reception

Scorpia

As *Fortuna* punches through the atmosphere, I realize a *rough landing* was an ambitious goal. Judging by the flashing emergency lights bathing the bridge neon green, it's too late to hope for anything better than a graceful crash. As the whole ship rattles and shakes around me, I grip the control wheel with both hands, fighting to prevent a nosedive. The craft groans and whines with the effort, audible even through the panicky wail of the alarm. We're still locked on the landing zone, as far as I can tell, but it's up to me to ensure we don't arrive as a flaming ball of bent steel and crushed limbs.

Not that there's much to do at this point. I've pressed all the buttons, pulled all the levers, and activated all the fail-safes. I've sprayed my mouth-guard with compressed air, the chill hardening it enough to prevent my teeth from shattering on impact. Now, I do the last things left to do: hold on tight and watch the surface of Gaia come closer, and closer, and closer.

The ship slows by the time she hits, but not enough for the

crash to be anywhere close to graceful. I slam back against my seat as *Fortuna* bumps and skids and slides across the planet's surface, metal screeching and scraping against rock. The vessel collides with something big, spins sideways, and grinds to a stop. The world leans left.

My chest strains against the safety straps. My knuckles are white around the wheel. I stay still, wrestling with my churning stomach. By the time I've subdued the urge to vomit, the alarms have quieted, and the lights have faded to a dim yellow. Nothing in the bridge is emitting flames or sparks or any other signs of impending danger. And, given the fact we haven't been blown to pieces by Gaian air control, it seems we made it into the landing zone. A sliver of the sandy stretch of ground is visible through the viewing panel, along with one rusty old ship that must have been abandoned here when the borders closed. That's probably what we hit earlier.

One hand peels off the wheel, then the second. I rub my mouth-guard until the warmth softens it into rubbery goo again and spit it into my palm. With my heart still thumping in my chest, I let out a breathless laugh.

The ship's banged up and the cockpit reeks of alcohol, but we're still in one piece. As far as I'm concerned, that makes this a great success. The world is spinning, my systems are fried, and Momma's surely going to chew me out for this, but we survived. I grin as I pocket the mouth-guard, unclip myself from the safety belts, and let my forehead fall to rest on the wheel.

"You did it, baby," I say, rubbing the control panel. "You got us here."

My stomach bubbles again. I shut my eyes, listening to the familiar creaks and grumbles of the ship as it settles. Given the rough landing, Momma will probably check on the cargo before she barges in here, so I have a few minutes to relax. But a steady, insistent beep soon draws my attention. I raise my head and glance at a screen on my right. Bold letters blink at me: *New Transmission Received*. Receiving a transmission after landing usually means a client is contacting us now that we're within range, but when I see the source, my stomach drops.

Titan. The message is from Titan. We haven't visited that war-ravaged rock in three years, because the only goods worth smuggling to Titan are weapons, and not even Momma is cold enough to sell bombs into a war her own son is fighting in. There's no reason for us to receive a transmission from Titan unless it involves Corvus.

A lump forms in my throat, making it hard to swallow. Corvus hasn't contacted us once in the three years he's been gone. He's made it damn clear he's done with us. But if he was killed in action, one of his superiors might pass the word to us as a favor to Momma. Taking a deep breath, I reach out, my hand hovering over the button to play the message. All transmissions are supposed to go straight to Momma—but if my brother is dead, I don't want to hear it from her mouth. I hit the button.

The image is dim and pixelated, but the sight of Corvus's face still knocks the air from my lungs. I lean forward, one hand reaching out to touch the screen, my eyes locked on his blurred image. His face is turned to the left rather than facing the camera head-on, and shadow falls across him. Between the lighting and the picture quality, his face is little more than a blotch of olive skin on my screen, but my memory fills in the details: his sharp features and distinctive nose, his kind eyes beneath thick brows. His dark hair, previously worn long and shaggy, is cropped short, and stubble shadows the lower half of his face. He's thirty years old now, three years my senior, but he looks as though his time away has aged him double.

Corvus clears his throat, the sound fuzzy with static. I tear my eyes away from his face and search the area around him for clues about the nature of the message—is he injured? Is he in trouble? But there's only a blank gray wall as a backdrop.

"This is a message from Corvus Kaiser for space vessel *Fortuna*," he says. Even aside from the static, his voice is strange to my ears, so clipped and serious. "At the end of this month, I will have served my required years in service for Titan. My enlistment is over." He pauses and looks offscreen. There's a muffled sound—maybe a distant explosion—but after a moment he looks back, seemingly unconcerned. "I'll be in Drev Dravaask. You can reach me through General Kel Altair." He reaches a hand forward, but hesitates. He looks directly into the camera for the first time. "Get me off this damn rock, Momma," he says, his voice catching on the last word, and the recording ends.

I let out a slow breath.

Realizing I'm still touching the now-empty screen, I draw back my shaking hand and wipe my eyes, trying to process the raw shock of the news. All these years, I went back and forth between hating Corvus and missing him, hoping he would survive and trying to convince myself I didn't care if he did. Now, seeing his face for the first time in three years, I have no idea how to feel.

Even if he did live, I never imagined Corvus would contact us after his enlistment. He abandoned us, after all—abandoned *me*—with no warning, not so much as a note to remember him by. He made his choice very clear: He's loyal to his home-planet over us. But now that he's gotten tired of playing soldier, he expects us to swing by and pick him up? Welcome him back like nothing happened?

I clench my hands in my lap, a wave of bitterness surging up despite the part of me that still aches to have my brother back. With a haze of whiskey clouding my thoughts, it's impossible to make any sense out of my tangled emotions. A large part of me is grateful for that.

But I'm getting ahead of myself. Just because Corvus is asking to be picked up doesn't mean Momma is going to do it. She's drilled it into us our whole lives that blood always comes first. Corvus betrayed that idea when he left us, and Momma isn't the forgiving type. This transmission might be the last I see of my brother. I guess I should be grateful that I got one last glimpse of him, and be content to know he's alive out there, somewhere.

Before I realize what I'm doing, I hit the button to play the message again. But rather than my brother's face, the screen flashes with a green warning box: *Access Denied*.

"Shit," I mutter. In the time it took me to watch and process Corvus's message, Momma must have gotten to the transmission and changed the access settings. Which means...

Right on cue, the sound of approaching footsteps reaches my ears: a slow and deliberate tapping, not heavy enough to be the twins and not rapid enough to be Lyre. I wipe my eyes again, willing myself to get my emotions under control before she gets here. I can't let Momma know I viewed that transmission before she restricted access to it. She's going to be pissed off enough about the rough landing, and I have no idea what viewing the message from Corvus will do to her mood.

Preoccupied with that, I almost forget the bottle of whiskey I was sipping in orbit. I glance around, hoping to hide it in the last seconds before Momma arrives, and curse as I see its shards scattered all over the cockpit floor. No wonder the smell is so intense in here—and that was my last bottle of my favorite Devan corn whiskey. I scramble to slide the glass into a corner with one boot but freeze as the metal door screeches open.

My mother's lined face is suited to scowling. Her hair and clothing are mussed, and there's a red mark on the olive skin of her forehead from one of the safety straps, but none of it softens her severity. If she was affected by Corvus's transmission, she doesn't show it.

She stands in the doorway, arms folded over her chest, and gives a loud, distinct sniff. I glance again at the whiskey and glass coating the floor and bite the inside of my cheek. Momma suspecting I peeked at that transmission is the least of my concerns right now.

"What the hell kind of landing was that?" Momma asks after a long silence, her sharp brown eyes shifting to me. "You trying to break my ship? Or just the cargo? You know those plants are delicate." I bite my tongue to keep from spewing something that'll earn me a slap. My mother steps closer and sniffs again. "You been drinking behind the wheel?"

"Of course not," I say, rising to meet her. "Captain," I amend, and stumble across the slanted floor. The world lurches around me, and I grab onto my chair for support, well aware that this isn't helping my argument. "I had the bottle waiting, was gonna celebrate when we landed," I lie once I steady myself. "But it broke when things got rough."

My mother's expression doesn't change. I release the chair once I'm confident I can keep my feet. I'm a head taller than her, long and lanky while she's short and solid, but my shoulders slump as if in desire to make myself smaller than her. I fold my arms across my chest, realize I'm mirroring her posture, and uncross them again.

"There was some kind of malfunction as we entered atmosphere," I say. "Autopilot failed, but it was too late to turn back. I had to land by myself." I meet her eyes and raise my chin. Messy or not, I managed the landing on my own, and that's nothing to scoff at.

Momma continues to scrutinize me. I've gotten all too used to that critical look over the last three years. Before that, she wasn't quite so harsh on me. We never really understood each other, but she mostly ignored me. On rare occasions, I could even make her laugh. That changed after Corvus left. All of a sudden she was watching me all the time, always ready to criticize. *"You're the oldest now. You have to do better. You have to stop thinking of only yourself."* Eventually I realized she was expecting me to step into Corvus's role in the family. It had never occurred to me until then that I might want to be in charge myself. Ever since, I've been trying to live up to the impossible task of filling his shoes.

As the silence thickens and my anxiety grows, my whiskey-loosed tongue fights its way free of my better judgment.

"Guess you should've listened to Lyre about getting the new parts back on Deva."

My mother's hand cracks across my face before I see it moving. I reel back, slipping on spilled liquor, and barely keep my feet.

"Don't lie to me, girl," she says. "You think I can't tell when you've been drinking? You're lucky you didn't get us all killed."

I press a hand to my stinging cheek and breathe deeply. It was stupid to think I could fool her, but I couldn't help but try.

"You should be thanking me. I got us here in one piece. Pretty damn good, given the situation, if I do say so myself."

My mother grimaces. As I let my hand drop to my side, I search her expression for some sign of emotion. Surely she should feel something after seeing the face of her eldest son for the first time in three years...and surely, not knowing I watched the transmission, she'll at least tell me that he's still alive. But Momma is silent, staring down at the remains of my whiskey bottle with an expression like stone.

"Something you want to say?" I prompt, and she glances up at me.

"Cargo bay in ten minutes," she says. "Family meeting."

Without waiting for a response, she turns her back and heads for the door.

As the metal door slams shut behind her, I sigh and run a hand through my hair. Of course Momma would never have a private conversation with me about anything remotely emotional. She'll probably just make a short speech to the whole family, let us know that Corvus survived his enlistment. I won't be surprised if she leaves out that he wants us to pick him up. After seeing Momma's cold expression, I'm sure she doesn't intend to allow him back. And that's probably for the best—or at least, I'm going to keep telling myself that it is.

I wait until the footsteps recede and Momma starts in on one of the others, her shouts echoing through the metallic hallways of the ship. Once it's safe, I head for the door. I need to check on my ship before this "family meeting" and get my emotions under control by the time Momma makes the official announcement.

Outside the cockpit, the middle deck is in disarray. The kitchen and dining room are strewn with utensils, freeze-dried meals, and a mess of other things I can't identify. More concerning, there's a distinct smell of smoke. I pick my way through the room, grabbing onto bolted-down furniture for support, but it doesn't seem to be coming from here.

On each side of the room are entrances to the personal quarters. On my left is Momma's, flanked by the twins'. Someone who didn't know my mother might've thought it was sweet of her to place our youngest closest to her, but I know the truth. The big twins are our muscle, which makes right between them the safest spot on the whole ship.

Across the disaster of a deck are the entrances to the other three rooms. Mine sits nearer to the cockpit, and at the opposite end, closest to the engine, is Lyre's room. Between them is the bunk that once belonged to Corvus, now packed with storage overflow. After that transmission, the sight of his door feels like another slap to the face. I tear my eyes away and continue onward before the bitterness surges up. There are more important things to focus on right now, such as where the hell that smoke is coming from.

Rather than heading down the spiraling stairwell to the cargo bay, where one of the twins' low voices alternates with our mother's, I pass to the back of the ship and descend to the engine room, smacking the pressure pad to enter. As the metal divider slides upward, I'm greeted by a face full of smoke.

Eyes watering, I push through until I catch a glimpse of my sister in one corner of the room, lost among the mess of colorful wires and mismatched mechanical parts that make up *Fortuna*'s oft-repaired heart. Lyre is bent over some piece of machinery, muttering curses under her breath. I wait, fanning smoke away from my face. One of my boots taps against the metal floor, but the sound is swallowed by the other noises in the engine room: hisses of air, mechanical clinks and clunks, and the steady *thump-thump-thump* of the huge main fan keeping the engine cool. The smoke gradually clears, and our tiny engineer straightens up with a grumble, wiping her gloves on the pants of her oversized jumpsuit.

"You lighting my ship on fire again?" I ask. My sister turns and scowls through the dissipating smoke. It's not very intimidating considering she's barely five feet tall, especially with a smear of dark grease across her face and her curls wrestled into a ridiculous knot atop her head, but she scowls nonetheless. At only twenty years old, she's already mastered our mother's trademark expression.

"*Your* ship?" she asks, placing a gloved hand on her hip. "It's not yours. Maybe you should remember that next time you think about crashing it."

"Oh, come on." I'm hearing an awful lot of complaints, considering I managed to land the ship without a single explosion to speak of. "I got us here with the engine on fire, didn't I? You should be thanking me."

"Thank you, oh glorious pilot, for not *quite* managing to kill us all."

"You're very welcome." I smile and bow. When I straighten up

26

again, Lyre is still frowning, this time at the engine instead of me. "Something fried my systems halfway through landing," I say, more seriously. "What gives?"

"The thermal control system is damaged and the left coolant pump needs—"

"Maybe a little less specific."

Lyre sighs, pushing a stray curl out of her face.

"To put it simply, nothing unexpected," she says. "I've been telling Momma we need parts since Deva. She threw out some excuses about 'prioritizing' our funds."

"Well, I'd say it's a priority now."

"It should've been a priority before the crash landing." Lyre yanks off her greasy gloves and lets them fall to the floor one at a time. "I'm not leaving this planet before we fix my ship," she says, and stomps past me.

"*Your* ship? I dunno if that's—"

"You reek of alcohol, by the way," she says over her shoulder as she clambers up the stairs, making a surprising amount of noise for such a tiny woman.

I shake my head as the door clanks shut behind her. Apparently my family is all about the dramatic exits today, but at least this one works in my favor. After double-checking to make sure that nobody's coming down the stairs to bother me, I make my way to the far corner of the engine room. There, I pry the cover off an air vent and pull out the box inside.

The black cube is a couple inches in each direction, punctured with small holes to allow airflow, and sealed with four pressure-pad-controlled locks.

"You still alive in there?" I ask, shaking the box and pressing my ear against it. Something shifts within. "Good. You're gonna make me a lot of money, little one." I tuck the box into the front pocket of my jumpsuit and head to the cargo bay.

This room is the biggest area of the ship, though right now it's mostly full of metal boxes tied down in neat rows. It looks like they were secure enough that the landing didn't topple any, which is lucky for me, as I'm sure I'd have gotten more than a single slap and an earful of scolding if they weren't. The twins are lost somewhere among the cargo, muttering to each other. Since I'd rather not get dragged into any manual labor, I dodge through the rows and head for the far side of the cargo bay.

Momma waits there, arms folded over her chest. Lyre stands a few paces away with her hands clasped behind her. I take a deep breath as I approach, steeling myself to hear the news I already know. It's a good thing I already saw that transmission; wouldn't want to have a breakdown in front of the whole family, especially not when I'm meant to lead them one day. Maybe Momma will be impressed by my stoicism, if she doesn't suspect right away that I viewed the message. I stop right between my mother and sister, glancing back and forth between their mirrored frowns.

"Is this the family meeting?" I ask. "Twins not included?"

Momma gestures for me to lower my voice.

"I don't need them getting all riled up before a job," she says, casting a look toward the stacks of cargo. "This is between us three for now."

"Sure, sure," I say, and wait. Momma takes her time clearing her throat and brushing off the front of her jumpsuit. Though Lyre must be dying of curiosity, she's completely still and silent, ever the attentive student.

"Guess I'll keep this short," Momma says, but her lips twist one way and the other, as if loath to let the words free. "I got a transmission from Titan when we arrived," she says, finally.

Beside me, Lyre lets out a small gasp and presses a hand to her mouth. I force my eyes to widen and my mouth to drop to feign surprise, but the effort goes wasted. Momma isn't looking at either of us, just staring down at the ground with her expression as guarded as ever.

"Is Corvus...?" Lyre begins in a small voice, but doesn't finish the thought. She sounds so frightened that I almost forget myself and chime in that he's still alive, but I hold my tongue.

"He's fine," Momma says. "His enlistment is over. Once this job is finished, we're heading to Titan to pick him up."

This time I don't have to fake the shock. I gape at Momma, the news so unexpected that my mind can't seem to process it. Even knowing that Corvus was alive, never once did I imagine that he would actually return.

This moment should be happy—part of me *is* absolutely overjoyed that my older brother will be returning—but resentment rises up in the back of my throat nonetheless.

"He's...you're letting him come back?" I ask, once I manage to force air back into my lungs. Momma and Lyre both look at me like I'm a complete idiot.

"Of course I am. He's our blood," Momma says.

"That didn't seem to matter to him when he left," I say. "He chose to stay on Titan. He picked his home-planet over us."

"And now he's coming back," Momma says with a scowl. "Stop being such a damn brat, Scorpia. You should be grateful." She waves a hand before I can retort. "Family meeting over. We'll talk more after we get this job done."

She turns her back and walks away, heading toward the lockpad that opens the surface ramp. Lyre glances at me. I glower at her silently, waiting for her to make some snippy comment or, worse, voice her agreement with Momma. But after a moment, she lowers her eyes, murmurs something about checking on the engine, and rushes up the stairs with her head down.

I thought I was ready for this, but I'm not. The news that Corvus will be returning hits even harder than the knowledge he survived his enlistment. If he wasn't coming back, maybe I could have finally let him go. Maybe I could have finished grieving the brother I thought I knew. But now...now it's like the scar has been ripped open again. My chest feels tight and my thoughts muddled, bouncing back and forth between joy and anger and fear. Somehow, through the chaos of my emotions, a cold and logical concern bobs up.

When Corvus was still here, he was next in line to be captain. Next in line to inherit *Fortuna* and run the family business. After he left, Momma's pressure on me made it clear the responsibility became mine instead. But if he's coming back...what does that mean for me?

"Wait," I say, turning toward Momma. She doesn't stop, doesn't even slow, so I rush to catch up with her. "We need to talk."

"Nothing to talk about," she says without looking at me. I hurry forward, swinging around to step between her and the lockpad on the wall. She scowls up at me, eyes hardening in a warning expression that very nearly sends me scurrying, but I hold my ground.

"You know exactly what we have to talk about."

"Out of the way, girl," she snaps. I waver and finally step to the side. As she punches in the code for the ramp, one side of the cargo bay hisses open and begins to gradually fold outward. "Focus on the job. We'll talk about the ship afterward."

"But—" Before I can get another word out, she pushes past me and heads for the nearby supply closet. I run a hand through my hair, stomach souring as I chew on those last words. She knows exactly what I want to talk about, and she's dodging the issue intentionally. "Bullshit," I mutter, and head toward the supply closet she disappeared into.

As the ramp lowers, the crimson glow of the planet's constant day spills into the cargo bay. I grimace and raise a hand to ward it off while I walk. My eyes will adjust to the color difference soon enough, but the red-tinted light always makes my head hurt after a week on *Fortuna*. I prefer the brighter yellow lighting of the ship, and the twenty-four-hour day/night cycles programmed into it. They're both modeled after the generation ships that brought humanity here, which were designed to mirror their home-world. But Gaia, like all the planets, has one side locked forever facing the red star at the center of the system, and its people live in a constant state of midday. It's the only way *to* live, since the dark side is too cold for anything to survive there. The constant light makes it difficult to keep track of hours or days or any time at all, which is why all the planets agreed early on to stick to Earth's ancient system.

I duck into the supply closet after Momma. She's already pulling on her hooded poncho and green-tinted goggles, part of the usual Gaian attire. I grab my own equipment off a shelf labeled with my name, pushing aside the heavier gear meant for Titan and grabbing the gloves that Gaians customarily wear.

"Corvus chose Titan's people above us," I burst out as I dress, unable to contain the whirlwind of my thoughts inside my head. I hop on one foot as I pull my pants on, and nearly stumble into the dust-covered cryosleep chamber in the corner. "He's been gone for three years. In Titan's war. We don't know…" I trail off as Momma grabs her scarf and leaves the closet, completely ignoring me. Mumbling half-formed complaints, I pull on the rest of my equipment, check to ensure the box is still snug in my pocket, and grab a clunky handheld comm from the stack. The thick square device is rudimentary for Gaia's level of tech, but it's enough to keep me in contact with the rest of the family if we end up separated.

Once I'm ready, I head out into the sunny, red-dyed cargo bay and join Momma where she waits for the ramp to finish lowering.

"Not another word," she says, holding up a hand. "Focus on the job. That's the last time I'm gonna say it."

I'm familiar enough with her tone to know pushing more will get me a smack, so I grit my teeth and hold my tongue. My thoughts continue stewing as we wait for the ramp to complete its slow and rumbling process.

I keep trying to convince myself that Momma would never hand the ship to Corvus, not after he's been gone for three years doing stars-know-what on that damned, desolate planet. We all know what the war on Titan is like. Whispers of it reach all the way to Pax—the story of a planet torn in two by civil war shortly after it was settled, and the endless cycle of brutality and revenge that has carried on ever since. I've seen the war with my own eyes during my family's visits, the blackened battlefields and rows of frozen, uniformed bodies. I've seen a lot of things in this system, both beautiful and terrible, but never anything as horrifying as Titan.

And Corvus, with his easy smile and gentle hands, was never a fighter. Frankly, I'm surprised he survived. But I'm damn sure the parts of him I loved didn't.

An unexpected surge of grief hits me at the thought. I swallow hard to force down the lump in my throat. I've done enough mourning for my brother; I need to focus on what comes next. If Momma does give the ship to Corvus—Corvus the soldier, the killer, not the brother I loved—then he could be even harsher than her. Since he's obviously so invested in Titan, he'll probably want to use the family business to feed the war machine. Can I live with that? Can my siblings? They have an option, after all. Maybe it will be the final straw that drives them to leave *Fortuna* and return to their home-planets.

That fear always haunted me back on Nibiru. It was so much nicer than Gaia that I worried the twins would decide to stay when the rest of us went to live on the ship with Momma. Corvus was the one who assured me it would never happen. *"They're not really Nibiran. They're Kaisers,"* he told me. *"Anyway, why would they want to leave? They'll always have us to look after them."*

Momma told us that blood comes first, but Corvus made me believe it. Now I know it was all bullshit.

Then again, maybe he wouldn't give our siblings the option to leave. Maybe he'll immediately replace us with his own people, since he so clearly prefers them, and leave us stranded and freezing on Titan. Once, I never would've believed my brother would do that. He was always so adamant that he was planning a better future for all of us. But that was before he left.

I can't live as an illegal off-worlder without a home again. Surviving off scraps, hiding whenever the law passed by, grappling with the constant terror that someone would notice I don't belong... I barely survived it once. Even on Nibiru, with Momma supporting us financially and neighbors willing to spare some kindness for a bunch of kids, my anxiety drove me to start drinking. And now? I doubt even Nibirans would have much sympathy now that we're adults, let alone the obsessively patriotic Titans. My little siblings were too young to understand back then, but now it's laughable to imagine Lyre trying to stomach scavenged food, or the twins trying to be inconspicuous. It'd be a lot less funny when one screwup could get them jailed or killed.

But I'm not going to let any of that happen. Whatever Momma's decided, or thinks she's decided, I have one more chance to prove myself before we meet up with Corvus. This side job of mine is the perfect thing to prove to her and my siblings, once and for all, that I deserve to inherit *Fortuna*. When I sell the little treasure in my pocket and show Momma the profit, she's going to be damn proud of me.

My thoughts are cut off by the thud of the ramp hitting the

surface. I blink and focus, gazing out at the expanse of Gaia revealed by the open side of the cargo bay. My mother heads down without a glance my way, each step making the metal ramp vibrate.

I pause on the threshold, take one last, deep breath of the familiar smell of *Fortuna*, and follow her. My boots clomp along the ramp as I descend, and a breeze ruffles my hood. Gaia has plenty of its own problems, but its climate is a breath of fresh air after spending our last job on sweltering, rainy Deva.

Gaia, along with the other planets, built huge landing zones like this when interplanetary trade and visitation was commonplace. Back then, this zone would've been full of anything from trade ships to tourist vessels to mercenaries looking for work. Now, the borders are closed to anyone but official government personnel and exceptions like my family. The flat expanse of space is glaringly empty except for us, some very old and rusty spacecrafts that must have been abandoned long ago, and a few unmanned delivery drones marked with Pax's flag. Drones can't deliver as much cargo as a ship like *Fortuna*, and they can be taken down by anything from weather to programming glitches to pirates like the *Red Baron* crew. But for most human-operated ships, it's simply too difficult and expensive to risk traveling between planets, so the drones have to do. We're among the last of a dying breed, surviving only because my siblings' unique birthplaces allow us to bend the law.

As I step out into the sand, I look up at Nova Vita, huge and bloody red in the sky. The planets arc out from the star in various crescent shapes—watery Nibiru is the closest, followed by little Deva and dusty Pax. Far off in the opposite direction is frozen and war-ravaged Titan, dwarfed in the Gaian sky though it's at least three times the size of Gaia in reality. I'm one of the few people in the whole system who can boast of having been to each of them, and a few dozen times at that—with the exception of Pax, which we visited on one especially illegal trip that required us to wear full antiradiation space suits. Yet every time I look up from a planet's surface, I get a pang of longing to explore that vast emptiness between them.

I'm torn from my thoughts by someone clearing their throat. I turn toward my mother, standing a few paces away with both hands in the air. I raise my eyebrows at the strange pose and the furious expression on her face.

"What...?" I cut off, finally noticing what she's seen. A dozen armed and white-uniformed Gaian officers are circling the ship, with more still trickling out from behind *Fortuna*, where they must have been waiting for us to exit. Most of them have their hands on their weapons, and all of them are now staring at me.

I sigh and put my hands up.

CHAPTER FOUR

Soldiers

Corvus

After Ivennie's rush to find me, I'm not sure what to expect when I walk into the cafeteria, but my steps slow as I find my other three team members casually enjoying breakfast. This room, like the rest of the outpost, is built to fit ten times our number. Despite the many tables and the vastness of the room, my team is nestled close together on the same side of the same bench. Considering how huge Sverre is, they barely fit. Daniil and Magda sit shoulder-to-shoulder beside the heavily tattooed blond, a thick blanket draped over the both of them. Daniil has an arm looped around Magda's waist, and she leans her head against his shoulder. I suppress a hot spark of envy in my throat. *Jealousy is a disease of the soul*, I remind myself. But no matter how many times I silently reiterate the Titan saying, the feeling remains.

"Corvus," Daniil says, noticing me first. The lanky, olive-skinned marksman sits up straighter and removes his arm from Magda's waist. The blanket falls off one of her shoulders, and she frowns at him. He doesn't even notice, smiling at me instead. "Good morning."

Daniil Naran was assigned to my team early on, when I was not yet one of Altair's most favored sergeants, but merely a new soldier eager to prove myself. At first, I didn't understand why they had sent an asset like Daniil to someone as unproven as me. He was more experienced than I was, trained in interrogation techniques, and exceptionally talented with a sniper rifle, without a single blemish on his service record.

I initially assumed he was sent by Altair to help keep me safe, as a favor to Momma. But the truth spilled out when he was drunk one night: Daniil was the product of a Titan mother and a visiting Paxian. Not full Titan blood. He's slimmer and darker-skinned than the majority of Titans, but that wouldn't have been enough to pull much attention to him if he hadn't tried to use his mixed planetary heritage to avoid military service. It didn't work, but merely trying was enough to make him look borderline traitorous. If he had ended up in any team other than mine, he wouldn't have lasted long.

"How nice of you to join us," Magda says, her pale, sharp face pinching. As usual, her tone has a bite to it. And—as usual—the sound of it warms me anyway. She tosses a lock of long brown hair over her shoulder and leans away from Daniil. She's our newest other than Ivennie, and the closest to my own age, since she legally delayed her mandatory service to have children—the one reason Titans respect. She's also been making trouble, mostly for me, ever since she arrived. She's always prodding at me, distracting me, chipping away at the wall I maintain between myself and my team. Months ago I decided it would be best to find an excuse to reassign her, and yet I keep finding reasons not to.

I'm really not in the mood to deal with her and Daniil jostling one another to get my attention. Despite the words I parroted to

Ivennie earlier, Titan relations are...quite a bit more complicated than familial feelings, and I still have trouble navigating them. The three stifling weeks at this outpost have been particularly bad, especially after the loss of Uwe and the arrival of the new recruit. I avoid eye contact with any of my soldiers as I head to the food they've collected on the end of the table. Since there clearly isn't a pressing issue, I might as well eat.

"One of you should be on patrol," I say, heaping steaming rice into a bowl and dropping a few gelatinous protein cubes on top. Once they begin to melt, I crumble freeze-dried algae over the top. Sverre taught us all this method of using the army's stock rations. The others all raved like it was the best meal they'd ever had, but none of them have ever tasted Nibiran fish, or fresh Devan fruit, or even Gaia's simple but artfully arranged cuisine. Here, even when I'm full, I never feel fully satisfied.

"It's still early," Magda says. "It's not time for the daily stroll for another fifteen minutes."

She smiles. Already trying to get a rise out of me, as if I haven't given enough lectures on the importance of staying on guard out here.

"So what's the problem, then?" I ask, trying not to let her get under my skin. She'll only enjoy it. She tilts her head, as if not understanding, so I add, "Ivennie said you were looking for me."

"Oh, yes." Magda's voice takes on a fake note of sweetness. "We were merely wondering if there was any word from the old bear."

Meaning they wanted to bother me into coming to spend time with them, and Ivennie is too new to say no. I suppress a sigh as I sit on the bench across from the others, stirring my food into an unappetizing brown mush before taking a bite. At least it's warm.

Ivennie hovers to the side with her own bowl, frozen in indecision about where to sit. After a few moments, Magda gestures to her, and she gratefully darts over. As she sits next to her, Magda steals Daniil's half of the blanket and wraps it around the other woman instead, rubbing warmth into her arms.

"No word yet." I focus on my bowl of food instead of on my team and their casual affections. "But I trust that the general has us here for a reason."

"Altair wouldn't waste our time." Sverre's voice is a quiet, rare rumble. "He knows our value." I nod to him, glad that at least one member of my team isn't acting like an impatient child. Sverre has been at my side the longest of all. It took me weeks to earn the trust of the very patriotic Titan, who hails from a small village to the east and had never met an off-worlder before me. It also took one thorough beating in hand-to-hand combat when he decided to challenge me. But ever since I bested him, I've had his loyalty, and found myself grateful for his presence in new ways every day.

"Yes, yes, we all know Altair is unbearably wise." Magda sighs. "It's just that it's very cold out here, and boring, and I miss the taste of beer."

"Can't help with the beer, but surely I kept you warm and entertained last night?" Daniil asks, feigning offense.

Magda lets out a full-throated laugh, nudging him in the ribs. I shove another bite of food into my mouth, unable to bring myself to mentally repeat the jealousy mantra again. It's a lost cause.

"If you're so bored, then we'll have a change of pace today," I say, once I trust my voice to stay neutral. "We could use some combat exercises after spending so much time on our asses. And we'll extend our usual patrol. I don't like how quiet it's been. We can't forget how close we are to enemy territory."

"Combat exercises and patrols?" Magda wrinkles her nose. "You truly have the worst idea of entertainment. Must be those Gaian sensibilities of yours."

Everyone laughs, aside from Ivennie, who shoots me a wide-eyed, uncertain glance.

"I'll take that as volunteering for the first patrol," I say, unwilling to show Magda that her comment chafes even though I tell myself she's merely teasing me. None of them would have poked fun at me in such a way before she showed up.

"It was a joke, Sarge. Surely they have jokes on Gaia?" She tilts her head to study me, waiting to see if I'll take the bait.

Before I can formulate an answer, the scream of an alarm pierces the room, booming around the empty space of the cafeteria. The lights turn pale green. I'm on my feet in an instant, with the others close behind.

"Are we under attack?" Ivennie asks, round-eyed, her voice barely audible above the noise. "All the way out here?"

This outpost is isolated and far enough from the front that it would be highly unlikely for the enemy to strike here. Even if they did, I checked the radar not an hour ago, and there was no sign of anyone approaching. And yet, the alarms are sounding…and as we were just discussing, there's no doubt in my mind that General Altair has us placed at this remote location for a reason. As much as I want to believe this is a false alarm, merely a nearby movement of our own troops or a particularly nasty storm approaching, my gut tells me otherwise.

"I'll check the radar. Daniil, to the rooftop. The rest of you ensure the entrances are secure. Report immediately if you find anything."

The casual chatter of breakfast was less than a minute ago, but the mood shifts immediately, and we change with it. I slide into my role of sergeant without a moment's pause, and at once my friends become soldiers. Their spines straighten, their eyes harden. Together, we move to face whatever trouble has found us.

As I race toward the surveillance room, reports trickle in from the others. The main entrance is secure. The hangar is untouched. No perimeter breach, no sign of an attack. Still, my tension mounts.

When I reach the radar, I breathe a sigh of relief. It shows a shift in the landscape, a nearby cliff that must have crumbled. Nothing more than a landslide. No sign of the enemy or any other movement, so it's likely that a recent storm knocked something loose, and it gave way to gravity. I shake my head and shut off the still-screeching alarm.

Just when I'm starting to relax, my comm crackles to life once more.

"Corvus," Daniil says. "I think you need to see this."

CHAPTER FIVE

Bad Business

Scorpia

I bite back a string of curse words as the Gaians stare us down. Every ship arriving on Gaia is greeted by a party of customs agents, and Momma has contacts who ensure we don't encounter any trouble with them. But these aren't customs agents. These people, with their stiff-shouldered white uniforms and long black gloves, are Gaian law-enforcers. Which means Momma's contacts aren't among them...and which also means they're fully armed and ready to spray us full of holes at any given opportunity.

Something is wrong. I resist the urge to grab the package hidden beneath my poncho, or hightail it back into *Fortuna*, or do anything else to call attention to the fact that I have something extraordinarily illegal tucked into my jumpsuit.

"Well, look at this. I had no idea we were so popular on Gaia." I puncture the bad joke with a nervous laugh. None of the officers spare me a glance.

"Shut up, Scorpia." I glance over my shoulder at the familiar whisper to see Lyre waiting at the edge of the ramp, her hands also held aloft. Rolling my eyes, I turn forward again.

"What's this about, officers?" Momma asks, pretending like I never spoke. Her words come out smooth as silk, though she's standing between a dozen armed law-enforcers and a recently crashed ship full of contraband. "We're a registered ship who received full permission to enter your airspace." She looks at me, awaiting confirmation.

"Oh, yeah, they waved us in. It's all squared away," I say, and shut my mouth before any jittery laughter can escape. My body rattles with nerves, liquor sloshing uneasily in my stomach.

"This is *Fortuna*, correct?" asks the officer who seems to be in charge, stepping in front of the others. She's a tall, brown-skinned woman with hooded eyes beneath straight eyebrows. Her crisp white uniform is decorated with gold buttons and a number of metallic pins whose meaning I don't recognize.

"That she is."

"Hold where you are. We have a flag on that ship." I swear under my breath as the officer pauses to say something into her comm, a sleek, chrome device much more updated than the ones we carry. "You're Captain Auriga Kaiser?" she asks, looking up again.

"Yes, ma'am," Momma says. "Gaian citizen."

"And your crew?"

My mother hesitates. The officer sees it and frowns.

"They have work visas," Momma says. Right on cue, a shadow of suspicion darkens the officer's face. She stands up straighter, looks at us harder. None of the planets are friendly to outsiders, but Gaia has always been especially xenophobic, and it's only gotten worse in recent years.

"Names and birth-planets," the officer demands.

"This is Lyre Kaiser, Devan citizen," my mother says, while the officer records the information in her comm. "The twins on the ship, Andromeda and Apollo Kaiser, are citizens on Nibiru." The officer's lip curls. It's been fifty years since the Nibiran-originated plague that devastated Gaia, but Gaia hasn't forgotten it, or the incredibly rare Interplanetary Council meeting in which all the other planets voted against their plea for reparations.

After a pause, Momma jerks her head toward me. "And our pilot, Scorpia Kaiser. Space-born."

As a couple of the other officers murmur, the one in charge looks directly at me. Such attention, from a woman in such an unfortunately familiar uniform, makes me break out in a cold sweat. As an illegal off-worlder child, I learned early to fear Gaian law-enforcers. But I force a smile through the terror and flicker the fingers of one hand in a wave.

The woman's expression is almost pitying. It seems even a Gaian can find sympathy for someone like me, without a legal home anywhere in the whole system. My siblings' birth-planets were a calculated move by Momma, exploiting a legal loophole to grant her access through closed borders, but a calculated home is a home nonetheless. At least it gives them an option. They have somewhere to go if they decide life on a smuggler vessel isn't for them. They could make the same choice as Corvus if they wanted.

And then there's me: the screwup, born early on a ship waylaid by pirates. We were only one day out from Deva. If I had waited one day to join the world, I would've been born on the surface and declared a citizen. Momma wouldn't have been turned away at the border and forced back to Gaia with a failed shipment, and we wouldn't have ended up broke and stranded here for seven years.

I grit my teeth and push the thought away, aching for a drink despite the rumbling in my guts.

"Hm," the officer in charge murmurs, turning back to my mother. "Thank you." She touches her earpiece and goes silent.

My head is starting to spin. It likely has something to do with the fact that I'm quickly transitioning from "drunk" to "hungover," but the situation isn't helping matters. Between the crash and Momma's announcement, I thought today couldn't get any more screwed up, but here we are.

I drop my head to obscure my expression from the officers and mentally run through a list of reasons Gaia's government might flag a ship. Most of it, unfortunately, is something we've been guilty of at one point or another. We're certainly not innocent of importing contraband right now. Is it possible one of Momma's contacts ratted us out, or that a previous shipment was tracked back to us? If we get caught, my mother might get jail time if she's lucky, but the rest of us will likely die right here in the landing zone.

Each of the planets is wary of outside tech and life-forms, but Gaians have the strictest policies of all. I was able to weather the hatred as a child, but Corvus could never understand why the locals hated us so much. He was always so desperate for everyone to like him. So Momma, who grew up on Gaia, sat us down and tried to explain it.

When they first left Earth, humanity worked together for the species' survival. But the people who arrived in Nova Vita were several generations past the original emigrants. Over the long journey, people went lifetimes without seeing a world outside of their own metal walls, and each ship had already developed distinct cultures by the time they arrived here.

Settling on different planets further divided us. The colonists took apart their generation ships, using the materials to construct their first homes and more. By the time they discovered that Pax had such hostile wildlife and rampant radiation, or that Deva's native plants were often deadly, or that Gaia's population was far too large for the planet's unfruitful soil to support, or any of the other endless problems, each was too busy dealing with their own share of troubles to help the others when they asked for aid.

Many people died in those early days, and by the time the planets managed to agree on treaties and trade routes, resentment had sprouted. Soon new differences popped up—like attitudes toward the alien artifacts they discovered on every planet but Pax. Some, like the statues, are useless relics. Others—weapons, mostly—turned out to be useful tech that people found ways to activate. Most were wary of the mysterious Primus tech, but Gaians were eager to embrace it, while Nibirans banned it entirely, insisting that such technological obsession and hubris was what led to the rapid depletion of Earth's resources. Soon other sticking points arose as well, such as issues with the legality of Devan plants, and moral concerns over the genetic tinkering and dubiously safe tech implants that Paxians insist are necessary to survive on their world.

Now, it's been almost two hundred years since humanity settled here, and it seems the planets can hardly find anything to agree on anymore. For Gaia, the Nibiran plague carried by a traveling family was the final straw. After that, Gaia shut its borders to all interplanetary travel except for drones and its own citizens. The rest of the planets swiftly followed suit. After the appointment of their latest and most extreme president, I suspect the only reason Gaia allows any trade at all is that they haven't found a way to fix their notoriously poor agriculture.

I won't pretend to understand much about interplanetary politics, but I'm familiar with their consequences: closed borders, tightly regulated imports and exports, and absolutely zero tolerance for rule-breakers. If they were arrested, my siblings could petition their home-planets for extraction, but that rarely works; no government is eager to claim responsibility for smugglers, especially not with tensions between planets as high as they are. I don't even have that long shot of an option. If Gaian law enforcement decided to gun us down here and claim we pulled our weapons first, nobody would bat an eye.

All things considered, the situation is not good. Not a damn bit good at all.

I turn at the sound of footsteps on the ramp behind me and swear as I see the twins paused there with a crate over each broad shoulder.

Though they're the babies of the family at nineteen years old, the twins are both a head taller than me and built as sturdy as hunks of steel. They're the palest of all of us—still not the pasty white of many Titans, but between the height and their skin tone, it's easy to guess they have some Titan blood. Both twins have Momma's dark eyes and wavy brown hair—Apollo's is down to his chin, Andromeda's down to her chest, each with a dramatic undercut on one side. Aside from being unreasonably tall, my youngest siblings are also gap-toothed, empty-headed, and extremely prone to solving problems with laser-fire.

Drom lets her cargo drop with two heavy thuds and reaches for the blaster on her hip. Pol is a half second behind his sister.

"No, no, no," I say, nearly tripping over my own feet as I scramble out of their way. "You morons—"

Both twins halt with their guns half out at a sharp whistle from our mother. Drom glances over at her, glances back at the officers who now stand with weapons drawn, and slowly holsters her gun and raises both hands in the air. Pol again follows her lead. I release my breath and scoot back to my previous position, hands still held aloft.

"This treatment is absurd," Momma says, somehow retaining her calm despite the dozen guns now pointed at the heads of her youngest children. "Check your records. I've done a hundred runs like this over the years; there's no reason we should be flagged this time."

The head officer remains silent with a hand to her earpiece and a wrinkle between her thick eyebrows. The others say nothing and don't lower their guns. The package is hot and heavy in my pocket.

If these officers search *Fortuna*'s cargo, we could end up all right. We know how to keep our contraband well hidden, tucked away among the legitimate cargo, stuffed into nooks and crannies and hidden compartments. This shipment is biological, too, which will make it harder for scanners to identify among the legal produce. These officers won't find anything amiss unless they do an extremely thorough search, and if they call in customs agents who are more suited to the task, Momma's contacts should be able to help us out.

But my little box is a very big problem. One half-assed pat-down will find it, and once they have that, it'll justify a top-to-bottom scan of our whole shipment.

"Really sorry about the landing," I blurt out, nerves making it impossible to stay quiet. "We had a system malfunction. The thermal...something." I glance back at the ship, tilted heavily to one side and already thoroughly scuffed before this incident. "Though honestly, it was a pretty good job given the situation."

There's a long pause.

"Anyway," my mother says, "our cargo is some freeze-dried fruits and veggies from Deva. I'd be happy to give you a look. Hell, I'll give you a sample if you like."

"That won't be necessary," the officer in charge says. She removes her hand from her ear, pockets her comm, and folds both hands behind her back. "But we do require you to come with us."

I glance left and right, calculating which way is more likely to save my life if this ends in a blaster fight. Neither direction is promising.

"What exactly is this about?" my mother asks. Before the officer can answer, she flicks a hand. "Relax, you two."

48

Both twins guiltily remove their hands from their weapons and raise them again. My chest feels constricted. It's only a matter of time before something in this situation blows up, and it's more than likely going to be the dumbass twins.

"Classified," says the woman in uniform.

"Well, pardon my rudeness, but I've heard tales of scrappers out here pretending to be officers," Momma says. "Mind if I see some documentation to ease my worries?"

The woman confers with her earpiece before stepping forward and flashing the screen of her comm at my mother. Momma's shoulders tense. I tense, too. I'm sweating beneath my hood, my heart beating fast. Any second now, one of these jumpy officials, or one of my trigger-happy siblings, is going to let loose a round of laser-fire. And then there will be a lot more lasers, and blood, and all in all, it'll be very bad business.

"Thank you, Commander Zinne," my mother says. "I'll come along. Let me and the crew get our things together."

"Just you," Zinne says. "No crew."

In the silence that follows, I hear the twins shift behind me.

"Yeah, that's not happening," Pol mutters. Drom begins to count our adversaries under her breath.

Not for the first time, I wish I was in the habit of keeping a blaster at my hip like every other member of my family. It wouldn't be all that useful in my hands, but at least it'd make me seem less like an easy target.

"*Fine*," my mother says again, this time through gritted teeth. "Give me one minute with them. We have plans for this cargo that need smoothing out."

Zinne looks like she wants to argue, but my mother doesn't have a face that allows much room for argumentation. This woman, even with her fancy uniform and almost a dozen guns in her favor, seems to recognize that. Momma treks back to the ship's ramp without waiting for an answer. At a gesture of her hand, my siblings and I cluster around her, our heads together and our backs to the law-enforcers.

"What's this about?" I ask.

"That woman is Talulah Leonis's head of security," my mother says.

"Oh," Lyre says, very quietly.

"Well, shit," I say.

The twins are silent. Pol's eyebrows are drawn together, his face blank of recognition; Drom is watching the officers and doesn't seem to be listening to the conversation. I smack her on the side of the head to get her attention. She shoves me back and nearly sends me toppling on my ass.

"Leonis is the Gaian president, idiots," I inform both twins, once I manage to regain my balance and dignity. "The one who thinks all off-worlders are scum? Whole family wiped out by the Nibiran plague when she was a kid?" I still remember Momma swearing and stomping all over the ship three years ago, when she found out Leonis was elected, raging about how an extremist like her was going to be terrible for business. Leonis ran on a platform of Gaian independence—aka complete seclusion. The moment this planet solves its food shortage problems, I'm sure even drone trade will be cut off entirely. Maybe eventually we'll be cut off, too, despite Momma's Gaian citizenship.

"Oh," Pol says. "Yeah, shit."

"So we shoot and run?" Drom asks.

"No shooting," Momma says. The twins groan in unison, and I let out a breath. "I don't know what's going on here, but if they wanted to arrest me, they would've already shot the lot of you and dragged me away in cuffs. I'm going to find out what they want. The rest of you will go to Levian and meet our contact at oh-nine-hundred hours like we planned, even if I'm not there." She turns her clear eyes to each of us in turn, waiting for a nod before continuing. "Lie low, don't take unnecessary risks. Scorpia, you're in charge while I'm gone. We clear?"

After a stunned moment, I break into a grin.

"Crystal," I say. Guess she isn't too pissed about the crash after all, if she's leaving me in charge. Maybe she was secretly impressed by my ability to think on the spot and get us here on time. But I know this is more than some victory prize. It's a test. It's always a test.

"I don't follow," Lyre says. "You say 'no unnecessary risks,' but you put *Scorpia* in charge again? After that crash landing?"

"She knows Gaia best," Momma says. The reasoning deflates my ego, but I'll take what I can get. "Any other questions?" Lyre opens her mouth again but closes it. She presses her lips together and shakes her head. I smirk at her, and she pretends not to notice.

"Good," Momma says. She reaches over to squeeze my shoulder, and when I meet her eyes, she holds them for a long moment before turning away. If not for the tightness of her grip, I would almost think this was a rare display of affection, but her eyes send a clear message: *Don't fuck this one up, Scorpia.*

I watch as she leaves us to hop into the government-issued hovercraft without another glance back. Two moments later, the cruiser rises above the ground with a mechanical roar; one more, and it's gone in a cloud of dust, zooming toward the gleaming Gaian capital city that's barely visible on the horizon. I keep watching until the craft is only a speck in the distance, my gloved hands clenching at my sides. When I shake myself out of it, I find all three of my younger siblings staring at me. Right—I'm in charge now.

"Wish we had a nice cruiser like that," I say.

"They didn't even look at our cargo," Lyre says, frowning.

"We've never been in Levian without Momma." Pol taps his fingers on his blaster. "Are we gonna be okay?"

"Don't be a baby," Drom says, shoving her twin. He shoves back. I step between them, holding my hands up. With these two, a playful scuffle can all too easily turn into a bloody brawl.

"Hey, relax, we're gonna be fine." I force a smile, trying to ignore the pressure bearing down on me. We *better* be fine. "Leave the thinking to me, all right? I'm the one in charge."

I don't voice the real question that all of us, myself included, want to ask: *What are we supposed to do if she doesn't come back?*

The clunker, as we refer to our four-yard-long, several-decades-old hovercraft, barely fits all our cargo, let alone any passengers. It also takes three tries to start and rises into the air with a loud and concerning whine from the engine. The flat, rusted vehicle hovers around my shoulder level, trembling like it's considering giving out at any moment.

The struggling machine is hopelessly outdated, a big metal contraption that resembles a raft one might find floating on Nibiru's waters. It has a bulky engine outfitted with solar panels on the back end, a steering wheel at the front, and little else in the way of utilities. The vehicle doesn't even have a roof, leaving both cargo and passengers open to the wind and ever-present sun.

But at least it can fly. Probably.

"Seems good to go," I say, turning to the others. Drom nods her agreement, but Pol gnaws his lower lip, and Lyre sucks a breath through her teeth.

"We should unload some of the cargo," she says. "Make two trips."

"That's a long-ass ride to do twice in a day." It'll take at least two hours to get to Levian, and I have a side trip to fit in before our official meeting.

"Well, it'll be longer if we break down halfway." Lyre taps a finger on her lips. "Maybe we could leave one of the twins with half the cargo."

"Hell no," say both twins in unison.

I could've told Lyre what the answer would be. Drom hates sitting around, and Pol hates being separated from her. It's obvious to me, but Lyre, who would rather spend time tinkering with the engine than talking to us, doesn't know how to think with anything other than pure logic. It's one of the reasons why she'll never be in charge of the family. But I shake off the thought of inheritance as my mind wanders to Corvus again. I have to focus on the situation at hand.

"Nobody stays behind," I say.

"I really don't think this is a good idea," Lyre says.

"You never do. And it usually works out fine anyway."

"*Fine* is a relative term."

"Well, you know what's not relative?" I wait for her to look at me before extending a middle finger in her direction. "The fact that I'm in charge."

Lyre sighs. I can almost see the gears in her head turning, examining a few more arguments before settling on resignation. Without another word of protest, she grabs one of the handholds on the side of the clunker and pulls herself up. She settles in the back, wedged between two crates, and frowns toward our destination.

Once she's up, the twins exchange a glance and shrug. Pol gives Drom a boost, and she gives him a pull. As they sit atop crates of cargo on either side of Lyre, the clunker drops a half foot lower in altitude.

I lurch backward, throwing my hands out to keep my balance, and regard the vehicle warily. Appearances aside, the thing seems like it's still holding up for now. Lyre is right, though. If our vehicle gives out halfway, we'll have a long, sweaty walk ahead of us, and a pissed-off customer, plus Momma's wrath.

But if we make two trips, I'll definitely miss out on my side job, and that can't happen. So I take a deep breath, throw on a smile, and pull myself up. I'm about to take the wheel but pause as my stomach lurches. I clap a hand over my mouth and swallow down bile.

"Drom," I call back once my stomach is under control, and beckon with one hand. She nearly trips over the cargo in her rush forward to take the wheel. I pat her on the back and squeeze myself onto the craft's floor between two crates. Lyre peers down at me with her ever-present frown, so reminiscent of our mother.

"Right," she says. "Almost forgot our fearless leader is still drunk."

I yawn instead of arguing and pull my scarf up to cover more of my face.

"Wake me when we get there," I mumble.

As I doze off, the shuddery movement of the hovercraft brings me back to the gentle rock of a hoverboat, and I sink into a half dream, half memory of Nibiru.

It was the day Momma was supposed to come home from a business trip to Gaia, but it was always a toss-up whether or not she'd arrive on time. So, Corvus decided we'd all spend the day together fishing on a hoverboat borrowed from our neighbors. The twins soon grew bored of it and began whining about wanting to see Momma. Corvus was trying to teach Lyre how to fish. She was always so eager to be his little assistant, but she was distracted by the twins, infected by their souring mood.

"She'll be here soon," Corvus said, already struggling to handle the fishing pole and Lyre, a nervous set to his jaw. We were nearly out of funds and any food other than dried algae.

"You two better be quiet before the akkorokamui hears you," I said, stretched out on my back on the floor of the boat.

"The what?" Pol asked, his forehead crinkling with worry.

"What, you haven't heard of it?" The twins shook their heads at me, Pol already sitting up and eager for a story while Drom was more interested in picking her nose. "Really? Never?" I flipped onto my stomach and crawled toward them. "The fisherfolk only dare speak of it in whispers, in case it overhears..." Both twins leaned forward as my voice dropped. "It lives underneath the waves, with eyes bigger than our boat and eight tentacles big enough to wrap around Vil Hava." I raised both arms and wiggled them, snaking closer. "And when it gets hungry, its favorite treat is... noisy little children!" I lurched forward to tickle them, sending both twins into shrieking fits of laughter.

"That's stupid. There's no such thing," Lyre said from the back of the boat, six years old and already mastering her face of disapproval. I glanced at her, dropping my hands, as she tugged on Corvus's sleeve in search of support. "Right?"

"Don't know," Corvus said, focused on fishing. But when he caught her disappointed look, he ruffled her hair and added, "You'll have to look it up in the digital library and report back to me."

Between the constant noise of the twins and Lyre fumbling with the fishing pole, we didn't catch any fish. But when we returned to our neighbors, I offered them a story for some of their previous catch. And I told them about a world where there was more land than water, with narrow streets crowded with people and huge alien statues with blank faces; a place with technologies they couldn't imagine on Nibiru—clocks built into flesh, and comms so small they could be worn around a finger. I don't think they believed half of it, but they laughed and laughed, and gave us the fish.

And when we got home, Momma was waiting. The twins ran screaming to greet her, followed by Lyre with one of her rare smiles. I stayed where I was, forcing a smile until the little ones disappeared. Once they were gone, I broke into relieved tears. Corvus stayed with me until they passed, wiped my face with his sleeve so Momma wouldn't see, and we went inside together.

A sharp turn jolts me awake. For a moment I can almost hear the waves, taste the salt-tinged winds. But then the current situation catches up with me and a familiar sour taste rises in the back of my throat. We're back on Gaia. I sit up, wincing at the growing pressure in my head. Any hints of a pleasant buzz have left my system, leaving nausea and a pulsing headache.

The first thing I see is Lyre, green in the face and clinging to a cargo crate. Pol sits atop a box with a wide grin, his hair blown wild by the wind. Drom is pushing the clunker to its top speed, but thankfully for us and our cargo, it's not really all that fast.

Ahead of us, the Gaian capital city of Levian looms up, metallic and shimmering. But all around us is...

"What the hell?" I lean over the side to get a better look. I grew up on the outskirts of the city, not far from here. We're flying over what should be Gaia's scraggly farmland. Last time we were here, this harvest seemed like it was going to be the best Gaia had managed to produce to date, with tall fields of black corn and dark expanses of budding orchards. Momma grumbled about Leonis's initiatives being bad for business.

But now, we fly over barren land. The fields are empty. Not just the one directly beneath us, but all of them as far as I can see in every direction. I squint at the dry soil.

"What's this about?" I yell over the wind, turning to face Lyre.

"No idea," she yells back. "Maybe they harvested already?"

It doesn't fit with the normal growth pattern, but Gaians are always fiddling in their labs, so it's not impossible they developed something to speed it up. I hope not, though. If the crop failed, it could double the profit on our legal cargo.

After the barren fields come the statues. As soon as I spot the glossy black protuberance of one poking out of a bank covered in deep red moss, my stomach flips.

As a child I avoided the Primus ruins, as seeing them from afar was enough to make every hair on my body stand up at once. The first time I saw one up close, I was about five years old, playing a game of tag with Corvus. I ran from him, fast and reckless as I always was, and back then my body was made of knees and elbows and too-big feet. A trip sent me tumbling all the way down a grassy hill, knocking my knee against something hard on the way down. At the bottom of the hill I sat up, head spinning and knee strangely cold, and turned to come face-to-faceless with a huge, tentacled statue. I sobbed the whole way back to the ship, clinging to Corvus's hand.

I shake my head, trying to push away both the feeling that the statue is staring at me and the memory of my brother.

Once we reach the outskirts of Levian, the architecture gets a lot more human. But unfortunately, it also gets a lot more Gaian. Their buildings are angular and severe, metal glossed to annoyingly reflective perfection. It almost hurts to look at the shiny buildings and the glimmering solar panels lining the rooftops. The windows all have their blinds pulled down to block out the constant light.

Though *Fortuna* will always be my home, I usually enjoy trips planet-side. I can appreciate the novelty of Nibiru's endless ocean or Deva's tangled black jungles, find beauty in the wild frontiers of Pax or the vast tundra of Titan. But Gaia . . . not only are creepy alien ruins far more abundant here than anywhere else, but my memories of the place flood back regardless of my attempts to drink them away. Memories of an empty stomach and Momma's long absences, of picking pockets and learning to lie. And most of all, memories of Corvus. Corvus teaching me to hold my breath as I ran past the statues so I'd be less scared, bandaging my hands after I scraped them escaping from the law-enforcers, giving me the last bite of food.

I grimace and bang a fist on the side of the hovercraft.

"Let's land," I shout to Drom. "We'll walk the rest of the way." I'm eager to get moving. It'll help get me out of my head, and anyway, flying this thing through Levian's narrow streets is always a nightmare.

Drom shoots me a thumbs-up. She weaves through some buildings on the outskirts of the city and slows in preparation for landing. As we round a corner, I realize at the last moment what she's headed for. I curse, the word lost in the wind.

Drom brings the clunker right up to the foot of a Primus statue and lands there with an ungraceful thump. I lurch forward, my stomach threatening revolt. After a few long moments, I swallow and stand up, trying not to look at the statue towering over us.

It stands at least twenty feet tall, pitch black and completely unblemished despite a thousand years of wind and rain and time beating down upon it. It's almost humanoid at first glance, with a head, body, and four limbs. But where the arms should be are slender, tentacle-like appendages, and where the face should be, the statue is smooth and blank.

The Gaians have constructed a small fence around the base of the ancient monument, plastered with warnings about getting too close. I'm not sure why they bother. You could unload a full blaster at one of these things and it won't chip its surface. The twins have proved as much on a previous trip. The aliens had some way to manipulate the material, given that there are knives and other objects made from it, but as far as humans are concerned, the stuff is indestructible.

At the very front, near the strange, bony appendages that compose the statue's "feet," is a golden plaque. *Scientia potentia est*, the engraved words read. Knowledge is power. It's so Gaian I want to vomit. The remains of the Primus are scattered across the other planets as well, with the exception of Pax. But none have ruins as prominent as Gaia's, and none put much stock in the creepy, worshipful obsession that the Gaians have toward the dead aliens. Scientists theorize that this was the Primus home-world, which Gaians consider a source of pride. To me, it seems like living in a home whose previous owners disappeared under unknown circumstances is a pretty terrible idea.

I clamber out of the clunker, refusing to look directly at the statue and risk having my reaction show on my face. When I turn to my siblings, I find both twins smirking and Lyre hiding a small smile behind her hand.

"Little shits." I turn my back to the monument and fold my arms over my chest, trying to ignore the hairs on the back of my neck standing at full attention. My siblings never fail to find it hilarious that I'm afraid of the Primus and everything they left behind. The twins are enamored with modified Primus weapons—not that we could ever afford such a rarity—and Lyre devours every book she can find on alien theory. None of them, it seems, have ever noticed the way Momma looks at these statues. And I know if my mother is afraid, I better be scared, too.

"All right," I say, gesturing to the twins. "You two keep an eye on the cargo while Lyre and I go see the broker."

I'd feel a lot safer with one of the twins accompanying us, but again there's the issue with separating them. It's probably for the best, anyway. The twins are way too big to avoid attention, seeing as they're both more than a half foot taller than the average man on Gaia. They're also way too eager for a fight, and Momma's the one person who can talk them down. Without her, they're too much of a risk to go traipsing through the city with.

"Keep your weapons hidden and try not to shoot anybody," I say. "And if you do have to shoot someone, hide the body somewhere clever."

The twins grin their identical grin, gummy and gap-toothed. I'm not convinced there's a single clever bone between the two of them, but they're Kaisers, and Kaisers are nothing if not resourceful.

Lyre and I leave the twins with the cargo and press deeper into the heart of the city, ditching the goggles that mark us as clear off-worlders. It's early enough that the streets are empty. While some of the other planets have looser concepts of time, Gaia sticks to a strict daily schedule.

Levian is laid out in a straightforward grid of streets that make up clearly designated districts. The buildings differ slightly from district to district but altogether are annoyingly similar to one another. Each district has at least one billboard or poster of President Leonis, giving the impression that she's always watching with her dark, sharp eyes. While political ads on other planets usually feature smiling, charismatic leaders, Leonis is stoic and imposing with her graying hair pulled back from her severe face. She's the latest in a line of progressively more ruthless Gaian presidents, taking the most extreme measures yet in an effort to combat the planet's struggles with food and population control.

I shudder, hurrying my steps. This place is creepy, but at least it's easy to navigate. It shouldn't take us long to get to the storage facility—but when we're a few streets away, the chimes of a bell sound up and down the streets, emanating from the speakers mounted on every street corner.

"*Shit*," I say, hurrying my steps. "Are we running that late?"

"It appears so," Lyre says with a sigh. She doesn't bother to speed up, already knowing we won't beat the rush. And of course, she's right.

First Bell marks 7:00 a.m. and the beginning of the Gaian workday. Gaians are nothing if not punctual, so the streets are already filling with people by the time the last chime fades into echoes. I groan, slowing for Lyre to catch up to me, and try to fall into the flow of street traffic. Everyone travels one way on the right side of the street, and the opposite on the left. Between that, the grid of the streets, and the tightly wound Gaian manners, it's the most organized crowd you can find anywhere in the system. Eerily so, like watching a hive mind at work.

Except, like usual, I can't seem to fit in. As we're pulled into the tide, I step on the foot of the man behind me, apologize to his disapproving frown, and immediately plow right into the person ahead when they stop. They glare at me over the top of a medical mask.

I start to offer my hands, palms up, in a quick Gaian apology, but freeze halfway through the motion as I realize why traffic has stopped. Five uniformed law-enforcers have formed a loose barricade at the crossroads ahead and are using glowing handheld devices to scan everyone's hands and eyes before allowing them through. I hang back as much as I can without disrupting the line, craning my neck in an attempt to figure out what they're looking for.

As the enforcers pull a startled-looking man aside, the crowd stirs uneasily around us, though they don't abandon their lines. When the man attempts to pull away from the enforcers, one of them jabs him in the stomach with a baton. He goes limp and they drag him away. I grimace, though no one in the crowd reacts other than to pull white filtration masks out of their bags and put them on.

Lyre and I pull our scarves up to cover our faces.

"What is this?" she asks, her eyes wide. "Should we try to find another way through?"

"If we step out of line, it'll call more attention to us." I chew the inside of my lip, noting that nobody else in the crowd seems particularly confused about what's happening, and turn to the woman beside me.

"I can't believe this," I say with a sigh. "I mean . . . really? Again? Is this necessary?"

Despite my best attempts to imitate the attitude of the crowd, her eyes narrow in suspicion.

"If it prevents another plague, it's a small price to pay," she says.

"Oh, but of course. I misspoke." I gesture a small apology. "I merely hope I won't be late to work. I have to make it all the way to Itsennen."

She inclines her head, the suspicion dimming as I name a district that's both far from here and known for its luxury shopping and restaurants.

"So long as you're healthy, it should be quick. Your employer will understand."

"Let us hope you're right."

I turn back to Lyre.

"Sanitation check," I murmur under my breath. "Don't panic, we'll be fine."

"Unless we brought something from Deva," she says in a low, frantic whisper. "You did throw up that entire last night—"

"That was the whiskey. Relax. We'll be fine."

Despite my words, my mouth is dry as we approach the sanitation checkpoint. Still, I force myself to strip off my gloves and hold out my hands like everyone else. As long as this machine isn't also configured to read Devan plant residue, I'll be fine.

"Good morning, officer," I say, keeping my eyes down like a Gaian would.

"Good morning." He scans my hands. "Have you experienced any coughing, fatigue, or stomach upset?"

"No, sir. No symptoms to report."

My heart beats double-time as I wait. But after a moment, he waves me through with the rest of the crowd, with Lyre following shortly.

"I don't like this," she murmurs as soon as we're out of earshot, glancing back at the checkpoint.

"It's probably just a cold going around. You know how Gaians are." I shrug and pull my gloves back on. "Anyway, we'll be out of here soon enough. Just try to blend in."

The crowd soon thins as people filter into buildings or other areas of the city. By the time we reach the familiar, square building on the edge of the factory district, the streets are almost completely empty again. I glance around to confirm we're alone before rapping my knuckles against the metal door.

After several seconds, it scrapes upward.

Lyre and I step inside, and the door slams shut behind us. We're left in a small, bare room with only a desk in the corner and a hawk-nosed Gaian standing behind it.

"Hey," I say, and pause. My mind grasps at nothingness for a moment before producing a name. I snap my fingers and smile. "Thudana! Been a while, huh?" She scowls at me, unimpressed. People seem to find me affable enough on other planets, but here it always feels like I'm doing something wrong. Gaian manners are too complicated, and I didn't exactly get a crash course as an illegal off-worlder. Corvus was much better at knowing the right thing to do. "Uh…" I glance at Lyre, who shrinks back with a shake of her head, never one for conversation with strangers.

Thudana pulls up the end of one glove to reveal a glowing digital clock etched there. The electronic tattoo reads in blocky white letters: 07:14.

"You're late," she says.

"Oh. Right. Sorry." Fourteen minutes late, and she's being pissy. Damn Gaians and their schedules. I extend my hands in a gesture of apology for the third time since my arrival here, resisting the urge to roll my eyes. "We experienced an unavoidable delay."

"At customs?" she asks, suspicion crossing her face.

"No, no. Ship malfunction. Nothing to concern yourself with."

"And where is Auriga?" Her lips purse in displeasure.

"Talking to our client," I lie. "Trying to make up for the delay." If this woman knew my mother was pulled away by law enforcement, she'd boot us out onto the streets. "She'll be here in a couple hours."

"We don't rent to off-worlders. Do you have permission to be in the city?"

Despite my many years away from Gaia, and the fact that I'm here legally this time, the implied threat still shakes me up. My tongue tangles on itself. Lyre nudges me, and I clear my throat.

"Of course we do. We're here rather than scattered in pieces across the landing zone, aren't we?"

"I can't rent space to anyone without a Gaian ID."

My lips form soundless words for a moment.

"You've done business with us many times before," Lyre says quietly, while I struggle to respond.

"I did business with your mother," Thudana says. "Your *Gaian* mother."

"Aw, c'mon," I say. "It's—"

"Illegal."

"Oh, now you're suddenly so concerned with the law?" I almost laugh. There's no way Thudana is unaware of the illegal business people use her rooms for. My mother has kept cargo here many, many times over the years. The two are practically business partners.

"*Scorpia*," Lyre hisses. Thudana, behind the counter, sits up straighter.

"I'm not sure what you're implying," she says stiffly. "This is a perfectly legal business. Which means we do not conduct deals with off-worlders."

I sigh, running a hand through my hair, and look at Lyre.

"Go wait with the cargo," I say. She frowns at me.

"But—"

"Now." I try to channel the firm voice Momma uses when someone's not listening to her. Lyre's frown lines deepen, but she turns and heads for the door. Once it's shut, I turn back to Thudana and lean across the counter, propping my chin up with a hand. "Okay, how much will it take for you to do business with us?"

Judging by the way she sizes me up, I wasn't wrong in the assumption this was a matter of funds. This woman doesn't care about the legality of doing business with us. She just wants to be compensated for the potential risk.

"I want a cut."

"My mom is already giving you one," I say, since it seems like a reasonable guess.

"A bigger cut," Thudana says.

"How much?"

"Ten percent."

I let out a low whistle and lean back.

"Not a chance." I pause, trying to estimate how much Momma is already giving her. If only she wasn't so damn secretive about details like this. I bet she told Corvus all this shit, but she never lets me in on anything. And the moment I say the wrong amount, Thudana will know I'm bullshitting and kick me out. "How does six percent sound?"

Thudana grimaces, scratches her nose.

"Eight percent and a deposit of five hundred," she says. I open my mouth, and she adds, "Refundable once it's all handled."

"Hm." I drum my fingers on the counter, pretend to consider the offer while I attempt to remember if I have that many credits available. This wouldn't be a problem if Momma gave me access to the business account, but she's made it very clear she doesn't trust me with the family funds. Like the rest of my siblings, I merely get a small cut of the earnings in my own personal account. We made a nice profit on Deva, but my last few nights there are a bit of a blur. Devan clubs are way, way too much fun. If I check my balance in front of Thudana, though, it'll make me look weak. She's already staring too closely at me. I need to make a call. "Deal."

I pull my square comm out of my pocket and hold it out. She pulls out her own, slim and chrome and updated like Commander Zinne's was. We hold the two devices with the screens facing each other until each one gives a beep of connection.

"Transfer five hundred creds," I say for voice recognition.

"Verified," Thudana says, meeting my eyes. We stare at each other, and I hope she doesn't notice that I'm sweating. If this transaction fails, I'll look like worse than a fool—I'll look like a cheat. Despite her relationship with my mother, she'd definitely call in the law if she thought I was trying to swindle her. And as an off-worlder, even a legal one, I won't get a chance to defend myself before they drag me to jail.

My device beeps. Hers follows. I let out a breath. Thudana pulls her comm back, her sour expression softening.

"All right," she says, and reaches under the desk to pull out a keycard. She waves it over my comm until it beeps. "You have access to room 306 for twenty-four hours. Get your cargo in, quick and quiet."

*   *   *

When I emerge from the building, I'm surprised to find the sky dark and gloomy, a stark contrast from the mild weather merely ten minutes ago. I tighten my hood around me and hurry back to the cargo, not wanting to get caught in the rain. Thankfully, the traffic is gone now that the workday's begun, and the sanitation checkpoints are gone.

I walk briskly, pausing to scroll through the contacts on my comm and send off a quick message: *I'm in Levian. Have something for you. Where should we meet?* A couple minutes later, a response pings back, containing only an address for what looks like an abandoned building in the Turill district. I grin. *Be there in 20*, I send back.

The twins are playing some kind of game on their comms when I arrive, while Lyre keeps a wary eye on the streets. Her eyebrows lift as she spots my smile.

"What did you give Thudana?" she asks.

"A heavy dose of my usual charm."

She rolls her eyes.

"Guess you can work it out with Momma." Her tone is bitter, but I can't help but savor the feeling of knowing something she doesn't. She stands and brushes dust off her jumpsuit. "Anyway, we've got about two hours until our meeting with the client."

"Two hours," I mutter. "Damn."

It's a tight time frame, but I can still fit in my side job if I go now. My siblings aren't going to like it, but I'm sure they're capable of moving some cargo and lying low for a couple hours.

"Get this shit off the streets," I tell the twins, and wave my comm over each of theirs to pass over the electronic key. "Room 306." The twins, thankfully, seem to be in an obedient mood, and rise with two crates each.

"You should get some rest," Lyre says, as I watch the two of them disappear around the corner. I glance at her, and she wrinkles her nose. "And a bath."

I shrug off the comments and push past her.

"Actually, I've got some business to take care of before the meeting."

"Excuse me?"

"It's gonna be real quick. I'll be back with plenty of time for the deal."

"Are you serious, Scorpia?" Her eyes go wide. "Momma left you in charge. You're supposed to be handling this."

I'm already stepping away as she finishes. I don't want to wait until the twins get back and have to run through the whole explanation again. Drom won't give a shit about me leaving, but Pol gets jittery when plans change, and I don't have time to waste on soothing his nerves.

"Already handled it." I hold my hands out in a placating gesture. "Like I said, I'll be quick. Just visiting an old friend."

"You don't have friends."

"Oof." I dramatically press a hand to my heart. She scowls, and I drop it and laugh. "Okay, you're right. Not a friend. It's a steamy, illicit love affair. That good enough for you?"

"Scorpia." I was prepared to walk away despite any further nagging, but something in her tone makes me stop and look back at her. She frowns at me, her arms folded across her chest, but the expression is worried rather than harsh. "Just tell me you're not doing something stupid because of this whole thing with Corvus."

I gape at her a moment before snapping my mouth shut. Annoyance surges up inside me.

"Mind your own business for once," I snap. "I don't need a babysitter. All right?"

Lyre presses her lips together like she's trying to keep words back. But just as I'm once again about to leave, she says, "I'm trying to help you." The words tumble out in a rush, like she's forcing them out before she can second-guess herself. I pause but don't turn around. "Look, Momma's gone and something's off about this whole job. You shouldn't be alone in Levian. Whatever you're doing, bring me with you. I can keep a secret."

I glance back. Her cheeks are red, but she meets my gaze steadily. For a moment I consider the offer. It could be nice to have a second pair of eyes and Lyre's sharp mind...but no. The thought is foolish. Lyre is probably just looking to steal some of the profit—and Momma's favor—for herself. Either that, or she plans to rat me out.

And I don't need her. I'm trying to prove I'm capable of running a job all by myself, without Momma or anyone else breathing down my neck. I have to do this on my own.

"Thanks but no thanks. I can handle myself, little sis."

I walk away before she can get another word in.

CHAPTER SIX

The Old Bear

Corvus

The rest of my team is already waiting when I arrive on the roof. They lean against the metal railing in uneasy silence, staring out at the frozen landscape around us.

Weak sunlight filters through the clouds today. It's mild weather for Titan, though the wind buffets us this high up. Since I didn't take the time to fully gear up for the outdoors, the cold bites at me, and I clamp my jaw shut to keep my teeth from chattering. The others didn't take time to dress, either, and are wearing unbuttoned jackets and billowing scarves in danger of ripping free.

I approach the roof's edge, shouting to be heard above the wind. "Report."

"Something weird, Sarge," Magda shouts back. Snippy as always, but her forehead is wrinkled with worry. I frown, leaning across the railing next to her.

This outpost rests on the crest of a small mountain and provides a generous look at the surrounding area. A sea of white and gray surrounds us, expanses of unmarked snow broken by rocky spires and deep, icy valleys. At first I thought the view was breathtaking, but after three weeks stationed here I'm beginning to find it dull.

It's familiar enough that my eyes immediately find the restructured cliff. As I saw on the radar, there's no sign it was triggered by anything unnatural. But there is…something. Something I can't quite make out amid the rock and snow sent tumbling by the landslide. I squint, leaning farther over the railing.

"At the base of the cliff…" I stop as it disappears. Maybe it was nothing more than the glint of light on the snow.

"Something's glowing in there," Sverre says.

That's what I thought I saw, but I was hoping I was wrong. If it came from anyone else, I might have doubted still, but Sverre speaks only when he's sure of something.

Ivennie stands back, chewing her lip in consternation. Daniil watches me silently. It's not hard to guess what worries them. This outpost may be near the border to Isolationist territory, but it's also in the middle of nowhere. We haven't seen a single sign of life, let alone combat, in the weeks we've been stationed here. For this to happen now, so close to us, can be no coincidence. And that glow hints at something not human-made.

Primus technology is rarer on Titan than on other worlds; there's evidence the aliens settled here, but their statues, and anything else they left behind on this planet, are buried deep beneath the ice. When someone goes through the trouble of digging it up, it's usually some type of weapon. Dangerous, volatile, better left untouched. The Isolationists embrace it despite the danger, insisting it is one of Titan's natural resources left for us. But my people, the Interplanetists, are more wary, insisting alien technology is too unpredictable, and we are better off trading with other planets than digging up ancient history we know too little about. Their fear borders on superstition in my opinion, but generally I agree with the sentiment.

"Get inside and be ready to move out," I say. "I'll contact the general."

While my team gears up, I sit in the briefing room on the basement floor of the building. Pressing a hand to the control screen calls up a holographic image of the surrounding landscape. I spend a few minutes scrutinizing it, searching for anything I might have overlooked, but find no hints of whatever we saw.

Altair answers my call almost immediately, his video image coming to life on a wide screen mounted on the wall.

"The old bear," as Magda loves to call him behind his back, is as pristine as always. His gray-shot hair and beard are neatly trimmed, his medal-decorated uniform perfectly immaculate. I'd place his age somewhere in the fifties, which is not so old at all on any other planet, but here marks him as a survivor.

"General," I say, pressing my fingers to my heart. The man is a war hero, a tactical genius, and my own personal mentor during training. I owe him my station, and much more.

"Sergeant Kaiser." He returns the salute. "I'm glad to finally receive a call from you. I take this to mean you have an answer for me?"

My tongue sticks in my mouth. I hadn't considered that he might expect that.

"I still have another week to consider, sir," I say, and pretend the flicker of disappointment on his face doesn't feel like a needle to my heart.

"I understand it's a difficult decision," he says. "But I hope you understand it's an offer I didn't make lightly."

"I am truly honored, sir. That's not why I'm contacting you today, though." He inclines his head, and I clear my throat and continue. "Something has happened nearby. A landslide uncovered an unidentified object, close enough to be visible to the naked eye from our position." I slide a hand across the touch-screen, sending a snapshot of our map to him, and wait for him to receive the transmission. "However, we're getting nothing on our radars. Would you have us evacuate the outpost?"

"No," Altair says, his eyes still on the map I sent him. "Your team is in no danger. In fact, this is the sign we've been wait-ing for." Altair is a composed man, not easily incited to emotion, but there's an unmistakable gleam of excitement in his eyes as he looks up again. "I know your time here may be almost done, Ser-geant Kaiser, but I need to ask this one last thing of you."

"I'm grateful to serve." The Titan saying has often tasted like a lie, but not this time. I'm happy to make myself useful to him and his cause one last time.

Altair nods his gratitude, and his hands move across the screen before him. A few moments later, a file appears on my own device. When I tap it, a three-dimensional image springs to life above the table.

"What am I looking at?" I reach out to touch the hologram with two fingers, rotating it. It's an image of an orb, its edges lumpy and indistinct, its surface moving in slow ripples. A faint light pulses from within.

"This is what you'll be retrieving from the site. It's a power source."

"Alien in nature?" The question is absentminded; the silence from Altair's end is both an answer and an indication I should not have asked it. "Apologies, sir. I forget myself."

It's not the sort of question that's asked here, especially from someone as low-ranking as me. Still, my mind turns over this new information. An alien power source. I've long wondered if the Interplanetists utilize Primus technology more often than they admit. But what use could they have for such a thing?

"Your radars won't be of any assistance," Altair says, which is just as much of an answer to my question as the previous silence was. "It may be buried beneath the ice, but if it was visible to you, it should be close enough to the surface for you to locate once you're on-site. I trust you will find a way to secure it."

"Your trust is not misplaced."

"Take the exosuits and any other equipment you need from the outpost, but no large machinery. You'll be a stone's throw from enemy territory. Best not to attract any unwanted attention."

"Understood."

"And, Corvus?"

I wait.

He leans forward, his gaze sharpening. "This is highly classified. Let no one see it. Do you understand?"

There are a dozen questions I could ask here—Does he mean I should hide this from my team as well? From our own people? What should I do if someone does see it?—but I know the answers already.

"Yes, sir."

"Go make your planet proud," General Altair says, and severs the connection.

As my superior's face disappears, I'm left staring at the still-spinning hologram above my table. A classified retrieval mission so close to the border...an alien power source buried beneath the ice...and so many questions, unasked and unanswered.

How convenient that Altair chose a team headed by me, an off-worlder with fewer qualms about the Primus than most, to keep watch at this remote outpost. I knew there had to be a reason for us to be here, and I suspect there is more to this mission than Altair is letting on. Thinking back to the hunger in his eyes when I told him what we saw, I'm absolutely certain of it.

CHAPTER SEVEN

Friends in Low Places

Scorpia

walk briskly, with my head up and my eyes forward, like I have somewhere legitimate to be. It's enough to keep the law-enforcers from bothering me. The streets are mostly unoccupied this early in the day, when everyone's just begun to work. I'm sure the approaching storm crackling overhead doesn't make anyone eager to be outside, either. The only people I pass are a few cleaners washing the streets after the morning rush and some enforcers on patrol.

I've always hated Levian, with its overly organized layout and blocky, near-identical buildings in neat little rows. The streets are too clean, not a single person or piece of trash out of place. Everywhere I look there are clocks, maps, and signs designating buildings or districts. The whole city is like an overly friendly neighbor trying way too hard to be helpful. It's especially shocking after Deva, where time has little meaning and the crisscrossing walkways seem to be thrown together at random. I love the playful chaos of Deva; on Gaia, I'm always tempted to break something just for a moment free from monotony. Growing up here was a nightmare. Being here now, when the streets remind me of playing tag with Corvus in the empty hours after Last Bell, is even worse.

Trying to shake off the memories, I pass from the heart of the city to the Turill district. It's an older area on the outskirts of the city, one that most people have moved away from as the city expanded south, infringing on areas that used to be reserved for arriving ships and related businesses. Turill is still clean and orga-nized, but the buildings are more worn down and dated, muted and monochrome rather than shiny and metallic. I pass by quiet residential areas and cafés, clothing shops that have fallen behind on trends, and outdated game lounges. There's even a very old and empty-looking building whose sign declares it CHURCH OF THE FIRST DIVINITY. I eye it, wondering if it's dedicated to an ancient Earth-based religion or to Gaia's creepier sect of Primus worshippers, but it's hard to tell from the building's understated appearance.

At the end of a long, straight alley, I find the building my cli-ent designated. The sign on the front of the building is blank, the shutters closed, as though the place is abandoned.

I knock: three quick taps, one loud thud, and another tap-tap. The door slides open eerily fast, and shuts itself behind me just as swiftly.

The lobby is small and irritatingly Gaian. A huge clock made of black metal decorates one wall. Gaians love to make their obsessive time-tracking seem like an artistic choice rather than a practical one. I always find the constant reminders of time restric-tive, and especially so now, when its hands tick away the limited minutes until I have to return to my family. If I don't make it back for our meeting with the customer, I'll never hear the end of it. *Especially* if something goes wrong.

I chew on my lip, but force myself to stop as the door on the other side of the lobby slides open. In the doorway stands a small

Gaian man with watery eyes and an almost impossibly wrinkled face. He crosses his arms in an X over his chest in a formal Gaian greeting, and I suppress a grimace as I return the gesture. Even the black market brokers on this planet are unbearably polite. I hate these kinds of pleasantries; they make it impossible to tell what anyone is really thinking.

"She's on her way," the man says. He gestures for me to step through the doorway into the second room, but I stay where I am.

"Wha—she is?" I ask, startled. "Shey?"

The man nods. I shift, eyeing the room with renewed suspicion. I don't like that he immediately knows who I am and who I'm here to see. I don't like anyone keeping tabs on me that closely, especially not for a job like this, but I guess that's what he's here for. Shey wouldn't have sent me here unless we could trust him.

"How long will it take?" I ask, drumming my fingers against my arm.

"Impossible to say," the man says, his expression inscrutable. "Security has been tight lately, it may be a while."

I sigh, and step farther into the building. This room is bigger than the first, and my eyes are drawn to the mural covering one wall, artistically depicting a meeting between a human and a Primus. The faceless Primus has its tentacles spread wide, light fanning behind it in an image of godliness; the human is bowing, humble, hands extended in supplication. Whether it's a sign that the man who owns this building is a Primus worshipper, or it's just a general, creepy Gaian thing, I'm not sure.

At the center is a tall, round metal table encircled with a ring of stools. The only light in the room comes from the yellow-tinted lamp hanging directly overhead, casting the corners of the room into shadow. By habit, I check each of them in turn before seating myself on one of the stools. Once I do, the old man is already gone, and the single door is closed.

As soon as I'm alone, my fidgeting breaks out in full force. First a finger tapping a beat on the table, then a leg jumping in place, then a soft whistling under my breath. Eventually, I jump to my feet and begin to pace in front of the eerie Primus mural. Again and again, my thoughts return to my family and what will happen if I'm late. Lyre is capable enough to handle a routine sale on her own, though her aloof attitude won't earn her any friends along the way. The twins, though…the twins rarely manage to stick to plans, and even more rarely listen to Lyre's voice of reason. In fact, they're more likely to do the opposite to spite her, and she still hasn't picked up on that over the years. Without me there, the deal will be at least twice as likely to end in excess bloodshed and a severe lack of compensation. And of course, Momma will blame me, like usual.

As soon as I hear the telltale *clunk* that means the door's about to open, I scramble back to the table, throw myself onto a stool, and assume a pose of casual relaxation. I can't have myself appearing nervous in front of a potentially skittish client. When she enters the room, her hood up and her face covered by a scarf, I slowly get to my feet, stretch, and flash a smile. As usual, she's dressed in the height of Gaian fashion, wearing a hooded white dress with stiff, squared-off shoulders and burnished silver buttons down one side.

"Hello, hello." I throw out a gloved hand to shake, quickly remember that isn't something Gaians consider polite after the plague, and cross my arms in an X over my chest in their traditional greeting instead. "Whoops, just got back from Deva," I say, both to smooth over the social blunder and pique her interest in what I brought. "Apologies about contacting you during the workday."

"It's not a problem," Shey says, returning the formal greeting. "I told work I had woken up with a cough, and they quite vehemently insisted I stay home."

She pulls back her hood and smiles warmly at me. My heart

beats faster in response, just like it did the first time I saw her a year ago, throwing away my latest profit in a ritzy Itsennen bar.

Back then, even with her hood still up and her face shadowed, just a glimpse of her face—light brown skin, broad cheekbones, dark eyes—was enough to make me do a double take. There was something familiar about her features, but I was too tipsy to place her.

I offered to buy her a drink. She declined without even glancing my way. But when the bartender noted the goggles around my neck and outdated comm, he demanded to see my visa, and all of a sudden I had Shey's attention. Usually, when Gaians realize I'm an off-worlder, they pull away from me. Instead, she leaned closer, her gaze curious rather than suspicious.

"Are you Devan?" she asked, noting that I had ordered corn whiskey from the planet.

"Nope. Just came from there, though, and this is much better than Gaian-made swill." I sipped my drink, eyeing her. "How about I give you one more guess, and if you're wrong, I get to buy you that drink?"

She smiled and looked me up and down. I turned fully toward her, inviting the scrutiny, unable to deny that her attention gave me a small thrill.

"No scars, so Titan seems unlikely," she said, tapping a gloved finger to her lips. "Not Nibiran, or the bartender would have reacted quite differently, I imagine." She tilted her head slightly. "So you're from Pax?"

"Good guess, but nope. I'm no gunslingin' Paxian rancher, either," I said, imitating a Paxian drawl, and grinned at her confusion. "You ever heard the term *space-born*?"

The conversation continued on for a couple hours and several drinks. She told me she was a scientist researching Primus technology. I hinted I was a purveyor of "off-world curiosities." And eventually, I sold her a Devan snake-snapper in an alley on the outskirts of Levian.

I was considering trying for a kiss when she looked up at me, the light on her face and a political ad for President Leonis on the wall behind her, and I finally realized why she looked so familiar. I should've walked away then. Hell, I should've run as fast as I could in the opposite direction. Instead, I asked, "So how can I get in touch next time I'm here?"

Against all odds, the president's daughter turned out to be a discreet client with a strong interest in Devan plants. Curiosity about anything off-world is a strange quality for a Gaian, since they're generally convinced that Gaia has everything worth having in the system. I couldn't help but find her interest endearing. We've met up a few times now, though after a close call last time, we decided to use the assistance of a broker and a safe house.

My mother would never let me do such a risky deal, but once I show her the profit I make, she's sure to be impressed. Shey's mother, on the other hand, would certainly have me put to death if she found out...but Shey's wallet makes it worth the risk. The pretty face doesn't hurt, either, though for the sake of our business relationship I still haven't tried for that kiss yet.

"Pleasant travels?" she asks. My mind flashes to *Fortuna* crashing into the landing zone and the law-enforcers leaving with my mother.

"Nice and smooth. You have any trouble getting here?"

"Not at all."

We're both good enough liars that the answers mean nothing. But I brush that off and gesture at the stools. I wait for Shey to sit first; that's a Gaian custom I know, mostly because Shey was shocked I didn't wait the last time I met her. Once she's settled, I sink onto the opposite stool.

We've barely seated ourselves before the old man is there with two glasses and a pitcher of iced water. That, at least, is something Gaians have plenty of—not like Titan or Pax, where I have to carry my own around. He sets them down on the table, bows his head toward Shey, and leaves us.

There's a long pause as I decide whether or not to jump right into business. I'm aware of every second ticking by, but not so keen on ruining my relationship with a good client, either.

"Uh, so . . . how's work?" I venture. Shey frowns at me.

"Classified, as usual," she says, her eyebrows arching, and I mentally kick myself. Of course. Shey does government work studying the Primus, and she's never keen to give any details about it.

"Right. Well. Just making small talk," I say.

Shey says nothing, but sits with her shoulders very stiff and her lips very firm. It could be because of my question, but it probably means I'm doing something else wrong. After a moment, I make a guess and grab the pitcher. Shey immediately slides one of the glasses forward. I pour for her and allow her to take the pitcher and pour me a glass as well.

Fucking Gaians, I think. The water is refreshingly cool on my tongue, but I can't help but wish it was something with more bite. Some hair of the dog would help with this swiftly developing headache.

"I don't come to this part of town often," Shey says. She sips her water delicately, holding the glass with both gloved hands. "I hope you have something that makes it worthwhile."

"Well, I don't often sell illegal goods to the daughters of presidents," I say, "so I can promise you that it is."

I tip my glass in Shey's direction and take another drink. Her lips tug upward, and she mirrors the gesture in a way that may or may not be mocking.

"A new Devan plant?" she asks.

"But of course." I never get sick of the way her eyes light up. "Though, you know, I can bring you other stuff if you want. There are a lot of fascinating—"

"No, thank you," she says before I can even finish. "I have no interest in other contraband."

She sounds almost offended by the question. I shrug, downing half my glass of water, and after a moment her expression softens. She looks down at her lap.

"I . . . believe there's a lot to be learned from them, that's all." She hesitates, and then blurts out, "And a blanket ban on Devan plants is just as absurd and illogical as Nibiru's ban of all Primus technology."

I laugh, setting my glass down.

"Well, at least we can agree on that." As much as I'd love to pass the day talking to Shey, my time is running short, so I reach into the pocket of my jumpsuit and pull out the box. It isn't impressive on its own, just a small, unadorned black cube, but Shey's eyes are hungry the moment she spots it. She pushes her glass aside and places her hands on the table with her fingers splayed. I bite back a grin and tap a finger on the box.

"This," I say, dropping my voice to an almost-whisper, "is a little something I found in the wild jungles of Deva, where human-eating plants threaten all those who stray from the civilized path." I run my hand along the edge of the box and press on the first of the pressure pads, which opens with a faint hiss. Shey leans farther forward still, her eyes very round. "I have seen many things in my travels, but this . . . this is something the likes of which I had never laid eyes on." I press the second of the four pads; another hiss; another inch of space closed between Shey and the box. "When I first saw it, I didn't believe locals who said it was a plant. Surely, I said, no plant can act like that. No plant can *move* like that. And yet . . ." I press the third. "And yet this one did."

I let the dramatic pause linger until Shey raises her eyes to meet mine. I press the last of the pads and move the lid aside.

Nothing happens. For a moment I fear I managed to kill the

thing on the journey, but—slowly, very slowly—a slender, leafy black tendril extends above the edge and pokes at the air around it. Shey gasps, pressing a hand to her chest. I hold a finger out just above the plant. The tendril prods once, twice, and begins to wrap itself around it.

It moves more slowly than clouds traversing the sky, but for a plant, it's almost alarmingly rapid. Personally I find the thing creepy, but I keep my smile plastered on as the vine tugs at my finger.

Shey leans forward, both hands clasped to her chest now, eyes locked on the tiny monstrosity. I can practically see the credits sliding into my account already. And luckily for me, Shey hasn't got a lick of savvy about the actual going rate. I have no shame in charging her as much as I think she's willing to pay. She's not going hungry anytime soon, and I have no qualms about ensuring that I never will again.

"What's it called?" Shey asks. She shifts closer, leaning farther over the table.

"The Devans called it a..." I pause, realizing *strangle-vine* isn't a particularly appealing name. "Creep-crawler, I think."

She's leaning so close now that I can smell mint on her breath and have to make an effort not to stare down her dress. A *considerable* effort, given that I've spent the last several days crammed into a spaceship with no company other than my family. She glances up at me, quirking one eyebrow in a way that lets me know I've been caught in the act, and I avert my eyes. I bite the inside of my cheek and focus on the vine, which is now brushing its leaves against my wrist. I need to keep my mind on the job.

"May I?" she asks, holding out one hand. A pale green clock tattoo glows just above her glove, reminding me I'm on a deadline, but I can never bring myself to rush with Shey.

"Sure." I pull free from the vine just as Shey reaches forward to take it, and our fingers brush. Even through my rough brown gloves and the white silk covering her own skin, the gesture feels strangely intimate—especially for Gaia, where hands touch so rarely. Shey's cheeks flare pink, but she refocuses on the plant as I pull back. She strokes a leaf with one finger and lets out a quiet laugh.

"It tickles," she says, and slowly turns her hand over, watching how the vine clings to her. "Reactive to heat, I wonder?" After a few more moments of watching the plant, she glances up at me through her long eyelashes. "How much?"

I swallow and turn my eyes up to the ceiling so I can think clearly.

"I'll give it to you for two thousand." On Gaia, that's approximately what one would pay for an old, beat-up vehicle like my family's clunker, a reasonably fine piece of art, or a hell of a lot of alcohol. On some of the other planets, it's a small fortune. When Shey doesn't respond, I lower my eyes to her. She's staring at me with her lips pursed, all hints of possible flirtation gone, if I didn't imagine them in the first place. "Fine. Eighteen hundred, because I like you."

"Don't be absurd," Shey says, her expression unchanging. "I'll give you one thousand for it."

I let out a surprised laugh.

"Is that a joke?"

She says nothing.

"Okay, look, I know you don't have much experience with this sort of thing, but surely you can appreciate the time and effort that go into an operation like this," I say. "Not to mention the danger it puts me in. Do you know what I had to go through to get this thing off Deva?"

In truth: not much. Obtaining the plant cost me precisely one sandwich, handed to a local child who dug it up for me. The strangle-vines grew like weeds on the outskirts of his village, and its people had to hack them away once a week so the plants wouldn't invade the fields and kill their crops. The most difficult part of the process was hiding the plant from my family. My mother immediately decided that the strangle-vines were useless, but I thought of Shey and her credits the moment I saw it.

"I will give you one thousand and no more."

"Then I had to check on it five times a day on the journey," I lie, continuing with my wheedling tale as if Shey hadn't spoken. "It didn't do well in the ship's climate. Probably why one of them has never made it to Gaia alive. You hear what I'm saying? This is the *very* first, one and only, Gaian creep-crawler." I point a finger at her for emphasis. Judging from her unimpressed expression, it's considered a rude gesture in Gaian culture, but I've had enough of their many rules right now. "And you could take it home today."

"Indeed," Shey says. "For one thousand credits."

"You know what, that reminds me, I didn't even mention the trouble we ran into with Gaian customs! They boarded us, scoured the ship. I would've flushed the plant if I hadn't known how much you'd love it."

"One thousand."

My still-pointing finger wilts, and I let the arm fall to the table with a thud.

"You're supposed to barter, not just keep repeating the same number. Haven't we been through this before?"

"I don't see the point in such games," Shey says, and bites her lip in a poor attempt to hide a smile. I roll my eyes and lean back.

"Twelve hundred."

"One—" Shey begins, and I throw up my hands.

"Fine!" I say. "Fine, fine, I give up. A thousand it is, you pain in the ass."

Shey grins, and I grimace back at her. It's mostly for show. A thousand is still a nice profit for a job like this, certainly nice enough to impress my mother, and still substantially more than most people would pay for such a useless thing. All in all, it's a success, though I'm not happy about Shey learning a glimmer of business sense. I was hoping to keep fleecing her, maybe bring in some bigger sales once I get my mother on board.

I'm so eager to close the deal that I unthinkingly spit on one glove and extend the hand to shake. When Shey physically recoils, her eyes wide with horror, I realize my mistake. I lean back and wipe my glove on my jumpsuit. The old business tradition was commonplace back on Deva, and would be fine just about anywhere else in the system, but of course Gaia is different.

"Oops," I mumble in embarrassment, and pull out my comm. "Like I said, I'm fresh out of Deva. Sorry."

Shey, breathing a visible sigh of relief now that the offending spittle-covered glove is gone, takes a moment to collect herself and pull up each of her gloves. She opens her mouth to speak, but is cut off by an ear-shattering *boom* from the next room over.

The table shakes from the impact. I scramble to my feet. My mouth opens, and out of instinct, I nearly call out for the twins— but I'm alone. Alone and unarmed.

"Oh, fuck," I say, looking at Shey. "You said this place was safe!"

Shey is staring at the door, one hand over her mouth, the other still hovering near the illegal plant. I snap my fingers to get her attention. She yanks free from the plant, shuts the box, and shoves it across the table at me.

"Whoa, whoa, this is yours," I say, pushing it back. My heart is starting to hammer. I'm majorly screwed if I get caught here, especially without my family to back me up. Plants from Deva are a class-one contraband item on Gaia. If I'm caught with one, there's only one punishment: death. Off-worlders don't even have a legal right to a trial. "You just bought it. It belongs to you."

"We haven't finalized the deal!" Shey protests, sending the box sliding back across the table.

"We were about to." Push.

"You're the criminal, you take it!" Push.

"I'm an off-worlder, *you* take it!"

I give the box a hearty shove, intending to send it toppling into Shey's lap. Instead, it flies right off the edge of the table and clatters to the floor, where the improperly closed pressure locks hiss open. I swear, take a step toward the fallen contraband, and freeze with one arm outstretched as the door leading to the lobby slams upward. I drop my hand to my side and step back.

The woman in the doorway is tall and uniformed in all white, with straight eyebrows and lips pressed into a thin line. It takes me a moment to place her face, and as soon as I do, I take another step back, eyes darting around to find an escape that isn't here. This is the officer who apprehended *Fortuna* and took my mother. The head of security of the Gaian president herself—the same president who's the mother of the woman I just sold an extremely illegal flora to.

"Yvette," Shey gasps, her eyes going very wide with recognition. "What...what in the world are you doing here? Did you follow me?" She sounds affronted at first. A moment later, the gravity of the situation seems to hit her, and her eyes fill with tears. "I... I..."

But the officer isn't looking at her. She's looking right past the woman she's apparently here to collect, and staring at me instead. I meet her gaze and know in an instant that she recognizes me, and how very, very bad that is. I force a weak smile, and the woman stands up straighter and raises her chin.

"Well, if it isn't the space-born Kaiser," says Yvette Zinne.

"Shit," I say.

CHAPTER EIGHT

Belly of the Beast

Corvus

My team gathers in the ground-floor hangar to prepare for our mission. Our five armored exosuits are lined up against the wall. Even unmanned, they look like towering metal soldiers awaiting orders. The durable four-legged spider tank we drove from Fort Sketa rests on the other side of the room.

Considering how close we'll be to the border, and all the mystery around this power source we're retrieving, I'm especially grateful for the equipment. I can't seem to shake off Altair's words. *"This is the sign we've been waiting for,"* he said. But a sign of what, exactly? What will we find buried beneath the ice? The questions keep rolling through my head, though I don't dare show any sign of hesitation as I explain the basics of the mission to my team. They're already geared up in their heavy gray-and-white uniforms, thick layers of waterproof thermal clothing covering them from chin to ankle. Sturdy snow boots, their soles designed to grip the ice, cover their feet. Their cloth masks and goggles are slung casually around their necks.

As usual, we prepare for the mission with a quick smoke. I dole out the hand-rolled cigarettes, thin paper wrapped around a mixture made primarily of black Sanita leaves. They contain enough of the stimulant to get the blood pumping and take the edge off fear and pain and cold. When I first arrived here, I hated the stuff. In training, my first taste of it made my head spin so badly that I almost passed out, much to the amusement of the other recruits. Now, the pre-mission ritual is familiar and calming.

"No large machinery on this mission," I tell my team as I finish my smoke and crush the smoldering remains under one bootheel. The numbing tingle of Sanita spreads through my veins.

Magda, our tank driver, groans in disappointment. I pause, waiting for everybody's attention.

"But we're taking the exosuits."

My team draws a collective breath. Magda's former disappointment disappears in an instant. Daniil's eyes light up, and he bounces once on the balls of his feet like an excited child. Even Sverre grins. All three of them head for the rack of mechanical suits mounted on the far wall. Ivennie, on the other hand, goes faintly green in the face.

"An exosuit?" she asks, pausing at my side while the others carry on. "I haven't... I've never... I mean, in training, but—"

I clap her on the back and propel her forward.

"You'll be fine."

She glances over her shoulder at me, and I falter at the look on her face. I've seen those wide, trusting eyes in the faces of many fresh recruits over the last few years, and too frequently watched the light die from them. I clear my throat and give her one last pat before removing my hand.

"Daniil will show you the ropes," I say, gesturing to him. He waves her over and begins explaining, resting one hand on her arm, while I head over to my own suit.

The exosuits are mostly identical, but the one meant for me has a black slash across its dull metal to mark me as the team leader. I flip open the small hatch on its chest—marked *Made in Pax* in blocky letters—and tap out my passcode. The suit opens, metal peeling outward to allow me to step inside.

I slip my feet into the fitted boots and slide my fingers into padded gloves. When I press my back against the armored shell, the rest of the suit closes around me, metal clicking and clacking into place like a second skin. Soon the suit covers me from neck to toe in several inches of protective steel. I step forward and it moves with me, machinery working to carry the massive weight of the rig. It feels deceptively light and easy to handle, but each of my steps makes a heavy *clunk* on the hangar floor. I turn and grab my helmet, each finger clicking as the metal joints move, and slip it over my head.

The helmet locks into place, molding to the suit's spine, and my world narrows to a thin slit. My breath echoes in my ears, tinny and too close. The Sanita dampens my nerves to a slight shiver but doesn't stamp out the anxiety completely. This machine has saved my life a hundred times over, but it never fails to feel like a metal death trap in these first few seconds.

Once I have a hold of myself again, I press a button on the inside of my right glove to activate my comms and am immediately greeted by Magda's laughter. The sound warms me—but I stifle the response. I shouldn't feel that way. Especially not shortly before a dangerous mission.

"What's so funny?" I ask, sharpening my voice.

Magda makes an effort to control her laughing fit, though a few more chuckles still slip through.

"Sorry, sorry," she says. "It's just . . . the new girl . . ."

"Do we really have to bring her?" Sverre's voice rumbles in my ear now, sounding considerably less amused. "She'll be a hindrance."

I turn to see Ivennie standing stiffly alongside the others, her arms held straight out. Daniil is still standing next to her, trying to shout orders that must be unintelligible now that her helmet is on.

"She'll be fine. It's only a retrieval mission." Strictly speaking, I'm not sure if that's true. But expressing any uncertainty will merely worry them more, and we need a full team in case the enemy shows up. So close to the border, we have to be prepared for that. If our outpost noticed whatever is happening in that valley, it's just a matter of time before the Isolationists do as well.

I walk over to Ivennie, waving a hand in front of her helmet to get her attention, and gesture toward the communications button on the hand of her exosuit. After a few tries, her panicked breathing fills my helmet. "There," I say. "You're fine. Take a lap around the hangar, get used to the feel."

After a few moments, she controls her breathing and sets off with hesitant, heavy steps to do as I say. I nod to Daniil, and he shoots me a thumbs-up before heading over to his own suit. By the time Ivennie completes her trip around the room, she's steadier on her feet and everyone is ready. All lined up in their suits, it's impossible to tell one member of my team from another. Serious Sverre, clever Magda, cheerful Daniil, and rookie Ivennie are all made equal by the exosuits. Four faceless soldiers awaiting orders. It always makes things easier.

"Let's move out. Keep a close formation and stay low. We won't be far from enemy lines."

"Yes, sir," Ivennie says with a little too much enthusiasm, while the others murmur quiet affirmations. Magda lets out a cough that I suspect is meant to hide a laugh.

As the hangar door opens, we take off, five gray blurs streaking down the mountain and across the expanse of white. The suits don't fly so much as they hover, propelled by jets from the hands and feet—but either way, they're damn fast. The wind whips past as I move, tearing at the metal suit, but inside it's insulated and warm. Between the armor surrounding me and the Sanita rushing through my veins, I feel invincible as I soar above the icy ground.

It's too difficult to turn my head and look at the others behind me as we travel, but a hatch in my arm reveals a radar I can use to track them. It shows four blinking dots behind me; three are steady, holding a tight formation, and the last one wobbles along but remains mostly on course.

As Altair warned me, the target doesn't register on my radar. But the closer we get, the more noticeable the pale, on-and-off glow becomes. I slow as I approach, and the others follow my lead. The site sits at the bottom of a small valley. If anyone shows up, we'll be completely vulnerable. We won't see them until they're on top of us.

"Daniil, dismount at the top of this ridge. You'll be our eyes while we're below."

"Understood." One of the identical suits hovering behind me sets down. Daniil steps out of the suit and pulls his sniper rifle out of its compartment in one smooth motion. He pulls on the protective goggles and balaclava hanging around his neck. Breath fogging up the air through his cloth mask, he sets up his gun on its stand and fits his portable comm around his ear. Once he's finished, he shoots me a crisp salute. If he has any qualms about being left cold, alone, and exposed here, he doesn't show them.

"Everyone else, on me. Eyes peeled. We don't know exactly what we're getting into here."

We close in slowly, approaching the site like it's a dangerous animal, but only ice awaits us. I shut off my rockets and set down, testing the frozen ground with one booted foot before moving forward to survey the area. A small black shape protrudes above the surface. I crouch down beside it, brush snow away. The smooth black surface is clearly Primus material. My mind flashes to a childhood memory of Scorpia crying at the foot of one of Gaia's huge alien statues, so scared she couldn't move until I helped her up, but I push the distracting thought away.

Down below us, something rumbles. A pulsing glow illuminates my team's helmets. They scramble backward, and I resist the urge to do the same as I glimpse the huge, dark shape beneath us. I take a deep breath, steadying myself for the sake of my team. It's impossible to fight the impression of a gigantic beast waiting for its chance to strike. But the thought is foolish. I scrape snow away from the ice, squinting down at the shape.

"The objective is below us." I tap my fingers on the surface. "We'll need to melt our way through. Daniil, you see anything up there?"

"Nothing but snow."

"Good. Let's get started."

Even with the heat our suits produce through their hands, cutting through the ice is a long process. After an hour, my neck is cramping and my suit is uncomfortably warm. Removing my helmet for a minute would cool me off, but I can't risk it, not even with Daniil's frequent check-ins verifying that we're alone out here. We're too close to enemy territory, and the more of the object we reveal, the brighter its pulses of light shine through.

Soon, we're rewarded for our patience as we melt our way through to what lies beneath the ice. It's hard to tell exactly what we're looking at, but we're all familiar enough with the sight of the strange black material the Primus used in place of metal. I'm prepared to deal with questions and uncertainty, but nobody says a word. Whether the silence comes from trust or mere obedience, I'm not sure.

I'm more used to Primus technology than the rest, having

grown up on Gaia, but I'm unsettled by whatever this is, too. I've never seen anything like it. The shape is all wrong for it to be one of the famous statues that Gaia is rife with, and it's much too big. Is it a structure? Some kind of huge machine? Impossible to tell.

After another hour of melting and chipping at the ice, I finally realize what we're looking at.

"It's a ship," I murmur. Despite my unease, excitement also prickles in my nerves. Humans have always known that the aliens must have traveled between the planets somehow, but to my knowledge, a ship has never been uncovered, not even on Gaia. And to think one was waiting on Titan, of all places. This craft is on the smaller side, not much bigger than *Fortuna* and built much more slimly and delicately. Though perhaps *delicate* is the wrong word, since the whole thing is made of indestructible alien material.

I instruct the others to work at the sides of the ship, and then the front, searching for a way into the vessel. They work in silence, though the comms occasionally pick up labored breathing. Once a large enough portion of the ship is revealed, I search for any sign of a hatch or opening. Finding none, I search again by running the hands of my suit over the smooth surface and knocking to search for hollow areas. My team stands back and watches in discomfited silence. Eventually, one of my fingers finds a subtle indent in the material.

"Help me pry this open," I order. They won't be happy about it, but we don't have any time to waste. After a brief hesitation, Ivennie is the first to step forward. Sverre is soon to follow, and lastly a reluctant Magda. Together, we dig our fingers into the barely noticeable edges of the hatch and pry it open. A wave of stale air leaves the ship, warm enough that it creates a fog around us for a moment before dispersing.

We all stand outside, scrutinizing the narrow entrance. The

interior is dark and appears unfrozen. It's barely large enough to allow one exosuit to squeeze through. Normally, my team would be tripping over one another in their excitement to be the first to reach an objective, but now they're silent. As we wait, the ship pulses again with a faint glow, the light shining brighter out the open hatch. Sverre curses quietly over the comms, and Magda takes a step back. They're doing their best to hide it, but they're frightened. Perhaps it's for the best; Altair told me not to let anyone see the objective.

"Wait for me here," I say.

"Sarge..." Magda starts, but stops herself.

"Spread out. Form a perimeter. Don't let your guard down."

Without further delay, I lower myself into the opening and drop down. Rather than thud heavily against the floor, my boots hit something soft and sink down a few inches. I scramble to turn on my light, and my visor illuminates a swathe of the darkness in front of me.

"Are you okay? What do you see down there?" Magda's voice crackles with static, although she's only a couple of yards away. I frown, tapping the side of my helmet with one hand.

"I'm fine. Hard to explain what I'm seeing. It's..." I trail off, shining light on my feet as I step forward. The floor is made of a spongy substance, soft enough that my suit's metal boots leave footprints as I move, though they spring back up to uniformity a few seconds later. I approach the wall and tentatively press my fingers against it. It doesn't have the same give as the floor, but the material seems to shiver beneath my fingers. Perhaps it's a trick of the light. "Alien," I murmur to myself, too quiet for the comms to pick up. I leave the wall and move farther into the ship. Perhaps I should be scared, but I can't fight my curiosity.

"Do...see...objective?" Magda's voice crackles in my ears, more distorted than before.

"Not yet." I pause as I reach a circular hole in the wall. Beyond it is a larger chamber, but my suit is too big to step through the entrance. I scrutinize it for several long seconds before reaching a decision. I'm aware of every second that ticks by with us so close to enemy territory, and I don't want to remain in here any longer than necessary. The quicker we get this done, the quicker we can leave. "I need to dismount," I say, hoping my team will pick up enough of what I'm saying to understand. "Think my comms will cut off when I go deeper. If I'm not out in ten minutes, come find me."

"Sarge, shouldn't we..." The rest of Magda's argument dissolves into static.

I raise my hands to my head and hold them on the pressure pads until my helmet clicks out of its locked position. When I raise it, silence awaits me. Cool air licks my sweaty skin. The wind whistles outside the ship, but the sound is distant. In here, everything is still and quiet. After a moment's hesitation, I fully open my suit and step out onto the spongy floor with merely my boots and uniform as protection, grabbing my portable comm and helmet as I go.

Despite the cold air slipping through the open hatch, it's strangely warm in here. A ship that's been buried under ice for stars-only-know how many years has no right to be this warm inside.

I step through the circular entrance into the larger chamber of the ship. Judging by its size, this must be the equivalent of the main deck. Like the rest of the craft, the floor is pliable, the walls softly rounded, a stark contrast to the hard metal angles of a human vessel. In a normal ship of this size, my breath and footsteps would echo in the emptiness. But here, a thick silence blankets everything.

I move through the chamber, adjusting my helmet's light to inspect various areas of the room. It's fascinating, but I don't allow myself to be distracted by the alien symbols on the walls, or the fleshy cords dangling from the ceiling, or any of the other odd things I pass. Everything about the ship is foreign and disorienting, including the fact that it gets warmer as I head toward the rear of the vessel. But all of that is banished from my mind as the glow pulses again. It ripples throughout the entire ship, briefly lighting the ceiling, walls, and floor beneath me, but something in the depths of the vessel shines much brighter than all the rest.

I follow the glow across the main deck and through another circular doorway, stepping into a small, oval-shaped room, not much larger than my quarters back on *Fortuna*.

There, dangling from the ceiling, is the power source I've been seeking. Slim black cords snake into it from both sides and from above, holding it in suspension. With each pulse of the orb, the cords shiver, a movement that travels down their lengths and continues to ripple through the walls and ceiling. The room is moving around me, pulsing in tune with the power source, like it's the ship's ancient, still-beating heart. When another, larger pulse occurs, the orb glows so brightly I have to cover my eyes.

The whole ship is full of movement, full of what almost feels like life. Struck by a sudden fear that the entrance could have closed behind me, I whirl around. But my light shows me that both circular doorways are still open, and when I concentrate I can still hear the distant howling of the wind outside. Relieved, I turn back to the power source. It's mesmerizing to watch it move. I've never seen anything like this before, nor even heard of one existing, even on Gaia. Despite the amount of alien artifacts there, most of them are inactive. With a power source like this, I can only imagine what someone could do, the types of long-dead technology they could awaken. It must be invaluable. And given the Isolationist penchant for Primus weaponry, it would also be incredibly dangerous in their hands. That must be why it's so important for my team to retrieve it before they do.

I move slowly forward and raise my gloved hands. There's no

reaction as they draw nearer to the orb, nor when I lay them on its surface, which feels hot even through my thick gloves. The pulsing beneath my hands again reminds me of a heartbeat, and I swallow back uneasiness and force myself to hold on tighter. I pull it toward me—first gently, then with more force, then straining as hard as I can. The damn thing won't come free.

"Fine," I mutter. I set down my helmet so the light illuminates the area and pull my knife from its sheath. The slick black Primus blade was a personal gift from Altair when he promoted me to sergeant—a weapon confiscated from the enemy, which he knew few of the Primus-wary Interplanetists would dare to use. I've never encountered anything like this before, but the knife can cut through just about anything.

The cords are tough. Even with the deadly sharp Primus blade, I have to saw through rather than slice. When it finally snaps, thick black liquid sprays out, splattering my hands and face with warm goo. I stumble back, panic flaring in my chest, frantically wiping at the spot where it touched my bare cheek. But after a few moments, I don't feel any effect other than a visceral disgust. Taking deep breaths to steady my heartbeat, I shake my head and wipe my gloves on my pants. Whatever the stuff is, it seems harmless. I turn to the next cord, hesitate for a moment, and begin to cut again.

By the time I'm halfway done, the pulse of the power source is weaker and less frequent, and I'm sweating from the effort and the heat it exudes. Black ooze decorates the front of my uniform, and I'm sure it's smeared across my face as well. It should be pooling on the floor, too, but instead the soft material seems to be absorbing it.

As I hack through the last of the cords, the orb comes free in my hands. Its pulsing ceases, though the pale glow remains. Severed cords dangle limply from the walls and ceiling, dripping black liquid.

A low sound reverberates from the walls around me. It starts like a quiet groan of anguish, but grows and grows—louder and louder until it's overwhelming, coming from every direction at once. My thoughts drown in the noise; my teeth vibrate in my head. I drop the orb and clap my hands over my ears, nearly falling to my knees. But just when I think I can't take the sound anymore, it dies away, and everything goes still. The ceiling, the walls, the floor—the steady, coordinated movement of the ship—all still.

Breathing hard, I lower my hands. The ship is quiet, with no signs that removing the power source will have any further effect. Steadying myself, I bend to pick up the orb again. It's lighter than I expected it to be, soft and sticky to the touch, still warm after being severed. I shrug off my goo-splattered jacket and wrap it around the alien object. I'm not sure how delicate it is, so I'll have to be careful.

The warmth of the ship is already dissipating now that the power source is disconnected, and if we didn't have the enemy's attention before that awful noise, we certainly have it now. It's time I got back to my exosuit. I tuck my wrapped prize under one arm and grab my helmet with the other, stepping carefully through the circular door and heading toward the front of the ship.

I'm almost there when something makes me stop. Once I might have ignored the quiet alarm bells ringing in my head, but not after these last three years on Titan. I duck to the side, out of the view of the front chamber, and listen. There—barely audible— is a snippet of what might be a voice outside. But why would a member of my team be out of their exosuit?

A moment later, the hatch creaks, and someone drops down into the entrance chamber. I wait, back pressed to the wall. I touch the comm in my ear, but the device is completely dead, its signal weaker than the one in my suit. If it's a member of my team coming in, they'll know that and call out to me any moment now.

I wait a second, two seconds, three. Only silence.

Cold resolve fills me. I'm not surprised; I always knew this was a risk, coming so close to enemy grounds, and the light pulsing from the unburied ship must have drawn them in. I click my helmet's light out, plunging the room into darkness, and slowly lower it to the ground along with the power source. Then I slide my knife into my hand and wait. After a few moments of shuffling on the other side of the entrance, an enemy soldier steps through.

Up close, the Isolationists don't look so very different than us. They never mentioned that in training. They showed us the different style of their uniforms—the tapered sleeves and square buttons, the gray armbands and rounded helmets, the points in their bodies that are the easiest to hit. They had us shoot and stab and lob grenades at targets printed with the image, rewarded us for destroying them, drilled it into our heads that this was our enemy. Them versus us. But training did nothing to prepare me for moments like these, when the enemy's helmet is off and I end up face-to-face with a young man wide-eyed with shock and fear. The Isolationists draft their soldiers quite a bit earlier, another fact they declined to warn us about in training.

It was hard the first few times. Now, I don't hesitate. The blade cuts cleanly through the skin of his neck. He goes down fast, bloody and gurgling. As gore splashes me, I think again of the black liquid spraying out of those cords in the ship, and my stomach lurches.

But there's no time for weakness. I thank the stars for the Sanita still fizzing in my veins, keeping squeamishness and worry at bay. If an enemy soldier made it here, that means he made it through my team. I grab my belongings and click into my exosuit. The comms are dead, scrambled either by the alien ship or the enemy or both.

Which means I'll be going in blind. But my decision is nonetheless clear—there's nowhere else to go. So I take a deep breath, tuck the power source under my arm, and launch through the hatch.

CHAPTER NINE

Code Blue

Scorpia

I sit in the back of the hovercraft with my hands cuffed in front of me, desperately trying to think of a way out of this. The vehicle rattles and shakes, battered by heavy winds and rain now that the storm has fully kicked in. The windows are tinted so that I can barely see outside. A dark screen separates me from the front of the craft, too, where Commander Zinne and Shey have been arguing ever since we got in.

"Such an unthinkable lack of responsibility," Zinne says from the driver's seat. "I would expect such a thing from off-worlder trash like the Kaisers, but you, Shey? I thought you were better than this. You placed the entirety of Gaia in danger with this foolish stunt of yours."

"The ban on Devan plants is ridiculous," Shey snaps back at her from the passenger seat, her shoulders set and her spine stiff. *She* doesn't get any handcuffs, which doesn't seem quite fair but also doesn't surprise me. "I needed it for research purposes. Did you know they're averse to Primus material? It could explain why—"

"I don't care about your reasoning," Zinne says. "You're not above the law."

They've been going back and forth for a while now, but Commander Zinne clearly isn't prepared to listen to any arguments. She certainly wasn't when she saw the strangle-vine trying to crawl out of the box, stomped on it until it stopped moving, and bagged it to throw in the incinerator later. She was similarly unsympathetic when she tripped me as I tried to run, ripped my gloves off, and handcuffed me so tightly my fingers went numb. She took my comm and dragged me out of the building kicking and yelling, right over the body of the broker facedown in the lobby. He must have tried to stop her from gaining entry—or maybe he just tried to run. Either one would be enough for an enforcer to fire on this planet.

The whole time, Shey trailed behind us, crying prettily. It got a little less pretty when she saw the body and the burnt laser-fire mark through his head. Maybe she's never seen her mother's zero-tolerance policy in action before.

At least I didn't end up like that, but I'm headed in the same direction.

"Do I get a lawyer?" I ask when their argument hits a lull. "'Cause I really think—"

"Shut up," Zinne says without turning around.

I shut up. As the security officer begins to rant again, I focus on trying to squirm my way out of my handcuffs, to no avail. These things are damn tight.

"Do you realize how quickly something like that could spread through our planet?" Zinne continues. "What kind of irreparable damage it could do? Devan flora are plant killers, Shey. Crop destroyers. Ecosystem ruiners." Gaia doesn't have much to destroy, as I recall, but it probably won't help my situation to point that out. "This could have been like the Nibiran plague all over again. There is a reason such things are illegal. There is a reason that breaking those laws is punishable by death."

I grimace at the reminder. While I haven't given in to total panic yet, I have no illusions about where this hovercraft ride is taking me: the death penalty. No trial. No chance to contact my family and get them to bail me out. I need to figure this out on my own, and time is ticking away. I look down at my handcuffs, suppressing a groan. I'm lucky that they're a simple pair of low-tech metal bindings, but my wrists are chafed raw already, and I'm nowhere close to being able to squeeze out. Drom boasts that she once dislocated a finger in order to escape from some, but I don't think I have the grit to do that without making enough noise to get Zinne's attention. Then I'd meet the same fate as that poor broker, plus a dislocated thumb.

"Hey, does Gaia have one of those off-worlder advocacy groups?" I ask, cutting off another rant on responsibility from the officer. She turns to glower at me.

"We do not," she says. "And if you keep squirming around like that, I'm going to tase you."

I go still, and she returns to berating Shey. It's slowly dawning on me that I really screwed up this time...possibly for the last time. I was caught red-handed selling a Devan plant to the daughter of the president. I'm about as thoroughly fucked as a person can be.

I've never been much of a planner. My survival depends largely on the occasional stroke of genius...or luck, as other people usually call it. But by the time the hovercraft stops and lowers to the ground, neither genius nor luck have struck, and I'm starting to get concerned. I'm not fond of the idea of dying over a stupid plant. I always thought I'd go down with *Fortuna*. Something dramatic, with fireworks and shit.

As Zinne comes around the craft and opens the door, I get a

glimpse of the long, flat metal building outside. I recognize the place—North Levian Containment Facility, a low-security prison in the rolling hills outside the city. Most commonly used to temporarily hold prisoners before they're either set free, moved somewhere more secure, or executed. I can guess which one they have in mind for me.

When Zinne reaches inside, I squirm away as best as I can in handcuffs, and look toward Shey in the front. The president's daughter is sitting with her spine ramrod straight and her eyes forward, ignoring our scuffle.

"Shey," I say, shouting to be heard above the howling winds outside. "Hey. Look at me. Are you gonna let this happen?"

Zinne curses as she tries to get a good hold on me, thwarted time and time again by my kicking feet and pointy elbows, growing only more slippery as rain splashes into the hovercraft. It gives me a few more seconds to try plucking Shey's heartstrings. There's no way she doesn't feel a little bit guilty about this. I've seen the way she looks at me; it can't all be fake.

"C'mon, Shey! Look at me! We're friends, yeah? You're not gonna let them kill me." The words come out confidently, but Shey doesn't react. My stomach sinks. "You're not gonna let them kill me," I say again, softer this time, almost pleading. "Right?"

Finally, Shey turns. Her eyes are red and her face drawn amid the mass of her thick hair. But damn, even with death looming in front of me, the lady is gorgeous.

"I'm sorry," she says. She reaches back and places a hand on my arm, giving it a gentle squeeze. The light touch makes my heart soar for a moment—then crash as she pulls back her hand and lowers her eyes. "There's nothing I can do. Goodbye, Scorpia."

With one final tug, Zinne yanks me away from my last hope and toward the prison where they'll decide my fate.

*   *   *

Zinne leaves me in a corner cell. The room is shut off from the rest of the prison by a thick metal door, its surface broken only by a tiny one-way slot for food and water. The walls facing the outside hold huge windows, high enough that they're impossible to reach with my hands cuffed, bars thick enough that I couldn't get through them even if I could reach. I have to stand near the door to avoid the rain leaking through.

As the door shuts behind me, panic hits fast and hard to my gut. I take in a shuddery breath, resisting the urge to throw myself at the metal and pound on it until my hands bleed. It won't help me. It didn't help me last time I ended up locked away in a Gaian jail cell.

Despite all the shit I got into during my childhood on Gaia, I was pretty good at getting out of it, too, and I've only been locked up like this once before. I was barely seven, but age doesn't matter when you're an off-worlder caught with your hands in a rich man's pockets. I was fairly confident the officers wouldn't have the stomach to kill me, though, and there's no easy way to ship an unwanted person off-planet. They would just throw me in a cell for a night, try to scare me. It worked, but not for the reasons they thought. It worked because that was the night we were supposed to leave.

My mother had finally saved enough money to gas up *Fortuna* and hire a skeleton crew to get us to Titan. She was to deliver what I later found out was a dozen crates of highly volatile Primus-tech grenades discovered on Gaia. But at the time, all I knew was that the ship was supposed to leave in six hours and I was locked up in jail. As I stared at that metal door, I was certain I would be forgotten on Gaia, and I would never see my mother or Corvus again—or *Fortuna*, or the stars I dreamed of every night. I screamed and hit the door for hours, and hours, and hours, until the skin on my knuckles split open and each punch left a bloody smear across the door. All the while, the guards laughed outside.

That same familiar terror sinks its claws into me now. I force myself to rest my forehead on the door instead of throwing myself at it, but my breath comes jaggedly, and that phantom laughter echoes in my ears.

"Momma won't leave," I tell myself. "She'll find me. They'll find me."

But what if they don't? What if they can't? What if they don't care enough to try? Momma's already mad at me over the debacle of the landing, and soon she'll have Corvus to replace me. Lyre will probably be happier with him in charge. The twins will miss me, but they're too dumb and obedient to ever come looking for me themselves.

I think of last time, when I emerged crying and bloody-knuckled and terrified to find Corvus waiting. I think of the way he smiled when he saw me, one of his eyes blackened from a scuffle with a guard, and held his hand out.

"Let's go home, Scorpia."

I take in a shaky breath and pull away from the door. No one is going to be waiting outside this time. Nobody is going to save me.

I turn away from the door and run my eyes over every inch of my cell. There's a small camera hidden in one corner, which I pretend not to notice, and nothing else of note. That done, I check through what I have on me. My boots are steel-toed and could serve as a weapon if I'm desperate enough. My jumpsuit is useless. My pockets...

"Oh," I whisper, as my mind flashes to the mouth-guard still stuffed in my pocket. The knot in my stomach loosens and the tension in my shoulders eases. A grin fights its way through the freezing terror. "Took you long enough, stroke of genius."

I turn my back to the camera and carefully maneuver the rubbery ball out of my pocket with my cuffed hands. Cupping my fingers around it, I bring it to my mouth and exhale. After a few repetitions, the warmth turns the substance gooey and pliable. I tear off a small chunk of it with my teeth and push it into the keyhole of my handcuffs.

I place the rest of the substance back in my pocket, and wait for it to cool and harden. After a few minutes pass, I give the handcuffs a simple twist, and they come free. I catch them before they hit the floor and hold them close to my body. The small freedom is enough to calm my racing heart.

"All right," I mutter to myself. "What now, what now?"

I move toward the lock on the door and scrutinize it as closely as I can without making it too obvious to the camera. Because this is a temporary holding facility, I'm hoping for something low-tech like the cuffs Zinne slapped on my wrists. Unfortunately, that's not the case. The lock can be opened only with a keypad from the outside. I bite back a curse, push away despair, and run through my other options.

When the guards come for me, they won't expect me to have my wrists free or a makeshift weapon in the form of the cuffs, so I could get the jump on them. That method might work for the twins, but I'm not much of a fighter. Lyre probably knows a million legal loopholes that could buy her time until the family found her, but I don't have much legal know-how, either.

I am, on the other hand, a pretty good liar. So that brings me to Option C.

Tucking my hands against me so my wrists still appear cuffed, I stumble back against the wall and let out my most dramatic wail of pain. I curl forward around my stomach and drop first to my knees and then entirely to the floor, contorting my body as though in terrible pain. The whole while, I force out loud, agonized groans.

Still crying quietly, I wait. And wait some more. I was hoping that would be enough for them to send someone to check on me, but then again, this is Gaia.

"Help me!" I yell, forcing the words to come out pained and pitiful. "It burns. Oh, please, it burns!"

It takes about ten minutes of yelling and screaming, but finally the metal slot on my door clanks open.

"Quiet down in there. You're disturbing the other prisoners," a guard says through the slot on my door. The voice is young, male. A rookie sent to do grunt work, most likely. Perfect. I look up at the slot, molding my face into an expression of agony.

"I need medical attention," I say through gritted teeth, and take a deep, gasping breath. "My stomach…it's like it's on fire. Please!"

"You were fine when you got here," the guard says, and starts to close the slot.

"W-wait! It must be that plant I swallowed."

There's a pause, a beat where I think he might ignore my words and leave me here.

"Plant?" he asks warily. "What plant are you talking about?"

"I…I don't know. Some black leafy thing with these pods hanging off it. I swallowed one when I saw the officers coming, thought I could hide it, but they caught me with the other one—"

The metal slot slams shut. Through the door, I can hear the hurried steps of the guard retreating. Running, not walking, because he has at least an inkling about what kind of plant I'm talking about.

Biting back a grin, I stay where I am, curled on the ground with my un-handcuffed hands hidden out of camera view.

If I know Gaians at all, they'll be sure to document everything—even an unregistered off-worlder thrown into a cell and soon to be forgotten. And if I'm right about that, the file likely includes both a name and a reason for arrest. In my case, that would be the import of class-one contraband: Devan flora. It should be enough to back up my story and get them sufficiently worried, especially if the guard realizes what I'm imitating.

Honestly, as far as Devan plants go, blood-boilers are relatively harmless. The pods are toxic, sure, but the kind of toxic that'll give you a good high. A few licks of one, and you'll end up with a hot tongue, a mild fever, and a pleasant buzz that lasts a few hours. Especially popular on Titan, I've heard... which is exactly where I once witnessed an unfortunate soul who had somehow ended up swallowing a pod. I'll never know whether it was the result of ignorance or desperation or a fit of madness, but within the hour, he had ripped off his uniform and was on the ground, writhing and sweating, his skin steaming in the cold air.

Momma made us leave before the end of it, but she explained what would happen in all its gory detail. When the toxic pod sits in your stomach, the fever it induces swiftly becomes a lot more than mild. It drives your body temperature up, and up, and up some more. Once it reaches a temperature of 110, the resin covering the pod melts, and it explodes. Violently. On hot days in Deva, just being near one of the plants is dangerous enough to cause a few deaths every year. When it's *inside* you, well... it makes a mess. And it's a mess that scatters the plant's sharp, tiny, resilient seeds all around the area.

Which means, if the Gaians want any hope of stopping blood-boiler plants from spreading through the local ecosystem, they'll have to drag me to a much more secure place than this cell. So I wait, patient, forcing out a few more groans of agony in case anyone's listening.

After a few minutes, the door clanks open. I fake an especially violent coughing fit.

The guard who enters the cell is armed and decked out in a full quarantine suit, including protective headgear. Still, he stays several feet back, his face pale and sweaty through the glass over his face. Poor Gaian has probably never seen or dealt with a Devan plant in his life, but everyone knows the stories about blood-boilers and brain-rot fungus and other floral horrors. As far as he's concerned, I might as well be a nuclear bomb right now.

"D-don't move," he stutters, voice muffled through the glass. He gestures with his blaster. I'm guessing he'll hesitate to use it, though. Getting potentially toxin-infected blood everywhere would only increase the chances of some kind of outbreak.

I nod, stay where I am, and make sure my handcuffs look like they're still secure until he's within striking range. Then I grab a tight hold of one of the cuffs, scramble to my feet, and swing the other into the side of the man's helmet. He stumbles to the side as the glass audibly cracks.

The man freezes, gloved hands outstretched, eyes locked on the break splintering across his helmet. He lets out a whimper like a cornered animal. I take off before he can recover, heading right out the open door and down the hallway.

From what I saw coming in, this place isn't heavily guarded. Just two turns and a couple prison guards stand in my way to freedom—if they haven't initiated a total lockdown based on my lie about the Devan plant. But so far, there are no screeching alarms or flashing lights or hordes of law-enforcers crashing down on me.

Heart surging with hope, boots pounding against the tile, I round one corner, another corner—and slide to a stop as I spot another guard. Her back is turned to me, her hand is to her ear, and she speaks urgently into a device wrapped around one wrist. She's too engrossed in a conversation to notice me enter the room.

"We're initiating a quarantine warning at the North Levian facility," she says, her words becoming audible as I creep closer. "Code

Blue. Requesting outside assistance. We're not equipped for a proper quarantine confinement." As she pauses, presumably listening to the answer, I move slowly and quietly toward her. If I can get close enough without her noticing, I can knock her out with these cuffs and be on my way. I hold my breath, sweat trickling down my forehead, and raise the handcuffs in preparation to swing.

"We're not sure," the guard says. I'm two yards away. "But, yes, she was brought in for possession of Devan flora." One yard. "According to her file…" The guard turns and comes face-to-face with me.

Her eyes widen. I curse and swing—too slow. She catches my wrist, twisting it, and the cuffs clatter to the floor. Her face blanches after the automatic reaction, eyes flashing to her thinly gloved hand where it touches my bare skin, her mind no doubt revisiting that quarantine warning. But after a moment, she fumbles for her gun with her other hand, grip tightening despite her obvious fear.

"The quarantine threat has escaped," she shouts, her voice ringing up and down the halls of the prison. "I need backup!" I struggle to break free of her grip, but it's useless; she's stronger than me. Before panic can take hold, an idea strikes me.

"You sure do," I say. "Here's a Code Blue for you."

I spit a mouthful of saliva into her face.

The guard gasps, reels back, and releases me to raise both hands to her face, which is twisted into an expression of abject horror. I don't blame her for it—as far as she knows, that mouthful of saliva could've been a death sentence. I'm not going to wait around for her to figure out that it's nothing more than an insult. I peel off before she can recover, sprint out the prison's door, and keep running toward freedom.

With rain falling in a sheet around me, I run until I can't run anymore. Even then, with my legs shaking and my lungs aching, I force myself to keep planting one foot in front of the other, stumbling over slippery rocks. At least the hills to the north of Levian are familiar to me and provide plenty of cover. Within twenty minutes, I'm halfway to the city and confident that no one's following me. My clothes are soaked through and I'm cold down to my bones, but at least the weather will make it more difficult for hovercrafts or drones to follow me. Gaia is used to mild weather; I've never seen a storm quite like this before.

Soon, the thrill of my escape has faded and been replaced by a sour taste in the back of my throat. Dread fills my stomach and weighs me down. I'm not sure how much time has passed since I separated from my siblings. But between my meeting with Shey, my imprisonment, and now this, I'm sure I've missed the meet-up time with my family's client. My share of that job would've been five times the amount I nearly got from Shey... and I blew it. All because of this stupid, botched side job.

Another failure for the list. Panic swells in my chest as I imagine Momma's reaction when I see her, so I force my thoughts to my siblings instead. What would they have done when they realized I wouldn't be there in time? Did they stay behind in Thudana's storage facility? Or go without me to meet the client?

Probably the latter, which is by far the worse option. Lyre would have taken the initiative. Lyre and the twins would've gone... the trigger-happy twins, who refuse to listen to a word that she says. I groan and shake my head, forcing myself not to imagine that scenario any further. It doesn't go anywhere good, and I don't need that weighing on my mind right now. I have my own shit to deal with.

It takes another thirty minutes to arrive at the outskirts of Levian. By the time I reach the city, I'm shaking with exhaustion and cold. I drag myself into the shelter of a nearby building to rest for a few minutes before moving onward.

Only then do I notice that the streets are empty. Not *nearly* empty, as they were right after the workday began, but utterly deserted. Wind howls down the empty street and rattles against the closed doors and shutters, which should both be open during the Gaian workday. Perhaps it's just the weather, but something about it makes the hair rise on the back of my neck. The whole city is eerily quiet.

Once I catch my breath, I force myself to my feet and move deeper into the city streets, pressing myself against buildings and keeping my eyes peeled for Gaian law enforcement. The interior of the city is no different than the outskirts: deserted, shut down, empty.

"Citizens of Levian—"

I jump as the voice booms through the rain, flattening myself against the closest house. But the streets are still empty; it's an automated message coming through the city's public service speakers.

"This is a warning for a quarantine lockdown in immediate effect," the recording continues, in the crisp and level voice that I recognize as Talulah Leonis, the Gaian president. "Please stay inside your homes, avoid face-to-face contact, and follow Code Blue guidelines while awaiting further instruction."

In the silence afterward, an incredulous guffaw escapes my mouth. I slap a hand over it to hold back a full-on fit of laughter. A lockdown. The whole city of Levian is on lockdown because of me. This may be the proudest moment of my life. If Corvus were here, he'd laugh for days about this.

My mood sours immediately at the thought. If Corvus were here, he'd be taking the deed to my ship right about now, I remind myself, and head toward Thudana's facility to find my family. I need to salvage this situation before I face Momma. This mistake can't cement my uselessness in her mind and determine the rest of my life.

Small patrols of officers wander the city, but they're easy to avoid considering how well I know the backstreets. I make it to Thudana's without a hitch, and wait for the nearest patrol to move away before knocking.

After a few seconds of continuously rapping my knuckles across the door, I stop and sigh. Of course she's not answering. The city is in a damn lockdown. I squeeze the bridge of my nose and try to force my exhausted brain to think of something. After a moment, I clear my throat and knock again, this time delivering three heavy thuds with my fist.

"This is Gaian law enforcement. Open up!" I yell in the gruffest voice I can muster.

The door slides open. I squeeze my way inside, pushing past Thudana and scrambling to the back of the room, leaving a muddy trail across her carpet. She scowls and slams the door shut behind me with one hand.

"Stop making such a racket, you stupid off-worlder," she snaps, bringing out her other hand from behind her back and revealing the blaster clutched in it. "You do realize I have a camera on that entrance?"

"Sorry," I say, holding my hands out in an exaggerated apology and trying to hide a smile.

"Where's the rest of the rabble?" she asks, scowling.

I blink.

"The rest?" She stares at me like I'm a complete imbecile. As I stare back, the truth sinks in and settles into a cold lump in my stomach. "My siblings aren't here?"

She presses her lips into a thin line and shakes her head.

"They left with the cargo an hour ago."

I force down a mouthful of curses. No need to panic quite yet.

"Did my mother come by?" I ask, hoping against hope. She shakes her head, and my heart sinks.

I turn to the door, picturing the empty streets of the locked-down city outside, all the paranoid Gaians hiding in their homes, the law enforcement patrols looking for anyone out of place—and somewhere, my siblings, carrying enough class-one contraband to get them the death sentence several times over.

And the Gaians will be looking for them, I realize for the first time since my arrest. It should have occurred to me much sooner, which makes guilt jab me right alongside fear. When Commander Zinne took me in, she knew my name. She knew which ship I arrived on. My arrest would have cast suspicion on the whole family. If they find them and search our shipment, my siblings will be thrown into cells just like I was. Or maybe they'll be shot, now that I've been declared an even worse security threat than before.

"Damn it," I whisper. If only they had stayed put. It's been an awfully long day already, and I'd really love to guzzle half a bottle of whiskey, drop into bed, and sleep for at least twelve hours. But my siblings are out there, and likely stuck knee-deep in a mess of my own creation. So I have to go out. The city may be on lockdown because of me, and the enforcer patrols no doubt have my face on file, but my siblings are counting on me.

I sigh, roll my shoulders back, and glance at Thudana. My gaze travels down to the blaster in her hand.

"How much to borrow your gun for a few hours?" I ask.

CHAPTER TEN

The Objective

Corvus

I launch out of the ship and into a whirlwind of motion and laser-fire. Over two dozen Isolationist soldiers in gray uniforms are swarming the alien ship, more cresting the ridge around us. Two of my exosuited soldiers are on the ground, grappling with five enemies each. Only one is airborne and focusing fire on the heavy antiaircraft gun set up on the ridge, the kind of weapon meant to take down suits like these.

As soon as I notice the gun, it fires. Too late to dodge. The projectile smashes into my side and sends me careening off course. I slam into the ice, and the power source rolls free from its wrappings. Before I can grab it, another hit sends me sliding and dents my armor, making it difficult to breathe for a dizzying few seconds. I struggle to my feet and launch again, rolling out of the way of the next shot, but one of the enemy soldiers has already reached the power source.

Off to my left, an exosuited soldier goes down beneath a wave of enemies. One pulls out a knife—a Primus blade like my own— and takes aim at the back of the suit's neck, right at the pressure pads where the armor is weakest. Directly ahead, the Isolationist picks up the power source.

A sharp breath, a split second's hesitation.

I take aim at the woman holding the objective and fire as the knife comes down on my soldier's neck. Both bodies jerk in dying throes at the same time.

I launch forward, skimming across the ice, and grab the fallen power source. Part of me wonders if I should take off now, head back to the outpost alone, secure the objective above all else—but my suit is damaged, the propulsion weak and shaky. I won't make it. It's almost a relief to have that choice taken from me. Now, I can focus on the fight.

We're terribly outnumbered, but aside from the one fallen suit lying facedown on the ice, my team is holding their own. The enemy has no machinery, no exosuits like us, only their uniforms and their weapons. My team, armored in their suits, cuts right through them. But another volley from the antiair gun sends one of my group sprawling to the ground, their exosuit dented and smoking. They're immediately swarmed with enemy soldiers. I aim the pulse rifle built into my suit's right arm and take down five of them with a single burst of laser-fire as I fly past. These are easy kills, but that gun up on the ridge is a problem. If we lose our suits, we lose our one advantage.

I fly directly for the cliffside, dodging antiair shots as I go. One clips my leg, but I hold my course. At the bottom of the cliff, I touch down and jump directly upward. The suit propels me over the edge.

The moment I crest its peak, I open fire on the soldiers hunkered there, spraying laser-shots at the woman manning the AA gun and the others around her. But my suit is damaged, hovering too close to the ground, and an enemy soldier manages to grab my leg and drag me lower. One of his comrades grabs the fallen anti-air gun. I strain to pull away, but my suit whines and shudders, its thrust too weak. The antiair gun's barrel aims at me.

The shot lands directly on the already-dented torso of my suit. Metal crunches around my ribs, constricting my chest in a rush of sharp pain. The suit goes limp as I crash to the ground. It's dead-weight. I can't move, can't fight the enemy soldiers who rush me.

Panic paralyzes me. This is what I've feared every time I've stepped into this suit: that I would end up trapped, helpless. I fire off a round from my pulse rifle, but one of the enemies pins my arm and renders it useless. Another pries the power source out from under my arm.

"I need assistance now. *Now.*" The communication system is still offline, but I try anyway, fear and pain cracking my voice. I cough. It's hard to breathe, impossible to move. "Can anyone hear me? I need—"

I cut off as the soldier holding the power source hits the ground. Trapped as I am, I can barely move my head, so it's impossible to decipher the blur of motion. With the enemies distracted, I hit the emergency release and evacuate the suit. The metal creaks open with agonizing slowness, and I climb out onto the ice, yanking off my helmet last and tossing it aside. I gulp air, each deep breath sending pain jolting through my torso. At least one of my ribs must be broken.

The wind howls around me, heralding a storm on its way. All the enemies I see are dead on the ground. One of my team members hovers nearby, suit covered in dents and badly damaged. They struggle with their helmet before managing to pull it off.

My stomach twists as the figure inside is revealed. Daniil was our sole support from above. Regardless of the fact that he saved me, him being here means the rest of the team is completely exposed down below.

"Why aren't you at your post?" I shout at him, and his forehead creases with confusion. I know I'm not being fair. Without him, I'd be dead right now. Prioritizing his leader and the objective is exactly what he should have done. But the Sanita is starting to wear off, and my heart is pounding at the thought of the others. Magda, Sverre, Ivennie—one is already dead in the valley and the rest could be soon.

"I saw you go down," Daniil says. "I thought—"

"No. You didn't." He flinches back at the words. "Give me the suit and set up here."

"The helmet is—"

"That's an order, Naran. And give me your coat."

Whether it's the harsh tone or the use of his surname, Daniil blanches and rushes to comply. While he grabs his rifle and steps free, I pick up the power source, hiding it from Daniil's view. As soon as he tosses me his coat, I wrap it up.

"Guard this," I say, shoving it into his arms. "With your life. And don't leave your fucking post until the fighting is over."

"Yes, sir." Daniil doesn't make eye contact as he places the wrapped orb at his feet and sets up his gun, his body already shaking from the cold.

I dive off the cliff without a glance back. The cold air burns my face on the way down, completely exposed without the helmet. This is risky, but the objective is secure. Now I can worry about my team.

Minus the one I've already lost. That moment replays in my head, and guilt rises in the back of my throat like bile. Who was it? Which of them did I let die?

No time for that. The second I'm within range of the fighting, several of the enemy soldiers open fire on me. I raise an arm to shield my face, and their shots ping harmlessly against the metal. But this suit is badly damaged and fading fast; I can feel its engine struggling to keep me aloft already.

Both of my remaining team members are still suited. One is on their knees on the ice, fighting off waves of enemies. The second is still airborne, though judging from the fact that only three of their propulsion rockets are firing, not for long. I fly in to help the former, taking down three soldiers with my pulse rifle before the thing dies on me. I jam the trigger uselessly, growl in frustration, and swing my metal fist at one of the soldiers instead. He goes down with a crack of bone. I ram another one, turning her into a bloody smear across the ice.

With me in the fray and the antiair artillery taken out, the battle doesn't take long. The enemies are out-equipped enough that their superior numbers mean nothing in the end. They must not have expected so much heat from a remote outpost.

We're mopping up the last few soldiers when my borrowed suit gives out, collapsing into a heap of metal. I jam the emergency release, crawl out, and leave the broken machine behind as I stumble toward my downed team member.

Now that the fighting is over, my eyes are locked on that fallen suit and the body inside. Dread chokes me as my mind replays the fight over and over. Again and again I return to the moment I chose to chase the power source rather than save my team member. I made the choice I had to. I prioritized the objective, as I've been trained to do. In the middle of a fight, it was instinctual, easy. But now I have to face the consequences.

Which of my teammates will I find dead on the ice? Not Daniil, who is making his own gradual descent down the cliffside with his sniper rifle. Will it be steady Sverre, who never questions my judgment? Rookie Ivennie, who looks at me with such naked trust in her eyes? Or sharp-tongued Magda, who I care for much more than I should?

It's dangerous to care. I shouldn't have a preference about whose body I'm about to find. It isn't fair to my team or to myself, and it isn't logical. But my heart can't seem to heed my mind.

I struggle across the heavier snow of the valley, each step sinking several inches down, each lift of my legs straining already-exhausted muscles. The effect of the Sanita is almost completely gone now, along with the rush of battle, and the aches and scrapes on my body are solidifying into throbbing centers of pain. Each breath is a knife's jab to my ribs, a constant reminder of the blow I took. But I push forward until I fall to my knees beside the fallen suit, and grab the bloodied helmet with both hands. The mechanism that connected it to the rest of the suit is already severed. It comes free easily.

The moment the body's honey-blond hair comes tumbling free, relief washes over me. Guilt chases close behind, but it's not strong enough to overpower that initial relief. Ivennic is dead. I let her die. But only Ivennie. Not Daniil, not Sverre, not Magda. Not Magda. I thank the stars even as I curse myself.

Nearby, Sverre struggles out of the exosuit still stuck on its knees, struggling to pull one leg free from the dented metal. I school my features into a blank mask as he limps over, looking at Ivennie's body and then at me. He nods, his face stonelike. I nod back. A mutual understanding—this is terrible, but not nearly as terrible as it could have been. Soon Daniil joins us as well, his eyes downcast and his body trembling from the cold with no coat to protect him. He wordlessly passes me the still-wrapped power source.

Lastly comes Magda. Her suit, already half in pieces, falls apart the moment she lands. One side of her head is bloodied, but the rest of her is intact. Our eyes meet for a brief moment before her gaze slides to the body. She doesn't look up at me again.

I clear my throat and gather the power source into my arms.

"Objective secure. Let's get out of here before they send more troops."

Sverre and Magda attempt to bury Ivennie's body while I place the power source in a more secure bag and take stock of the damage. Daniil dons the coat I returned to him and tries to warm up, silent and shivering. By the time I've determined that each of our exosuits is too badly damaged to make the flight back to the outpost, the others have given up trying to dig through the hard ground, and snow has started to fall. An ugly storm is brewing, thick, dark clouds clustering directly above us. Titan weather is like nothing else in the system, calm one moment and a howling blizzard the next. Somehow these storms are impossible to track and predict by weather radar, which means too often that we end up in situations like this. At least we're properly geared out for the elements. Hundreds of Titan citizens die from the harsh weather conditions every year.

I crouch next to the last broken exosuit, tapping my gloved fingers against the metal. Much as I don't like it, there's only one answer.

"We'll have to walk back to the outpost." I straighten up, adjusting the strap of the bag over my shoulder. The power source rests inside, still giving off faint warmth through the bag's thick, waterproof fabric. "We'll return for the damaged exosuits with the spider tank."

"We're walking through the storm?" Magda asks, her voice cross. Normally, neither she nor the others would question me in a situation like this. But we're all cold and tired and hungry, and one of our own lies frozen on the ice, so I choose to ignore it.

"We have no choice. We can't stay here." I glance back at the alien ship. Tempting as it is to try to plug in the power source and hide from the storm, by the time it blows over we could be trapped by the snowfall. And the Isolationists will undoubtedly return, either for revenge or scavenging or both.

My team says nothing, their eyes cast downward.

"If we hurry, we can beat the storm," I say, though I know that we won't. The wind is already picking up around us, whipping the snow into painful shards, but there's nothing else to do. "Come on."

One by one, we set off across the ice, as the snow begins to bury the bodies we left behind.

CHAPTER ELEVEN

Responsibility

Scorpia

I head toward the warehouse where we were supposed to meet our customer, dodging Gaian patrols as I go. The rain is dying down now, though it's still shockingly cold for Gaia. Right now, President Leonis will want her citizens to believe she has the situation under control, so she'll avoid bringing in the big guns like air patrols and tracking drones to find us... but it's only a matter of time. Wherever my siblings are, they won't be safe for long.

If they're safe now, that is. They wouldn't have had any warning about the Code Blue before it happened, and if they didn't make it back to Thudana's, who knows where they could have ended up? Maybe a patrol caught them before they could make it to safety. The twins aren't exactly inconspicuous...

My anxiety is nearly unbearable by the time I reach the warehouse. I slink through the back alley to the rear entrance and pause outside to steady my grip on Thudana's blaster. The warehouse is quiet, but I have no idea what I'm about to walk into. I take a deep breath and yank the door open with one hand, leveling my gun at the inside of the warehouse as I step through the door.

Three answering blasters swing in my direction. I freeze, panicking for a moment before I realize the people holding them are my siblings. The relief in all of their expressions makes my stomach roll with guilt, but I force a smile.

"Miss me?" I ask, just before Pol squeezes the air out of my lungs in a bear hug.

"We thought you were gone!" His voice is muffled as he presses his face into my shoulder.

"Oh, come on, you know I always come back." I slap him on the back, and he releases me. While I regain my breath, I study the others. Drom gives me a nod, the relief I saw earlier already replaced by stony aloofness. Lyre is pale and shaky, but unharmed. "Anyone been in contact with Momma?"

"No," Lyre says. She wrings her hands. "We pinged both you and her an hour before the meet-up. Neither of you responded."

"So what'd you do?"

"Well... We went to the meeting. I thought that if something was up, it was better than sitting on the contraband with a known associate of Momma's." She falters. "Right?"

I realize, with a jolt, she's looking at me for approval—and noting my sour expression. But the bitter taste in my mouth has nothing to do with Lyre's admittedly smart decision, other than the fact that I wasn't the one to make it. I gesture for her to continue.

"We met up with the client and everything was going smoothly. But the sirens started as we were about to finalize the deal. As soon as the buyers heard the announcement about a Code Blue, they got spooked and left."

My stomach plummets. Damn, I really have the worst timing.

"So the cargo is...?" My siblings turn and look toward the

other end of the warehouse. There, stacked up against the wall, are the cargo crates, presumably still full of extremely illegal contraband. "Shit."

"We didn't know what to do with it," Lyre says. "We can't let the officers find it, obviously, but if we abandon it, then..." She trails off, but I follow the train of thought. The cargo is worth a fortune, and surrendering it would also make this whole trip pointless. Momma would be furious.

I chew the inside of my cheek. The deal was a failure, and now we're stuck with a bunch of contraband in the middle of a quarantine. This job—the job that was supposed to be my last chance to prove my worth to Momma—has become a complete and utter disaster, all because I tried to fit in that stupid deal on the side. I thought I could impress Momma by doing something on my own on top of the normal job, but instead I've ruined everything. We've had business go awry in the past, but it's hard to remember the last time a trip went this poorly. And now my siblings are all staring at me, hoping for me to save them.

"Okay," I say, my mind working. "Okay, okay...so..." There's only one answer, as hard as it is to swallow. "The officers will find us if we don't move, and we can't move with the cargo. We need to get rid of it." The thought of dumping something so valuable hurts, but we don't have a choice. This is evidence that could get us killed. "And we need a distraction that will let us sneak out of the quarantine. So..." I snap my fingers. "We've gotta burn it."

Lyre's face crumples, but she doesn't argue. The twins exchange a glance. Oddly, they both seem to be barely holding back smiles...but then again, they're always in favor of plans that involve arson.

"Sounds good," Pol says. "But you do know—"

"Yeah, I know how much it's worth. But we've gotta take the loss. You've got a lighter, right?" I gesture impatiently. After a brief hesitation, Pol shrugs and digs a slim metal device out of his pocket. "I'll tell Momma I made the call," I say, snatching it. "We don't have time to argue. Sanita leaves are supposed to be really flammable, right?"

"Yup," Drom says, while Pol nods along.

"And it's medicinal, right? Nontoxic?" I don't know much about Sanita, but I do know its leaves can be crushed into a pain-killing paste of some kind.

"Yup."

"Just do it already," Lyre says, already moving toward the cargo crates. She dumps one out on the floor. First comes a pile of freeze-dried produce, this one mostly mangoes and bananas. Then she pulls out the false bottom, and out drops a pile of black foliage.

Soon enough, we have a sizable mass of food and Devan plants lying on the warehouse floor. I bend down next to it and touch the lighter's flame to one curling black leaf of the Sanita plant. It lights up instantly. Though not all of the fruits and veggies take flame quickly, the Sanita burns almost alarmingly well and exudes a powerfully sweet smoke.

"That should do it," I say as I step back, waving smoke away with one hand. The cloying smell is already sticking to the inside of my mouth and nose.

"We should probably get out of here before we inhale too much," Pol says.

"Yeah, it's really—wait, you said this shit isn't toxic!"

Pol laughs. Beside him, Drom is wafting smoke into her nose.

"No, but it will get us nice and high," she says, and both twins display that damn grin of theirs.

"Wha—?" I stumble backward toward the door as the words sink in, covering my nose with one hand and trying to hold my breath. Lyre squeals, covering her face with both hands and running for the exit. "Are you fucking kidding me?"

"It's fine," Drom says, waving a hand dismissively. "I hear Titan soldiers smoke this shit all the time before battles. It'll probably help us."

"Yeah, and it'll make a good surprise for the Gaian officers," Pol says with a grin. He's been making no effort not to inhale the thickening smoke, but now he coughs, putting a hand over his mouth. "This is...kind of a lot of smoke, though."

"Let's get the hell out of here!" I yank the door open and let Lyre out first before waving at the twins. Pol yanks Drom by the arm, and she takes one last deep inhale before reluctantly letting herself be dragged along to the alleyway behind the warehouse.

The shouts of Gaian officers rise in the distance, likely responding to the plume of smoke forming above the warehouse. As the door shuts behind us, I lower my hand from my mouth and cough in a vain attempt to rid myself of the prickle in my throat. Every inhale brings a faint taste of sweetness.

Outside, the rain is now gone, the sky as clear as if it were never here. Strange, but I don't have time to ponder the weather right now. My siblings follow me to the mouth of the alley, where we crouch and wait for the officers to arrive. I'm tempted to ask the twins how much smoke I would've had to inhale to feel its effects, or what exactly those effects are, or how long I have until they set in—but maybe it's better not to know. It's not going to make a difference anyway. This diversion will give us one chance to slip past the Gaian patrols, and we have to take it. So I stay silent as we wait, and try not to wonder if the tingle spreading down my limbs is more than pins and needles from holding this crouch.

Soon a group of uniformed officers come running toward the warehouse. I press myself against the alley wall and hold up a hand to signal my siblings. Right as they pass by, I straighten, and the world sways around me.

"Okay," I whisper, putting a hand against the building to steady myself. I stare as it ripples beneath my hand, shake my head, and turn to my family again. "Move fast and quiet. We have one chance at this."

Shit. The effects of the Sanita are definitely hitting me now, strong enough to make my head spin. There's no way Titan soldiers fight like this; I must have inhaled too much. I would probably be panicking if not for the drugs dulling my nerves. But regardless, this is our one shot at making it out of here. We have to move, now.

I suck in a deep breath, take two steps forward, and fall flat on my face.

"Violation of off-world visa regulations, violation of Code Blue quarantine, possession of class-one contraband, possession of unauthorized weapons..."

An unfamiliar voice drags me out of the black void of unconsciousness. My whole body hurts, but mostly my nose. I groan, trying to touch it to assess the damage, but I can't move my hands. Instead, I peel my eyes open and squint in the sunlight. The voice prattles on as I try to make sense of the blurry world around me.

"Arson, ingestion of a prohibited substance, public intoxication, resisting arrest..."

"We only resisted a little," Pol says, somewhere behind me, and Drom chuckles.

"For the third time, please be quiet while I finish the list of infractions."

The world sharpens into focus as the danger of the situation hits me. I'm on the ground, hands cuffed behind me. Lyre is slumped at my side, unconscious and also restrained. The twins are seated back-to-back with us. And all around, forming a tight noose of uniforms, are Gaian law-enforcers. One in front notices me raise my head, and places her hand on her blaster as I try to wriggle out of my binds.

"Sir? This one's awake," she says, glancing behind me. The man who was speaking moves to my front, scrutinizing me for a moment before looking down at the comm secured around his wrist.

"Ah, yes," he says, tapping the screen with one slender finger. "This would be Scorpia Kaiser." He meets my eyes. "You have an additional charge. Terrorism." He glances over at the other officers. "She's the one who instigated the Code Blue."

I wince at the following shocked silence from both the officers and my siblings, wondering briefly if I could fake losing consciousness again.

"Scorpia, I'm going to kick your ass," Drom says.

"I'll explain later." If there *is* a later. My head is still foggy and my thoughts jumbled, but I know the situation we're in is incredibly dangerous. If the twins really resisted arrest while I was out—even just "a little"—they're lucky to be alive. Fear and guilt churn in my stomach, making it hard to breathe for a second. Damn, we are really in over our heads here, and it's all my fault.

"How long was I unconscious?" I ask, trying to turn toward the twins. I catch a glimpse of Drom, one eye swollen and dried blood caked on the side of her face, before the officer grabs my shoulder and yanks me forward again.

"No squirming," he says, squeezing hard enough to make me wince. I grit my teeth and glare at him as he releases me. My heart is pounding in my chest, but like hell am I going to give him the satisfaction of seeing my fear.

"About an hour," Pol murmurs behind me, once the officer looks down at his comm again. "Lightweight."

Despite the circumstances, there's a hint of barely contained laughter in Pol's words. I shut my eyes, guilt further wrenching at me. I'm sure the drugs aren't helping, but the twins really don't understand the situation we're in. None of my siblings know Gaia and its heavy-handed police force as well as I do. Apparently a thorough beating wasn't enough to get it through the twins' skulls.

"Then why haven't they moved us yet?" I ask, my voice tight.

"Don't know. They're waiting for something."

If they were going to imprison us, they would have done so already. So I know exactly what they're waiting for—authorization to kill. I lower my head, desperately racking my brains for something to get us out of here, but it jerks up again at the sound of an approaching craft.

The sleek white cruiser slows to a hover a few yards away from us, engines sending a cloud of churning dust in our direction. I shut my eyes and duck my head, but it still chokes me. By the time I finish coughing, the cruiser has landed. The four doors slide upward, and a stout figure jumps down.

A gasp escapes my mouth as I recognize Momma. I can't remember the last time I was so happy to see her. The feeling brings me back to my childhood, running toward home with law enforcement at my heels, certain that as long as I could reach my mother no one could harm me. That stupid, childish belief surges back now. Momma will figure something out. She always does.

But my smile dies as a group of white-uniformed officers exits the vehicle after her. My relief turns to confusion as they surround Momma. And yet, she doesn't seem concerned by their presence.

Before I can figure it out, another familiar face exits the vehicle, and certainly not one I expected to see accompanying my mother: Talulah Leonis. The president of Gaia is here.

My lip curls in distaste. Leonis is a woman known for her hard stances, and particularly the harsh regulations and punishments she doles out to off-worlders like me and my family. I've always hated her, and Momma has used some choice words to describe her practices as well. So why the hell are they together now?

Leonis is several inches taller than my mother, and startlingly reminiscent of Shey, aside from the lighter skin tone, graying hair, and fine lines etched into her face. She has the same dark eyes, broad cheekbones, and ramrod-straight posture, but she has no hint of Shey's warm smile or easy charm. She's exactly as stoic and tightly coiled as she looks in every political ad.

Momma stops a half yard away and folds her arms over her chest. She looks down at us, ignoring the law-enforcers who regard her with a wary eye, and presses her lips firmly together. She waits. Soon enough, Leonis stops alongside her, standing almost shoulder-to-shoulder as if they're old friends. The president's face, however, is an icy mask that doesn't quite manage to hide her contempt.

Beside me, Lyre begins to stir, blinking up at the president in sleepy confusion. The twins are unsuccessfully trying to turn their heads and get a look at what's happening. Nobody says a word, and tension crackles in the air. I should keep my mouth shut...and yet words spout out nonetheless.

"It's, uh..." I shift in my handcuffs, blow a strand of hair out of my face so I can get a better look at her. "It's an honor to meet you, Madam President." My words ooze with over-the-top politeness, and I flash her a very fake smile.

"Scorpia," Momma says, her tone frosty enough to make me wince. "Shut up."

I oblige.

"I hope you understand that you've put me in a difficult position," Leonis says. It takes me a moment to realize she's speaking to Momma, because she never looks directly at her. As if merely looking one of us in the face is beneath her. "The city is in an uproar. I was under the impression I was dealing with another Gaian, who understood the value of subtlety."

Momma's eyes flash with barely contained fury, but she keeps her voice calm.

"I can assure you, if your people hadn't pulled me away with so little warning, this never would have happened." She glances down at me, and I look away. "My children, unfortunately, did not have a proper Gaian upbringing. Though, from what I understand, your daughter was involved in this as well?"

Despite the situation, I have to bite my lip to hide a smile at that. I'm not sure what's going on, but it does feel good to hear Momma sass the Gaian president. After a moment, Leonis sniffs, turns away from us, and nods to the collection of enforcers standing at attention nearby. The man in charge perks up, so eager for orders that I want to gag. *Gaians.*

"Uncuff them," Leonis says.

I'm not sure who's more confused—me, or the officer receiving the orders.

"What?" we both say, as he looks at the president and I look at my mother.

"Ma'am, these are off-worlder criminals with an incredibly long list of offenses to their names," the officer says, gesturing in particular to me. "You want them released?"

"Was my order unclear, officer?" the president asks. Her tone and expression are both mild, and yet there's something steely and frightening in her eyes. I recognize the look from my own mother. This is a woman who's used to having her orders followed without question.

Still, the officer hesitates. I have to imagine this goes against every word of his training and code. He casts another look at me, the hatred stewing behind his eyes. I grin up at him. But a moment later, he controls his expression, nods, and gestures for the other law-enforcers to assist him in releasing us.

I bounce to my feet as soon as I can. Though my heart is still pounding, and I haven't a clue where this situation is going, I make a great show of stretching my arms above my head and making contented sounds. The head officer glares at me from nearby, his shoulders stiff.

When my siblings are released, they remain in a tight circle around me, warily eyeing the officers and glancing at Momma for cues that don't come. Pol takes a half step toward her, but stops as he realizes the president is still at her side. Lyre stays pressed close against me. Even Drom hesitates, her usual confidence gone in the face of such a strange situation. None of us are sure what to make of this.

"So..." I glance at the president. It's hard to look her in the face, after years of seeing pictures and videos. If Leonis had been in charge when I was here as a child, I probably wouldn't have survived. Since she came into power, she's enacted laws that made it illegal to help an off-worlder under any circumstances. I've heard stories of children dying on the streets begging for a sip of water. Gaians try to hush such tales, but I know in my heart that they're true. That's why I force myself to look at her. I want her to look into the eyes of someone she doesn't consider human enough to save, and let her see part of herself mirrored back. I take a deep breath before speaking, ensuring that my voice is steady. "We free to go, then?"

The president meets my gaze for the first time, and smiles. It's a small, tight motion that doesn't reach her eyes.

"This never happened," she says, once again somehow managing to sound conversational and threatening at the same time. She pauses. "As long as you disappear from my planet within the next hour, that is."

Momma clears her throat and jerks her head at us.

"You heard her," she says. "Back to the ship."

I stop on the threshold of the cargo bay. I had anticipated the space to be left empty after our last unloading, a reminder of everything we lost in this botched job—but instead, the bay holds five small, new crates. They're not our usual variety, either. These are highly polished steel containers with passcode entry pads, the kind meant for holding something expensive and probably volatile.

While I was busy getting arrested—twice—it looks like Momma was busy as well. And this confirms my suspicions. Leonis didn't pardon us out of the goodness of her heart. Momma made a deal. And while I've taken all sorts of morally questionable, highly criminal jobs in the past, this one turns my stomach in a way those never have. The others felt like necessity. This one seems like shaking hands with the devil.

Working with Leonis. Corvus's return. My own screwups on Gaia. Everything is starting to collide in a nasty way, like the universe is conspiring to make my world collapse on itself from multiple directions all at once. Is this what it feels like to have karma catching up with me? I'm not sure, but I do know that not even the ship feels like home right now. Every step forward makes my stomach drop lower.

But maybe that's because I'm approaching Momma. She's waiting near the stairs, arms folded over her chest, eyes tracking me as I trudge up the ramp. I force myself to stop and face her despite my desire to run and hide in the cockpit. There are a lot of things I want to say about Leonis, and Corvus, and the ship, and everything.

"Momma," I say, once I'm confident my voice won't shake. "Let me explain—"

She hits me so hard that a gasp rips out of my mouth and stars dance across my vision. Heat flares in my face and tears sting my eyes—from both pain and deep shame as I realize that all of my younger siblings witnessed that. Momma hitting me is nothing new, but she doesn't usually make it a public humiliation.

"I'm sorry," I whisper, so quietly I'm not sure she hears it. "Momma…"

"Get the ship ready for launch," Momma says, her soft voice made loud by the utter silence around us.

I shut my mouth, open it, shut it again because I can't trust the words that will come out. Momma's eyes are cold. The twins scoot past without looking our way, exchanging an uneasy glance as they head up the stairs. Lyre hits the button to shut the ramp before scurrying upstairs after them with one hand pressed to her mouth. Then, it's just me and Momma in the closed cargo bay. I swallow hard. I've been reprimanded by Momma many times before, but this feels different. In the past, I've always felt that her punishments were meant to make me better. Now, she looks at me like she's given up. It makes me want to curl up in a hole somewhere and never face the world again.

"Of course," I say, once I muster up words. I glance at the crates tied down on the other side of the bay. Maybe Leonis gave her an offer she couldn't refuse, something big enough to delay picking up Corvus. Surely the Gaian president wouldn't have any business in a war zone. "Are we still headed for…?"

"Straight to Titan," Momma confirms. "The Gaians repaired our engine. We're all set."

My shoulders slump. So much for another chance to prove myself before Corvus's return…and so much for this job being anything close to legitimate business. I'm burning with questions, but I'm already pressing my luck with Momma by delaying the launch this much. So after a moment I take a deep breath, nod, and jog upstairs through the messy middle deck.

The cockpit still smells like spilled whiskey, and glass crunches beneath my boots as I make my way to my chair, but it's comforting to sink into my usual seat. Here, at least, I feel equipped to handle whatever problems come my way. My hands go through the motions, prepping for launch, while my mind settles into a blank state. It feels good not to think, at least for a little while, and better to see my screens come to life and the lights turn red. I strap myself in, wrap my hands around the wheel, and start her up.

As *Fortuna* launches and we leave Gaia far behind, I allow myself to pretend for a few golden minutes that we're not headed toward worse trouble on Titan.

CHAPTER TWELVE

Our People

Corvus

The storm screams around us as we make the long trek back to the outpost.

The cold is constant and ruthless on this planet, but the current storm is harsh even by Titan standards. The wind rips at my heavy clothing as I lean into it, one hand raised to cover my eyes. I can barely see the others through the snow whipped into a haze of white in all directions. We travel for hours, guided by Magda's compass, and make little progress. But we have to keep going. Seeking shelter so close to enemy territory is suicide. If the storm trapped us, we would have nothing to do but wait to be found and slaughtered.

Finally, we're safely on our own ground. But everyone is growing weak and tired, lagging farther and farther behind. My ribs are in agony, this alien power source feels heavier with each step, and the weather shows no sign of letting up. We'll never make it to the outpost in these conditions. So I signal Magda closer and shout at her to take us to the closest shelter possible. I hate doing this, especially with something so valuable on our hands, but we have no choice.

After another hour's travel, when my legs feel ready to give out beneath me, Magda leads us to a small border town called Kisk. Built into a series of caves on the side of a cliff, the town is barely visible through the storm. I head for the first door I see and rap my knuckles against the stone in three heavy knocks.

After a silence long enough that I start to wonder if I'll have to break it down, the door swings open a couple of inches. A sliver of a man's face and the barrel of a blaster poke through. Behind me, I hear several clicks as my team draws their own weapons, but I hold up a hand to halt them. I carefully lower the hand to my heart, tap it with two fingers, and then pull up my sleeve to show the man the brand on my wrist. The cold air bites at my flesh, and I cover it again once I'm certain he's seen.

"I'm Sergeant Corvus Kaiser, under General Kel Altair," I say, shouting to be heard above the howling wind, though it sends fresh stabs of pain through my chest. "We need shelter through the storm."

The wind is louder than ever as I wait for his reply. The man squints at me, his expression hard to read. These are our people, and our people have a legal obligation to provide shelter and supplies when necessary—but that doesn't mean everyone is eager to do so. We may have to force our way in. But finally, the man nods and swings the door open. I'm grateful to step into the warmth.

Warmth is relative on Titan, of course, and the house is still cold enough for my breath to be visible, but at least we're out of the biting winds. I stomp my boots on the welcome mat to shake off the snow before continuing in, with a glance over my shoulder to ensure my team is performing the same courtesy. Magda, one booted foot already extended over the mat, rolls her eyes at my look and steps back to scrape off the ice.

"Thank you for the hospitality." I let my goggles fall around my neck and slip off my mask. The house is small, made almost comically so once my team steps inside and shuts the door behind them. Beyond the living room, I catch a glimpse of a tiny kitchen and another doorway that might lead to a bedroom. It's a modest living space, clearly not meant to accommodate such numbers. But if this man doesn't want to allow us past the threshold of the living room, I won't push him.

"Of course." The home's owner stands on the edge of the room, his blaster now in the back of his pants, his head lowered and two fingers respectfully pressed to his heart until each of us returns the gesture. "Happy to provide. My name is Kaalid Hort."

The others strip off their outer layers and make themselves as comfortable as possible on the man's sparse furniture. Sverre sprawls out across the ratty couch with a groan. Magda and Daniil fight over the remaining armchair until he stubbornly plops down and she just as stubbornly decides to sit on his lap. I roll my eyes at them and turn to our host. Hort is broad-shouldered and stocky, his tan skin worn and leathery but marked with few scars. I search for a war-brand on his wrist, but find it smooth and blank.

"Did you serve?" I ask, made wary by the lack of a brand.

"No," the man says, and gestures down at himself. "Bad leg. My wife did, though. Lost her life in the Battle of Vuuten. Now it's just me."

It's odd for a Titan to live alone; usually, a lone man would integrate into another family in the village. But perhaps Kisk is too small for that to be possible.

"She made her planet proud." It's what you're supposed to say, but the words never fail to sound hollow and cold to my ears. I've never heard of that battle, or of Vuuten, which must have fallen before I came here. Just one more in the endless stream of small victories and great tragedies that make up the war.

The man inclines his head in a nod.

"Do you need anything?" he asks. There's a hesitation to the words. Most people on Titan don't have much, especially in places like this, and providing for five soldiers is a tall order. *Four*, I remind myself, and shake off the image of Ivennie's face. It's still a lot to ask. This man will likely spend days with a half-full belly to make up for it. But my people are hungry.

"Yes," I say. "Food and drink. Something warm." I try to ignore the anxiety that crosses Hort's face before he bows his head.

"Of course," he says, and backs toward the kitchen. He pauses on the threshold, his gaze flickering to the closed bedroom door. A soft sound—a muffled word or a cough—comes from within. My hand moves to my blaster.

"You said it was just you," I say sharply. My team's conversation quiets as they note the tension. Daniil and Magda rise to their feet. The man holds up both hands, palms out.

"Wait," he says quickly. "I . . ." He stammers for a moment. "Let me show you."

I gesture toward the door with my gun, and the man sidles toward it, with nervous glances toward my waiting soldiers. He opens the door slightly and hesitates, giving me an imploring look.

"Please," he says. "Only you."

I frown. As much as I want to believe we can trust our own people, this could be a trap. My mind flashes to Uwe's death, the dirty-faced child in the sewer. After a moment, I gesture over my shoulder.

"Daniil, with me," I say. "Everyone else stays here."

Daniil is at my side in an instant, his weapon drawn. Out of the lot of them, I know he'll be the least eager to fire his blaster, but that doesn't mean he won't do it if necessary. And, if it comes down to it, he's also talented at forcibly extracting information. The man hesitates for another moment, but eventually nods and leads us into the room, shutting the door behind us.

The bedroom is dark enough that it takes my eyes a moment to adjust. It's a tiny room, with one bed and a small dresser. The man steps around the bed while Daniil and I exchange a glance. What could he have to hide in this room?

"It's okay," Hort says in a soft voice, gesturing. "Come and meet our guests."

On the other side of the bed, two small, pale figures rise. One is a boy—nearly a young man—with narrow shoulders and a mop of scraggly hair. The second is a girl, younger than him by at least a few years, with fair curls and a round face. Both look at us with wide eyes, the resemblance to their father clear.

"I'm sorry," Hort says, standing beside them with a hand on the girl's shoulder. "When we heard a knock at the door so late, I didn't know what to expect. And then..." He hesitates. "As I said, I'm happy to provide. But I know soldiers can be...rowdy."

I sigh, holstering my blaster, and gesture for Daniil to do the same.

"You could have gotten them shot," I snap at the man, who bows his head. "Never do something so stupid again."

Despite my harsh words, I can't blame him for hiding his children. I know exactly the sort of rowdiness the man speaks of. In fact, I've probably heard more accurate—and much worse—tales of soldiers' deeds than he ever has. Some people have no better ways to let off steam. And as much as I want to tell him that my team isn't like that, the words stick in my throat. I glance at Daniil, who shrugs at me, and Hort, who is staring down at the floor with his hand still protectively gripping his young daughter. My mind flashes again to that child in the sewers.

"Daniil, check them for weapons," I order. Hort's mouth opens, but shuts again, and he steps away as Daniil moves to pat them down. Once he's done, he nods at me.

"All right. They can stay here as long as they remain quiet. Now get us something to eat."

I leave the room before the man can say anything, with Daniil close on my heels.

"Nothing to worry about," I say, stepping into the room.

I'm surprised to find Magda and Sverre re-entering from the kitchen rather than waiting for us. Sverre has a bottle of frostroot vodka clutched in one hand and a grin on his face, and Magda is ripping pieces off an algae sheet with her teeth.

"We got impatient," she says without a hint of remorse, flopping across the couch before Sverre can reclaim his spot.

"Couldn't find any water, so I took this," Sverre says, uncapping the bottle and taking a generous swig.

A hint of shame in their behavior wriggles its way into my heart, but I ignore it and the look on Hort's face as he shuts the bedroom door behind him and sees them. At least I know I made the right choice in letting the children stay hidden.

"Water and something more substantial than algae," I order, and the man bows his head and moves to the kitchen.

First comes the water, and I have to order my team to briefly set aside the rapidly depleting bottle of vodka they're passing around. Soon Hort returns with a fresh pot of soup. The broth is thin, but it contains a surprisingly hearty amount of kale and carrots and pale pink frostroot.

"Village grown," he boasts, puffing out his chest. "We have a greenhouse with imported Devan soil."

He stays long enough to be polite before disappearing into the bedroom with his children, taking a small portion of the meal with him.

I help myself to a serving of the soup but wave away the vodka each time my team tries to pass it to me.

"Don't you ever relax?" Daniil asks me, after a few drinks have made him bold. He perches on the armrest of my chair, looping one arm around my shoulders and pressing his cheek to the top of my head.

"Job's not done yet," I say, not returning his touch but not pulling away. His nearness doesn't make me uncomfortable, precisely—but neither do I want to encourage it, especially with him. Daniil has never been shy about his feelings.

"Not much work to be done during a storm," he says, leaning against me.

Magda, now sitting on the couch with her legs draped over Sverre's lap, clicks her tongue at us. She eyes Daniil's arm around my shoulders, and I resist the urge to pull away from him. This is fine, I remind myself. This is normal for them. And even if it wasn't, there's no reason I should care what she thinks.

"Our dear sergeant's job is never done," she says, her eyes locked with my own though she's speaking to Daniil. "Because he always has to keep an eye on us." Her gaze flicks toward the bedroom doorway before returning to me. "Isn't that so?"

I tense, waiting for her to pry more or for one of the others to comment. But Sverre is busy eating and drinking as much as he can get his hands on, and Daniil ignores her. I choose to do the same, and busy myself moving our packs to the kitchen to open up more space in the crowded room.

By the time I'm done with the task, everyone is fast approaching drunk and the tension has thawed. I don't usually allow my team to drink much—it's a dangerous habit on a world like this—but tonight they deserve to relax. I indulge in a glass of it at their insistence, and tolerate the subsequent cheer with a roll of my eyes.

Situations like these always make me think of my sister. In years past, I never understood Scorpia's drinking, how she could spend all night puking and reach for the bottle first thing in the morning, insisting it was "the best hangover cure." Aside from those times, I always thought of my sister as happy. She was constantly laughing, cracking her stupid jokes at the most inappropriate moments. She could lighten the mood of any situation, a talent I sorely missed when I first came to Titan. Losing her felt like losing a part of myself—the good part, the part who knew how to laugh and how to show mercy. I thought her drinking was an affliction, a learned habit not dissimilar from her stealing and lying. Now I wonder if it was a crutch to dull the edges of a constant hurt, like it is for so many people on Titan.

That's why I refuse to drink much myself. I want to let this ache linger as long as it can. I owe that much to Ivennie, and the other hundreds of faces that haunt me. The guilt, the regret, the uncertainty tearing at me—I deserve it all. I failed Ivennie, and unless I decide to take Altair's offer, I'll be turning my back on the rest of my team soon. What will happen to them if I leave? How can I turn away after everything we've been through together? They need me. Likely much more than my family does. Watching them now and thinking about it, my heart tells me to stay. To protect them until I can't anymore.

After a couple of hours of drinking, the day catches up with everyone. Sverre and Daniil curl up on the couch together and exchange a few tired kisses before falling asleep. Magda, sitting on the floor with her back propped against the same piece of furniture, dozes off with her head leaning against Daniil. Exhaustion hits me as well, amplified by the aftereffects of the Sanita, and I nod off despite my intention to keep watch.

I'm not sure how much time passes before I wake. I jolt upright and wince as the movement jostles my ribs. The others are sleeping soundly, and the house is quiet, though the storm still rages outside. It's tempting to let myself fall back asleep in the company of my team, but instead I stand, cracking my neck and back as I rise to my feet. Someone needs to watch over the power source. I shouldn't have left it alone at all, but my exhaustion sabotaged me.

I walk into the kitchen, and freeze as I spot Hort in the corner. My mind races. I had assumed he retreated to the bedroom with his children, but he must have slipped out while I slept. Even with his back to me, it's obvious that he's shuffling through our packs on the floor.

The sound of me drawing my weapon stops him. He turns, face draining of what little color it has as he finds himself staring down the barrel of my blaster.

"I—I didn't mean anything by it," he stutters. "I—my family, we hardly have enough as it is, and with this—I was just looking for some food—"

He blathers on, but I stop listening as my eyes shift past him to my pack and the soft glow emanating from within. My stomach drops. How could I be so stupid as to leave it unguarded? If only I was less tired, if only I had woken when he left the bedroom… But after a moment, my heart grows hard and cold. *"Classified,"* Altair told me at the end of our conversation. *"Let no one see it."*

"Did you look?" I ask, cutting off the string of useless words coming out of the man's mouth. His mouth hangs open, and I steel myself further.

"No," he says, and I step closer, aiming my gun directly at his forehead. "I mean—I did, but I have no idea what it is!" His expression turns wild as he sees the look in my eyes. His own eyes dart around, searching for an escape or a weapon. But instead of going for either, he breathes, "Please."

I grab him by the arm and drag him toward the door. My team stirs at the sound of the struggle, and Magda raises her head. One hand reaches for her weapon, but I stop her with a quiet order. She watches me go.

"I won't say a word," Hort says, gripping my arm while I haul him outside.

Once I shut the door behind us, it's just me and him and the howling wind. The storm is starting to break, and the ground is covered in a fresh blanket of snow as far as the eye can see. Each step crunches through a few inches of it as I move forward and release the man. He stumbles and falls, his bad leg giving out beneath him.

"I'm sure you think you won't," I say, my voice flat. "But if the enemy comes here? If they threaten to kill your family and destroy your village? If they torture you? Then will you be able to hold your tongue?"

He looks up at me, his mouth working silently for a few moments before he manages a word.

"Please."

I grimace in disgust. Not an argument, not a denial—merely a *please*, again. I wish this man would at least put up a fight, at least give me some reason to consider doing something other than what I have to do. I crouch beside him so we come face-to-face. He's trembling in the cold, his breath coming in short puffs, but I'm barely aware of it myself.

"What's the nearest fort?" I ask. He stares at me. "Sketa?" He nods. "Run there," I say. "Run as fast as you can and don't stop. When you get there, beg to serve them however you can. Never speak of what you saw, and never come back here. That's the only way you'll be safe."

He continues to stare, jaw gaping dumbly, tears freezing on his cheeks.

"Do you understand?" I ask, my voice rising, and he snaps his mouth shut and nods.

"But my family—"

"The village will care for them."

"And my leg—"

"The storm is breaking. Go, now, and hopefully you won't meet any trouble on the way."

When I rise, he scrambles to his feet as well.

"Thank you, sir," he says, touching his fingers to his heart. "Thank you. Thank you. I will go, I promise."

When I don't say another word, he turns his back and starts to run. I'm thankful for the wind, then, because it stops him from hearing me move behind him. I inhale deeply and take aim at the back of his head.

He's not aware of the shot streaking toward him until he falls.

I stand there, breathing in lungfuls of icy air and staring at the splash of red across the white ground. Soon, fresh snow begins to cover it. I lower my weapon and tilt my face upward, staring at the stormy sky.

By the time I finish burying the body and return inside, the house is quiet. Sverre is still sprawled across the couch, one massive arm flung across Daniil. It takes me a moment to realize that Magda, now sitting in the armchair, is awake. She watches me, but I avoid her gaze as I brush off the worst of the ice coating me.

More than anything I want to be alone, but too much longer in the cold would be dangerous. So I head to the cramped space of the kitchen and lean on the counter. My hands burn and my face is numb. The pain in my ribs seems to grow worse with each breath. I should drink something, eat something more as well, maybe have one of my team members look after my wounds—but I can't bring myself to search through this family's cabinets after what I've done. From the look of the pantry, we've practically cleaned them out already anyway. No wonder this man was desperate enough to rummage through our belongings. If only I hadn't been so stupid as to leave the power source unguarded...

When I hear soft feet on the floor behind me, I shut my eyes.

"Not now," I say, low enough that I won't wake anyone else.

"Especially now," Magda says. When I say nothing else, she reaches for me.

In moments like these, it's easy to understand why Titans crave physical touch so much. It's the sole bit of warmth on this stars-damned world. Magda's fingers slip beneath my jacket and trace lines of fire across my icy skin, massage feeling into the half-frozen muscles of my neck and shoulders. I draw a shuddery breath as she eases the knots of tension.

I want to pull away before anyone wakes up and sees us. I want her to never stop touching me. I want . . . I want many things that aren't possible.

"You don't have to be so lonely," Magda murmurs. Her hands pull away, but before I can miss her touch, her lips replace them. She presses a soft kiss into the space where my neck meets my shoulder, slipping one arm around my waist and pressing herself against my back. I let myself lean into her for a moment—a dangerous moment—but then push her hands away. She steps back, and I turn. Her face is unreadable in the dim light. "Why?" she asks. "Why do you have to be so distant?"

Because to do otherwise would mean too much to me. Because I know it wouldn't be the same for her. Because I can't let myself grow used to this place . . . because I'm leaving, I've always known I'm leaving them behind, and my actions today solidified it. This is a reminder of who I'd have to become if I accepted Altair's offer and stayed here, and it is not a person I want to be. Even that person can't take care of my people here.

But most of all, I push her away because I don't deserve comfort. Not after everything I've done.

"Because I just killed and buried one of our people," I say, my voice quiet but cold as the storm outside. "Go to bed, Magda."

She jerks back as if I'd burned her. For a moment, she hesitates; and for that moment, I almost wish she won't leave. But I don't speak, and the moment passes, and she leaves me. I spend the night alone on the floor, my arms wrapped around the power source, barely able to shut my eyes.

CHAPTER THIRTEEN

Liar's Dice

Scorpia

The trip to Titan is usually mind-numbingly boring. Traveling between the other planets takes about a week, give or take a couple days, but Titan is so far out that it takes three entire weeks to get there from Gaia. Plus, there's nothing out that way except empty space and the icy rock itself, which is not exactly a place that invites visitors. Even for smugglers like us, it's rare for a job on Titan to be worth the fuel and time of getting there, let alone worth the risk of facing the volatile situation on the surface. So, it's unlikely we'll encounter anything more exciting than an occasional meteorite on the way, and autopilot can generally handle the trip on its own. Momma still prefers to have a warm body at the wheel at all times, just in case, but it doesn't have to be me any more frequently than anyone else.

But after the colossal fuckup that was our job on Gaia, everyone's tense and nervous and doing their best to avoid each other. It's not easy to do when we're all crammed on a small ship together, but we've gotten pretty good at it over the years. I spend each day awaiting my judgment from Momma...and yet, one week into our journey, she still has yet to punish me for what happened.

There have been little things, of course. I had to clean the whole cockpit and the main deck myself the first day after we left Gaia. She's restricted everyone's access to the media database, which makes shifts at the wheel duller than usual. She's locked up all our rations except for dry and tasteless algae sheets. She also hid as much of my alcohol as she could find, though that was only around half of it. And in a particularly cruel twist, she's staggered the twins' shifts so that their sleep schedules are opposite, making both of them moody and irritable, finding ways to pick fights with everyone else in the family because they don't want to admit how much they miss each other.

But Momma did most of these things the time Pol accidentally spilled a container of Devan spices she was saving for a special occasion. It isn't enough for what happened on Gaia—especially for what *I* did. I didn't just botch a job, I nearly got myself and everyone else killed. These punishments are annoying, but they don't fit the crime. I spend the week holding my breath and tiptoeing around, but Momma passes the majority of her time holed up in her room. She sends our schedules every morning, noting shifts at the wheel and cleaning duties and whatever other chores she assigns us, but otherwise it's like she's barely here.

Every day, I'm certain that my punishment must be coming soon. All the quiet hours without music or company or the distraction of a decent meal give me plenty of time to ruminate about what it could be. That's not even mentioning my uncertainty about the future, which sits like a cold rock in my gut, though I do my best to drink it away. I shouldn't, not with Momma already pissed off at me, but without anything to take the edge off, I'm afraid the fear will grow and grow until it paralyzes me.

Drinking keeps my emotions at arm's length, but I can't keep the thoughts out completely. My stomach ties itself into knots every time I think of facing Corvus again, and whether or not he'll return to his status as Momma's heir and favorite, along with my million questions about what's in our cargo bay and why we're working for Leonis. I'm so afraid of facing Momma's judgment that I can't bring myself to ask her about any of that. As desperately as I want to know, I keep telling myself that surely her anger will fade over time.

"But waiting without knowing what's coming is almost worse," I complain to Lyre when we both find ourselves in the kitchen at the same time. She's been avoiding me like the rest of my family, and the isolation is slowly driving me insane. I rip off a tasteless piece of algae with my teeth. "Maybe *that's* the punishment. Waiting for something to happen, imagining what it could be, all that shit."

"Or maybe she just doesn't want to talk to you," Lyre says, rummaging on the shelf to grab her own plastic-wrapped packet. "For good reason."

"Oh, come on—" I start, but she's already retreating to her room with her meal in hand.

After a couple more days, I decide I've had more than enough solitude. Approaching Momma still seems like a terrible idea, but surely my siblings can't stay mad at me forever. So I start scheming.

Pol is the easiest to hook. The moment I offer to share some of my secret alcohol stash, he agrees to meet. Lyre is a little bit tougher, but she comes around when I tell her I'll take her cleaning duty tomorrow. Drom, tired and cranky after a long shift at the wheel, demands I take her cleaning duty, give her a full bottle of vodka, *and* swap our next shifts, but finally we have a deal.

So, after Momma goes to bed, we gather in the kitchen to play our favorite game. The twins sit on one side of the table, Lyre and me on the other. Drom's eyes are shadowed and her face drawn, but she's smiling nonetheless, talking in a low murmur with her twin. It's the first time I've seen them together on this trip.

"Whose shift is it?" Lyre asks, placing a heavy bag of dice on the table, right next to the bottle of whiskey I've brought to share.

"Mine," I say, and scoff at her disapproving look. "What? I'm like, thirty seconds away from the cockpit. And we're out in the middle of nowhere. Let's play already."

"You better hope Momma doesn't wake up."

I shrug, even as my stomach twists nervously at the thought, and pour a drink for each of us.

"This is my best bottle, so savor it," I say, passing each person a glass.

Lyre rolls her eyes and mutters something, but tips out the colorful assortment of dice in the center of the table. Despite the tension still lingering in the room, we each scramble to grab five. Like every other game over the last three years, we ignore the extra set that remains untouched in the center, though this time my eyes linger on it. Twelve more days until we see Corvus again, and I still have no idea what Momma's plans are.

But now's not the time to think about that. Tonight, we're playing Liar's Dice, a tradition my siblings and I have had since we were children.

When we first started playing this game, we each had a set of five plastic, six-sided dice, like you're supposed to play with. Then Lyre decided to swap one of hers out for a weighted die that always lands on six, which we all caught on to after a few games. Next Drom broke one of hers in half—I'm still not sure how she managed to do so, but the thing was thoroughly unusable—and replaced it with a lopsided metal die that somehow never lands on one. Soon enough Pol brought in an eight-sided die as a joke, which became an accepted part of the game as soon as we saw how much the changed statistics annoyed Lyre. And so it went.

At this point, our collection is about half original dice that work as intended and half an assortment of others. Part of the game is figuring out which you've ended up with and which the others are holding.

It's a mess of a game, probably completely incomprehensible to anyone outside of the family, and the only one we ever agree on playing.

"Shit," Pol says, hefting one die in his hand. "Think this one's weighted."

"Shouldn't have told us that," Drom says. "Too late to swap now."

"Maybe I'm bluffing."

"We all know you're not bluffing."

"Come on, let's go," I say.

We down our drinks, drop our dice into the empty cups, shake them up, and flip them over on the table. I glance around at my siblings' reactions to their hands before I check my own, noting the wrinkle on Lyre's forehead, Drom's slightly raised eyebrow, Pol biting his lip. Then I cup my hand around my glass and lift the edge to peek at my own assortment of dice. One, three, four, six, and another six.

"Who goes first again?" Pol asks, despite this being the millionth time we've done this.

"Oldest," I say, still considering my dice.

There's a pause.

"That's you, Scorpia," Lyre says.

"Oh. Right." Just when I had gotten used to that, word of Corvus's return has my mind all screwed up again. I shake my head and focus on the game, setting my cup down and rolling the numbers through my mind. Calling sixes is the obvious play . . . or I could lie my ass off.

"Five fives," I say, making eye contact with Lyre to my left. It's a baseless estimation at best, and should mislead the others that I have at least one five on the table. But more importantly, it's low enough that it should make it impossible for Lyre to win unless she makes a risky call—which she won't.

"Seven fives," she says without missing a beat. Low enough that it's not risky, but high enough that the game shouldn't last long enough for me to win, either. Predictable enough. I make a face at her and turn to watch the twins, whose play styles tend to be... interesting, at the very least.

Drom checks her hand again before speaking, a hint of a frown crossing her face.

"Nine fives."

I scoff. She went too high, as usual, especially considering that I don't actually have any fives on the table.

"No way," I say, leaning over to elbow Pol. "Call the bluff."

But he won't, of course, not when it's Drom, and especially not with other people encouraging him to do so. Pol checks his hand, looks back and forth between us, and checks his hand again.

"Well, think about the statistics," Lyre says. "According to—"

"Ten fives," Pol declares, cutting her off.

"Aw, bud, I didn't want to have to do this to you." I shake my head, grinning. An easy win for me. "Too bad. Liar!"

Pol groans as we all lift our cups. I peer around the table, eyeing everyone else's dice.

"You didn't have a single five!" Pol complains, leaning over to look at my hand. "Why do you always do this shit?"

"Only six of them on the table," I say with a laugh after counting them up. "Drom, you could've gotten Lyre."

"Yeah, fuck off."

My siblings slide their glasses and the bottle to me. Winning the hand means I get to pour everyone else's drinks. Usually the idea is to get everyone else as drunk as possible, but seeing as this is *my* bottle of good whiskey, I give barely a splash to everyone except myself. They all grumble as they take them back, but these rules, at least, we always follow.

As soon as everyone has their cups back, we drink, shake, and flip again.

Though the night may have started out on a sour note, we soon fall into the easy rhythm of the familiar game. Lyre wins the next round, and then me again, and then Drom in a particularly lucky callout. Soon the laughter and jokes are flowing steadily, though we all keep our voices hushed for fear of waking Momma. Something inside me eases, like I've let out a breath I was holding for too long. This is how things are supposed to be. This is how *we're* supposed to be.

And then, halfway through the fifth hand, the lights turn green. In the second it takes for me to realize what that means, the emergency alarm begins to blare.

"Shit," I say, scrambling out of my chair and sending a couple of my dice toppling to the floor.

"Get to the wheel," Lyre yells at me, while the twins stare— Drom at me, and Pol at Momma's room. I take off down the hall as her door bangs open, her yells drowned out by the noise, and dive into my chair in the cockpit. Thank the stars I didn't drink enough to be well and truly drunk yet. Still, with the alarm wailing and all of my screens screaming warnings at me, it takes me a few moments to realize what I'm looking at: a large object, moving toward us, fast. It's something I haven't seen in a long time, but I know exactly what it means.

I let out a string of curses and slam a fist to shut off the emergency alarm.

"Incoming!" I bellow down the hall for the rest of my family to hear. "It's the *Red Baron*!"

A moment later, I hear the metal *thunk-thunk* of their grappling hooks hitting the side of our hull. I barely have time to grab a hold of my armrests before *Fortuna* is yanked sideways.

CHAPTER FOURTEEN

Loyalty

Corvus

Once the storm blows over, the outpost is a simple walk away. My team is quiet. No one speaks of last night, but I know they must be aware of what I did. The silence weighs heavily upon my shoulders, though none more than Magda's, who won't even look at me when I give orders. Daniil—the only one who knows the full extent of my guilt, including the children we left behind in that room—keeps stealing furtive glances at me, while Sverre seems doggedly determined to pretend he doesn't notice anything is wrong. Everyone is tired.

By the time we reach the outpost, my mood is sour enough that I smoke more Sanita without offering any to the others, trying to dull my jittery nerves and the pain in my chest. My breath comes in shallow, painful bursts. The others stand in the hangar and wait, avoiding eye contact with me, though Magda and Sverre exchange wordless questions with their glances. Once I'm done, we set off in the spider tank. First, a quick trip to retrieve the broken exosuits from the site of the battle, which thankfully goes without a problem. Once that's done, we head to Fort Sketa to meet the general.

I sit in the back of the tank with the bag containing the power source on my lap. Ever since the incident with Hort, I've been loath to take my hands off it. Magda is at the wheel, Daniil and Sverre manning the guns. The space is built for five—a normal team's size—and the emptiness left by Ivennie's absence is impossible to ignore. It makes the already-uncomfortable travel by tank nearly unbearable.

The spider tank is designed to travel through dangerous terrain, able to navigate across ice and up almost-vertical cliffs, but the four legs plod along in jerky motions that always sicken my stomach. Even after three years on Titan, I'm still not used to land vehicles, too accustomed to the smoother travel of hovercrafts that are common on every other planet. Here, the extreme winds and unpredictable weather make them too dangerous to operate.

It takes an hour to reach Fort Sketa. By the time we arrive, my stomach is revolting, my mood worse than before. The trip here, the incident last night, the battle before, my upcoming conversation with Altair...with all of it together, my nerves feel raw and exposed. I grind my teeth together, fighting the urge to smoke more. But the last of the Sanita hasn't worn off yet, and my team is already giving me sidelong glances. Normally, they would be fighting like children over who gets to climb out the hatch first, but now they wait, tense and uncertain, for my order.

They must think I've gone soft, reacting so strongly to two deaths yesterday. They still don't know that if this conversation with Altair goes the way I hope, I'll be leaving them—and soon.

"Get some food, and medical attention if you need it," I say, moving toward the hatch when none of them leave their seats. "I'll meet you later."

"Yes, sir," Daniil says softly. Everyone else is silent, and I don't look back as I climb out and head inside, clutching the bag with the power source tightly under my arm, though it jostles my injured ribs.

Fort Sketa is one of the larger bases of Interplanetist operations. Only one stout, windowless story of the building shows aboveground, but it continues far down beneath the surface. The hangar is crowded as I move through it, full of teams arriving and leaving, the air thick with shouted orders and clouds of breath in the chilly air. A few thousand soldiers occupy the fort at any given time, ready to be dispatched to the front or one of the nearby cities.

I ignore the busy noise and movement all around me and head straight to the elevators. The woman operating them salutes me as I approach. I speak Altair's name like a passcode, and after confirming on her comm that he's expecting me, she holds back the rest of the crowd and sends me down into the depths of the fort alone.

When the elevator doors open again, the air is several degrees warmer and more humid. My breath is no longer visible in front of me as I walk down the hall, past a number of locked doors and an even higher number of cameras, to the door bearing Altair's name. I pause outside, taking a deep and painful breath to ground myself, and knock.

"Enter."

I do so, my fingers already to my chest in salute. The room is small and plain, decorated by a few sparse pieces of furniture and the helmet of an old exosuit hanging like a trophy on the wall behind the general. Fluorescent lamps bathe everything in pale light.

Grizzled and broad-shouldered, General Altair sits with his hands folded on the desk in front of him. Standing, he towers over me, but even seated, he has an unmistakable gravitas that demands respect without a word. His uniform is marked with his years of service and many honors, but the scars crisscrossing his face and hands say more.

"Sergeant Kaiser," he says with a nod. "I'm glad to see you well."

"The same to you, General."

His eyes move to the bag over my shoulder, and his expression shifts to eagerness. I step forward to set it on his desk, but Altair nods toward it rather than gesturing for me to sit.

"Show me."

I carefully remove the orb from its case and place it atop his desk. Its soft glow lights Altair's smile.

"Very good," he says without taking his eyes off it. "Yes. You've done well. These are hard to find, and extremely valuable. I trust nobody else saw it?"

"One civilian. I took care of him."

"I see." He nods. "An unfortunate necessity. Good work."

I wait, hands clasped behind my back, but he says no more. After a few moments, I clear my throat.

"Sir." The word comes out almost apologetic. "There's also the matter of my discharge from service."

Even with Sanita dulling my nerves, my heart is pounding. I've spent three long, painful years waiting for this moment, but now, it also means turning down Altair's generous offer.

"Ah." His smile disappears like a switch being flicked. My mouth goes dry, and I swallow hard as he gestures for me to sit. He produces a bottle and two glasses from his desk, and pours us each a couple of fingers of vodka. I haven't eaten yet today, and my stomach gurgles in protest, but it would be rude of me to reject the tradition. So we clink glasses and drink together, while my stomach ties itself in knots in anticipation of what he'll say when we finish.

"I take that to mean you aren't interested in the promotion I offered," he says as he sets down his glass, wiping his mouth with the back of one hand.

"Truly, sir, I am honored by the opportunity," I say, setting down my own glass and trying to maintain my composure. "But as you know, my family is waiting for me. And I...I have a life elsewhere to consider."

Altair drums his fingers on his armrest. His eyes are focused on something past my head.

"In truth, few people end up leaving after the minimum three years, you know," he says, after a long pause. "They either die in the service or pledge their life to it. Fight until they can fight no longer. They realize their planet needs them. Their people need them."

Beneath the numbing tingle of Sanita, an alarm rustles in the back of my mind. What is he trying to do? Make me feel guilty? Make me reconsider? Surely he knows that I've always meant to leave.

"Perhaps they have nothing to return to," I say, choosing my words carefully.

"Perhaps." Altair leans back in his seat. I remain seated stiffly, my hands folded in my lap. "Or perhaps they realize that people are looked at differently here when they don't bear the scars of war along with the brands. As they say, the only honorable discharge is—"

"When the breath leaves your body," I finish softly. I'm suddenly very aware of how alone we are right now. Far underground, away from my team, farther still from my family. It never occurred to me how very easy it would have been for Altair to not send my message along to Momma. It never occurred to me that he could have had someone else deliver the power source and officially discharge me, as well. Why did he bring me here? The question rises up in my throat, but I swallow it down and wait. Silence stretches between us until it seems ready to snap.

"Of course, your situation is different," he says, finally, and I let out a breath. "You have a home off-world. A choice. I understand,

Kaiser, I truly do. I never expected you to stay, no matter how good of a soldier you make."

I don't know how to respond, so I merely nod my head.

"I suppose I should be grateful you served at all. I know how this war must look to your off-worlder eyes." I stay silent. There's no safe response to such a statement. "And I'm not a fool, either. I know the conflict here is as nonsensical as the rest of the system thinks it is. Settling here was a mistake, and we should have realized it long before now. This world is barren. Hostile. It wants to be rid of us. If we had only managed to pool our resources rather than fight for them, to focus on leaving this place rather than trying to survive it...If we had united like the nations of Earth did when it came time to leave their planet..." He trails off, shrugs. "But it's too late for that now. The Isolationists will never agree that this planet isn't enough for us, nor grant us enough peace to open the secure trade routes we need. Even aside from that, there's been too much bloodshed." He shakes his head. "There will be no end to this war. And if there was, what would it leave us with? This planet is no great prize."

I shift in my seat. I'm unsure why he's telling me this, but I know his words are dangerous. Titans try very hard to convince themselves that they're fighting for something. I almost had myself convinced of it, enough so that his words unsettle me.

"I've been grateful to serve my planet, sir," I say. "I'm not sure what you're suggesting."

"I'm suggesting we give the Isolationists what they want: a planet all to themselves. Let them freeze and starve here, if that's what they want so very badly. Let them rot."

"And what about us?" I realize after the words are out that the *us* isn't entirely appropriate. I'll be gone soon, and whatever Altair is planning won't apply to me.

"Our side has always known that the answer to our problems lay outside of Titan," he says. "We've always argued for trade, for open borders, for agreements with the other planets." He pauses, his tapping fingers going still and his eyes searing directly into mine. "I was going to speak to you about this if you accepted my offer," he says. "But if you're planning on leaving...hell, might as well give it one last shot." He leans forward in his chair while I remain silent. "Our side has argued for many radical things, but until now, no one has been so bold as to suggest we could leave this place entirely."

My brow furrows.

"There's nowhere to go," I say, before realizing that isn't exactly true. My chest constricts, and I can barely bring myself to speak for dread of the answer it may bring. "Unless your plan is to invade one of the other planets?"

"No. I'm tired of war," Altair says. "What I want is somewhere new. Somewhere we can start fresh, free of this bloodshed and these grudges." He pauses. I still don't understand, but I wait for him to continue rather than interrupting his thoughts. "When we left Earth, we couldn't be one hundred percent sure these planets would provide a home, either. I find it hard to believe the rest of the universe is as empty as people say."

"But we have no ships."

In response, Altair's smile grows into something less bitter, more genuine. My thoughts race. Titan may be poor in many ways, but it is rich in a few things: quartz, iron, and oil. And we have factories to refine them, to create steel and silicon, and to build solar panels to export to the other planets. People may sneer at Titan, but in some key ways, it has the most potential of any planet in this system. If someone wanted to build a ship—to build a *fleet*—then, theoretically, Titan would be the place to do it. And if they have more power sources like the one I found...if they have a way to use them in human-made ships...exodus could be possible.

But in a place where homeland means everything, to merely

suggest such a thing would be traitorous. I hesitate, weighing each word before I speak again.

"How would the other generals feel about such a plan?"

Altair's smile fades. His eyes wander past my head again.

"I suppose we'll find out when it's ready," he says, his eyes moving back to focus on me. My breath hitches as I understand. What he's suggesting—what he's doing already—*is* traitorous, and he has no qualms about it. He searches my face before continuing. "When the time comes, I'll need people like you at my side. People who are intelligent enough to see beyond these stupid, bloody battles and this pointless war."

Pointless. Though I believe most of what he's saying, that word rankles. How many people have I watched die—and how many have I killed—for this war, on his orders, to hear it called pointless now? I've spent so much time trying to convince myself that it had to be worth something.

"I apologize," Altair says, no doubt reading my expression. "Pointless is the wrong word. For now, this war is necessary. The point is survival, for you and for everyone else on Titan. But I've grown weary of war, and as the years go on, I find it more and more difficult to see a way for it to end." His eyes hold mine captive. "What I'm saying, Corvus, is that I know you want to leave because you think this place is a death sentence. But I've seen what you're capable of—what your heart holds—and I know you're too good to go running back to your family of criminals. Especially after what your mother did to you."

The reminder makes me go cold. My words are stuck in my mouth. I didn't think that Altair knew. I didn't think that anyone here knew. Momma told me that it would be too dangerous if people realized I wasn't serving out of choice. That people couldn't know that I was only here because she left me nowhere else to go.

"There is another option for you," Altair says, tapping his finger on his desk to punctuate the sentence. "Another life for you, with us. With me. With your team and a future that you will help lead us to."

A *no* is ready on my lips, but I pause. Momma, Scorpia, my little siblings, the ship that's always been my home...I've spent so long thinking about returning to them. But is that where I belong? Will I be able to live as a smuggler again, with no honor and no scruples? If I go home now, with everything I've done and all the ways I've changed, will they accept me? I don't know what's happened while I've been gone, but I know that nothing will ever be the same between us again. I'm not sure if I can forgive them for leaving me, or if they can forgive me for what I've become. I doubt even Scorpia will recognize me, regardless of how inseparable we were in the past.

And maybe this is where I belong now. Maybe I've adapted so thoroughly that I might as well stay. Maybe my team and my planet's people need me more than my family does. If I stay here, I'd be treated as a war hero. I'd be given a position of leadership under a general I respect. And if Altair truly seeks a future free from the war, I wouldn't have to resign myself to being the monster I had to be over the last few years. I could forge my own path, become who I want to be.

I wrestle with my thoughts quite a lot longer than I ever thought I would.

"I'm truly honored that you would consider me," I say quietly, keeping my head bowed and my eyes down in a show of respect. "And I have no doubt that you will succeed at leading Titan's people toward a new and better future."

"There's a *but*, I suppose," Altair says. I glance up at him and drop my eyes again.

"But I must decline," I say, as he already knows I'll say. "It's time for me to go home."

For a long moment, there is only silence. I clench my hands on my lap, keeping my head down. Altair is a good man, and I respect him, but I've never before had to disagree with him. Or, rather, I've never had the opportunity to consider disagreeing. I'm not sure how he'll take it now.

He sits back in his chair, folding his hands in front of him.

"So be it. I wish I could say that I'm surprised." He laughs, the sound abrupt and surprising, and my head jerks up. "Oh, stop looking at me like you're a puppy expecting to be kicked. You've served your years, Corvus, and you've already been officially discharged. You don't have to do everything I say."

I let out a breath, tension draining from my shoulders. Still, I don't relax fully. Altair doesn't seem angry, but he's a man who masks his feelings well. I don't intend to overstay my welcome any more than necessary. I stand, bowing my head, and unstrap the gun from my hip to set it on his desk.

"Thank you, sir."

"The medical wing should have civilian clothes you can change into."

I nod and slide my black Primus knife out of its sheath as well, but Altair waves a dismissive hand.

"That was a gift. Keep it."

I go still, hesitating for a moment with the knife held out in offering. Part of me wants to insist on leaving it—shedding all reminders of these three bloody years—but perhaps it would be good to keep a memento after all. I nod again, slipping the knife back into its sheath on my leg.

"Thank you, sir," I say once more, my voice quiet this time. "I hope you know I'll always be your ally."

"Maybe one day we'll do business together," he says with a wry hint of a smile as I step toward the door. "We'll leave for Drev Dravaask first thing in the morning. I'll make an exception and allow you to accompany me on the armored train one last time." I nod my head in grateful acceptance, though the reminder shocks me—as of tomorrow I'll be a civilian, with none of the advantages of being a soldier on Titan. "And I suppose I should tell you in advance. I'll be meeting with your mother while she's on-planet as well."

I pause halfway to the door. I shouldn't be surprised that my mother isn't coming to Titan just to collect me. Of course she'll have business to conduct after three years away, and Altair is an old contact of hers. Still, Momma would meet with him for only one reason. The thought of her selling weapons into the war I recently left—the war that people I love are still fighting in—makes me uneasy. But it isn't my place to say anything, not to the general or to my mother.

"Thank you for warning me," I say before the silence grows too thick.

"Of course. And, Sergeant Kaiser?"

I pause with my hand on the door, but this time I don't look back at him.

"You've made your planet proud."

CHAPTER FIFTEEN

Red Baron

Scorpia

The floor tilts and the ship groans. The whole vessel shakes as *Fortuna*'s engine struggles to pull in the right direction, but she's fighting a losing battle. The *Red Baron* is a hell of a lot bigger than us and will have no problem dragging us close enough that they can force their way inside.

Once I'm sure I can keep my footing, I follow Momma's shouts down to the cargo bay. Lyre is carrying gear out of the supply closet, and the twins are already armed to the teeth—knives strapped to their legs, guns slung over their backs, grav-grenades at their hips. I check in the supply closet, but as I thought, everybody's already grabbed the good shit. We have only a few sets of body armor, which have been claimed by Momma and the twins, and the weapons are all taken as well.

"Spare a blaster?" I ask Drom as I emerge, but she grunts and pushes past me to grab her armor from Lyre. "Aw, c'mon, you have enough weapons to neutralize an entire planet!" I shout after her as she walks away. Pol moves to join her near the ramp door, but I grab his arm and yank him to a stop. "One blaster. Please?"

He scrutinizes my face.

"You drunk?"

"What? No. You saw how much I drank. I'm not a lightweight."

He sighs, unclipping a laser pistol from the back of his belt and delivering it into my waiting hands. He places it very delicately, as if it's fine china rather than a weapon powerful enough to blow a hole through someone's skull.

"Don't lose it."

"I'm not going to lose my only gun."

"That's exactly what you said last time," he mutters, but hands me a smoke grenade as well before he follows his twin.

I turn to Momma, who is bent over the cargo. The five crates are tightly secured enough that the impact doesn't seem to have rattled them.

"Our cargo is volatile," she says, turning back to us. Her eyes are bloodshot and ringed with shadow. I nearly forgot that it's been almost two weeks since we were face-to-face. I'm curious what has her so worried that she's been losing sleep—but whatever it is, she's all business now. "We're going to have to go on the offensive. As soon as they force the ramp open, Pol and Drom, you're going to board their ship. Force them off and don't back down."

"Their ship?" I ask. The *Red Baron* has a small crew for a ship of its size, but they still outnumber us. The adjustable bridge they use to board us provides a good choke point, where only a few of them can move through at a time. We usually take advantage of that when we fight against boarders, and the crates provide good cover, too. No matter the cargo, the things are made of metal and can take a few hits meant for us. But if the twins push through to the other side, they'll be completely exposed.

"Did I stutter?" Momma snarls, her eyes meeting mine for the first time. I clamp my mouth shut.

Maybe I shouldn't be shocked, but I am. She's never acted this way about a shipment before. Even when we've transported weaponry, I've never seen her so paranoid about its safety. This has to mean either the cargo really is *extremely* volatile, or Momma is paranoid about anyone getting close enough to see it...or both. Enough that she's willing to risk our safety to protect it.

"When they push through, you and you"—Momma points at Lyre and then at me—"are going to follow. Move past while the twins are distracting them. Lyre, you need to disengage the locking mechanisms and cut us loose. Scorpia, cause a distraction, pull as much heat off her as you can. Come back to meet up with us when you've done your jobs. As long as we get free, we can outrun them."

I exchange a glance with Lyre, who looks utterly terrified at the prospect of heading onto the ship. "Cause a distraction" is my usual role, and one I'm comfortable with, but Lyre is never on the front lines. Her brain is much more valuable when it's not in danger of being blown out.

I don't like this. Neither does Lyre, but she doesn't look eager to speak up, either. At least the twins look pleased with the plan, each of them grinning from ear to ear in anticipation of the fight. Still, I notice Drom rubbing an old scar on her left forearm. She got the ugly, circular mark during a previous fight with the pirates, shortly after Corvus left, when we were still getting used to his absence. I still remember the way she screamed and Pol cried, the blood soaking the med bay, Momma muttering about her possibly losing the arm. When Drom notices me looking, she stops and scowls at me.

"Any questions?" Momma asks, in a tone that seems to strongly advise against the idea.

"Where are you gonna be?" I ask despite that, realizing she left herself out of the plan she laid out. As usual, she looks at me like I just blurted out the stupidest thing she's ever heard.

"With the cargo. Where else?"

A cheeky reply rises on the back of my tongue—*I dunno, maybe helping carry out your own insane plan?*—but I bite it back. Momma's right, it was a stupid question, one I should've known the answer to before I asked it. Time and time again, she's made her priorities clear, and this is no different.

"Got it, Captain," I say with false cheeriness, and accompany the words with an over-the-top Titan salute, pressing two fingers to my heart. I realize a moment too late that it's probably in bad taste, considering where we're headed and all, but I don't think she even notices me. She's already taking her position behind the cargo, crouching behind one of the metal boxes. She pulls out a heavy-duty, Titan-issue pulse rifle, resting its barrel on the top of the crate in front of her.

I sway on my feet as the floor rocks beneath me. That must be our ship making contact with the *Red Baron*. We've been through this enough times that I know what to expect. It's illegal to outfit ships with weapons, and no planet will let you land with them, but the *Red Baron* has found a technically legal way to launch an assault with those magnetic grappling hooks. They'll keep us pinned to their side and hack our security pad to force the ramp open directly into their ship's loading zone, leaving our cargo bay vulnerable and waiting to be plundered.

Right on cue, the high-pitched whine of machinery starts on the other side of the ramp. That would be them plugging into the hatch and accessing our security system, which means we have only a couple of minutes before they're inside. The twins take their spots on either side of the ramp, backs pressed against the wall and guns at the ready. I lift my borrowed blaster and position myself near the supply closet door.

Lyre hurries over and crouches beside me. Her eyes are huge, but the hand wrapped around her slim-barreled laser pistol is steady.

"We're gonna be fine," I whisper to her.

"Fine? *Fine?* We're about to board a pirate ship!"

I have no retort for that, so I shrug and glance over at the twins. As much as I'm trying to project confidence, I'm worried about our chances here, and this plan puts them right in the line of fire. They're still smiling like it hasn't occurred to them that they should be frightened, but then again, that's usually the case. Even when they were children, they were prone to tumbling headfirst toward danger with grins on their faces. Pol might be the more reasonable of the two, but he doesn't have the good sense to back down from a bad fight, either, especially not if his twin's going in.

Just because they're not afraid doesn't mean they shouldn't be. Momma told me my job was to pull fire away from Lyre, but maybe I can help the twins out as well.

"I've got an idea," I say, turning to Lyre.

"Oh, no."

"It's—what do you mean 'oh, no'? It's a good idea!" I dart into the supply closet and start pulling various supplies off the shelves, searching for what I need. Stars, we have too much shit, and none of it is organized in any reasonable fashion. I don't even know why the hell we have an adjustable bridge folded up in here, like the one the *Red Baron* is using to board us.

"One minute till breach, Scorpia," Lyre calls. I curse and scramble. A few moments later, I dart out with my arms full of goggles.

"Heads up!" I call out, and toss a pair to each of the twins. Pol catches his, eyebrows rising as he looks down at them. Drom, who is busy scratching her nose, gets hit in the face with hers. She catches them before they fall, and shoots me a look that makes me take a step back. "Sorry, sorry. You're gonna need these."

"Night vision?" Pol asks, pulling his over his head and letting them dangle around his neck.

"For what?" Drom asks, shoving them into her pocket.

"You'll figure it out."

A moment later, the ramp screeches as it's forced open. My heart races. Having a plan in mind makes me feel better, but it's not going to make this first part of the fight any easier. I have to hope that the rest of my family will handle their own while I do my part to help them. We've never lost anyone in a scrape with the *Red Baron*'s crew, but it's not from a lack of trying on their part, and we've had some close calls. Both twins have a number of nasty scars from the pirates, and Corvus was nearly killed in one particularly brutal fight about five years ago. The only reason he lived is that Captain Murdock dragged him over, beaten and bloodied, and gave him back to Momma as a "gift" for surrendering. Part of me thinks they keep us alive for their own entertainment. The pirates wouldn't know what to do with themselves if they couldn't fuck with us.

"Good luck," I tell the twins. Pol grins at me, while Drom rolls her eyes, focused on the ramp as it gradually creaks open.

"Scorpia, move your stupid ass out of the way," Momma shouts at me from the rows of cargo, the barrel of her pulse rifle aimed at the door. I cast one dour look back at her before jogging across the cargo bay to join up with Lyre again.

"I hope you know what you're doing," she says, but pockets the goggles I hand her nonetheless.

My response is swallowed by the metal-on-metal screech of the cargo ramp ripping fully open, leaving the belly of *Fortuna* exposed to the *Red Baron* and its occupants.

The *Red Baron*'s crew is a bunch of strays from all over the system—much like ours, but bound together by greed rather than blood. My family might be smugglers, but the *Red Baron* crew can't even keep their smuggling half-honest. Instead, they're pirates, stealing from other ships like ours. *Especially* ours, since their captain, Aldrin Murdock, has a long-held grudge match with Momma.

Momma's tight-lipped about what exactly went on between them, but I've pieced together that she learned the tricks of the trade on the *Red Baron* when she was younger, and that she ended up stranded on Titan of all places when they parted ways. Momma must have done something to pay Murdock back for abandoning her, because now he hunts us down whenever he can. We've had our asses kicked and our cargo stolen more than a few times over the years.

So at times like these, I thank the stars for the twins.

The moment the ramp is lowered, the *Red Baron*'s crew rushes forward from the adjustable bridge. Three of the pirates come through, armed and built nearly as big as my younger siblings. I barely get a glimpse of them before a smoke grenade goes off. The room erupts in obscured chaos, shouts and laser-fire seeming to come from every direction at once. Momma's pulse rifle fires off steady bursts amid the fray. Drom tosses a grav-grenade that throws two of the pirates screaming and flailing into the air, and Pol forces the third back with a steady stream of laser-fire. But more soon rush forward to aid their fallen comrades and renew the assault.

I move forward along the wall of the bridge, avoiding the thick of the fighting. Lyre is gone from my side already, having disappeared into the smoke when I wasn't paying attention. Or maybe I was the one to leave her behind. No telling now—I need to keep going. I toss my smoke grenade ahead of me as the first begins to dissipate.

I nearly fall on my face as I transition from my own ship to the *Red Baron*, the few-inch drop onto the other deck catching me by surprise. Thankfully, the laser-fire and shouting from the nearby fight drown out the sound. Our one advantage here is that the *Baron*'s crew won't expect us to rush forward onto their ship, and if I give us away, we'll lose that.

Eventually, the footsteps fade and the smoke clears, leaving me in an empty hallway. This ship is huge, and I'm not familiar with its corridors, but I assume the breaker room will be somewhere on the lower deck.

As I jog through the hallways looking for a way down, I try to push away my concerns for both Lyre and the twins and focus on my own job. I have enough to worry about myself. My path should take me down to the heart of this very big ship. If all goes well, I'll be able to cut the lights and give my family—prepared with their goggles—the upper hand in the fight...but that assumes I can figure out how to manage it, and that I don't get killed along the way. I'm not much of a fighter. The idea of killing has always made me squeamish, and thus far I've managed to avoid it. But unfortunately, that makes me a liability for my family in fights like these. Usually the best thing I can do is stay out of the way.

Luckily, the twins and the promise of cargo beyond them must be drawing most of the attention right now. The ship's halls are empty except for me, though I hear shouting and footsteps and laser-fire not too far away. I pass through a mess hall, down the stairs, and through the middle deck, following the sound of the engine. Their engine is quite a bit larger than ours due to the ship's size, and a whole lot noisier. Down belowdecks, the sound is a constant, jarring rumble.

Which means I don't hear the pirates around the corner until I come face-to-face with them.

With two guns aimed in my direction, I freeze and slowly raise my hands in the air, eyes darting from one face to another. My heart skips a beat as I recognize both of them.

The first to step forward is Captain Murdock's right-hand woman. Izra Jenviir is a lean, middle-aged woman with paper-white skin and hair so pale it looks almost silver in the light. A crater of red scar tissue takes up the space where her left eye should be, and a black rectangle on her right wrist covers an old Titan war-brand. Everyone says she's a deserter—not to her face, of course, if they like to keep their teeth inside their mouths—but I've always had trouble imagining her running from anything. She's a half head smaller than I am, but that doesn't make her any less terrifying.

She also, apparently, has a gun for an arm now.

"That's new," I say, eyes flicking toward the strange device wrapped from her elbow to the tips of her fingers. I recognize the slick black shine of Primus material, but I've never seen anything quite like this before. The thickest section reaches from the pirate's wrist to her elbow, with several other, spindlier parts circling out from around it to encapsulate her arm like a long, thin rib cage. Though her arm is mostly intact, the weapon is attached directly to her flesh, pieces of it plunging into her fair skin. Looking at it makes me queasy. "Looks...nice?"

When she turns her arm to the side, something clicks, and the rib-like sections slowly peel outward. The thing emits a low hum that makes every hair on my body stand up at once. She aims her wrist at me, and I jerk back so fast that I slam into the wall.

"Hey, hey, what did I tell you?" her companion says, stepping forward and holding a hand out in front of her. She gives him a withering look, and he smiles in response. It drops off his face as he turns to me. "This one's mine."

Orion Murdock may not be the captain's son by birth, but he's been living on the ship ever since the cap picked him up as an orphaned Devan street kid, so everyone refers to him as such. The *Red Baron*'s pilot is a lanky man a handful of years older than me, with deep tan skin, loose brown curls, and a shadow of stubble across an angular jaw.

"Hi again," I say. He spits at my feet, his pretty features twisted in a scowl.

"Can I trust you to kill her instead of fucking her this time?" Izra asks, glaring at him.

He grimaces. "That was one lapse in judgment."

"Two, actually," I say, thinking back to our tryst. "There were two lapses in judgment."

Then Izra looks at me again, and my tongue shrivels in my mouth. I gulp.

"Trust me, I deserve to be the one who kills her," Orion says.

"Then do it already."

"I'd love to. Slowly and painfully and such. But we might need a hostage, and a useless pilot is perfect for that."

With two guns and Izra's glare still aimed at me, I keep my mouth shut and keep my eyes on the—barrel? Mouth? I'm not sure how to refer to the front end of her freakish alien gun arm. *Mouth* somehow seems more accurate.

An explosion rattles the ceiling above us, and we all look up.

"I'm guessing they need your help with those twins," Orion says to his shipmate. "Leave this to me."

With a growl under her breath—an actual *growl*, which nearly makes me piss myself—Izra shoves past me and stalks toward the stairs, every step slow and menacing despite the immediacy of the situation. Orion moves closer to me, his blaster still aimed at my face.

"Okay, hostage," he says in a low voice, pressing his gun against my cheek. He pauses, glances at Izra's back as she disappears around the corner, and breaks into a broad grin. "Pretty convincing, huh?"

"Honestly, you laid it on a little thick," I say, and we both burst into laughter. He lowers his gun, and I let my arms drop to my sides. "Been a while. How's it going, friend?"

"Oh, you know, same as usual." He props one arm against the wall behind me, leaning close enough that I can't help but admire his distracting face. That stupid face is the reason I hesitated the first time I aimed a blaster at him. I'm grateful for it now, though, as it was the beginning of a beautiful, mutually beneficial arrangement. Both of our crews think we hate each other's guts so much that we insist on killing the other ourselves. In reality, whenever our ships clash, we find a way to weasel our way out of the situation and hide until the worst of the fighting is over. I do worry about my siblings, but to be honest, I'm so useless in a fight that I usually only make things worse when I'm around. "What are you doing all the way out here near Titan?"

"I should ask you the same," I say, leaning back against the wall and folding my arms behind my head. Judging by how relaxed Orion is, we aren't at risk of discovery here.

"Believe it or not, we have legitimate business out this way," Orion says. "But when the captain spotted you on the radar, he couldn't resist the temptation."

I scoff.

" 'Legitimate business.' As if, you vultures."

"Believe what you want," he says. "Seems we're turning a new leaf. After this little scuffle, of course." Before I can ask what he means by that, he continues, "Anyway, I've got a bottle of Devan whiskey with your name on it back in my room." He places a hand on my waist, pulling me closer. "Shall we?"

"Damn, that sounds nice." I bite my cheek, dragging my eyes away from his face. There's no time for that, or for prying into the *Red Baron*'s affairs. "But I can't. Actually, I need a favor."

Orion groans.

"I hate when you say that."

178

*　　*　　*

It takes some wheedling, but Orion owes me after I saved him from getting his ass beaten by the twins last time we met, so eventually I talk him into taking me to the breaker room. I bloody his lip and walk him there with my gun at his back just in case we encounter anyone on the way.

"You'll only have about five minutes," he says on our way there. "Then someone will either fix it or activate the emergency lights."

"Five minutes will be plenty." Before we round the corner to the room, I lean forward to kiss him on the cheek. "Thank you, darling."

"Yeah, yeah. Next time it's your turn to play the hostage."

"But of course."

My smile dies as we step into the breaker room, and I realize we're not alone. Sitting in one corner, comm in his hand, is none other than Captain Murdock. Orion tenses in front of me, and my skin crawls. I've rarely come face-to-face with my mother's old boss and our longtime enemy, as he prefers to avoid doing his own dirty work. He's not a big man, but there's something frightening in his dark eyes and the smile that stretches across his grizzled, olive-skinned face as he sees us. I remember him smiling like that when he dragged Corvus back to Momma, remember the way Drom screamed when she almost lost her arm.

Swallowing back fear, I remind myself that I have the advantage here, and press my blaster into the back of Orion's neck.

"Put down the comm," I say, "or I'll—"

"Intruder in the breaker room," Murdock says into his comm before I finish speaking. I curse under my breath. Calling my bluff, or does he just not care? Either way, we're about to have company. Even if I run for *Fortuna* now, I'll never make it. The one way out is to pull off my initial plan. But this room is a mess of panels and wiring, handwritten notes stuck all over the walls. I have no idea which one controls the lights.

179

"I will shoot him," I say, hoping I sound tougher than I feel. "Tell me which one is the light switch."

"Headed out to Titan, huh?" Murdock asks, leaning back in his chair. I slowly move Orion through the room, glancing around at the various notes in the hope I'll see something useful. "Picking up that brother of yours?"

"Aw, how kind of you to ask," I say, panic rising as I see nothing helpful. "Afraid it's none of your business, though."

He lets out a low chuckle. "Is that so?"

My eyes slide to him and his stupid smile, unsure what that means. But of course, he's only trying to distract me. I jam the barrel of my blaster against the side of Orion's head hard enough that he lets out a gasp.

"You want me to shoot him? Is that it? Tell me!"

"Come on," Orion pleads, either genuinely frightened or doing a damn good job of pretending. I'm not sure which of us he's talking to. But Murdock raises a blaster of his own, casually taking aim at his adopted son.

Shit. *Shit.* Would he really shoot Orion? Footsteps approaching in the hall outside mean I'm about to be screwed either way. I frantically glance around the room, and finally, my eyes snag on a panel behind the captain's head. *Main deck lights*, a note next to it reads in sloppy handwriting. And then, under it: *Bottom deck lights*. Of course it can't be simple.

Murdock shuts one eye to aim. Heart pounding, I pull my blaster away from Orion's head and point it at the bottom panel. I shove Orion to the floor as we both fire. Pain sears the side of my head as the lights go dark.

I fall to my knees, gasping in pain, warm blood splattering from the left side of my skull. It hurts too badly for me to tell exactly where I'm hit, but I'm still alive. If I want to stay that way, I have to focus.

Captain Murdock fires again, a flash of light in the darkness, but it goes wild as I scramble to the side. I clap a hand across my mouth to stifle my breathing.

"Stop, stop," Orion cries out, still on the floor somewhere. "You almost hit me, Dad!"

"Oh, shut up," Murdock says, but doesn't shoot again. I remove the hand from my mouth and grab the goggles still dangling around my neck. As I slip them on, they jostle the injured side of my head, and I bite back a cry of pain. That shot must have caught me right in the ear.

Once the goggles are on, I see Orion still pressed against the floor but unharmed as far as I can tell. Murdock swings his blaster back and forth, searching for me. I hold my breath and straighten up, taking aim at the panel for the main deck lights. I fire off a shot and immediately duck into the outside hall. Out here, the dim glow of a few emergency light sources remains, but not nearly enough to provide reliable sight. The reinforcements Murdock called are stumbling around in the darkness, swearing and calling for their captain.

The *Red Baron*'s corridors are dim and green-tinted, but visible with my goggles on. Hopefully this darkness will give us an edge, and hopefully Lyre can get her own job done so we can get off this piece-of-shit ship and back on course.

Judging from the considerably increased number of pirates I encounter on my way back to my family, the lack of power has drawn them away from the promise of loot on our ship. The *Red Baron* has become a mess of pirates struggling their way toward the breaker room. None of them seem properly equipped to deal with the blackout, making them easy pickings for me. I dispatch a few as I go, shooting at legs and delivering blaster strikes to the backs of heads, and leave a trail of groaning or unconscious pirates that would make the twins proud. There's a certain sense of satisfaction to besting fighters who could normally snap me like a toothpick. But after my last conquest elbows me in the face and very nearly manages to shoot me, I decide I'm done playing warrior for the day. I sneak past the next few I see, which is easy enough given how loud and clumsy they are.

I've made it to the mess hall by the time the world suddenly brightens, and duck beneath the nearest table just in time as a small group of beefy pirates run through. Once they're gone, I slip off my goggles and find the ship lit in its usual pale yellow glow. They must have managed to turn the power back on, which means I better get the hell out of here before everyone I passed on the way comes back to find me. Heart thumping in my chest, ear throbbing in pain, I run for home.

In the next hallway, shouting and laser-fire reach my ears. I skid to a stop, but as I recognize Drom's voice crying out, I sprint forward again.

When I round the corner, I find both twins cornered by Izra and another pirate. Pol's shoulder is bloody and his posture hunched; he's still on his feet but disarmed. Drom is on the floor beside him, her face crumpled in pain. A serrated spear of black Primus material, which must be a projectile shot from Izra's gun, pierces through the meat of her calf.

Fear spiking through me, I open fire on the two pirates. The man goes down with a grunt, but Izra whirls to face me, raising her terrifying weapon. The Primus gun hums as it reloads a shot.

"Orion said he'd take care of you," she growls.

"Orion's bleeding out on the engine room floor," I lie. Her eye widens. "That's what he gets for being cocky. You better run if you wanna save him."

My finger itches on the trigger, but I'd rather avoid further fighting if I can help it, especially with more pirates headed this way. Izra hesitates. But after a moment, she bends down to help up her companion and drags him down the corridor toward the engine room. We both keep our weapons trained on each other as she passes.

As soon as she's gone, I rush to the twins.

"Oh, stars, that looks bad." I bend down next to Drom but can't bring myself to try to yank the spear out of her. It will probably just do more damage. "We need to get back to the ship. Now. Help me, Pol."

Drom lets out a cry of pain as we both work to lift her up. Shouts down the hall announce pirates approaching quickly.

We race as fast as we can manage down the corridors of the enemy ship. They're gaining on us fast, and by the time the bridge to *Fortuna* comes into sight, I'm shaking from exhaustion and terror.

"Lyre!" I shout as I see her peering out from the entrance. "They're coming. Please tell me you cut us loose!"

Lyre nods, her eyes very wide as she sees the state of us and hears the pirates close behind. I push Drom at her and turn to deter them with laser-fire, slowly backing toward the ship while my younger siblings hobble forward. Only when they've made it do I turn and race to follow. I slip on the blood-soaked corridor and nearly lose my footing before stumbling into the safety of the cargo bay.

Momma is still crouched behind the storage containers, pulse rifle trained on the ship's entrance, blood smeared down the side of her face. A shocking amount of dead pirates are piled in the cargo bay in front of her, none even close to reaching her. Their bodies are so thoroughly riddled with holes that Momma's weapon must have been at work. Bile rises in my throat at the sight. Usually, our skirmishes don't end with quite so many bodies, but it seems Momma really wasn't screwing around this time.

Sometimes it's all too easy to forget the things my mother's done to build up our family business, and the things she's willing to do to defend it. Even after all our familial bickering, seeing her like this fills me with a childish sense of awe. No wonder the pirates don't seem eager to follow us here.

"Let's go," Momma barks once we all stumble on board, shutting the ramp behind us and effectively ruining my moment of admiration. Pol and Lyre ease Drom to the floor near the stairs, and she leans her head back and shuts her eyes with a groan. Momma has already started checking on the cargo crates, with barely a glance to spare for her injured children.

"Drom's hurt," I say. "She needs medical attention ASAP."

"She'll get it as soon as we're out of here," she says without looking up, moving to the next cargo crate. "Get a move on."

I grit my teeth, resisting the urge to say something I'll regret. A glance around confirms that I'm not the only one who's noticing Momma's neglect. Both Lyre and Pol stare at her in shock, and Drom is shaking in pain. But, as much as I hope for support from them, nobody speaks up.

"Get her to the med bay and strap in," I tell them, and reach down to squeeze Drom's shoulder before I head for the stairs.

We're lucky that we all made it out. For now, this is the way things have to be. But after today, maybe, just maybe, one day I'll get a chance to make sure fights like these go a lot differently.

For a moment I'm caught in the daydream, but the sound of something pounding against the cargo bay yanks me back to the present. I clamber up the stairs to get us the hell out of here.

CHAPTER SIXTEEN

Of Traitors and Cowards

Corvus

Part of me is tempted to spend the night in solitude and leave in the morning without another glance back. Maybe it would be easier to do so, for me and my team. They'll still have each other. And soon enough they'll forget my face, like all the others who came and went.

But these past few years have taught me the consequences of leaving without saying goodbye. When I was drafted, Momma encouraged me to leave a message for my siblings to help them cope with my departure. I couldn't bring myself to do it, or to beg for something to remember them by, and I've spent three years regretting both of those things. I've wished for a reminder of Scorpia a thousand times over in moments when I desperately needed something to keep me afloat.

And as eager as I am to leave this war behind, as much as I never fit in with my team in the way they wished I could, they've been as close to a second family as I could ever find. We have fought and bled and killed together. They've followed my orders without question or hesitation, even knowing that I'm an off-worlder who could never truly understand their ways.

I stop in the medical wing to apply a healing salve to my injured ribs, along with a pure Sanita paste to numb the area. While Titans are certainly good at blowing one another up, they're also good at patching themselves together again, with medical technology far beyond most of the other worlds. By the time I leave, my breathing is already coming easier, and when I wake up tomorrow, my ribs will be knit back together already. Just another day in the war. The part that comes next will be much harder.

Though I pick up civilian clothes, I drop off the outfit in my room rather than changing immediately. I'm not quite ready, not yet. Heart heavy, I go to find my team in the mess hall, where they're huddled over bowls of steaming soup and tall glasses of beer. Their conversation falls silent as soon as they notice me. I move toward a seat across from them, but stop at the last moment, deciding to stay on my feet.

"I'm going to keep this short." I sweep my eyes over my team's faces, all turned toward me with expressions of uncertainty, though I can't bring myself to meet Magda's eyes. I clear my throat to get rid of the lump rising there. "I'm leaving. Tomorrow."

"What?" Sverre is the first to speak, his voice slow and rumbling, his forehead wrinkled in consternation. "Did the general promote you?"

"We'll find a way to follow you," Magda says fiercely. "He can't expect you to leave us all behind."

Daniil is silent, his eyes locked on my face. I meet them for a moment before looking away.

"No." I keep my voice steady. "I'm leaving the service."

Now a shocked silence answers me. Magda shakes her head, her face disbelieving.

"No, no," she says. "Don't be an idiot. Where will you go? What will you do?"

"We know you've been through a lot lately," Sverre says, as reasonable as always. "But that doesn't mean you have to leave. You need to reconsider."

They still don't understand. All of them know that I'm an off-worlder, but I don't think any of them truly considered what that means. For most Titans, there is nothing beyond their icy planet, nothing beyond the constant war. But not for me.

I take a deep breath.

"I mean that I'm leaving the planet."

There's a moment of silence. Another. I watch as understanding dawns on the faces of my team members. Daniil's head sinks down, his silence still unbroken. Magda is frozen, as if her body hasn't caught up with whatever is going on inside her head. Sverre clears his throat. A flash of something like hurt crosses his face, then disappears. He shrugs.

"Well. Good for you, I guess," he says, and takes a sip of his beer.

I almost allow myself to relax. But all at once, Magda springs up and lunges forward as if she means to climb right over the table to get to me. Sverre grabs her before she can, sending his half-full cup of beer sloshing across the table. I take a step back. Magda's eyes are cold with anger.

"You bastard," she spits at me, loud enough that several heads at nearby tables turn toward us to witness the spectacle. My cheeks burn, but I raise my chin, maintaining eye contact with her. "You coward. How dare you abandon your people?"

I should have expected this. Titans are nothing if not loyal—their love for their war-torn homeland is an integral part of their identities. And Magda, most of all, is loyal to a fault. I swallow thickly and try not to let her words get beneath my skin.

"Really? A coward?" My voice is low but hard. "After everything I've done?"

"Everything you've done so that you can run with your tail tucked between your legs?" She laughs, a cruel sound with none of the warmth I normally find in it. "It means nothing now."

"It means something to me!" Despite my best intentions, my voice rises to meet her shouts now, enough for the words to reverberate in the huge room. As the echoes die away, silence falls. The entire mess hall is quiet around us.

Magda's face is twisted in contempt, Sverre won't look at me, and Daniil sits with his hands covering his face. After a moment, Magda shakes off Sverre's grip and folds her arms over her chest.

"I understand now why you always stayed at a distance," Magda says, her voice soft but icy. "You and your Gaian attitude, poisoning all of us with your secrets and your selfishness and your jealousy. You were never one of us, you filthy off-world traitor."

I flinch as if she struck me, the words stabbing deeper than any physical blow could. For a moment I stand and stare at her, struggling to find something to say in return. I want to scream and rage at her, to grovel at her feet for forgiveness, to say something, anything that will fix this before I lose my chance to ever have a proper goodbye. But I can't. She's already made up her mind, and there is nothing I can say now that will make her forgive this.

So I turn and walk away, like the coward she accused me of being.

The rush of blood is so loud in my ears that I barely hear the footsteps behind me. I make it halfway down the hallway, fists trembling with rage and hurt at my sides, and whirl around when a hand touches my back. I almost swing a fist out of instinct, but stop short as I see Daniil.

"What do you want?" I snarl at him. I can't take any more punishment from my team. Magda's cold eyes are seared into my brain, tangling with memories of her warm hands against my frozen skin. Magda is lost to me now. I don't want my memories of Daniil's smile sullied as well.

"Sarge—"

"I'm not your sergeant."

Daniil's face is pained.

"Corvus," he says. There are clearly more words on the tip of his tongue, but he hesitates, and instead throws his arms around me. I embrace him without hesitation. We remain like that for several long moments, our arms wrapped around each other, heedless of the bustle of other soldiers and army personnel passing through the hallway around us. My heart aches as the hard shell of my anger melts away.

"That wasn't the goodbye I wanted," I whisper.

"I know. Me neither."

"I don't want to abandon—"

"I know. I know."

The foot traffic in the hallway around us has slowed to a trickle now, leaving us essentially alone. We stay close together, in the kind of long embrace I've always held myself back from these past three years. It doesn't matter anymore. I have nothing left to lose.

"I need to ask you something," he says, close to my ear. I can feel his heart jumping in his chest.

"Anything."

"Your family... they're smugglers."

My stomach drops. I have an inkling where he's going with this, but I hope I'm wrong.

"That's not a question."

I try to lean back, but Daniil grips my arm, his voice lowering to a whisper.

"How much would it take to transport a person?"

I sigh. There it is—the question I was hoping he wouldn't ask, and all the truth it implies. Apparently Daniil is hoping for more than a goodbye after all. *Treason*, a small voice in the back of my head whispers, but I push it down. As much as I want to be angry with him for asking, I can't help but understand. I brush his hand off my arm and take a step back.

"You can't ask things like that," I say, speaking low but firm. "And we don't smuggle people. We don't even have the capability for it. We're a small ship."

Devan plants are complicated enough to transport. *Fortuna* is too small of a vessel to hide anything close to a living, breathing human, even if we had some way of getting them onto a planet once we reached it.

"Surely you have a deep freezer." He avoids eye contact, his voice still hushed but rapid. "If I was in cryosleep, you could—"

"*No*." There have always been whispers about it—that if you enter a planet while technically dead in cryosleep, and come back to life when you awaken, it would make you a legal citizen. I'm sure some idiots out there have tried it, but I've never heard whether or not they succeeded. Regardless of that, and the impracticality of smuggling a frozen off-worlder, what he's suggesting is danger-ous. "I don't know what rumors you've heard, but it's not viable. It's only a fifty percent chance that you'll wake up at all, and no telling what the side effects will be even if you do." I let out a huff of breath, shaking my head. Humankind has been struggling to perfect cryosleep technology for centuries, with no success as of yet. Most people who go under wake up with memory loss, or nerve damage, or worse. They don't wake up as the same person who went under—if they wake up at all. "You must know all of this, Daniil. Why ask it?"

My teammate looks at me for a long moment. He lets out a soft sigh, his shoulders slumping.

"I don't want to die here." His cheeks flush with shame. Only on Titan would that admission be said with such a self-loathing expression. "I don't want to be another death in a never-ending war." He looks down. "And I will be, if I stay. A fifty-fifty chance would be miles better than what I have here."

We haven't spoken of Daniil's secrets since he first spilled them to me—his heritage, the way he was dragged unwillingly into service—but I still remember them well. Daniil is barely more Titan than I am in peoples' eyes, and when I leave, he'll be all alone. I'd like to believe the others will take care of him...but who knows how much will change. Who knows how much my decision has already affected things, after seeing that hatred in Magda's eyes. I realize now that her last words to me—*filthy off-world traitor*—must have burned Daniil as well.

"Please," he says, when I say nothing. "There has to be a way. Don't leave me here."

My heart is heavy. Stars, I want to help him. I love Daniil—not quite in the way he wishes I did, but I love him nonetheless. And despite my determination to walk away, I can't deny that part of me wishes I could rescue every member of my team from this awful war. Especially Magda...but Magda will die for her planet someday with a smile on her face. She would never come with me. And Daniil would.

Momma will never agree to it. For all her unscrupulousness and credit-grabbing, we've never transported human cargo. Never. Especially not a Titan deserter, since aiding one amounts to high treason on this planet. And Altair will know it was me. We'd never be able to return. But how can I say that to Daniil when he's looking at me like this?

Maybe there is a way. Maybe Pax, at least, could take him. The laws aren't so strict there, and the borders not so well defended, and he might have an argument for citizenship if his father is truly there. Most people think a life on Pax isn't worth the risk, but it has to be better than here. If Momma agreed to make the trip...it could be possible.

"I'll try," I say. I can see that he doesn't believe me, so I step forward, take his hand, and squeeze it in mine. "I can't promise you anything, but I will do everything I can. Stay in Sketa. I'll contact you before we leave the planet."

He looks down at his hand clasped in mine for a long moment, swallows hard, and nods.

I don't need to tell him that it's a slim chance. But despite knowing that, I feel a glimmer of hope. Perhaps I can do one last thing before I leave this awful place. One good thing to redeem myself for all the terrible deeds I've done.

And after abandoning me to the war for three years, Momma owes me one hell of a favor.

CHAPTER SEVENTEEN

The Verdict

Scorpia

In the aftermath of the fight with the *Red Baron*, I can't help but feel jubilant. For once, something went our way. And for once, I played a part in our success rather than screwing everything up. No one can say that our plan would have gone nearly as well without my brilliant idea to shut off the lights. Which means, of course, that I have to remind everyone every chance I get.

"Pretty smart," Pol says.

"It wasn't your worst plan," Lyre admits.

"Should've fuckin' thought of it about five minutes earlier," Drom says, gesturing to her bandaged leg, which turned out to be a considerably less easy fix than my injured ear.

And Momma, who has given up secluding herself in her room, rolls her eyes and says, "Congrats, you did your job for once." Which, honestly, is probably the nicest thing she's said to me in a few years.

So, when Momma announces we're having a family meeting, it doesn't fill my stomach with dread. Maybe this time I won't get yelled at about something or other. Maybe she's not mad about my mistakes on Gaia anymore. Maybe she's finally going to tell us what this job we're running for Leonis is about, or what the plan is once we meet up with Corvus. Titan is less than a week out now, after all, and she still hasn't given us any details.

We all gather in the cargo bay after dinner. Lyre waits patiently with her hands clasped behind her back, while Pol leans against the wall and Drom sits at his feet with her injured leg stretched out. We managed to get the alien spear out of it and patch up the worst of the damage, but she'll have to wait until Titan for proper medical care.

I come to a stop between Lyre and the twins and shove both hands in my pockets. A couple minutes later, Momma arrives and stands near the ramp, gazing around at us. She still looks tired, but more composed than when the *Red Baron*'s attack caught us off guard.

"First of all," she says, "I know these last few weeks have been pretty rough on everybody. I've had a lot to think about, and those pirate bastards always pick the worst time to show up." She shakes her head. "But, as usual, we proved to them that we're not such easy pickings. We all did well in that fight."

Momma meets my eyes, and inclines her head in a small nod. For a moment I'm too shocked to react, but as her gaze moves away, a flush of pride and a broad grin break out across my face. I glance around to see if anyone else noticed. The twins seem oblivious, but Lyre catches my eye and smiles.

"That said, I think it's about time I told you all something," Momma says, drawing my attention back to her. "As you all know, as wrong as things went on Gaia, I was able to secure another job for us on Titan. And, well…" She pauses, and I'm shocked to catch a glimpse of something close to emotion on her face. I can't remember the last time Momma showed any feelings other than anger. I shift uncomfortably, my joy over her praise dimming with uncertainty. "This is a big one, kiddos," she says, and smiles. Actually smiles. "It's the biggest job of my life. Big enough that...well..."

As she pauses again, I realize where this is going. My breath catches in my throat, and I bring my hands out of my pockets and stand straight up.

"This run to Titan is going to be my last job," Momma says. "It's time for me to settle down somewhere. Retire."

Lyre gasps. Pol's mouth drops open. Drom's face is stony, but she reaches out to place a hand on her twin's leg. I stare at my mother, holding my breath. A lump of feelings wells up inside me—dread, fear, anticipation. Because I know what comes next. If Momma's leaving, that means someone has to be left in charge.

And I may have screwed up on Gaia, but it has to be me. It *has* to be. Especially after I proved myself during our run-in with the *Red Baron*. Why else wait until now to make the announcement? That nod of approval Momma gave me had to mean something. And who else would she give the ship to? Corvus? Even if Momma is letting him back on board, it's ridiculous to hand *Fortuna* to him the moment he returns to the family. He's been gone for years. We don't know who he is now. Despite all her complaints, there's no way Momma would leave us in the hands of someone who might as well be a stranger. She must have been hard on me because she knew this was coming. All those reminders about me being the oldest now were preparing me for this.

"It's been a long run," Momma says, "and a good one. But I'm getting old now, and you're experienced enough to handle yourselves without me. I think I've earned myself a few years of rest." She pauses, flashing her teeth in that startlingly unfamiliar smile again. Somehow, it makes her face look older, softer, more tired. "And so, I have one more announcement to make."

This is it. This is the moment I've been anticipating my whole life. The moment Corvus and I whispered about when we were younger, though we always imagined it would be him rather than me taking the helm. It's the moment when the thing I love most in the world finally becomes mine. My ship, my home, my life. *Fortuna*. And with the ship, I'll slip into the role my mother played for so long: the head of the family. It's a staggering amount of responsibility, but I'm ready. I have to be. I bite my lip, fighting back a smile. No more worrying about Momma's disapproval, and no more dealing with people like Leonis. Things are going to change with me in charge.

"As you know already, Corvus's enlistment on Titan is over, and we'll be picking him up while we're there." She takes a deep breath and meets my eyes. The beginning of a smile melts off my face as my heart stutters with sudden fear. "Corvus will be returning to us. And once we're reunited, he will inherit the ship and take his rightful place as the new head of the family."

"What?" The question slips out of my mouth before her words sink in, my voice so quiet I'm not sure anyone else hears it. I blink, blink again, trying to process it.

Corvus. The family business is going to Corvus. *Fortuna* is going to Corvus. Corvus, who abandoned our family to fight in a war on Titan, who chose his home-world above his blood. Corvus, who hasn't contributed any of the sweat and tears I've sacrificed to the family business over the last few years.

He left. He betrayed the family name. He betrayed *me*. And Momma's giving him the ship? I glance around the room, hoping for one of my siblings to speak up so I don't have to, desperate for at least one of them to seem as upset as I am. But nobody will look at me. None of them seem surprised by the decision, which hurts worse than Momma's words.

"Fucking Corvus? Are you kidding me?" I'm not aware of how

loud I say it until I hear the phrase echoing around the cargo bay. I lean forward, my hands balling into fists at my sides, glaring at my mother. It all surges up—the anger, the resentment, the unfairness of it all. Momma used me. She let me believe for years that I could be the one left in charge . . . and the moment her precious golden child comes back, she's ripping it all out from underneath me. She must have known this would be her decision the whole time. Maybe I was the only one who didn't.

"This is bullshit," I snarl. "Bull. Shit." The anger is blinding. If I wasn't so exhausted, I could be more eloquent—could argue my point rather than bubbling over in rage—but right now all I want to do is pour out all the things I've been holding in for years. I step forward, raise a finger, and point it in my mother's face, right between those icy eyes and their disapproval. "Fuck Corvus," I spit at her. "And fuck you, you cold-hearted, stars-damned *bitch*."

Lyre lets out a strangled gasp, and one of the twins mutters something unintelligible. But I keep my eyes on Momma, hoping her face will reflect some fraction of the hurt swelling in my own chest.

My mother gives me an unimpressed look and jerks her chin. A moment later, I'm dragged backward, one of the twins on each arm. I didn't even notice Drom standing up. I sputter and kick, but my siblings barely seem to notice.

"Time to go," Drom says.

One twin would've sufficed, and with the two of them, I have no chance. Drom's injury barely hinders her. I spit curses as they haul me away from Momma and up the stairs. They pull me out to the middle of the deck and drop me there, letting me stumble and fall to my knees. By the time I manage to collect myself, Drom is already halfway down the stairs again, grumbling about her leg. Pol is still standing beside me. His arms are wrapped around himself, his eyes wet and red-rimmed.

"Wipe your damn eyes, you big baby," I say. I know he's not crying for me, or for Corvus. Hot anger boils inside me, making it hard to feel anything else. "We all knew she'd leave us eventually." I clench my hands on my knees, remembering him blubbering on Nibiru every time Momma walked out the door. "Like always."

My little brother wipes his eyes, looks down at me for a long moment, and walks away.

Once I'm alone, I sit back on my heels and shut my eyes. It's been a hell of a day. And it's shaping up to be a hell of a life, if my mother is really leaving Corvus in charge.

It's been three years since I've seen him, my older brother with his easy grin. Momma always loved him most, and not without reason. He was always the best of us. He was better than me at everything, aside from maybe lying and drinking, and never once boasted about it. He was the golden child, and I loved him too much to resent him for it.

He would've made a perfect captain if he hadn't left.

I can still feel that gut-punch of disbelief that hit when my mother told me he was gone. Corvus didn't warn me, didn't hint to any of us that he was considering staying behind on Titan. We all knew about the warrant on him and the trouble it caused our business trips there. But I never considered he might give in. I was nursing one hell of a hangover and didn't even think to check if he was on board before we launched the ship. It wasn't until we were a half day out from Titan that I noticed he wasn't in the kitchen preparing dinner like he usually did.

"He decided to enlist," my mother said when I asked her. "I tried to talk him out of it, but you know how he is. Never could talk him out of that 'honor and glory' horseshit."

I thought it was a joke until I searched the whole ship myself, from cockpit to engine room, and found him nowhere. Momma wouldn't even give me access to send an interplanetary message. Instead I ripped his room apart, certain that he had to have left something for me—a letter explaining himself, some trinket to remember him by, *something*—but he had left nothing but the hole of his absence.

It hurt. Three years later, it still hurts, but I'd almost resolved myself to the idea of never seeing him again. Plenty of people go off to die in the war on Titan. Most of them, actually. And Corvus was always more suited to stitching wounds and cooking meals than putting holes in people. He was the gentlest of all of us. He was the good one.

"You finish your tantrum yet?"

My mother stands over me. The emotions she showed during her speech are gone now, replaced by her usual icy expression.

"Thought you would be pleased by the news," she says when I don't speak. "Aren't you grateful to get your big brother back?"

"No." The lie burns on the way out, but I spit it anyway. I grind my teeth together and breathe out through my nose. "I want my ship." So much for maintaining my dignity. I sound like a child and I know it.

My mother lets out a huff of breath that could be either a laugh or a sigh.

"The ship's never been yours, and it never will be."

Never. I grit my teeth as my eyes sting, willing them not to overflow. I put a hand on the wall to steady myself and rise to my feet, drawing myself up to my full height so I can look down on my mother.

"I know *Fortuna* better than anyone else," I say, "and I pilot her better than anyone ever could. You know it's true."

"It's not enough."

"It's..." I had a multitude of arguments waiting on my tongue, but I wasn't ready for that. My mouth hangs open dumbly before

I snap it shut. "The hell do you mean 'it's not enough'? The ship is my *home*, it's always been my home, I've got nowhere else to fucking go!"

"Then you best stay on your brother's good side."

I stare at her, realizing for the first time that she knows exactly what she's doing to me. It's not like she hasn't thought this through. She's placing my entire life in Corvus's hands—after he already betrayed me once. In one cruel twist he could take away my home, my job, my family, everything I care about. What the hell will I do if he decides to kick me out? No planet will take me, and even in the unlikely event I can secure a spot on another ship, it will never be mine like *Fortuna* was.

And no matter what happens, I'll always be as helpless as I am now. I'll never have the control of my life that I've always craved.

"We haven't talked to Corvus in three fucking years," I say, struggling to keep my voice level. "We have no idea what the war has done to him! He could've been paralyzed. He could've lost his damn mind, he could've..." I trail off as a surge of pain makes it too hard to speak. When I start again, my words come out quiet and empty of venom. "Even aside from that, he's already made it damn clear where his loyalties lie, and it's not with the family."

"What did you think was gonna happen?" she asks. "Did you notice the state that Gaia was in? Did you notice the tension on Deva? This system is changing, Scorpia. Things are getting worse, not better, especially for people like you. Something big is coming, and I need to know that someone is taking care of my family when I'm gone."

"I can—"

"You can't even take care of yourself! Look at the mess you got yourself into on Gaia." She barks a laugh at the surprise on my face. "What, you think I forgot about that? You think one clever ploy on the *Red Baron* excuses it? You got yourself arrested twice, botched the job, triggered a quarantine. If I wasn't there to drag you out of trouble, you and your siblings would be dead right now, all because of *you*. You really think you could handle the responsibility of an entire ship? Of being in charge of the whole family?" She shakes her head, turning away from me. "I feel sorry for you. I do. But I built this business from nothing, and I'm not going to let you destroy it."

Shock leaves me at a loss for words for once. I always knew I disappointed Momma—she made that very, very clear—but I never realized how much. These three years, I've let myself believe that maybe I could step up to fill Corvus's shoes. She *let* me believe it, with all her bullshit about me "being the oldest now" and needing to be "more responsible." But with what she's saying now, it's clear she never would have let me. I have a sinking feeling that even if Corvus wasn't coming back, this conversation would've come one day, maybe when Lyre was older and ready to take the helm instead of me. She was never really going to give me a chance.

After a moment, Momma sighs.

"Look," she says. "I know it's not your fault. Not really." Her face softens a bit, and she reaches over, placing a hand on my shoulder. I stiffen under the unfamiliar touch, so surprised I can't seem to move or speak, and instead brace myself in preparation for another inevitable verbal blow. "You know, when I was younger, I made a lot of hard decisions so that you kids wouldn't grow up like I did. You're the only one I failed with. Corvus, too, I guess, but he was less affected by it. He never took to that life. Didn't absorb it, not like you and I did." She shakes her head. "I clawed my way up from that life. I got us both out. Yet you still act like you're stuck there, surviving day-to-day rather than thinking about the future. And you can't run a ship like that."

Momma's never talked to me like this before. The raw honesty makes me uncomfortable—and makes me wonder what she's really trying to say. Finally, it hits me.

"So that's why you hate me?" I ask.

"What?" She seems genuinely taken aback.

"Because I'm your failure."

For a moment she's silent, her forehead creased. But then she rolls her eyes, scoffing.

"Don't be so melodramatic." She turns her back to me. "One day you're gonna realize this was good for you."

I remain in place while my mother heads to her room. As the door shuts behind her, I stare down at the floor and swallow hard. I'm not going to scream, or cry, or break something, though the urge is there. There's no time for that, not when I have a mere week before we complete the job on Titan and my mom hands the ship over to Corvus.

But once Momma is gone…once she's gone, she doesn't get to decide what happens anymore. Just because she's decided to hand the ship to Corvus doesn't mean it's going to stay in his grasp. I don't have to listen to him, or to her, or to anyone. I don't have to wait and see what my traitor of a brother will do when the fate of our family rests on his shoulders.

Trying to impress my mother is a lost cause. I see that now, and I also see that it's completely unnecessary. I'm a Kaiser, and Kaisers don't grovel and say *please* when they want something. It's certainly not what Momma did to build this business. She stole, and she lied, and she cheated her way into getting her ship and her fortune. And I'm prepared to do the same.

Corvus left us. He's no true Kaiser. But I am, and I'm going to prove it. After that, I'm going to launch into space and wander the stars in *my* ship. Fuck what my mother says. She'll be gone soon. And one way or another, I'll take this ship and make it my own.

CHAPTER EIGHTEEN

Veteran

Corvus

The next morning, I wake early to head to the train for the sake of avoiding unwanted company. The station is just below the surface, chillier than the lower levels of the building, and the ceiling trembles under the weight of activity in the hangar above. I stand near the tracks, bundled up in the ragged clothes I scavenged from the medical wing. They're too thin to warm me much and don't fit well—but neither does my uniform anymore, and I don't want to arrive in Drev Dravaask wearing it. As of today, I'm no longer a soldier.

When I first arrived on Titan, underground rooms made me feel caged and nervous. Especially so in places like this, where the ceiling occasionally shakes loose clouds of dust, and the rumble of trains along the tracks makes it feel like the whole building could collapse on top of me. Over the years it's become normal. Now, for the first time in a long time, I wonder if it will feel strange to walk in the sunlight again.

I turn to salute General Altair when he arrives, and he nods to me, scrutinizing my clothing with a flick of his eyes.

"Morning, General."

"Morning, civilian."

The general's voice is crisp and businesslike, yet somehow the word sounds like an insult coming from his lips. I suppress a frown, and we wait in silence for the train to arrive. When the armored vehicle grinds to a stop on the platform and the doors slide open, we both step on board and seat ourselves on the hard metal benches. Though the train is nearly empty today, we sit at opposite ends.

The compartment is cramped and dimly lit, and when the train takes off again, the whole vehicle shakes as it races along the tracks. Still, it's much faster than travel by spider tank, and more convenient than the slow, cramped elevator shafts that civilians use to get to and from Drev Dravaask. I'm lucky that the general granted me access to the armored train, which links all the major forts and cities of our territory, normally reserved for active soldiers.

Altair is quiet for the ride. Though he accepted my choice to leave, I know he doesn't respect it. He's disappointed in me, and I wish that it didn't bother me so much. It makes me want to try to explain to him why I have to leave, to tell him about Uwe and Magda and my family, but I know that making excuses will only earn me contempt. So I shut my eyes, listen to the rattling of the train around me, and try not to think about everything I'm leaving behind and the uncertainty ahead.

The general leaves my side the moment we step out of the train station. Without my team, my uniform, or my family, for the first time, I realize that I am completely and utterly myself—and completely and utterly alone. Perhaps it is impossible to be one without the other.

*   *   *

The underground fortress of Drev Dravaask is beautiful. It's warm enough that I take off my outer coat, and not overcrowded with people and buildings like the major cities of other planets. There is a simple elegance to its architecture and a surprising kindness in its people. They all nod or smile at me as I pass, or press their fingers to their hearts if they notice the brand on my wrist. I return the gesture without thought, drinking in the quiet. It's so peaceful here compared to the rest of Titan. Neither the storms nor the war can touch this place. Drev Dravaask has held its ground for over a century while cities around it crumbled. The stability allows people to build lives here that do not revolve around war. There are restaurants and shops, bars and inns, families that aren't missing pieces. Of course, there is also a huge military recruitment center near the heart of the city, and posters advertising the perks of service on every street corner, so it is not possible to forget entirely.

Momma's message instructed me to meet my family at the Blackbird, a bar and inn that the first person I ask is eager to direct me to. I stop along the way to eat, treating myself to an expensive restaurant that claims to serve "exotic Nibiran delicacies." What they call "fish pastries" is a very poor attempt at reconstructing the Nibiran street food, with dry bread, a bare hint of curry flavoring, and only fish-flavored protein cubes inside, but it's still leagues better than army rations.

By the time I reach the Blackbird, though, my stomach is queasy from food so much richer than it's used to. The sight of more recruitment posters sickens me further. When I spot the HALF-OFF DRINKS FOR SOLDIERS sign in the window, I pull down my sleeve to hide my brand, the thought of the special treatment discomfiting.

Whether it's my scarred face or my gait or something else entirely, the bartender still marks me as a veteran right away. He proudly displays the brand on his own brown skin as he insists on giving me my first beer free despite my protests that I'm no longer on active duty, and marks down the price for the room I rent, too. Once the key is in my hand—a physical key, so strange and outdated, since hardly anyone on Titan carries a comm—I find myself grateful for the excuse of the beer to keep me at the bar a bit longer. I may be alone now, but the distant-but-constant presences of people around me have provided a distraction. Once I go into that room and shut the door, it will just be me and my thoughts until my family arrives tomorrow.

I savor the taste of the beer, dark but sweet, and the quiet buzz of activity in the rest of the bar. It's barely the afternoon, but there's a group of uniformed soldiers sitting in one corner enjoying a leave of absence, and what looks to be a jubilant family gathering in the middle of the room.

"Their daughter's off to Fort Sketa for basic tomorrow," the bartender says, jerking his chin at the smiling blond girl in the midst of the festivities. "Maybe you could give her some advice?"

She doesn't look like she wants advice. She looks like she's never been so excited about anything in her young life. And why shouldn't she be excited, with the tales this city has surely fed her about the war?

"It's better to go knowing nothing," I say, and finish my beer as quickly as I can before retreating to my room in the upper stories.

I barely make it to the toilet before I vomit up my pastry and beer, both far too much for a stomach used to army rations. I flush my mouth out with water and move to a bed that feels too soft to sleep in. When I lay back on it, it feels as though I'm going to sink and sink until I disappear.

Staring up at the ceiling in the silence, I finally let myself wonder what it will be like to see my family again. Merely imagining that moment unleashes a surge of emotions I've been trying to repress, and the questions that come along with it.

Will they cry when they see me again? Will *I* cry? How will Momma react if I do? Will she feel sorry for me, or will she think I'm weak? Does she miss me? Do the rest of them? I was trying to keep this simple, to remove myself from my emotions and focus on the practicality of escaping this war. Now all my fears and my hopes rise to the forefront of my mind, so closely intertwined that I can't focus on one or the other.

I've spent these last few years trying to think of my family as little as possible. All the memories I've been subduing well up now, filling my mind with a million small things I've missed about them. The gangly, fearless twins, quiet Lyre with the secret little smiles she shared only with me, and Scorpia's capacity for bold laughter in the face of despair. I hope she was able to hold the rest of them together, to lighten things up for our younger siblings like she always did for me. Stars, I miss her, despite all her flaws.

And Momma...Momma, whose stern looks made me feel like scum on the bottom of her shoe, whose rare praise meant more than anything else in the world. I miss her, too, though it hurts to admit.

In the early days, I used to think of them all the time. When I curled up, freezing and alone, in the barracks, I would tell myself stories about them to get to sleep. I wondered what kind of people the twins and Lyre would grow up to be in my absence, and imagined Scorpia shirking off her many bad habits and stepping up to take care of the family. They were foolish thoughts, and likely hurt me more than they helped, but they were all I had for a while. The one thing that kept me going was the hope that I would see them again.

I've done such terrible things for a chance to see them again.

But now, as the day approaches, part of me dreads it. It's been three years since I've seen or spoken to anyone in my family. Three years. I don't know who any of them are anymore, and they won't know me. They'll be expecting the brother they knew before, and he's a person I barely remember. I wonder, will the realization come slowly? A gradual, sinking disappointment? Or will they realize it the moment they look at me, see every sin laid bare on my skin, as visible as the scar on my face? I'm not sure which is worse.

When I shut my eyes, for the first time in a long while, my thoughts return to the last time I saw my family. While the others were off drinking and gambling, as they always did in Drev Dravaask, Momma told me she needed a favor. I didn't even think to question what it was; I was just eager to do whatever she asked of me and return to my siblings before they got themselves into too much trouble.

She led me to the steps of the recruitment center. Still, I didn't understand.

"Corvus," she said. It was hard to tell in the dim lighting, but her eyes looked almost wet. That was the moment I realized something was horribly wrong. My heartbeat grew so loud in my ears that I barely heard her next words—about mandatory service, the warrant for my arrest, her clients getting wary of working with her. How my formal education and leadership experience would put me on the fast-track to be an officer. That one of the generals was a contact of hers, and he would look after me.

"It's only three years," she said, "and I'll make sure you're not just another grunt for the meat grinder."

"You're leaving me here?" I asked, once I forced air into my lungs. It felt surreal, like this couldn't really be happening. "You want me to fight in the war?"

"Not want. I would never want this for you." She grabbed my chin, forced me to look at her. "I need you to do it. Things are

getting bad in the system, and one day they're gonna hit a break-
ing point. When that happens, we'll need connections on Titan.
We'll need connections anywhere we can get them, but *especially*
Titan. Do you understand?"

Reluctant as I was to admit it, I did understand. Interplanetary tensions had been on the rise for a long time. The growing extremism on Gaia, Deva increasing prices on their exports,
Pax shipping weapons to Titan despite criticism from the rest of
the planets, Nibiru's heated condemnation of Primus technology . . . Yet I never imagined it could come to war, as Momma was
hinting at. But if she was right, if it did come to all-out warfare,
Titan's military expertise and wealth of raw materials would suddenly make them one of the most powerful planets in the system.
Having contacts here would be invaluable.

But would it be worth me going to war? Worth the very likely
loss of my life?

"Think of your family," Momma said. "Think of your siblings."

I already was. Three years without them by my side. But I forced
myself to think further. If I refused, turned against Momma, I
believed my siblings would follow me. But follow me where? There
was no place for them on Titan. No hope for a better future for all
of us. I thought of all those whispered conversations with Scorpia,
all those dreams we had built up, and my chest ached.

"Okay, Momma," I whispered. "I understand."

"That's my boy," she said, and released me. She took a deep
breath, closed her eyes for a second before opening them again.
When she spoke, her voice was a fierce whisper, too quiet for anyone to overhear. "Just remember, you'll never be one of them.
Don't buy into the propaganda bullshit." She pulled me into a
hug, the only one I could ever remember getting from her. "You're
a Kaiser, not a Titan. Don't forget that."

And I never could.

CHAPTER NINETEEN

Titan

Scorpia

We've got this, right, baby?" I say aloud, running one last check on *Fortuna* before we land on Titan. One of my legs jumps, the heel of my boot tap-tapping on the floor. I trail the tips of my fingers along levers and screens, making mental check marks. All my indicators look good, all my systems are running clean. She's as ready as she's gonna be, and so am I. This is one landing worth staying sober for. "You and me, *Fortuna*. You and me."

The moment we hit atmosphere, my nerves dissipate into a rush of adrenaline that makes me feel like I'm floating. I'm barely aware of my hands moving over the control board or my eyes roving the screens; instead the incoming information merges with my own thoughts, which flow seamlessly into responses from the ship, as if *Fortuna* is an extension of my body, another limb.

Heavy winds coming in at forty-five degrees. Slow vertical descent until—there. Winds pummel the ship, making her groan and shake around me, but I grit my teeth and ignore it. *Fortuna* can handle a little storm, I know she can.

I add more kick to get us over a swift approaching mountain, passing close enough to the peak that my entire body clenches—but we pass by without a scrape. Course correct, three degrees west. We're on target now. Good. Now we need to come down slow…slower…maybe not that slow. There. There's the sweet spot. Set the wheels down in three, two…

My back slams against my seat as we touch the surface, thrusting my mind back into my body. I blink rapidly, grip the control wheel, and ease us into a stop. The wheels slip on ice, but I fight the urge to slam on the brakes, knowing they'll find purchase eventually—and they do. *Fortuna* comes to a stop just inside the shelter of the rocky cave I was aiming for.

This time there are no alarms wailing, no smoke, no flashing warnings. We made it. It wasn't a perfect landing, but I'll be damned if it wasn't the closest I've ever gotten. I sink back in my seat with a satisfied sigh. The feeling is almost as good as being drunk.

For a minute I stay in my seat, half expecting Momma to come in and congratulate me on a landing well done. Once the lingering adrenaline drains away and leaves me clearheaded, I realize how foolish that is. The only time she ever barges into the cockpit is when I screw up. Since things went according to plan, she's likely already moving on to step two, along with the rest of my family. I sigh and climb to my feet, giving the control wheel an affectionate thump before following the voices down to the cargo bay.

The moment I reach the bottom of the stairs, a pile of assorted clothing hits me in the chest, and I scramble to catch it before it falls.

"The hell took you so long? Gear up," Momma snaps at me, while I blink at the pile of equipment in my arms. "There's a storm warning. We need to reach the city."

The rest of my siblings are already half suited up, donning the protective outer layers and heavy boots necessary to brave Titan. At first I'm surprised to see everyone dressed for the surface; usually Lyre, at least, prefers to stay behind on the ship while we're here.

But of course, everyone must be eager to see Corvus. I'm the only one who seems to hold any reservations about our big brother's return to the family. A sour taste in the back of my mouth chases away the lingering sense of accomplishment from the landing.

"Right," I mutter, setting the pile down and starting the process. I swear, there's always a storm warning here. Titan's surface is pretty much one big, angry, everlasting storm. While I pull on my jacket, I glance over at Momma, trying to find some hint of approval in her constant scowl. But I shake off that instinct, reminding myself of our last conversation and my determination to stop sucking up to her. Nothing I do will ever be good enough, and I need to stop caring either way. Instead, I look around at my siblings and prompt, "How about that landing, though?"

"Just hurry up," Momma snaps, and then turns her anger on Pol, who is having trouble detangling his goggles from his gloves. I sigh, shaking my head and plunking down on the floor to make it easier to strap on my boots. Lyre, standing nearby and already fully geared, glances down at me.

"It was a pretty good landing," she says. I glance up at her suspiciously, certain there must be some kind of insult or trick hidden in the statement, but before I can respond, she turns her back and heads for the ramp. I frown down at my boots and their knotted laces instead.

"It *was* a good landing," I mutter to myself, and hurry to finish prepping before the rest of my family leaves me behind.

The cave is warmer than the rest of the surface, close enough to an underground hot spring that *Fortuna* won't be buried under ice

212

and snow while we're gone. Still, pinpricks of chill immediately inform me of every patch of skin I left uncovered in my haste to suit up. I hiss at the shock of it, pulling my gloves up and readjusting my scarf until I'm properly protected from the weather. The city of Drev Dravaask is merely a half mile or so from our position, but a half mile can be brutal in this weather. Given the winds, we'll have to travel on foot rather than use the hovercraft.

Three Interplanetist soldiers wait at the bottom of our ship's ramp when we emerge. They're wearing considerably less protective gear than we're equipped with, their breath forming white clouds around their mouths. Their faces are covered in cloth and their uniforms are bulky, but judging by the way they shiver, it isn't enough. Momma approaches them and speaks to the one who nods to her first. She has a twin at each elbow, both of them carrying a gun in one hand and a stack of sealed cargo crates in the other.

I draw closer, intending to listen in on the conversation, but the wind whistling in my ears makes it impossible to hear a word of it. Whatever the exchange entails, it ends with Momma waving us down the ramp. She hits the button to shut the ship's entrance, and the three soldiers escort us out of the cave, past a handful of delivery drones, and toward the city.

The weather is even worse without the cave's shelter breaking the wind, a howling storm that tugs at my protective gear like an angry beast. On another job, I might've made some excuse about staying back to watch the ship. But this isn't just any job, so I grit my teeth and follow. Lyre is close on my heels, her small shoulders braced against the wind. I have to stop twice along the way to help her after she slips on ice. By the end she's clinging to my arm, despite my attempts to shake her off. Up ahead, I see Momma doing the same to Pol, leaning into his bulk when the gusts buffet us. Drom is limping, her leg clearly still bothering her.

Drev Dravaask is flat on the surface but for a few ice-covered

213

bumps and ridges that are barely discernible from the rocky tundra all around. When we draw closer, though, a group of soldiers emerges from out of nooks and behind rocks, converging on us from all sides and joining the three already escorting us. There are at least a dozen of them, hard-eyed and armed. I draw closer to Momma and the twins, and Lyre presses herself against me.

Even knowing these soldiers are from the Interplanetist side we're working with, it's hard not to be intimidated by the group of them. Titans have a hollow look in their eyes that I rarely see anywhere else in the system. Drev Dravaask is one of the better spots to be posted—a big city, well fortified, far from the thick of the fighting—but these soldiers still bear the marks of war. I spot gaunt cheeks and frostbitten fingers, puckered scars and red-stained gauze wrappings. One of the women near me is sucking on a blood-boiler pod like her life depends on it; her left boot has a hole in it, and the naked toe visible through it releases puffs of steam.

Momma places two fingers over her heart in salute, and I grimace and look away. Titan displays of patriotism are almost as strange to me as Gaia's obsession with dead aliens. Of all the planets in the system—even proud Gaia—Titan is the only one where I've seen people exchange actions and words declaring their loyalty on a daily basis. The Titans must be aware that their planet is objectively horrible, but they're eager to proclaim their love for it, as if they can make it tolerable through sheer force of will. I guess it's hard to convince people to die for something they hate.

Momma exchanges a few words with the soldiers—I hear something about "Gaia" and "General Altair," whose name I recognize from Corvus's transmission—and shows them her visa. One soldier waves away the others and leads us over to a rocky outcropping. He crouches next to it and shoves snow aside until a metal handle becomes visible. When he yanks it open, it reveals a dark tunnel descending into the earth.

Drom goes down first, ignoring the man's offered hand despite being hindered by her wounded leg. Pol helps Momma through next and follows. I push a shivering Lyre ahead of me to accept the soldier's help, making me the last one through.

As the hatch closes above us, I yank my scarf down and take a deep breath of stale air. It's still cold in here, but not the kind that'll turn your extremities black in a few hours of exposure.

A light source sputters to life ahead. It's just enough for me to see how close the tunnel walls are and get a glimpse of the sloping path ahead, with my family descending into darkness. The path is narrow, but after a few minutes, we reach a flat platform large enough for us to stand side by side. Pol has a pale red light stick clenched between his teeth, his arms full of cargo crates. The others cluster around him, their faces blurry in the dim lighting.

The elevator is a rusty, low-tech thing, and we're all forced to crowd onto the five-by-five square walled in by metal railings. A number of these machines are scattered throughout the city to allow traffic in and out. I'm sure there are more efficient and safe ways to enter and exit the city, but those are saved for more important people. For off-worlders like us, this old machine has to suffice.

As usual, everyone but the twins clusters in the middle once the creaky descent begins. Pol leans as far over the edge as he can without falling off, dangling the light stick, while Drom grins and jumps in place. The movement shakes the whole platform, making Pol grab onto the railing and Lyre squeak. I stay where I am, stomach queasy with the remembrance of the last time we were here, and the image of Corvus staring down at the city, quiet and stern, while the rest of us goofed off around him.

Drom jumps again, making the elevator sway hard enough to shatter my memory and nearly send me onto my ass. Pol laughs around the light stick in his mouth, and Lyre grabs Momma's arm.

"Cut that shit out," Momma says. Drom shrugs and stops, grinning nonetheless, and Lyre steps away from Momma and folds her arms over her chest. I study the lights of the swiftly approaching city. Somewhere in there, my brother awaits.

At the bottom, Pol ditches the light stick, and we follow a path marked with fluorescent lights. The city of Drev Dravaask is carved into the earth beneath the surface of Titan, dark and damp caves forming homes and businesses and more. The surface of the planet is too cold, too stormy; water freezes up there, and plants won't grow, and people die slowly and numbly without realizing that they're dying. Down here, close to the hot springs that run beneath the surface, it's a handful of degrees warmer.

It would be easy to be miserable in a city like this, but the people of Drev Dravaask find pockets of happiness in their cold underground world. As we head inward, a trio of soldiers sways past us arm in arm, belting a severely out-of-tune version of Titan's planetary anthem. A cluster of children giggle in an alleyway, fingerpainting dirty words on the walls. A hunched street vendor with a face full of battle scars hands a carefully wrapped meal to a gaunt teenager on the street corner.

All things considered, the place is kinder than Levian and safer than any of Deva's gilded cities. It doesn't hurt that it has the cheapest booze in the system, either. If not for the cold and the war, I might be able to enjoy myself here.

And if we weren't heading to meet Corvus, of course. I can't forget about that. The landing and post-success high were a momentary distraction, but now the knowledge weighs heavily on my shoulders as we trudge through the city streets. Soon—too soon—I'll be face-to-face with my brother for the first time in three years. I still haven't decided what I'm going to say, or do, or feel about it . . . or more importantly, how exactly I'm going to steal my ship from him. I have a tentative plan, but some part of me is holding out until I see Corvus. Maybe he'll change his mind about coming with us—or maybe Momma will take one look at him and decide that he's not the right person to be in charge.

Or maybe, just maybe, Corvus won't be as changed a man as I'm fearing he'll be. Maybe he'll have some explanation for why he left us. Maybe he'll be the brother I remember, and we'll cry and make up and my fears will all dissipate, and I'll feel safe with my future in his hands after all. It all depends on how this meeting goes.

Damn do I need a drink.

I'm considering sneaking off to the bar to grab one before the meeting when Momma stops. I follow her gaze to a building ahead, a tall and narrow structure with neon letters above the doorway declaring it THE BLACKBIRD. Beneath that, a smaller sign reads HALF-OFF DRINKS FOR SOLDIERS. Conversation and laughter and light leak out of the windows on each level, stretching out far above us.

"This is the place," Momma says.

I glance up at the windows, half expecting to see his silhouette waiting in one of them, but of course they're empty. Still, my heart starts to pound in my chest. We're so close to the moment I've been both hoping for and dreading for the last three years. As Momma heads inside, with Pol and Lyre close behind, my feet stay glued to the ground. Fuck, I'm not ready. I'm not even close to ready.

"The hell are you waiting for?" Drom asks, clapping a hand on my shoulder as she's about to pass by.

"Oh, uh, I just remembered that I should—"

She forcibly propels me into the building before I can finish the lie. Even with her injured leg stiff and her gait uneven, I don't stand a chance against her.

My protests die down as we enter. Sloshed patrons, fueled by steady streams of cheap liquor, play drinking games and cluster

217

around space heaters. I immediately attempt a pivot toward the bar, but Drom marches me toward the stairs the others are heading for.

"Oh, come on, at least let me grab a drink!"

"We'll drink to Corvus later," Drom says, shoving me up the stairs so hard I nearly fall. I glare at her over my shoulder, and she grins back. It's hard to tell whether she thinks she's helping or is just being an asshole. I sigh and trudge upward, shaking her hand off.

The floors above hold quiet hallways lined with doors. We're lucky that Titan, unlike Gaia, has need for inns like these. With soldiers moving between cities, and refugees fleeing areas affected by the war, places like this can turn a good profit. Judging by the soft conversation floating out of some of the rooms, a decent number of them are currently occupied. We keep moving, heading all the way to the fifth floor before Momma exits the stairwell and heads down the hall. She stops outside a room near the end and knocks.

I take a small step back, my heart thudding in my ears.

"Hey, I've got an idea," I say. "Maybe I'll go down to the bar and grab us a round—"

The door swings open, and the rest of the words die in my throat as I see Corvus standing in the doorway.

Parts of my brother are the same as I remember them. He has the same stern eyebrows and bumpy nose, the same narrow shoulders and lean build. But his hair is cropped shorter than he ever wore it before, and his face is shadowed by a bristly beard, and his frown lines are nearly as deep as Momma's. The thick scar that cuts across the left side of his face is new, and so is the black, numbered brand on his right wrist. The worst, though, are his eyes. They're two dark pits in his pale olive face, ringed with shadows that weren't there before.

His eyes flicker over the rest of the family before meeting mine. We look at one another across the space between us.

My chest is tight and airless. Stars, I want to hug him. I want to hit him. I want to cry and shout and tell him that I missed him, that I'm glad he's alive, that I hate him for leaving, that I'm scared he's not the same brother I loved so much before. I will myself to crack a joke to break the tension, to say something, anything, but the words stick in my throat.

Corvus speaks first.

"Hey," he says. "Been a while." His voice is rough, and his eyes bore into mine as if the words are meant for just me.

"Sure has." I try to speak in the same way, but it comes out too quiet, too uncertain. I thought I was ready for this, but seeing him is like a punch to the stomach. I clear my throat, search for something to say.

We're intercepted by a blur of a body. Pol throws himself at our older brother without hesitation, flinging his arms around him and squeezing himself tight against his chest. Corvus stiffens in response, both hands balling into fists as if he's ready to fight. After a second he relaxes, one muscle at a time, like it's hard to make himself do it. He leans into our brother. One hand rises hesitantly and cups the back of Pol's head, ruffles his hair in the way he did so many times when we were children.

"Well," Corvus says, his voice muffled through Pol's still-tight embrace, "you certainly got big, Apollo."

With a jolt, I realize how different the twins must look to him. They were barely sixteen when Corvus left, and though they were always big for their age and fast on their way toward being huge, they were rangy and still growing back then. The last time my brothers saw each other, Corvus was taller than Pol by a few inches. Now, our baby brother towers above him.

I fold my arms over my chest in an attempt to crush my rising emotions. As much as I want to be happy and enjoy this moment for what it is...I can't. I just can't. There's too much at stake. So instead, all I feel is a swiftly growing ache for a drink.

My brothers' moment is soon interrupted by Drom slamming into both of them in a bear hug. Then Drom is laughing, and Pol is crying, and Corvus's expression is obscured—but I can almost imagine him flashing that broad smile he wore so often in years past. A lump rises in my throat. I turn away, fighting back the overwhelming urge to join my siblings in their group hug and pretend like everything is the same as it's always been. Maybe if I can swallow my pride and force myself to join them, everything will go back to normal. But I can't, and it doesn't. Every moment that passes, every moment of silence without Corvus giving me an apology or an explanation or anything more than that simple *hey*, only seems to widen the void between us.

Lyre stands back from the commotion as well, eyes narrowed at Corvus like he's a particularly difficult engine problem in need of fixing.

"So that's our new captain," she says under her breath, and I force a bitter smile as anger flares in my stomach.

Still, I can't help but watch again as Momma steps forward to meet Corvus. The twins disentangle themselves from their older brother as they notice her approaching, falling back to leave nothing but empty space between him and our mother.

CHAPTER TWENTY

A Family Reunion

Corvus

When Momma puts her arms around me, my heart almost betrays my mind. It would be far too easy to let myself sink into this moment, to let myself enjoy this rare show of affection from her. Stars, I used to work so hard for this. I used to push myself to the very limit for a pat on the shoulder or a smile. Some secret part of me must still crave that affection and approval, because right now I'm almost willing to forget the last three years and let everything go back to the way it was.

"I'm so proud of you," Momma murmurs in my ear, too quiet for the others to hear. Despite these past few years—despite everything—those words reverberate down to my bones.

As she releases me and my gaze returns to my siblings, my heart hardens again. Each of them is a walking reminder of what I've missed over the years. The twins grew up while I was away. I can't believe how damn *big* they got, or how hard-eyed. Lyre has shadows under her eyes and a suspicious set to her mouth that wasn't there before. And Scorpia, usually so ready to chip away at tension with her laughter, wears a brittle lie of a smile and won't look me in the eyes. She's treating me like a stranger, as I feared she would.

I missed them, all of them, so badly that the ache in my chest became a constant part of my existence. But I can't seem to bring myself to voice it. If I let my emotions out now, I'll crumble beneath the weight of them, and I can't let that happen in front of Momma. I can't let the cracks show. She'll still expect me to be her perfect son, and I don't want her to realize the toll the war has taken on me until I'm safely on board that ship.

"We-ell," Scorpia says, breaking the silence. "I for one could use a drink. Anyone else?"

So much for her shaking that habit. I hesitate, hating the immediate urge to glance at Momma and check if she approves or not. Three years at war, and it seems I'm no stronger than I used to be.

"You offering to pay?" Drom asks, when no one else says anything.

"Oh," Scorpia says, as if it had just occurred to her. "Well you see, I would, but..."

"Let's handle the necessaries first," Momma says, cutting her off. "Drom, I transferred some credits to your account so you can get that leg looked at. Anyone else need anything while we're here?"

"Pol has a bad tooth," Lyre says. He scowls at her, and she steps aside before he can shove her.

"It's fine," Pol says. "I don't want them poking around my mouth."

"It's not fine. It's gross."

"Get it taken care of, Apollo. You know it's cheaper here," Momma says, silencing their squabbling. "The rest of you can do whatever you like, but Corvus and I have business to attend to." She nods her head at the small metal crates stacked on the floor. "Pick those up for me."

Of course. Business. Altair did warn me—though Momma didn't give the same courtesy before now—so all I feel is weary resignation. I thought I would have more time with my siblings, was even enjoying the familiar bickering between them, but I'm not in any place to complain with my ticket off-world in Momma's hands. So I obediently bend down and grab the crates, wondering what Momma is offering Altair that's small enough to fit in these little containers.

"Right, business first, of course," Scorpia says. I expect her to follow up with one of her sarcastic salutes or dumb jokes before sidling off to the bar downstairs. Instead, she sticks her hands in her pockets and flashes Momma a sharp smile. "I was thinking I should come along, too."

Forehead creasing, I look at Momma, who is studying her with narrowed eyes.

"Why?" Momma's flat tone makes it clear how she feels about the idea.

"Oh, I mean, were you really planning on just showing up with your soldier son on display like a trophy?" Scorpia asks, still smiling, head cocked like she's surprised she has to explain. "That'd be a little on the nose, don't you think? At least with me along you can pretend it's a family affair."

The not-so-subtle jab surprises me, and so does Momma's lack of shock. My eyes shift back and forth between my mother and sister. There's a tension underlying the conversation that I can't pinpoint, something I don't remember being there before. Since when does Scorpia talk to Momma like that? And since when does she care enough to attend business meetings? She used to be the first one to sneak away to the bar when business came up, like Lyre and the twins are doing right now, leaving me standing between my mother and sister with this awful silence.

"Scorpia is right," I say, earning myself two shocked stares. I look right at Momma when I say it, ignoring Scorpia's eyes on me. "They'll be offended if they suspect you're using me as a prop."

Momma sighs.

"Fine," she says, and gives Scorpia a meaningful look. "But you let me do the talking. One wrong word and you're out."

"I know when to keep my mouth shut," Scorpia says. Even after three years apart from her, I know a lie when I hear one, but Momma sets her jaw and chooses to ignore it. She heads for the stairs without checking to see if we're following. Scorpia hangs back, and finally looks up and meets my eyes. For a moment I think she's going to thank me, or welcome me back, but instead she only gives me a long, silent look and heads for the stairs.

As we follow Momma through the dim streets of Drev Dravaask, Scorpia's eyes burn into the back of my neck. She stays a few paces behind, watching me. The scrutiny makes me self-conscious, less about the surface-level differences she notices than everything that lies beneath. Am I really so transparent? Can she see the dozens of horrible secrets lurking beneath my skin? Does she already mistrust me?

I'm so focused on Scorpia that I forget to keep an eye on our surroundings. I hear a thud and a brief scuffle of confusion behind me, and turn to see Scorpia regaining her balance after a collision with a dirty-faced girl who can't be older than ten.

"Sorry, miss," the kid says.

"My bad." Scorpia is already glancing at me instead of watching the child start to slip away.

I step forward and grab the kid's wrist before she can disappear, yanking it high enough that her feet scrabble for purchase on the ground. She squirms and yelps, but nobody on the street spares us a second glance, save for my family. Momma watches with a stony expression, while Scorpia looks on in faint horror.

"What the hell are you doing?" she hisses, glancing around as if expecting someone to be scandalized about this. Clearly, she doesn't know this city like I do. I focus on the girl in my grasp, giving her a shake and a scowl.

"Give it up, kid." In response, the girl glowers up at me and lets out such a foul string of curse words that Scorpia raises her eyebrows. I shake her again, yanking the wrist farther upward so she barely touches the ground with the tips of her toes. "You want me to break your wrist? Let's have it."

Still swearing violently and balancing on her tiptoes, the kid reaches into her pocket with her free hand. A moment later, she produces Scorpia's comm and tosses it down. It clatters to the ground near Scorpia's feet. She blinks down at it before scrambling to pick it up, her face flaring red.

"You little shit," she says, doing a poor job of hiding the fact that she's impressed.

"You know what they teach us in the service?" I ask the girl. "That if we catch someone stealing, we should take a finger. And if they're already missing a finger…" I grab her free hand and yank back the sleeve, revealing a hand with four fingers and one stump. "Then we should take the whole hand."

The girl's eyes find the brand on my wrist and go round with fear.

"I didn't know," she babbles. "I didn't know she was with you. She looks like an off-worlder. If I knew she was with a soldier, I would never have done it!"

"*Corvus*," Scorpia hisses, staring at me. I ignore her, biting back frustration. I know that she must see her own younger self in this girl—as I often did when I first came here—but she doesn't get it. Things are different here. This kid needs to learn, now, or she'll get a much harder lesson next time she tries this shit. Most people won't be as forgiving as me. The last one already wasn't.

"You're lucky my sister has a soft spot for strays," I say to the girl. "Watch yourself."

I release her. She's gone in a blink, scurrying off into the shadowy alleys outside of the main street's light. Even after I let her go, Scorpia keeps staring at me, her eyes flickering over my face like she can't believe what she sees there. I turn to her, waiting for her to say whatever it is she wants to say to me. But she merely shakes her head and pushes past me to stand by Momma.

"Enough fucking around, we have a meeting to make," Momma says, and continues walking with Scorpia beside her. I follow after her, this time keeping one eye on the streets around us and the people who occupy them.

We meet General Altair at a squat gray building in a dim corner of the city. It's unmarked and windowless, but the small cluster of soldiers standing at attention outside makes its purpose clear enough.

"We're selling to the military?" Scorpia asks. I shoot her a sidelong glance, again surprised that she's so interested in business affairs, but her expression is more uneasy than curious.

Momma lets out a dry laugh.

"Who the hell else would I sell to on this rock?" she asks, and heads inside. I follow her, swallowing the apprehension in my throat, and Scorpia trudges after us.

Altair waits in the lobby, looking as composed as ever in his uniform. I salute him without a second thought as I approach, and Momma mirrors the motion. Scorpia does the same a half second later. Rather than speak here, the general instructs us to leave the cargo behind the desk for security reasons, and he and two other soldiers escort us upstairs.

We travel up a few stories of the building, past multiple pairs of uniformed guards, and all the way back into a private meeting room. Momma and the general sit across from each other at the main table, relegating Scorpia and me to a pair of chairs against one wall. The soldiers leave us to wait outside. Scorpia's eyes follow them and flicker to me once they're gone. Her gaze hovers on the war-brand tattooed on my wrist for an uncomfortably long time, as if she just noticed it. I resist the urge to hide it from her scrutiny.

"Thank you for accepting my request to meet," Momma says, bowing her head to the general with her fingers pressed against her heart once again. I avert my eyes, irritated by the sight of her miming a motion that has become so meaningful to me over the last few years. I know she doesn't believe any of the things it's supposed to mean. "I haven't done business here in a long while, so I appreciate the opportunity. And you won't be disappointed with what I'm offering. The product I have here is... unique, to say the least."

"You've always been a reliable business partner, and your son served me well," Altair says with a nod. "I look forward to seeing what you have to offer."

Even when he mentions me—praises me, nonetheless—he doesn't look in my direction. As though I don't exist. One of my hands curls into a fist at my side as I fight down a flash of anger. Altair did warn me that the end of my service would be seen as dishonorable, and Magda confirmed as much. Still, to be treated so differently from a couple of days ago, when the only thing that's changed about me is a uniform, rankles. Maybe Momma doesn't understand Titan culture as well as she thought, if she expected my presence here to be useful.

Altair pours two generous drinks to start the proceedings. Momma clears her throat.

"Pardon my off-worlder manners, but as you recall, I don't drink," Momma says. Usually she's eager to imitate planetary manners as closely as possible, from Gaian hand gestures to Titan salutes, but this is one matter she's never budged on.

"My apologies. It's been a while." Altair reaches for her glass, but Momma stops him with a wave of her hand.

"For the sake of tradition...Corvus?"

She gestures without turning to look at me. Calling me to her side like a dog. I grit my teeth and, for a moment, indulge the thought of refusing her just to prove that I can. The fantasy passes quickly. It would serve no purpose but to anger her and embarrass us both in front of the general. I move to her side and take the glass like the good soldier and obedient son I am. Altair and I down the glasses at the same time, and I return to my seat with the weight of his eyes on my back. *What does he think of me?* I wonder. His face is inscrutable when I glance over. Scorpia, on the other hand, stares at me with open distaste.

"I'm going to be perfectly frank with you," Momma says. "What I'm offering you is a chance to end the war."

I suck in a breath through my teeth. That could mean a number of things, but Momma wouldn't pull a lie out of nothing.

"If you wanted to sell bullshit, you should have gone to Ives or one of the younger generals," Altair says. "I don't buy promises. So tell me, what is it? A weapon?"

"It is. But not the kind you're used to."

Unease sours my stomach. I should be glad that a new weapon is going to my side of the war, but somehow I can't be. I thought leaving the service would mean leaving the bloodshed behind. But now, I'm just a different part of the war machine. A less honorable one.

Rather than speak, Altair gestures for Momma to continue.

"This is a specialty, freshly discovered piece of Primus technology, which I'm exclusively offering to you," she says.

The room goes very still. Primus technology. All this time,

Altair and the other generals told soldiers like me that they didn't believe in using it. That it was too dangerous. I let myself believe the mission to retrieve that power source was to prevent it from falling into enemy hands. The fact that Altair isn't immediately appalled by Momma's suggestion says otherwise.

"What kind of technology are we talking about?" Though Altair's voice is level, his interest is obviously caught. "A bomb?"

"Think bigger," Momma says. "A biological weapon. The kind with the potential to take out many, many more than a bomb would." She leans forward, smiling conspiratorially. "And the best part is…it won't cause any damage to structures or resources. It will affect only people, and anything they leave behind will be yours for the taking."

A chill runs up my spine as my mind conjures an image of some alien bio-weapon eating its bloody way through enemy ranks. Part of me hopes that Momma is bluffing, or at least exaggerating. I try to tell myself that it's just if it's only used on our enemies, that it could save people like Magda and the rest of my team… but I can't bring myself to believe it. Something about this feels wrong. And since when does Momma deal this kind of product? How did she manage to get her hands on such a powerful alien weapon?

The conversation drops to hushed tones. Though I try to follow it, my attention is drawn away as I notice Scorpia fidgeting in her seat beside me. She crosses and uncrosses her legs, taps a finger on the armrest, scratches her arm. Her eyes roam the room, never staying in one place for more than a couple of seconds. I shift in my seat. Every time I try to home in on the conversation between Momma and the general again, my attention is snatched away by Scorpia's squirming.

I know my sister is naturally restless, but if Altair notices her doing this, he could take it as a sign of anxiety, and anxiety as a sign of guilt. If he has any reason to suspect we're lying to him, this could go downhill very quickly. I know how Altair deals with potential threats: swiftly and ruthlessly. My status as a veteran won't grant us much protection.

"Stop fidgeting," I murmur, keeping an eye on the general to make sure he can't hear me. "You're going to make him nervous."

"I'm not fidgeting," Scorpia says, chewing on a nail. I rip my eyes off the general to give her a look.

"You're literally doing it right now."

Scorpia bites down on her middle finger and lowers the rest of them, turning so the gesture is hidden from the negotiations. She's always been difficult, but this behavior is getting under my skin in a way it didn't before.

"I see you still haven't grown up over the last three years."

"Is that what happened to you?" she asks. "Thank the stars I haven't, then. It seems miserable."

"I grew up a long time ago. One of us had to."

"Oh, boo-hoo. Poor Corvus, must've been so hard being Momma's favorite."

I grimace. I always hated when my siblings called me that, and now it's even more infuriating. How can she still think that's true? I know I should keep my mouth shut—should be the mature one—but I'm getting sick of staying quiet while she gives me this attitude. Why does she have to be like this? Why does she have to make it so damn hard? I hoped this reunion would be a happy one, but instead I feel the same with my family as I did among my team: stuck on the outside.

Despite my better judgment, I open my mouth to say more—but Momma glances over her shoulder at us, and I shut it again. Scorpia and I both straighten up and go silent.

"Scorpia, go get the cargo," Momma says.

"Me?" Scorpia points to herself, glancing between me and Momma, before getting to her feet. "Well, all right."

Once she's gone, Momma gestures for me to come over. Again, I obey, leaning close for her to whisper.

"Go outside and wait for Scorpia," she says. "When she gets back, take the cargo and tell her to go back to the others."

I pull back, staring at her. It seems I wasn't the only one to notice Scorpia's fidgeting—or maybe Momma's been waiting for an excuse to get rid of her ever since we arrived. But why use me to do it? Maybe it's solely because she doesn't want to argue with her daughter in front of a client, but it feels needlessly cruel. I've seen the way Scorpia looks at me already. She distrusts me.

But I don't have a choice. Not when my future is sitting in Momma's palm. Maybe that's what this really is: a test of my obedience. A test I need to pass, unless I want to risk being left behind again.

"Understood," I murmur, and nod to her before heading outside to wait. I shut the door behind me.

Uncertainty flashes across Scorpia's face the moment she rounds the corner and sees me waiting. Her steps slow, and she stops a few feet in front of me. Five small boxes are stacked in her arms. After Momma's words, I'm shocked again by the size of them—could something so tiny really hold an end to the war?—but tear my thoughts away to focus on my sister instead. When I gesture, she grudgingly hands them over, and steps toward the door. I stand in her way.

"It's time for you to go back to the others," I say, forcing myself to meet her eyes and watch the shock and hurt flash across her face.

"What?" she asks. "You've got to be kidding. I didn't do anything wrong. Why is she cutting me out?"

I stay silent, not trusting myself to speak. Part of me wants to reach out for her, tell her I'm sorry, that I'm on her side—but I can't right now. She seems on the verge of eruption, and we can't afford to have her make a scene with the general on the other side of this door. Once this deal is secure, once we have a moment alone without Momma, then we can go back to the way things used to be. It'll be us against the world again.

"Great," Scorpia mutters. "Just great. The golden boy's back, so who gives a fuck about me, right?"

Before I can even think about responding, she lets out a huff, turns her back, and storms off. I watch her go, guilt heavy in my stomach—but I have no other choice. I need to be what Momma wants me to be, at least until I'm safely off this planet. Then... then I'll try to fix everything.

Altair and Momma are still seated in the negotiations room when I reenter. At Momma's gesture, I set the cargo beside her and sit on the sidelines. I can't stop thinking about the look on Scorpia's face when I told her to go, but I push down my guilt as far as I can manage. This situation is just as dangerous as the war, and just like in battle, there's no room for emotions here.

"First things first," Momma says. "Let's see what you have."

"Very well." Altair reaches under his desk and pulls out a metal box of his own. He sets it on the desk between them and carefully removes the top. I suppress a gasp as I recognize the faint glow emanating from within.

The power source. The heart of the alien ship. The very thing I worked so hard to bring him. He's trading it for some alien weapon? Though I know it's unreasonable, somehow this deal feels like a betrayal, both to me and to the general I thought Altair was.

Then again, the fault is my own as well. I never asked what the power source was for. I never even thought to ask. I just followed orders, as always. As I'm doing now.

"Beautiful," Momma murmurs, leaning over to peer into the depths of the box. "President Leonis will be pleased."

President Leonis? Somehow, the more I learn about this deal, the more confused I become.

Altair replaces the box's top and nods to her.

"Now, show me what you've brought."

Momma reaches down, opening the boxes one after another and placing four glass vials on the desk. They seem almost completely clear at first glance, but when the light hits them, a barely perceptible glimmer of color appears in their depths. I frown. Is this really a weapon that can end the war? It looks so small, so insubstantial, especially in comparison to the things I've seen here on Titan...though in an odd way, the swirling colors remind me of the steady movement on that alien ship. The longer I look at the vials, the more they fill me with unease—and yet, at the same time, it's hard to look away.

Momma stiffens upon opening the last box, pulling me from my thoughts. Altair is busy studying the other vials, but I watch her, my own body tensing at her quiet alarm. After a long moment, she shuts the box, straightens up in her seat, and folds her empty hands on her lap.

"As you can understand, the president had a few reservations about Gaia's first interplanetary deal of this magnitude," she says, her face unreadable, her tension subdued but not gone. "At her request, we will be holding on to the final vial until the power source is secure on our ship."

Altair tears his eyes away from the vials. The corners of his mouth tighten.

"That wasn't part of our deal."

"Well, it is now."

I glance back and forth between the two of them, unsure if I should say something. Neither is outwardly hostile yet, but the tension is palpable. My heart rate rises. Why would Momma change the terms of the deal at the last minute? She knows as well as I do how suspicious Altair can be. I think again of Momma tensing the moment she opened the final box, how quickly she closed it. The box that Scorpia retrieved and brought here. My blood goes cold.

No. She couldn't have taken it. She knew how much danger it would put us in. She wouldn't do that. Would she?

"Then I have an additional condition as well," Altair says, rising from his seat. "You will accompany one of my sergeants to test the weapon before the agreement is finalized."

"Don't be ridiculous. I'm no soldier."

"And I'm no fool. I will have the weapon demonstrated or the deal is off."

Momma is silent for a long moment. I know she hates to get her hands dirty in such a way. But what choice does she have? She's merely a middle-woman between two planets. She has nothing to negotiate with.

Then she glances at me, and my stomach drops as I see her calculating eyes. She does have one option. She could send me in her stead. *Please*, I think at her desperately, though I can't bring myself to speak. *Please, no more. Don't send me back to the war.*

"Fine," Momma says, her eyes snapping back to the general. "As you wish."

Altair nods briskly.

"And will the former sergeant be accompanying you?" he asks without looking at me.

I don't miss the *former* jab. I press my lips into a grim line and look away from him, waiting for Momma's answer.

"He will not. Unless you'd like to leave a group of off-worlders unsupervised in the city?"

I try to hide my shock. As much as I hoped for this, I didn't expect it. She's actually sparing me from this. She's letting me stay.

"Fine," Altair says. "He stays. You and I will leave immediately."

I rise with them, and move over to Momma before she leaves.

"What should I tell the others?" I ask. She looks at me, her face unexpectedly soft, and raises a hand to touch my cheek. I stay completely still, discomfited by the affection.

"My boy," she murmurs. "I really am so proud of you." I stare at her, unsure what to say to that. After a moment, she lowers her hand, and her face hardens as if that moment of vulnerability never happened. "Tell them I'm attending to business and I'll be back in the morning." She grimaces. "And tell your sister I'll deal with her when I get back."

My mind races as we step into the hallway outside. So Scorpia did take the vial, as I suspected. But why? What is she planning? My sister must have known how much danger this put us in.

One of the soldiers stops to block my path as Momma and Altair head farther into the building. Momma looks back at me one last time, hesitating as if she wants to say something more. But instead, she nods silently and follows Altair. I watch until they disappear around the corner, trying to ignore the dread thickening in my stomach.

I'm being foolish. Momma will be back in the morning, and she can handle herself. She's not the one I should be worrying about. But Scorpia, an unaccompanied off-worlder alone in Drev Dravaask, possibly with a weapon of mass destruction in her possession... now that's a situation that could result in disaster.

CHAPTER TWENTY-ONE

A Risky Game

Scorpia

Fucking Corvus. I storm down the stairs of the building, seething and swearing under my breath. Less than twenty-four hours back with the family and he's already reclaimed his spot as Momma's favorite. Even after he abandoned the family, even when he's so obviously changed, she still loves him the most. I hate how quickly Momma forgave him. How quickly she decided to choose him over me. I'm sure it's only a matter of time before the rest of the family does the same.

Unless I can do something to change their minds. I pause at the bottom of the stairwell and pull the vial out of my pocket, watching the omni-colored shimmer swirl inside. Looking at it makes me feel queasy. Of course it had to be alien shit.

On our journey here, I thought about stealing a peek at what we were carrying, but my plans were always cut short when it came to opening up those damn crates. When I retrieved them for Momma here, I realized she must have some contingency plan, some way for another family member to open the crates if something happened to her. And of course she'd choose Corvus.

So, of all the stars-damned numbers in the galaxy, Momma chose Corvus's military identification numbers. The same digits tattooed on his wrist. I might laugh if not for the bitter jealousy filling my stomach.

I push the vial back into my pocket and compose myself before I enter the lobby, plastering on a smile as I approach the bored-looking young man behind the front desk.

"Hi," I say, placing my palms on the desk and leaning over. "I'm here with Captain Kaiser. I'm supposed to go talk to…"

I pause, recalling Altair's words. *"If you wanted to sell bullshit, you should have gone to Ives."*

"General Ives?" I guess. "Where can I find them?"

He glances up at me briefly before dropping his eyes again, fiddling with a comm even more outdated than the one I carry.

"Recruitment center, probably," he says, and taps away at his screen.

"Right. Thanks."

Outside, I take a deep breath of the cold city air and break into a smile, pushing thoughts of Corvus and my mother far from my mind. If this vial is as powerful as Momma claims it is, I'll be able to make a hell of a lot of credits off of it. Enough credits to be able to support myself and my younger siblings. If I can get back to them before Momma and Corvus do, maybe I can use that to win them over before Corvus steals their hearts, too. I can give them a choice, and make one for myself as well, rather than being completely at Momma's mercy.

Part of me loathes the thought of carrying this vial, let alone selling it to someone without knowing what it does. But this is my last chance to control my own fate, and I have to take it.

*   *   *

I don't know Drev Dravaask well, but the recruitment center is the easiest place in the whole city to locate. I follow a trail of bold neon signs and obnoxious posters right up to its steps. FIGHT FOR YOUR PLANET, one banner declares, with an image of a standard-issue pulse rifle. FOR HEART, FOR HOMELAND, another reads, depicting a beautiful young woman with her fingers over her heart and her eyes turned skyward.

The building itself is sturdy and square. Colorful banners hang from the windows, depicting Titan's flag and the Interplanetist symbol. Young soldiers, each branded but otherwise yet unmarked by the war, hand out flyers on the street side. Titan's planetary anthem plays from speakers behind them, loud enough that they have to shout to be heard above it. While everyone on Titan has to serve a compulsory three years of their life, offices like these are eager to sign people up for longer contracts with better benefits.

As I walk up to the tall double doors, I imagine Corvus—younger, fresh-faced, scarless Corvus—approaching them three years ago, and shiver. I still don't understand how or why he would do that. Most Titans know only the glorified bullshit propaganda tells them, but he knew what the war was really like. And from what I've seen of him now, it changed him in all the ways I feared it would. Part of me feels bad about the way things have already soured between us . . . but he's the one who abandoned me, I keep telling myself. And he's the one who's still wrapped around Momma's finger. Maybe once I have my ship and my future secure, I'll be able to find a way to mend things. But not now. Right now, I need to seize my last chance and secure some money and power before Momma gives everything to Corvus.

I walk through the double doors, past the soldiers and the flags, and directly up to the front desk. This one has five receptionists at work, each of them young and disgustingly full of Titan patriotism.

Four of them are already engaged with visitors, including a strikingly handsome young man who's speaking to no less than three girls feigning interest in the service, so I approach the last and clear my throat. She smiles up at me, her fingers poised over a holographic keyboard.

"I'm here to speak to General Ives," I say, trying to sound confident.

"Do you have an appointment with her?"

"No, but I've been sent directly by General Altair. Trust me, she'll want to see me."

The bullshit works. Soon enough, a soldier appears to escort me upstairs. He leaves me in a hallway on the third floor, where a uniformed woman who must be the general waits.

Ives is a handsome, well-muscled woman not much older than Corvus, with shoulder-length brown hair and sharp blue eyes. Like most Titans, she's startlingly pale. While General Altair was all aged expertise and tightly coiled control, Ives is one of the youngest generals I've seen on this planet, and she has a dangerous look about her. Her eyes track me as I approach, though the rest of her body remains perfectly still. Her smile is sharp-edged.

"I don't know you," she says. The words are somehow a statement, a question, and a threat all at once.

I swallow, fighting down nerves. As annoying as Corvus was back in that room with Altair, I know he was right. I can't act antsy here, not if I want her to trust me. These people are eager to be suspicious if given half a reason. I find my mind wandering to Shey as an example of how to compose myself, though the mental image of her brings a surge of pain and betrayal with it. I square my shoulders and lift my chin as I press my fingers to my heart.

"My name is Scorpia Kaiser," I say. "Eldest daughter of Auriga Kaiser, captain of the *Fortuna* and loyal supporter of the Interplanetist cause."

"Kaiser." Her eyes crinkle in recognition. "As in Sergeant Corvus Kaiser?"

It's a strange feeling to hear my brother referred to in such a way, with a title I wouldn't have known to call him, but I force a smile.

"The very one."

"One of Altair's favorites," she says, with another knife's edge of a smile. "I heard he had family off-world."

"We all serve the cause in our own way."

"True enough." She studies me. "So your family knows General Altair, then. Why are you here instead of with him?"

"My mother is seeing him right now." Better to slide in some slivers of truth when I can, lend more believability to the story. "He suggested you might be interested in a piece of our product as well."

"Product?"

"Weapon."

Now that catches her interest. Her eyes narrow into a calculating look, and she gestures to a nearby doorway.

"Let's talk, then."

After we sit, she pours us two drinks, as Titans customarily do. Vodka has never been my favorite, but I'm grateful for anything to take the edge off. I cast a glance around the room as I down it, trying to gather useful information, but it's plastered with recruitment posters rather than anything personal to Ives. The room is warm enough that I take off my outer coat for the first time since leaving the ship, draping the fabric over the back of my chair.

On Titan, as soon as the drinks are finished, small talk is over and business begins. So I jump straight into it.

I take a deep breath, put on my best saleswoman smile, and pull the vial out of my pocket. I hold it up to the light, illuminating the shimmering liquid inside it. Ives leans back in her chair, eyes following the vial's movement, expression impossible to read.

"Primus tech," I say. I'm not sure where I'm going with this, or how the hell I'm gonna sell something that I don't understand, but I need to start talking before she catches on that I'm nervous. "There's a reason people fear it. It doesn't behave like our technology does. It lives, breathes... changes." I run a thumb over the container, and the liquid inside ripples in response. "It goes above and beyond anything our technology is capable of. It's—"

"So what is it?" Ives asks, cutting me off. She taps the fingers of one hand on the desk, her eyes on me rather than on the product I'm trying to sell.

"It's a weapon," I say, trying to sound confident despite her obvious and well-earned dubiousness. "A biological weapon beyond what humankind has—"

"You've already made that clear," Ives says. "But what does it *do*?"

Shit. This is the part where I have to lie like I've never lied before. For all my efforts to investigate, and everything I gleaned from Momma, I haven't the slightest idea how to use it, and I can't exactly offer a demonstration. Plus, if I give details, Ives will know I'm a liar as soon as she uses it. If I do this right, on the other hand, she could be a lasting business contact, one not linked to my mother in any way. I'm going to need that if I intend to take over the family business.

I take a deep breath, lick my lips, and lower the vial. Even if I was willing to take my profits and never come back to Titan again after this deal, I don't think I can bluff my way through a step-by-step explanation of an alien weapon I have no understanding of. But maybe I don't need to.

"If you wanted to sell bullshit, you should have gone to Ives," Altair had said.

"How about I skip the gory details and get right to the point?" I ask. "I'm selling you a weapon that kills people, quickly, and does

241

no structural damage." I set the vial down on the table between us. Ives's eyes follow it, and flicker up to meet mine again rather than remaining there. "And more importantly...I'm selling you an end to the war."

Momma's words make a good closing line, but Ives doesn't look as convinced as I had hoped.

"You really expect me to use a weapon without knowing what it does?" she asks. "What kind of general do you think I am?"

"Well, I heard you were the kind with ambition," I say with a shrug. "I mean, Altair has already agreed to purchase the vials. He thought you might want a piece of the glory, but if not—"

"How generous of him to share some of it, for once," Ives snaps. She grinds her teeth together, and I stay quiet, worried I struck the wrong nerve. "If Altair suggested me, there must be a reason." She taps her fingers on the desk, staring at the vial. "It must be dangerous. That's probably why you're avoiding giving me details, too."

How convenient for me that Ives is weaving her own story.

"I didn't think you were the type to shy away from a little danger," I say, leaning into it.

"I'm not." She pauses and shakes her head. "But this is too much risk for me. I'm not going to send my people into the field with alien technology I don't know anything about. I don't know *you*. There's something off about this."

Damn it. Ives might be a young and hungry general, but maybe I underestimated the value of trust when it comes to deals like this. Altair knows Momma, but I'm a stranger to this planet, with nothing to back up my reputation. My stomach sinks. I force myself to keep my smile.

"That's perfectly fair. I understand." I slowly rise and take my time grabbing my coat, giving her a chance to stop me. She doesn't. "You were at the top of Altair's list, but I guess I'll move on to the next. Thank you for your time, General Ives." I salute her and head for the door, still moving slowly, still hoping. When I pause in the doorway and glance over my shoulder, she's staring down at her comm rather than at me, and my stomach drops further. I guess this is really it. Maybe I will try to track down another general, or...

"Wait."

I bite back a grin before I turn to face Ives again.

"Yes?"

She sets her comm aside.

"I just received word that one of Altair's teams is headed to Vin to test out a new weapon." I don't have the slightest clue where or what Vin is, but I nod as though I do. She scrutinizes me. "You said no structural damage?"

"No, ma'am. It's biological in nature. Only attacks living things. People, animals."

"But my own people won't be harmed?"

"Not as long as you're far enough away." She frowns, and I quickly make up some specifics to satisfy her. "Drop it from up high, and make sure you're at least ten miles away by the time it hits. And don't enter the area for at least a month afterward."

Ives's face is thoughtful, but I see the hunger in her eyes and know I have her. At this point, she's confirmed that Altair has already given the go-ahead. If she hesitates much more, he'll get all the glory. After a few moments, she gestures for me to sit, and I happily obey, slinging my jacket over the back of the chair again.

"Okay," she says. "If even half of what you're saying is the truth, I cannot allow this weapon to slip out of my fingers. I'm prepared to offer you five hundred thousand credits for it."

It takes every ounce of my willpower to keep my jaw from dropping. I was expecting this weapon to sell for a lot... but that's more credits than I've possessed in my entire life. No wonder Momma is all set to retire on this deal. *I* could retire with this on most planets, if I had anywhere I could retire to.

I'm so shocked that I let the silence last too long.

"I'm not sure if you're familiar with local manners, but this isn't a bargaining situation," she says, shifting in her seat. "I've made my offer. Take it or leave it."

"I see." I already knew that, but I'm willing to let her believe I'm ignorant to explain away the shocked pause. "In that case... yes. That price is acceptable."

Ives smiles that sharp smile again.

"Excellent."

My heart thumps with nervous anticipation. This is it—I'm about to close out the biggest deal I've ever made in my life. With this amount of credits in my account, I'll be able to take care of my siblings once Momma is gone, no matter how things go.

"This will save a lot of good people like your brother," Ives says.

I pause as a sudden, sick feeling surges up inside my gut. I think of Corvus out on that battlefield, and of everyone else out there right now, fighting in the never-ending war without knowing why they're risking their lives. And of all the people like Leonis, sitting on her pretty little planet and selling shit like this into the war.

People like her look at the Titans the way they look at all off-worlders, the same way they look at me—like something less than human. But they are human, and it's humans that will suffer at the hands of this weapon. Ives says I'll be saving people like my brother when I make this deal... but I'll be killing just as many. Their blood will be on my hands. I may be a lot of things, but I've never been a killer, and selling this weapon is no better than using it myself.

This vial could contain any number of things: explosions and fire, or slow decay, or more horrible fates I can't even imagine. I think of the alien statues back on Gaia and the cold needles that sink into my chest when I lay eyes on them. They were a species with so much power and so much knowledge, and they still managed to go mysteriously extinct. Gaia plays with too many artifacts that they really shouldn't. There are too many angles that I don't know. I have no idea what I'm handing over to this woman.

Shit, shit, shit. My conscience sure picked a hell of a time to spring to life.

As Ives reaches for the vial, I close my fingers over it and pull my hand back.

"But of course, I'll need to check with my mother to solidify the terms," I say, and suppress a wince at the furious look she gives me. I force a smile in return. "And you can feel secure knowing the results of Altair's test. I'll be back in the morning to give you our final answer. How does eight o'clock sound?"

Ives leans back in her chair, irritation evident in every small motion as she settles back into place.

"I see," she says, folding her arms on her lap with obvious restraint. "Fine. I will see you then."

Despite her neutral words, I can see in her eyes that I've made an enemy. Maybe I'll be able to fix this if we do future business... but more likely, I've just burned this bridge along with losing out on those credits. And for what? My stars-damned *conscience*? Every one of my instincts screams at me to make this right somehow, but instead I rise to my feet.

"Thank you for your time, General." I offer a hasty salute along with my words, grab my coat, and rush out the door. Ives watches me as I go, her expression so cold that I half expect soldiers to apprehend me on some silent cue from her. But the only thing to follow me out of the building is my own self-loathing, and that's bad enough.

By the time I make my way back to the Blackbird, I'm numb with cold and desperately in need of a drink. I was so close today. So damn close to everything I ever wanted. Five hundred thousand credits would have given me a chance to seize leadership, a way to take care of my younger siblings. The deal was *done*, and still I managed to screw things up. Now I have nothing. I'm completely at the mercy of whatever Momma—and soon, Corvus—decides to do with me and my siblings. After seeing who he's become, I have no doubt Corvus will lead us down the same path Momma always has, if not a worse one. So much for our dreams of a better future.

Then again, maybe this is for the better. Maybe this deal proved that I'm not cut out to lead this family after all. I had myself so convinced that I was the right person for the job, that I deserved it, but now I'm starting to see the weakness in myself that Momma must have always sensed. Corvus never would have given into his conscience like that. He would have done whatever it took. Hell, Corvus survived three years in Titan's war. If I was in his shoes, my damn conscience would have gotten me killed the first time I had to pull the trigger.

And now I have to face Momma and deal with the consequences of stealing that vial. I've already spun a lie that I hope will convince her, a rambling tale about getting hostile vibes from General Altair and securing one of the vials in case the deal went south. I doubt it will be enough to satisfy her, but then again, nothing I do ever is. I would've bolstered my courage on the way over, except that I'm so broke I can't even afford a stars-damned drink. Five hundred thousand credits...why the fuck did I just throw that away?

The moment I step into the bar on the first floor, I'm immediately distracted by the clink of ice on glass, the sharp smell of alcohol, the happy drunken singing from a group of soldiers in the corner. When the man closest to me takes a long swig of whiskey, I imagine the liquor sliding down my own throat and swallow hard, almost tasting it. The hole in my chest yawns wide, filling me with want.

I rip my eyes away from him and look around for my family. I spot Drom's towering form first; she's in a dim corner of the room, either flirting with or threatening some fresh-faced soldier boy—hard to tell with her. She must have had her leg treated, since she's not avoiding putting weight on it anymore. Pol is among the drunk soldiers I noticed before, laughing with them as if they're old friends. Lyre is also easy to find for once, seated at a table with a ring of scowling faces, her small fingers wrapped around a handful of dice. An assortment of trinkets, drinks, and other belongings sits in front of her.

Corvus is harder to spot, but eventually I notice him sitting at the end of the bar, hunched over a beer and as alone as he can manage to be in the semicrowded room. Momma is nowhere to be found. I pause, chewing my lip and trying to decide what to do. If Momma is upstairs, I could go face her and maybe earn some points for not trying to avoid punishment.

But I'm not ready to face anyone from my family, not before I'm numb enough to think clearly again. If only I wasn't completely broke. I'm not eager to try stealing on Titan and lose a finger for my trouble. Then again, there is one other reliable way to get free alcohol that works just about anywhere in the system.

I survey the bar and sidle up to the first lonely-looking soldier I see, a man a few years my junior with a shaved head and sad blue eyes.

"You look like you could use some company," I say, and flash him my most winning smile.

Soon enough I'm pleasantly drunk, and careening quickly toward being even drunker. I'm laughing too loud, talking too much, unsteady on my feet—but I can't stop. Every time I pause for a moment it all seeps in again. I have to keep trying to drown my thoughts. Drown myself as much as possible. I don't want to feel anything anymore.

The soldier buying my drinks seems to be of the same mind. His name is Alvid, though I keep forgetting it. The burn marks covering both his hands look recent, but he's reluctant to talk about them. Or anything at all, really. But I can talk enough for both of us, and he seems content to listen, those sad eyes never leaving mine.

It might be a decent night, if not for the day that came before it. And if not for Corvus shooting me sideways looks from the bar. The rest of my siblings are minding their own business— Lyre gambling, Pol chatting it up with various soldiers, and Drom enjoying her own companion for the night—but Corvus radiates judgment from his seat in the corner.

When Alvid excuses himself to take a leak, I can't help myself anymore. I slide onto the barstool next to my brother.

"What is it?" I ask. "You have something to say to me?"

"No." He remains facing forward, not looking at me.

I tilt my head, studying his stony face. I don't know what I'm doing here. Maybe I'm looking for some sign of the brother I remember, the brother I miss. Or maybe it's just the same self-destructive instinct that drives me to the bottle, again and again, even though I know I'm going to regret it in the morning.

"No, come on, what is it? You disapprove? Don't tell me you're still a prude after three years on Titan," I say, laughing. The rest of us always used to tease him about how seriously he took romance. But he's not laughing now. He only grimaces, reaching for his drink. I push it out of his reach with one finger.

Corvus lets out a long sigh.

"Have you always been this annoying?" he asks, turning to face me fully.

"Absolutely," I say with another laugh, though there's a deep ache in my chest cutting through the numb drunkenness. "You just used to have a sense of humor." He snatches his drink and turns away,

248

but I keep going. "Is that one of the many Titan army require-
ments? You have to sacrifice your sense of humor?" I lean closer.
"Or was it only your humanity? I forget."

He slams his glass down on the counter hard enough to make
me jump, his other hand curling into a fist. When he turns to me, I
flinch. I barely recognize him with the look on his face.

"Do you ever think about anyone other than yourself?" The
way he asks it, with a cold and casual cruelty, cuts deeper than
the words themselves. He's never spoken to me like this before.
While I stare at him, he lets out a disgusted sound and shakes his
head. "Of course you don't. Go fuck yourself, Scorpia."

A moment of silence passes. Then I let out a weak laugh and
stand.

"You too, huh?" I murmur. "Fine, then. Fine."

I don't know why I'm surprised; Corvus has already made it
clear he stands with Momma. Once he's in charge, he'll probably
be worse than her. Everything he's said and done since returning
to the family proves that I can't trust him anymore. But after my
screwup today, I'm in no position to do anything about it other
than try to drown the hurt.

As I stumble away from the bar, I see Alvid is back. I make my
way over and grab his arm, though he's barely steadier than I am.

"Let's go to your room," I say, and after searching my face for a
moment, he nods.

Upstairs, we shed layers of clothing on our way to the bed, our
breath the only sound in the quiet. His scarred hands are surprisingly gentle on my skin.

Please, I think, as my lips crash against his. *Please let me feel
something that doesn't hurt. Please let me forget myself, just for a little
while.*

249

CHAPTER TWENTY-TWO

Sirens

Corvus

My body is already half out of bed by the time my mind wakes up. One hand reaches under my pillow for my knife while the other searches for the rest of my gear. When I find only empty space beneath the bed, I pause, remembering. I'm not in the war anymore. The dark shapes stirring in the dim room around me are my siblings, not my team. We're in Drev Dravaask, not a war zone.

I let my shoulders slump, breathing hard, and look down at the knife in my hand. No longer in the war zone, but something did wake me up. For one dizzying moment I wonder if the sound was merely a product of my imagination, just another nightmare chasing me into the real world.

But Pol rolls out of the other side of our bed and stumbles over to the window, one hand scrubbing at his eyes. He yanks up the metal shutter and peers down at the street below. The sound spills into the room then: a high-pitched wail, ringing on-off, on-off, on-off in increasingly louder segments before starting over again.

As I shake off the last remnants of sleep, fear forms a pit in my stomach. I've heard this siren before, in other cities and forts, but never here. I don't know that the evacuation sirens have *ever* been sounded in Drev Dravaask, the underground fortress, the heart of Interplanetist territory. Why would it, when we're so far from the front? And why would it ever be safer outside the city than within?

Drom, feet hanging off the couch and a pillow over her head, lets out a muffled groan.

"Shut the damn window," she mutters, still half-asleep, and throws her pillow at Pol without opening her eyes. It thumps against his chest and falls to the ground, but he doesn't even look at it, instead staring at me and the knife resting in my hand. Light from the window illuminates his silhouette.

"What's happening?" he asks.

"The city's evacuating." My stomach rolls. Evacuation sirens in Drev Dravaask. A city that's a fortress, and at least a hundred miles away from where the fighting should be.

The morning after Momma handed Altair a weapon she promised would end the war.

"We need to go," I say, getting out of bed.

"I'll get Momma." Pol heads into the hall. I suspect he won't find her there, but I need to get my other siblings up before I deal with that. Outside, other patrons are already evacuating.

"Get up, Drom," I say, and move to the other bed, reaching down to shake Lyre's shoulder. "Lyre, Scorpia, wake up. We need to go."

Lyre, curled around a pillow, blinks up at me in sleepy confusion. "Huh? Scorpia's not here."

"What?" As my eyes adjust to the darkness, I notice that she's right. The other side of the bed is empty, its sheets neatly folded. Scorpia isn't here, and she never was. My mind flashes back to her stumbling upstairs with that soldier—and the fight we had beforehand. "She never came back?" The others all trickled in when they were done with their entertainment for the night, just like we always did in the past.

Next door, Pol's knocking has increased to a steady bang loud enough to cut through the rest of the noise.

"No," Lyre says, sitting up and running a hand through her stray curls. She yawns again. As she wakes up fully, she seems to remember that she's been determined to be cold toward me. She sniffs and shoots me a glare. "What's the big deal?" she asks, and then her eyes go wide as she notices the knife in my hand.

"There's no time." I shove my knife into its sheath and yank Lyre out of bed despite her protests. Outside, Pol is throwing his shoulder against the door. I usher both of my bleary-eyed sisters into the hall. By the time we make it out, the other guests in the hallway have made their way downstairs, and the door to Momma's room is swinging loose on one hinge. When Pol emerges again, I know what he's going to say.

"Momma's not here."

Panic hits me so hard it makes me nauseous. Either Momma left me again, left all of us—or something worse has happened. But my little siblings are looking at me, so I ball my trembling hands into fists and force myself to shake off my fear. That look and this feeling are all too familiar. The sensation of being needed by someone, and all the pressure that comes with it. I'm tired of it. Far too tired. But they need me right now.

"Let's get to the lobby," I say. "Maybe Scorpia and Momma are waiting there."

They won't be, but at least it will get us moving. And at least the gravity of the situation seems to be hitting my siblings, because they're quick to obey. Every floor we pass through is deserted, and so is the bar on the first floor. A half-poured drink and uncorked bottle of vodka still sit on the counter, and someone's cracked comm rests near a sticky puddle on the ground. Drom looks around the room with a frown, while Pol paces behind her and Lyre frantically presses the screen of her comm.

These people left in a hurry, and we should do the same. Yet I can't bring myself to say so out loud. Momma could be with Altair's soldiers still, or back at the ship. But Scorpia would never leave us. She has to be here in the city, somewhere.

Though the wrinkle of frustration in Lyre's brow says it's pointless, I dig my comm out of my pocket to check if she's been in contact. There's nothing from Scorpia, nothing from Momma, but a multitude of missed calls from Daniil a couple of hours ago. My stomach sinks. With everything that's been going on, I didn't even think to ask Momma about him.

But more concerning, there's a message from Altair buried in the midst of Daniil's attempts to contact me: *Kaiser, report to me immediately.*

Yesterday, he wanted nothing to do with me. What does he want now? Unless . . . A chill trickles down the length of my spine as I remember that last glimpse of him and Momma yesterday. Again, I'm struck with conviction that the timing of this evacuation can't be a coincidence.

I switch my comm over to the news feed. My device still hasn't been disconnected from the military network. When I see the updates scrolling across it, I suck in a sharp breath.

Vin has fallen. No survivors.

We've lost contact with the troops sent to Vin.

Reports of unknown illness in Il Yask. Initiating quarantine.

Il Yask down. Quarantine failure.

Kelivskyny infected.

Kelivskyny down. Initiate immediate evacuation of all nearby cities.

I scrutinize the updates, trying to make sense of them. Vin is a city near the front, a hotly contested strategic point that recently fell under Isolationist control. That could have been where Momma went to "test" this weapon with Altair's soldiers.

But Il Yask is a fort under our control, and Kelivskyny one of our cities. I paint the destruction across a mental map, tracing a path from their side of the border to our own—a line straight through the heart of our territory. Whatever is happening, if it continues, it will cut through Fort Jaalis, Fort Sketa, where I left my team—and then Drev Dravaask.

And though the reports don't specify, I have a sinking suspicion that I know exactly what this is, and why Momma didn't make it back to her room.

We've lost contact with the troops sent to Vin.

I rip my thoughts away from that trail and try to focus. I can't afford to think about that right now. Judging by the time stamps on these updates, we don't have long until the destruction reaches us.

But while Momma can handle herself, leaving Scorpia is as good as killing her.

If we stay, we could all die. Yet, despite everything that's happened between us, the decision is easy. I can't leave her behind.

"Head to the ship," I tell my other siblings. "Prepare for launch. I'll find Scorpia." I almost forget to add: "And Momma."

And maybe I have a chance to save someone else. I turn to my comm again, scrolling through my contacts and starting to type. If I can get my team to meet me here before the destruction hits, we can escape together. *Magda, I know we ended things badly…*

"Don't be ridiculous," Lyre says, tearing my attention away from the screen. "We can't separate right now."

"We have to," I say. *But something terrible is happening. Come to Drev Dravaask—*

"I'm here, I'm here, I'm here!"

Relief surges through me as I turn toward the stairs. Eyes

bloodshot, hair sticking out all over the place, hopping on one foot while trying to slip her boot onto the other—she's a mess as usual, but I've never been so happy to see Scorpia in my life. She stumbles as she reaches the bottom of the stairwell, and comes to a halt, chest heaving.

"Whew," she says. "That siren is not doing my headache any favors. What's, uh, what's going on? Where's Momma?"

She pauses, no doubt taking in the somber looks on all of our faces. I clear my throat and exit out of the message I was typing. There's no time, and it was a long shot anyway. I need to focus on my family, as much as it hurts to put Magda and the others aside.

"We don't know where she is. The city's being evacuated," I say. Shock crosses her features, followed by suspicion, and then horrified guilt. Like me, she must suspect this is our fault.

"That a normal occurrence?" she asks.

"No."

"Then please tell me you know a way out faster than those clunky elevators."

I take a breath and nod.

"There are service tunnels for soldiers," I say, leaving out that it's treasonous for me to take anyone but Titan military through them. I have a growing suspicion that it won't matter. Whatever happens on Titan today, I doubt anyone is going to have time to punish me for something as insignificant as that.

"Let's get going, then," Scorpia says. Thankfully, this time, no one argues.

My comm buzzes in my pocket. I sneak a glance at the screen to find another incoming call from Daniil. Heart heavy, I shut down the device. I have to save the people I can.

I turn back to my siblings, who are watching me and waiting to be told what to do. Almost like soldiers. Even Scorpia is silent for once.

"Stay together and follow me."

*   *   *

Though panicked crowds amass in other areas of the city, the soldiers' tunnel is empty by the time we reach it. The exit is hidden in the basement of a now-deserted factory. Some of the machinery creaks onward though the stations have all been abandoned. The heaters are still on, speaking to how swiftly the place was evacuated.

Judging by the time stamps on the messages I received, the army had word of the danger long before the city's alarm sirens went off. Crisscrossing boot tracks in the mud at the mouth of the tunnel indicate they were in a rush even with that advance notice. *Vin has fallen. Il Yask down. Kelivskyny down.* Drev Dravaask will surely follow. I think of all the civilians stuck waiting for elevators with no idea what's coming for them, and swallow down guilt. This city is huge, and there's no way it can evacuate in time, but that's not a problem I can fix. Saving my family will have to be enough.

My siblings peer up at the dark tunnel hesitantly. Lyre clings to Pol's arm, and he rubs her back with one absentminded hand. Scorpia squints in the dim lighting, her eyes bloodshot. Drom keeps glancing over her shoulder. I force myself to keep a stony face, hiding the conflict I still feel.

"This leads to an old factory near the caves," I say. "It'll be a quick walk to the ship from there."

Unless we find soldiers waiting to apprehend us the moment we walk through...or soldiers waiting at the ship to jump us and steal it...or unless even this route isn't fast enough for us to escape the doom that's coming for the city. A million things could still go wrong, but I can't let my siblings know that. I step into the darkness without hesitation. Ten feet in, I realize no one is following, and turn. "It's safe. I've been through before."

No one moves. The twins exchange a glance, while Lyre looks behind her at the stairs up to the factory, and Scorpia stares down at her half-laced boots. Drom's the one who finally speaks.

"We haven't heard from Momma. She could be trapped in the city."

"We don't have time for that," I say, choking back the real truth: that I suspect Momma is nowhere near us, and we have no chance of reuniting with her, now or ever again. They don't need to know that yet. It will only make them panic. "Drev Dravaask has never been evacuated before. Something terrible is coming." Something our family brought here.

Drom keeps her arms folded over her chest. Pol's hand drops from Lyre's back. His eyes narrow, features twisting into an expression I recognize from his younger years—the expression that means he's determined to be unreasonable. Drom may be stubborn, but Pol is worse. He's emotional.

"We had time to wait for Scorpia," he says, before I can cut him off.

Scorpia's eyes meet mine before skittering off again.

"You knew I was close," she says. "Can't we have this conversation back at the ship?" But even she sounds hesitant, as though part of her doubts what she's saying.

"Right. We have no idea where Momma is." My voice comes out harsher than I expected. Once, I was good at dealing with moods like these from my younger siblings. Now, I'm used to having my orders followed. My team would never question me like this in a moment of crisis.

"You're the last one who saw her," Lyre speaks up, twisting a curl around one finger. "What did she say?"

"She said she'd be back in the morning, but clearly that isn't the case. We can wait for her on *Fortuna*."

"I'm fine waiting right here," Drom says, planting her feet and leaning back in a casual stance. Pol stays tense, his eyes tracking my every moment, like he expects me to throw a punch.

"We're not going anywhere without Momma," he says.

257

"You idiots," Lyre says, but puts a hand over her mouth—likely afraid anything she says will only set the twins off, as it so often has in the past.

My jaw tightens. This is ridiculous. Wasting any further time could get us all killed. So it looks like I'm going to have to handle this the way I handled insubordination in my team early on, such as when Sverre thought he could challenge me. I stride straight up to Pol, ignoring that I have to look up to meet his eyes, and lean close.

"Listen to me," I say, my voice firm. "We do not have time for this shit. We're going to the ship. Now."

The little brother I knew before would have crumpled at my tone alone—but that was when he was sixteen years old and quite a bit smaller. Now, he smiles at my words, tilting his head in an exaggerated motion that emphasizes the height difference between us.

"Oh yeah? Are you going to make me?"

"If I have to." I hope it doesn't come to that. But if it does, I'm not afraid of Pol. He's always been more bark than bite. Then again, maybe Pol isn't the one I need to be afraid of. Drom's circled behind me while I wasn't paying attention to her.

"Just try it," she says, and shoves me forward, sending me stumbling into Pol. His lip curls as he shoves me back again. I dig in my heels and manage to regain my footing.

"Back off," I snarl at them, hands clenching at my sides. "I don't want to hurt you."

Both twins laugh at that. Anger pulses through me, a rising heat in my chest burning away my resolve to avoid violence. The twins may be bigger than me now, but they have no idea what I'm capable of. If I take down Drom first, I can end this quickly. Then they'll listen to reason. If I take her by surprise—

No. No. I take a deep breath, cold air stifling the flames. These are my siblings, not soldiers I need to put in line. As tempting as it is right now, I don't want to make them fear me. Surely there's a better way. I always managed to calm them before. I was the one who taught Momma the best way to talk them down from a tantrum.

But those memories seem very far away now, and when Drom jabs a finger into my back, it takes all of my willpower not to pivot and punch her in the throat. Perhaps noticing the growing rage in my expression, Scorpia finally steps forward, hesitating for a moment before she pushes between me and Drom, her hands held up. She puts her back to mine and forces our sister to take a step back. Some of the tension in my shoulders eases once I'm no longer surrounded.

"Okay, this is stupid," Scorpia says, swiveling her head to make it clear she's addressing both twins and myself. "You guys seriously think Momma needs *our* help? She's smart, she's resourceful, she knows people in this city. There's no way she's still around. She's probably back at the ship already, wondering why her idiot children haven't joined her yet. You guys can punch through your issues later; we need to go."

Relief hits me. She's stepping up, and it seems to be working. But though her words look to be calming the twins, they cause a spike of panic to break through my simmering anger. What she says could be true—Momma may have found a way back to the ship already. If the air-strike team made it safely, they could have dropped her there. And if so—if so, she could have left us behind already.

My comm beeps in my pocket. Another news update.

Fort Jaalis is down.

My pulse quickens. One fort stands between the spreading destruction and Drev Dravaask—the fort where I left my team— and we still need to make it through this tunnel and to the ship.

"Let's get the hell out of here before Momma decides to take off without us," I say, turning my head to speak to Scorpia over my shoulder. "We should—"

I cut off as pain explodes in my jaw. I stumble back into Scorpia, sending her staggering into Drom. They fall to the ground in a pile of limbs, both cursing and struggling, while I whirl to face Pol.

"We came here for you," Pol shouts at me, though I barely process his words through a red haze of anger. "For *you*. How dare you say she would leave—" His eyes widen a half second before my fist crashes into his face.

He stumbles back, shock flickering across his expression, before taking another swing at me. I dodge this one, and hit him again, hard enough to make his head snap back.

"We're done here," I say, but Pol's expression darkens. He throws himself at me. I hit the ground beneath him. A moment later we're a thrashing mess, him spouting insults and throwing wild punches, while I grimly struggle to pin him down. His elbow collides with my nose, spilling a rush of blood down my chin. I grit my teeth and flip him off me, twisting one arm behind his back and pressing my weight down. Breathing hard, blood dripping off my chin, I hold him on the ground. Still he thrashes, boots kicking up dirt, spitting out a steady stream of *fucker* and *coward* and *traitor*.

Filthy off-world traitor.

Rage sears my insides. One quick twist of his wrist, one satisfying pop and crack, and he'd never dare speak to me like that again. How he can dare to do it now is beyond me. Have I not done enough for this family? Sacrificed enough? After everything, this is the homecoming I get? I twist his arm harder, thinking of his fist striking my face, Scorpia's scathing words, Momma using me as a prop to sell the stars-damned weapon that's already wiped out three cities, Magda's last words to me in Fort Sketa—

Pol's insults cut off in a cry of pain. The sound jolts through my anger, immediately reminding me of my little brother falling and scraping his knee, or accidentally burning himself on the stove, or being bullied by his twin. I relax my grip, guilt flooding me as I come back to my senses, cooling the heat in my chest. I remember now. I remember the right way to do this. I lean down, speaking the words I so often spoke to Pol when he was a child, red-faced and thumping his small fists against my chest while I stood immobile and patient.

"That's enough, Apollo. That's enough."

After one last, vain struggle to escape, the fight leaks out of him. He goes still except for the rapid rise and fall of his chest. Once I'm certain he's done, I release him and get up, spitting a mouthful of blood off to the side.

The first person I see is Lyre, eyes wide and both hands over her mouth. Closer to us are Drom and Scorpia, still tangled on the ground.

"Sorry, sorry," Scorpia says, a leg hooked around Drom's knee to prevent her from standing, one hand smashed against her face while the other presses into her stomach. "I'm trying to—I just— My leg is—" She looks up and notices me standing. A moment later, she scrambles to her feet without any apparent effort, brushing herself off and leaving Drom winded and confused on the ground. "Well, that's done with," she says. But when she looks at Pol, pushing himself up from the ground with one hand pressed to his bloodied nose, her expression shifts to shock. She looks at me. I drop my gaze and wipe blood off my lips.

My comm beeps again. *Fort Sketa has fallen.*

I shut my eyes for a brief moment and think of Sverre, who never turned his back on me. Daniil asking me to save him. Magda. Magda smiling with the wind in her hair, with her lips on my neck. Magda before everything crumbled. I make a silent promise to remember her like that.

This time, when I walk into the tunnel, the rest of my family follows.

CHAPTER TWENTY-THREE

LOSS

Scorpia

We reach *Fortuna* without trouble, but Momma isn't there.

Everyone scours the ship, clinging to the same hope that she could be hiding somewhere—except Corvus, that is. He stays near the ramp, right next to the pressure pad that will close it. His knuckles are still stained with our brother's blood, and I can barely bring myself to look at him.

At least it's solidified something I was already suspecting: This man is not the same one who left me. The brother I knew would never raise a hand against any of us. He was always the anchor, the safe house, the one who would let the little ones scream and hit him all they wanted and still kiss their foreheads and tuck them into bed that night.

Pol, even with his face a mess, searches the hardest for Momma. And when he doesn't find any trace of her on board, he storms right out onto the surface again, ignoring everybody's protests. Though I hang back in the cargo bay, I can hear him shouting for her at the mouth of the cave outside, his voice carried by the wind.

Drom hovers on the edge of the ramp, looking toward her twin. One moment she takes a small step forward as if to join him; the next, she shrinks back as if to flee. After a few moments of teetering indecision, she lets out a frustrated growl and turns to the rest of us clustered in the cargo bay.

"What the hell are we going to do?" she asks, her gaze ping-ponging between Corvus and me.

I lick my dry lips. Now's the moment I should speak up if I want to solidify myself as our future leader... but I never wanted it to be like this. I glance at Corvus to see if he'll answer, only to find him staring back at me looking as lost as I feel.

As soon as our eyes meet, we both turn away. Embarrassment rises in my throat before it's overtaken by panic again.

Outside, Pol is still yelling for Momma. Beyond him, Titan is dying—and somewhere, Momma is cut off from us. Alive or dead, I'm not sure. And I don't know if it matters either way.

Waiting five more minutes could be the last chance to bring her back to us. Or it could get us all killed for nothing.

"Those antiradiation suits from Pax," Corvus says, drawing me out of my thoughts. "We still have them?"

"Uh..." It's hard to think about things like suits when Momma is still out there, but I force myself to picture the bulky orange outfits. "Yeah. I think so. You think those will help?"

"They can't hurt. Lyre, go get them," he says. She looks up at me instead of him. When I nod, she scurries off.

Corvus glances over his shoulder at her as she disappears into the supply closet, and then at Drom, who is pacing back and forth with her hands behind her head, muttering to herself.

"We can't wait much longer," Corvus murmurs, barely audible over the howling wind outside.

"I know," I say, my throat tight.

But neither of us give the order.

My heart thumps painfully in my chest, every beat reminding me of the passing seconds we're spending here. We don't know what's happening out there, or how it's spreading. It's possible we're already infected with something and it just hasn't hit us yet. But it's also possible we're not, and another minute here could change that. I'm painfully aware of every gust of wind bringing swirling dust and tiny ice particles into the ship, the danger in each breath I take. But surely Corvus is the one who has to make the call.

Lyre emerges from the supply closet with her arms overflowing with suits. She hands them out, dropping the last two on the floor before starting to put on her own.

"This is pointless," Drom says. "We don't know what the hell we're dealing with."

"Just put it on," Corvus snaps.

I ignore the nagging feeling that she's right as I slip off my bulky Titan gear to pull on the quarantine suit. When I get to the helmet strap, I notice my hands are shaking. I shut my eyes for a moment before I finish. The rest of my siblings have donned the suits as well, even Drom despite her protests. The two leftovers remain crumpled on the floor—Momma's and Pol's. I swallow the lump in my throat and pick one up, handing it to Drom. One suit still lies on the floor. Stars, our family was so close to being whole again.

But someone has to make a decision.

"Take this to Pol and tell him to get back in the ship," I say, talking loud enough to ensure everyone can hear me despite my helmet.

Drom takes the suit, her brow furrowing.

"He won't come without Momma."

I take a deep breath. Wherever Momma is, she won't or can't answer. It's possible she's already dead, one more victim of the hell she brought to this planet. Even if she's not, there's a reason she isn't here. And if we keep waiting, we're all going to end up dead. Yet still the words stick in my throat. What if I'm wrong? What if I'm just screwing things up again?

"We can't wait any longer," Corvus says. "Drag him if you have to."

Drom blinks at him, then at me. I know exactly how much we're asking of her. Not only sending her back to the surface to brave potential danger, but asking her to force Pol onto the ship against his will, rip him away from his hope of Momma returning. This could break their relationship as badly as Corvus broke ours. Drom may poke and prod and tease Pol—and occasionally start fights that end with blood and missing teeth—but this is different. We both know it. And yet, it has to be done.

"Go, Drom," I say.

She nods and heads for the ramp, her jaw and shoulders both set in firm lines. I watch her go, and wonder if Momma ever feels like this when she gives hard orders—like her insides are tearing themselves apart and her willpower barely prevents her from opening her mouth and saying *I didn't mean it, please come back.*

"Anything on the comm?" I ask, glancing back at Lyre. She looks up at me, biting her lip, and shakes her head.

"This is the right call," Corvus says. Somehow, that makes me feel worse rather than better.

I step onto the ramp, far enough out that the wind tears at my suit, and stare at the bleak landscape of Titan. Drom's bright orange figure treks across the white, struggling against the wind and the ice. Pol is so far away that he's dwarfed by the yawning cave and rocky tundra around him. He's just a small figure with both hands cupped around his mouth, screaming himself hoarse. Beyond him, something catches my eye—movement, possibly— and my heart surges. But when I look closer, there's nothing there.

I frown, rubbing a gloved hand across the front of my helmet in case something is smudged there. It must have been a trick of the light, sun glancing off snow. Or maybe some hope-induced hallucination. I sigh and turn to head back into the ship—and I see it.

A black cloud rolling over the white tundra, shivering and stretching as it moves like ink spreading through water, reaching all the way from the surface to the sky.

I gasp. The inky darkness disappears as soon as I turn toward it, but now that I know what to look for, I see the telltale colorful shimmer in the air. I know what it is. We brought it here. And it's coming closer, fast.

"Get back to the fucking ship!" I scream as loud as I can, hurting my own ears in the bubble of the helmet. I rip it off my head and scream it again, loud enough that Pol turns toward the sound of my voice. After one painstaking moment he begins to walk toward the ship, but not fast enough. Not nearly fast enough. The shimmering cloud behind him is catching up by the second.

Drom must hear my voice as well. But instead of turning toward the ship, she starts to run toward her twin.

I lurch forward a step, ready to run to them myself, but stop. I'll only slow them down. And I need to be here, need to be ready to launch the moment they're safely on board. I stare after Drom, heart in my throat, hoping to all the stars in the universe that my decision to send her out there won't get them both killed. I back into the cargo bay without taking my eyes off them.

"Lyre, we need that ramp closed the second they're back on board," I say without turning, watching as Drom reaches Pol. She pushes the suit into his arms, says something, and sprints back toward the ship. After a moment of fumbling the helmet onto his head, Pol follows, matching her pace now. Thank the stars, he listened.

But that cloud is gaining on them.

"Are you sure we can't wait a few minutes longer for Momma?" Lyre asks in a small voice. "We have the suits now. They might—"

"I'll handle it," Corvus says, already moving over to the pressure pad. Despite my mixed feelings about his return, I'm grateful he's here now, when we need him. He'll do what's necessary.

"But—" Lyre turns toward me, and cuts off with a gasp. Her head whips back toward the ramp, and her face goes white. "Oh, stars, I see it now." She shrinks back against the wall. "We're dead," she whispers. "Aren't we?"

"Scorpia, get to the cockpit," Corvus says. He, at least, isn't losing his shit yet, but I feel like I'm about to.

"I will." But I can't bring myself to move. I don't know if I'll be able to take off without knowing if they made it. We're already leaving Momma behind. I'm not sure how much more loss I can take right now.

The twins are fast, legs pumping them over ice and stone much more quickly than the rest of us could move, but the cloud is gaining on them. My heart thuds in a steady, rapid beat, and a mantra in my head matches its pace: *please, please, please.* One slip, one stumble, and they'll never make it.

When Corvus hits the pressure pad early, I nearly lurch forward to stop him before I see his intent. This damn rusty ramp is always slow, and it's slower still when it's half-covered in ice and snow. It creaks upward slowly, slowly, as the twins cross the last stretch of ground to the ship and the deadly, shimmering air looms up outside.

Drom makes it first, leaping to clear the partially shut ramp and stumbling to a stop against the wall beside Lyre. She whips around to watch Pol dive in after her, landing belly-first in the cargo bay with a grunt and a clink as his helmet hits the floor. A few moments later, the ramp shuts behind him.

Outside, I picture that black cloud devouring us—but there are no signs of the shimmering air within the ship. Maybe it's only a matter of time, yet I can't bring myself to run for the cockpit.

If this thing is going to worm its way into our ship, we're already doomed. For now, I just want us all to be together.

Once he catches his breath, Pol climbs to his feet. His helmet is unstrapped and askew, one glove on and the rest of the suit still bundled in his arms. He lets it drop to the floor and leans against the closed ramp door, his breath fogging up the inside of the visor.

"We can't take off yet," he says in between pants. "Not without Momma. We have to . . . we have to . . ."

He trails off. My response dies in my throat as I see him raising his ungloved hand and staring down at it.

"What? What is it?" I ask, taking a step forward, and then I see. A faint shimmer on the tips of his fingers, like a dusting of light. It slowly climbs up to his arm.

"Oh, fuck," Pol says. He takes a step backward, as if he can escape his own hand, and looks at Drom. He opens his mouth to say something, and crumples.

I catch him before he hits the floor, stumble beneath his weight, and drop to my knees with his head cradled in my gloved hands. Black froth bubbles out from between his lips, splatters on the inside of his helmet. He gasps for air, the sound an awful gurgle in his throat. His eyes roll back in his head.

"No." I yank his useless helmet off, toss it aside, and press my hands to the sides of my brother's head, worries about contagion far from my mind. I try to hold his head still while the rest of his body writhes. "No, no, no. Please no. What do we do?" I tear my eyes off Pol and look around the room, frantic. "Somebody . . . somebody do something!"

Drom is staring down at her twin in blank-faced shock. Lyre backs toward the stairs with both hands held up, her eyes wide. After a moment that feels like an eternity, Corvus lurches forward and drops to his knees next to me. He shoves my arms away and yanks Pol onto his side. Black goo spills out of his mouth.

"Andromeda, help me lift him," Corvus says. He stands up, lifting Pol's shoulders off the ground. Drom is frozen. "*Drom*," he snaps. "Fucking help me now!"

Drom blinks like she's coming out of a dream, and finally moves, grabbing her twin by the legs and hauling him up. Pol's body convulses, an awful, wet cry ripping out of his throat. The sound tears at my insides, and I have to physically restrain myself from reaching out to him. I can't do anything now. I'll only get in the way. Corvus will handle it. He's always been the one who takes care of us.

"Med bay," Corvus says, and pushes forward when Drom doesn't move. She stumbles and moves numbly, blindly, in that direction. I try to follow, but Lyre throws an arm in my path.

"Get us ready to leave," she says. Her face is streaked with tears and her arm is shaking, but her voice is firm.

"No," I say. "I need to—"

"You need to do your job and let Corvus do his."

"But…" I take a step back. She's right—of course she is—but I can't tear my eyes away from the sight of them over her shoulder.

"Go!" Lyre shouts.

I cling to that last glimpse of Pol before the three of them disappear around the corner, committing the memory of his face to my mind, just in case… just in case. I want to do something, anything—or at least be there for the end of it. But Lyre is right. We need to get out of here before we all end up like Pol. I take a deep breath, turn, and run for the cockpit.

It's possible bringing Pol on board means we're all doomed anyway, but I have to hope. Hope, and do what I can to save what's left of my family. I grit my teeth, blink away tears, and start the launch sequence, flipping levers and hitting buttons and typing in my personal command code.

For the first time ever without Momma aboard, I prepare the ship for launch.

CHAPTER TWENTY-FOUR

Consequences

Corvus

Titan is dying. Momma is gone. It feels as though the entire world is collapsing around me, but right now I have to focus on Pol seizing in my arms. His muscular body arches and contorts, his breath a pained gurgle, his eyes rolling. I nearly lose my grip on him, but we manage to lift him onto the nearest table in the med bay. As soon as she lets go of him, Drom steps back.

"I need your help," I say, meeting her eyes. They're wide, her face drawn and pallid. Her chest rises and falls rapidly. Drom could face a million firefights with a grin and a war cry, but now, her fear is palpable. She's no soldier under my command, just a nineteen-year-old girl whose twin is dying in front of her. Still, she takes a deep breath and nods at me, ready to follow orders.

Pol spews out another mouthful of black goo, so reminiscent of the liquid running through the cords on that alien ship that my stomach lurches. The sound of his breath is a terrible thing, wet and struggling. I don't know what the hell is happening to his body, but I'm familiar enough with the sound of choking.

"Get him onto his side," I say, rushing to the cabinets. I rustle through the shelves and containers. After three years away, I still remember the med bay's layout. Aside from the pills and quick-fix kits, it's shocking how little the rest has changed. "We need to help him breathe."

Drom sets her jaw and grabs Pol, turning him onto his side the same way she saw me do it. She lowers her helmeted head toward him and whispers words too quiet for me to overhear.

Once I find what I'm looking for, I push the tube down Pol's throat and slip the mask over his face. His breathing eases as the device clears a path and takes the pressure off his struggling lungs. Still, his body jerks, his eyes rolling and shifting and mostly white.

Drom looks down at her twin with a stricken expression.

"He's dying, isn't he?"

I turn away, rummaging through medical supplies and searching for an answer other than *I don't know* or *yes, he is, say your goodbyes*. I fill a syringe with an anticonvulsant and a painkiller. It's not time for goodbyes just yet.

As the medicine floods his veins, Pol's body slackens, his eyes fluttering shut. He's finally unconscious, which is likely a blessing for him. Drom doesn't relinquish her grip on his shoulders, as if she's trying to anchor him here.

"I'm doing what I can," I say.

Or, rather, I already have. I've cleared his breathing passages, stopped the muscle convulsions, taken away his pain. But I'm treating the symptoms, not the cause. I have no idea what other chaos this thing is wreaking within his body. I could run some scans, perform some tests... but I'm not sure there would be a point to it.

He's within the jaws of this weapon, and I have no way to pry him free. I have no idea how to even try. I've seen all manner of disease and injury in the war, both natural and human-manufactured, but this alien monstrosity is beyond my capabilities.

Drom and I stand on either side of the table, staring down at our brother as his breathing gradually weakens. With one gloved hand, I carefully brush his hair back from his face. It's very pale, save for the blossoming bruises where my fist struck it earlier. He needs me now. I can't lose it. But I can't bring myself to fight the voice inside my head insisting that it's pointless. I'm going to lose him, like all the rest. Just like I lost everything and everyone on the planet I left behind.

A screen on the wall crackles to life, and Scorpia's voice comes through the tinny speaker.

"Corvus? Let me know when Apollo...u-um...when you're ready to launch."

Drom looks at me wordlessly. I swallow hard, unable to bring myself to respond to either of my sisters. We need to strap in before Scorpia can get us off this planet. I can secure Pol to the medical bed, but...with the pressure of lift-off and the fact that I won't be able to get to him, he'll never make it.

Before we launch, I need to say my goodbyes to my brother and to all the people I'm abandoning to die on Titan. General Altair, proud and noble and looking toward a better future—and my team, who would have followed me anywhere, who hated me for going somewhere they couldn't follow. Magda, Sverre, Daniil.

Daniil, who I almost managed to save. My mind flashes to that last comm call from him, the one I declined as I fled with my family. I promised to help him, and in those last frightening moments on Titan, he thought of me. What would he have said to me? Was he looking to say goodbye? Or calling to beg, once again, for that long-shot chance at saving his life? One last, desperate chance, surrendering himself to the dangers of cryosleep to be smuggled off-planet for a new life . . .

My thoughts stutter, pause. Rewind. I raise my head and look at my brother on the table, with his shallow breaths and weak heartbeat, both fading with every passing moment. Apollo is dying. He will die, if I don't do something. But perhaps I can give him one last, desperate chance to live.

"Andromeda," I say, looking up at her. "Where do you keep the cryosleep chamber?"

We find the machine shoved into a forgotten corner of the supply closet, along with an adjustable bridge and other supplies I don't recall ever using. The device sheds dust as we roll it through the cargo bay to the medical room and alongside the bed holding Pol. I type in the commands, and the top slides open to reveal the rectangular interior—much like a freezer, or a coffin.

Horror and fragile hope battle across Drom's face as she helps me lift Apollo's limp body from the bed and lower him into the chamber. When I let go, she carefully arranges him with his arms at his sides. Her shoulders are shaking, tears streaming down her face beneath the helmet.

"This is the best thing we can do for him," I say, keeping my voice firm despite my own self-doubt. "Go strap in for launch. I'll handle the rest."

She takes one last look at her twin and bolts from the room with a muffled sob.

I step forward and look down at my brother. "I'm sorry, Apollo," I murmur. He's so still already, the only sign of life the faint rise and fall of his chest, which will soon stop, too. "I'll see you again." I close the lid.

Once I strap myself into a launch chair in the med bay, I give Scorpia the go-ahead. As the ship rumbles and shudders away from the carnage of Titan, battered by the planet's ever-present storms, I shut my eyes and will myself to hold it together until we find a way to make this right.

Scorpia finds me in a metal chair beside the cryosleep chamber, my head in my hands. I sit up as I notice her come in, trying to regain some sense of dignity. I can't let my family see me like this. They'll need someone to be strong—and I've always been the strong one. If they see that this has broken me, the rest of them will crumple, too.

She's still dressed in her contamination suit. When she sees that I've already shed mine—after scrubbing the cargo bay and medical room as thoroughly as I could manage—she takes off her helmet and takes a deep breath of sanitized air. Her eyes are red-rimmed, and the moment she's free of her suit, she pulls a flask from her pocket and takes a long swig. As she lowers it, she finally seems to notice the cryosleep chamber—really notice it.

"Oh, shit," she says, and rubs a hand across her face as if trying to wipe something off. "I forgot we had that thing. Is he...did you...?"

"Yes."

Scorpia takes a deep breath and drops her hands to her side.

"Stars, Corvus," she says, the relief evident on her face. "You..."

"Don't." I can't handle gratitude right now, not when we both know how much of a long shot it is that he'll ever come back.

She lets out a shaky breath and takes another swig from her flask.

"Okay," she says. "Guess we need to talk about what comes next. I punched in the coordinates for Gaia, but I wasn't sure where we're headed."

I can't handle that right now, either. I'm not sure I can handle anything at all after how much I've lost. I'm numb for the moment, but I can feel the grief hovering over me, waiting to crash down in a wave that's certain to drown me. It's impossible to think about how to move forward when I'm still struggling with the weight of everything left behind.

"We need to do whatever we can for Pol," I say, because that much is obvious even through my haze of grief. "That comes first. The longer he's under, the harder it will be to wake him up."

"Right. Yeah." Scorpia livens up at that and begins to pace the small room. "Well . . . that thing came from Gaia. Maybe it's not a bad idea to start there."

Gaia. During all of this, I had almost forgotten that the weapon Momma was selling came from there. Directly from the president, as I recall. This wasn't just some weapons deal; it was an interplanetary agreement.

As the realization hits me, I sink back in my chair, raking fingers through my sweat-sticky hair. I almost let myself believe that what happened back on Titan was a mistake—a case of alien technology gone horribly wrong. I thought it was Momma's greed that caused that catastrophe.

But President Leonis would never make a mistake like that. She wouldn't let something loose on another planet without knowing exactly what it was going to do—and she would never do anything so risky without a reason.

"Shit," I say hoarsely. "Do you understand what we just did, Scorpia?" She stares at me, her feet coming to a stop. "We started a war."

CHAPTER TWENTY-FIVE

Legacy

Scorpia

I renew my pacing, taking a swig from my flask. Now that Corvus points it out, it seems so obvious. This was never just some job. Leonis used us to fire off the first shot of a war.

"But why?" I think aloud. "Why would she want to go to war?" My mind wanders back to the barren crop fields I saw on Gaia, the sanitation checks. Something strange was happening there. I should have paid more attention to it, especially given that we made a deal with Leonis afterward, but I never got the feeling they were preparing for interplanetary conflict.

"Does it matter? It's already done." Just when I thought we were starting to get somewhere productive, Corvus is slumping back into the stance I found him in: head down, face in his hands. Like the weight of everything is physically pressing down on him. I can empathize—he's lost even more than the rest of us—but I can't let him collapse under it. He's the one who survived a war, the one who's supposed to lead us. Titan proved I'm not cut out for it, so we need him.

"Leonis is linked to all of this. We need to figure out what she's planning next," I say. "So . . . why would she use us to launch the attack? And why Titan?"

Corvus grimaces at the mention of his home-planet, like it hurts just to hear the name. Thinking too hard about Titan drags my own thoughts down a painful path, too—to Momma. If she was here, she would know what to do. She'd know how to save Pol. I take a deep breath and subdue my emotions with another long drink of whiskey.

"Well, let's go back to the issue with Pol," I say, and wipe my hand across my mouth. Maybe thinking about him will help both Corvus and me focus. "Like I said, the Gaians made this thing, or at least discovered it. And they know the most about alien tech to begin with. But without Momma, we have no access to Gaia. We won't be able to leave the landing zone."

"We won't even make it there," Corvus says dully. "Leonis clearly intended for us to die. We'll be shot out of the sky."

"Okay. So Gaia is a no-go. Where else? Maybe a doctor on Deva? Or Pax?" Deva is a more developed world, but Paxians are nothing if not innovative, with all their built-in tech and playing with genetics.

"No one's going to go near a Primus disease," Corvus says.

"They might if we throw enough credits at them," I say, and pause as dread hits me. "You have access to M—um, to the business account, right?"

"No." He raises his head to look at me, his eyes mirroring my horrible realization. "You don't?"

"Not a chance," I say, and huff out a hopeless laugh. "Oh, stars. So we're totally broke, too?" I take another long swig. If only I had sold that damn vial, we'd be in a much better position right now. Five hundred thousand credits could've been enough to give us another option, and instead we have nothing. Damn my conscience. Changing my mind didn't save Titan, it only screwed us over now. If I hadn't been so weak, we wouldn't be in such a dire situation. "Okay...so a war's starting, Leonis wants us dead, *and* we're broke. What else have we got?"

While Corvus stares at me in mute hopelessness, I realize the answer to my own question. Unease turns my legs to jelly at the thought, but I force myself to push back my fear, and reach into my pocket. I shiver as my fingers close around the alien vial. I nearly chucked the thing out the air lock the moment we were in open space, but I stopped at the last second. It's too valuable to throw away. Maybe the only thing of value we have, now.

"Well...I do have something to bargain with," I say, and pull the vial out. When I hold it up, light illuminates the swirling colors within. I shudder as it reminds me of the similar shimmer spreading up Pol's arm, his look of shock, the sound his body made when it hit the floor—

"Why the hell did you bring that on board?" Corvus snaps, rage bringing him to life. He's on his feet in an instant, grabbing for it, but I step back and pull it out of his reach. "Give it to me."

"Whoa, hey, wait." I block him with the hand holding my flask. Whiskey splashes across his shirt, and he glowers at me. "This is the only leverage we have right now. We could use it as a threat against Leonis, or even sell it—"

"No. We're flushing it out the air lock," Corvus snarls. "That weapon just killed my home-planet. Maybe that doesn't mean anything to you, but it does to me."

"Of course it means something," I say. "But there's nothing we can do about that now. Our brother is still alive, and we can still help him. We need to look at the bigger picture—"

"The bigger picture? Is that what you told yourself when you helped Momma kill Titan?"

He grabs for the vial again. When I block with the flask, he knocks it out of my grasp, sending it clattering to the metal floor. We both freeze as whiskey pools around our feet, realizing how easily that could have been the vial in my other hand. I take a step back.

"I had no idea what we were transporting," I say, trying not to erupt and provoke him even further. Neither of us are thinking clearly right now, and there's a dangerous look in his eyes. I'm talking to my brother—but I'm also talking to a Titan soldier. I need to remember that. "I doubt Momma did, either, or she would never have been on the surface when it went off."

Corvus stares at me. His eyes are hollow, hard. "If not for you, she wouldn't have been."

"What?" I stare at him. "What the hell are you talking about?"

"You stole that vial," he says, nodding toward the weapon I'm still holding behind my back. "It made Momma change the terms of the deal. Made Altair suspicious." He pauses, as if trying to hold himself back, but the words come out anyway. "That's why he insisted she go with them to test the weapon. That's why she didn't escape with us." He takes a breath. "She chose to let me stay. To go with him alone."

Guilt hits me so intensely it nearly knocks my legs out from under me. Tears spring to my eyes despite my best attempt to keep them down. Stars, I really know how to fuck things up. All of this is my fault. And yet—

"You... You knew that this whole time?" I ask. My voice starts as a whisper, but soon climbs louder. "You knew back on Titan and didn't say anything?"

"You wouldn't have listened. You would've panicked."

"So instead of trying, you decided to hurt Apollo? To let us wait long enough for him to get infected by that thing?" I'm shouting now, tears running down my face, but I can't stop myself.

"None of you listened to a word I said until I hit him," Corvus shouts back. His fists clench at his sides, though the rest of him stays still. "None of you listen—"

"And why should we?" I shove him with my free hand. It barely moves him, which only makes me more furious. "Why should any of us ever trust you again with how you've been acting? After you left us to fight in that stupid fucking war?" I'm tired of dancing around this issue, especially if he has the nerve to argue morality with me. "I'm sure you've managed to convince yourself that was some *noble* thing to do. You must be so pleased with yourself. You made Momma proud, and who gives a shit how much it hurt anyone else, right?"

I expect Corvus to be angry at my words, maybe even wounded, but instead his expression wrinkles in pure confusion.

"What?" he asks. "What did you just say?"

"You left." My voice rises, as if that will drive the point home. My chest aches. I want to see him angry, to see him hurt. But he just stares, silent, his brow creased. It makes the bitterness swell until my eyes burn and my voice shakes. The words tumble out before I can finish thinking them. "We . . . we were supposed to take care of each other. You knew I needed you. And you left. You left me, Corvus. And you didn't even leave a fucking note!"

A wave of tears comes along with the words, and I force myself to stop, raising a hand to my eyes as if I can hide it. I suck in a breath that trembles in my throat on the way out.

"You . . ." He starts, and pauses. He takes a deep breath. "You think I left because I wanted to?" There's a tinge of uncertainty, almost of hurt, but a moment later his face clears. "Momma said I left because I wanted to fight in the war," he says, as if explaining something to himself.

". . . What? You wanted to . . . to fight for your planet. To keep your citizenship." My eyebrows knit together. "You wanted to do the right thing, the honorable thing. Try to be a hero on your home-world. You wanted..." I trail off, my mouth going dry.

Corvus raises a hand and rakes his hair back from his face. His mouth opens and closes twice before he speaks.

"All this time I wondered how you could've left me there," he says, his voice very quiet. "How not a single one of you would've rebelled against her decision. How *you* would have accepted it."

"I don't understand," I say, though I do, the horror of it turning my insides cold. I don't want to believe it. But I can see the pieces falling into place now, see the story that makes a whole lot more sense than Corvus choosing to abandon us to fight. Corvus, a soldier? He could never even manage pickpocketing without guilt driving him to tears. The words catch in my throat, but I push them out. "Momma forced you to stay on Titan."

Part of me still desperately hopes that he'll say no. Because the lie, as much as I hated it, was so much less horrible than the truth.

Instead of speaking, he merely nods.

I let out a shaky breath, unable to muster up words. Maybe I should be happy to learn that my brother didn't abandon me. Not of his own accord, at least. That should make me feel better. It should fix things between us. Part of me aches to reach out to him, pull him against me, but I can't bring myself to. The gap between us is still there, only more painful now. The lie might have been what pushed us apart, but the truth isn't enough to pull us back together. Not after years of hurt. Not when we've both become such different people.

Another realization creeps up on me as the silence between us lengthens. I've been telling myself that Corvus is strong enough to be the leader we need right now. But instead, he might be broken worse than I am.

"Where do we go from here?" I whisper, raising my eyes to his face again. He's staring down at the floor, his expression shadowed. "What the hell are we supposed to do?"

He doesn't answer.

Days pass in a haze of alcohol. I stay as drunk as possible to keep myself from drowning, and spend nearly the whole time in the cockpit to keep us on course. We're still headed for Gaia, since Corvus hasn't suggested any better ideas. Matter of fact, he hasn't spoken to us at all. After our conversation, he became practically catatonic—leaving the rest of us stuck in limbo, waiting for him to get his shit together.

Shortly after Titan, we pass another spacecraft, an unmistakable blip on our radar, and my pulse races. There are only so many ships that could be out here with the borders closed, and we know the *Red Baron* is around. I hover with my hand over the emergency alarm. But after a tense few minutes, it passes by, and I let out a breath of relief. Thank the stars whoever it is didn't intend to mess with us, though they're in for a nasty surprise if they're headed for Titan.

I wonder how long that alien weapon stays active. Will people ever be able to live there again, or has the planet been permanently ruined? But that trail of thought leads to Momma, and the truth about Corvus's enlistment, and Pol's frozen body in the cryosleep chamber, and a whole lot of other things I can't deal with. Even the sad blue eyes of that soldier I spent the night with still haunt me, and I've already forgotten his name.

So I turn back to my bottle.

When the door opens, my head whips up so fast that the cockpit spins around me. There's a bitter taste in the back of my mouth, and my eyes are filled with grit I can't blink away. Shit, I must've fallen asleep at the wheel. I sit up straight and clear my throat, trying to look as sober as possible as I turn to see which of my siblings has interrupted me.

Lyre stands in the doorway, her arms folded over her chest. My vision is too blurry to make out much of her face in the dim light, but given the stance, I can imagine her familiar frown of disapproval. Just like Momma's. I grimace, reaching for my bottle, and curse as I find it empty.

"What do you want?" I try to snap, but the words blur together in a mess of drunken syllables, which only makes me angrier. I shouldn't be angry—this is the first time I've spoken to my sister since we left Titan, I realize with a jolt—but I can't help it. I thought we were all in mutual agreement to be alone. "It's the middle of the night."

"Early morning, actually," she says, annoyingly calm in response to my sharp tone. She glances at the fallen bottle and back up at me. "You should have woken me up if you weren't in a state to fly. I can take the wheel for a shift."

"I'm in a fucking fine state, thanks." Despite my words, exhaustion pulls at my eyes and limbs, reminding me that I *am* due for a rest. I sigh and push myself to my feet.

Once I'm upright I instantly stagger, the room lurching around me. Lyre scoots out of my way without a word. I lean against the dashboard for support and place one shaky foot in front of the other, reminding myself that she's watching me. But as I move toward the main deck, my boot catches on the slight step, and I stumble and fall hard on one knee.

"Shit," I mutter, and cover my mouth as bile rises in the back of my throat. I breathe hard through my nose, eyes shut, willing myself not to vomit. Not now, not here. Not in front of Lyre. I must look pathetic.

"Damn it, Scorpia," Lyre says from behind me. A moment

later, her small hand grips my free one. When I open my eyes and look up, she pulls me to my feet with a loud sigh and slips an arm around me. "You can't keep doing this."

"Why not?" I ask. "Who's gonna give a shit?"

She wordlessly nudges me ahead. I step slowly, focusing on my footing, while she stays by my side and takes as much of my weight as she can handle. I frown down at her.

"You're helping me," I say, that fact only now reaching me through my drunken stupor. I study her face, but nearly lose my footing as a result, and have to look down at my own boots instead. "Why?"

Again, Lyre doesn't answer. She pauses in the kitchen—leaving me leaning against the dining table—to fill a metal canteen of water.

"Drink," she says, pressing it into my hands.

I drink the canteen in three big gulps, and she fills it again before resuming her post under my armpit. Together we make the unsteady trek to my room. The moment she releases me I crumple onto my bunk, stretching out on my back with a long sigh. Lyre sets the water on the shelf beside my bed, and hesitates there, looking down at me.

"I need to tell you something," she says. "Are you going to remember this conversation?"

Her serious expression sobers me enough to pay attention. I raise myself up on my elbows, scrutinizing her. She points at the water, and I take a long drink before answering.

"Yeah, sure. What's going on?"

"I've been monitoring the radio and radar while the rest of you have been...busy," she says, lowering her eyes. "I've noticed an unusual number of unmanned drones flying out to Titan. I thought the other planets must have noticed that something had happened. And today, we picked up a message from Deva." She glances up to check I'm still listening, and nods at the water. I drink. "They know Titan has been destroyed. There's going to be an Interplanetary Council on Deva. All of the leaders have already agreed to attend."

"An Interplanetary Council?" I repeat, trying to shake off the drunkenness and focus. This is a big deal. The last council was before my lifetime, held to determine whether or not Nibiru was at fault for the spread of the plague on Gaia. After that ended with Gaia closing its borders to visitors and the other planets soon following suit, no one was eager to try again. None of the current leaders have ever met in person before now.

"As long as we aren't delayed, we can make it on time," Lyre says.

"Leonis will be there instead of on Gaia." I sit up completely now, taking another long drink of water. "And we can land on Deva safely..." As a thought occurs to me, I pause. "What did Corvus say?"

"I haven't told him yet," she says. "I came to you first."

"Why?"

She hesitates for a long moment.

"Because I think you're the one who will do what's necessary."

"Me?" I nearly laugh. Me more than Corvus, the leader, the former soldier? Then I remember what he told me about his enlistment on Titan, and my amusement dries up. Maybe he's not the person I've been imagining him as.

"Corvus has barely left the medical bay since Titan," Lyre says. "He's crumbling. He has no plan. If you come up with one before he does..."

She trails off, letting me fill in the rest. She's telling me there's still a chance to seize control. To be the leader, just like I wanted for these last three years. I never imagined anyone else might want that for me, too—and yet here Lyre is, helping me. She chose me. Still, self-doubt creeps up.

"Momma wanted Corvus to be in charge," I say.

"Well…" Lyre pauses, biting her lip. "It doesn't matter what Momma wanted. She's not here. You are. And we're counting on you." Her face reddens, and she abruptly rises to her feet, turning away from me. "Try not to forget that," she says without looking back, and leaves me with my thoughts.

As badly as I wanted to lead this family for the last three years, the thought frightens me now. I failed my siblings on Gaia when I got us all arrested, and again on Titan when I walked away from that deal with Ives. We can't afford another screwup or crisis of conscience. Right now, we need someone as calculating and hard-willed as Momma. She always protected us. It was probably for her own selfish reasons, but she still managed to get us out of trouble, and stars know we're good at finding it. Maybe her iron grip on the family was the only way to keep us safe and together, especially when it comes to hard situations like this.

But since she's not here anymore, maybe I can be the next best thing after all.

CHAPTER TWENTY-SIX

Cracks

Corvus

I startle awake as I hear footsteps, fumbling for the knife at my hip. As Scorpia enters the doorway, both of us freeze.

I remove my hand from the knife's hilt. Our last conversation still seems to echo in the space between us. All that shouting and all those tears, followed by days of silence. I've been sinking into my grief here, sleeping in a metal chair beside the cryosleep chamber, checking Pol's vitals even though they never change.

I can't bring myself to leave his side or wander the rest of the ship. I'm too overwhelmed already without trying to absorb the fact that I'm here again under the worst possible circumstances. The ship looks just the same as I remember it. I've imagined returning to *Fortuna* so frequently over the last three years, but now that I'm here, it doesn't feel anything like home.

Only once, exhaustion drove me to try going to my own bedroom, but I found it filled with storage containers. No one bothered to clean it out for my return. The moment I realized the only other option was to sleep in either Pol's or Momma's room, I retreated back here.

I know my siblings need me right now. I know they're expecting me to take charge. But how am I supposed to lead them when I'm drowning in guilt? Again and again my mind returns to my team, to Pol, to Momma. I've replayed my last moments with her a hundred times. She told me she was proud of me; she chose to go alone to test the weapon. Did she know what that choice meant? Does it matter?

"Good morning," Scorpia says, pulling my attention back to her before I can sink any deeper into my thoughts. Her eyes are bloodshot and her hair greasy, rings around her eyes suggesting she hasn't been sleeping much better than I have, but at least she doesn't look drunk yet. Just hungover.

I clear my throat, shifting in my chair, but can't come up with anything to say.

"I, uh, wanted to let you know that I'm calling a family meeting," she says.

Which is what I should've done. Would've done, if I hadn't been wallowing in my emotions. I need to pull myself together.

"About?" The question comes out harsher than I intended, though my anger is directed at myself. But Scorpia, to my surprise, breaks into a small smile.

"I've got a plan," she says, and races upstairs before I can ask more. I heave a sigh and push myself to my feet, cracking my sore back before heading up to the kitchen.

Everyone is already waiting when I arrive. Lyre is perched on a chair with her knees pulled up to her chest, chewing a thumbnail. Drom has her chin propped up with one hand and her shoulders slumped. Scorpia is standing at the head of the table, right behind Momma's seat, with a mug of coffee in her hands. She shifts from foot to foot, full of either nerves or excitement or both.

The moment I take a seat at the opposite end of the table, she bursts out:

"Okay, so this is a little crazy, but I think it's all we got."

Our younger siblings glance from her to me. After a moment's hesitance, I nod.

"Go on."

Her smile widens, verging on manic.

"So, last time we talked, we decided going to Gaia was our best option," she says. "The problem was how to land on Gaia without being instantly killed, and we still don't have a solution to that. But!" She raises a finger dramatically. "As Lyre told me this morning, Leonis isn't going to be on Gaia by the time we get to that part of the system, anyway. She's going to be on Deva, where the leaders of all the planets are meeting to discuss the fate of Titan."

Suspicion nudges me. Neither Lyre nor Scorpia shared this information with me before now. They've been talking together, without me. I glance at Lyre, but her eyes remain on Scorpia.

"You think we can land on Gaia while she's absent?" I ask, unwilling to be completely cut out of this conversation.

"No, no. I'm sure she's given orders to shoot us on sight. But we *can* land on Deva, and we might be able to get to Leonis there. She won't be expecting us."

"We could also get to the other planetary leaders." Hope sparks inside me. I'm not sure why Scorpia is fixated on Leonis when there are so many other opportunities. "We can go in front of the council, testify about what happened on Titan. We have the vial as proof—"

"No," Scorpia says. The interruption sends a wave of anger through me; I'm not used to being cut off. But I bite my tongue, letting her speak. Quarreling will help no one. "First of all, that plan hinges on the other leaders actually believing us, which is unlikely. Who's gonna trust a bunch of criminal off-worlders?" She glances around the room. "Like Momma always said, they're never gonna accept us. We've only got each other. Right now, Pol needs us, and the person with the best shot at saving him is Leonis."

"The woman who just eliminated an entire planet's worth of people," I say slowly, wanting to make sure she understands what she's saying. When she suggested going to Gaia, I never imagined she meant negotiating directly with President Leonis. We've seen where deals with her lead.

"You know, I've also been thinking about why that is." She walks as she talks, pacing the length of the table. All eyes follow her. "There was some weird shit happening on Gaia last time we were there. Dead crops, et cetera. And food has always been Gaia's major problem. So why would Leonis make a move against Titan? Titans don't have much to eat, either. But they do have one thing going for them."

"Ice?" Drom suggests flatly.

"Aside from that." Scorpia smiles at her, but she doesn't return it.

"Raw materials," I murmur, thinking back on Altair's plan to escape Titan. "Enough to build a fleet."

"Yes." Scorpia snaps her fingers and points at me. "That must be what she wanted. But building a fleet takes time. Leonis won't make any drastic moves right away. I say we talk to her now, blackmail her with the vial and the info we have, make her fix Pol. Then we get the hell out before this war really gets going, and find somewhere safe to hide until it's over."

"Or we could go forward with what we know," I say. "Ruin all of Leonis's plans before she can begin them."

Scorpia's expression dims, like she's surprised I don't agree with her. But what the hell is she thinking? Leonis destroyed Titan. Betrayed us. She killed Momma, nearly killed Pol. If I could get close enough, I'd murder Leonis myself, not bargain with her.

"You're not getting it," she says, holding my gaze. "Even if the other planets *do* believe our story, it implicates us, too. We're the ones who brought that weapon to Titan." She shakes her head. "If we go forward, Pol dies, and the rest of us will end up in jail."

"Look, I care about Apollo as much as any of you—"

"Do you?" Drom interrupts. She sits up straighter, leveling me with a glare. "'Cause it didn't look like that back on Titan."

"That…" Guilt gnaws at me as my mind replays our fight again. I had never hurt one of my siblings before. Never. "That was a mistake. But—"

"We can't afford to make any more mistakes right now," Scorpia says. "We've only got one shot at this." There's a triumphant look in her eye. Too late, I see this for what it is: She's taking control, right now, right in front of me. I thought I didn't want the responsibility, but I forgot what it's like to be forced to follow orders you don't agree with. And I never imagined Scorpia would be like this. She's going to lead us on a suicide mission.

I need to stay calm. Find a way to get through to her and the others rather than letting the divide between us become deeper. I need to stop this from happening.

"I know this is a difficult situation for all of us," I say. "And I know I've been gone for a long time." Lyre and Drom probably don't even know the truth about that, I realize. "I want you all to know it was never my decision to stay behind on Titan. I…I had to." I can't bring myself to blame Momma directly with her loss still so fresh, but I pause to let it sink in before I continue. "Now I'm back, and I need you all to listen to me when I tell you this is not the path we want to go down. I've seen where this line of thinking leads."

I look around, gauging their expressions. Drom's face shifts from confusion to shock as she understands my confession about Titan. Lyre's face is guarded, unreadable. Scorpia studies them, sipping her coffee, and waits.

"Stars," Drom mutters finally. "No wonder you're so fucked up."

Despite my best intentions, anger flares in my chest. I just poured my heart out, made a plea for morality, and that's all she has to say?

"I'm fucked up?" I push out from my chair and stand, slamming my hands on the table with a resounding bang. "Scorpia's talking about negotiating with Leonis, and *I'm* fucked up?"

As my shouts die down to echoes and then utter silence, I notice the way they're all looking at me—their mingled expressions of horror and pity. My stomach sinks. No one's going to respect someone they pity. No one's going to follow me.

"Well," Scorpia says, and sips her coffee. She circles behind Momma's chair and leans against the back of it. "Anyone else opposed?"

"I think we should at least arrange to speak with Leonis," Lyre says. She glances at me, but quickly looks away again. "It seems like a logical course of action. She knows the most about the weapon."

"If you think it'll save Pol, I'm all for it," Drom says. She's sitting up straighter now, no longer quite so defeated.

"Okay." Scorpia meets my eyes across the length of the table. "I'll set course for Deva, then."

"This is fucking ridiculous," I say. "I can't believe you. Any of you. I thought you were better than this."

Before any of them can respond, I storm away from the table. Scorpia takes a step toward me, as if to follow, but stops.

I walk straight to Momma's room, anger overriding my hesitance to enter her space. As the door shuts behind me, I lean back against it, taking deep breaths to calm the storm brewing in my head.

On Titan, I justified every horrible thing I did as a way to return to my family. Now I'm here, and we're heading down a road no better than the war I left. And just like on Titan, I'm pushed to the outside. Walled off from the rest. There, I was too much of a Kaiser to ever be truly Titan. Now, it seems I'm not really a Kaiser, either. I belong nowhere.

Maybe I don't deserve their acceptance. Maybe the war has taken too much of me, and the violence that's taken root inside me will grow and grow until it's the only thing left. It certainly feels like it right now, with anger taking up so much of my chest that it's difficult to breathe.

I sweep my eyes over the room, searching for...I'm not sure exactly what, but I know I came here looking for something. Some window into Momma's mind? Something to help me understand? I thought I had moved past her betrayal, but now the wound has been torn open again. How could she not only throw me into the war, but let my siblings believe I abandoned them by choice? I'll never get a chance to ask now.

Nor will I ever know the truth about our last moments together on Titan. How much did she know about those vials? Did she understand the choice she was making when she went with Altair rather than sending me? Whether it was intentional or not, I would be dead if not for her...and Titan would be alive. I can't seem to rectify those two truths.

Whatever answer I'm seeking, I don't find it here. Her bedroom is almost completely empty, hardly different than the bunks belonging to me and the rest of my siblings. It's disappointing somehow. I slide open the closet, but the thought of going through her clothes feels invasive, so I shut it again. I can't bring myself to pull out the bed, either; now that I'm here, I can't imagine sleeping where she did.

Trying to ground myself, I cross over to the sink and splash water on my face. The face in the mirror is worn down, world-weary; older than I remember looking, but not as old as I feel. Frown lines are starting to form around my mouth, replicas of the ones that marked Momma's face. I drop my eyes from the reflection before opening the medicine cabinet behind the mirror and rifling through it. It holds some pill bottles—none of them labeled—and a small, half-empty bottle of rare Gaian wheat whiskey, which gives me pause. Shoved into the very back, hidden and folded in half, is a photograph. I pause, hesitating briefly, and unfold it. My breath catches.

It's me and my siblings as children on Nibiru. I'm standing on the middle, smiling, one arm around Pol's shoulders and the other holding Drom far enough away that she couldn't pinch him, as she loved to do right as someone snapped a photograph. Lyre stands to the left, her round face almost comically serious, while Scorpia displays a huge, crooked grin and two thumbs up to our right. Momma must have taken it, because she's nowhere to be found in the picture itself.

I put it back. Shut the cabinet. There's a hollow feeling in my chest that grows and grows as I stare at the sunken eyes in my reflection. I'm not sure what hurts more: the knowledge that Momma, always so opposed to sentimentality, still kept that picture here, or the fact that her face isn't in it. She kept this for herself but left us nothing.

Anger blooms to fill the emptiness. One of my fists lashes out, and glass cracks beneath my fist. The pain is satisfying, distracting, so I hit it again, shattering the mirror.

The trip to Deva passes in a blur. The ship may be full, but it feels empty, and my siblings and I lurk through the quiet hallways like ghosts. Scorpia spends her time either in her room or the cockpit, with liquor on her breath and little to say to any of us. Lyre has been sleeping down in the engine room, obsessively monitoring the radio for further news. Drom only shows her face during brief visits to the kitchen.

And I am alone with my nightmares. They haunt me every time I fall asleep in my brother's bed, a thousand accusatory faces floating behind my closed eyes. The grief I've been trying to hold at bay rolls over me, as if the ghosts of my past can sense what my family is about to do. Pol, Momma, my team, the general, all the innocent lives wiped out on Titan. Sometimes in sleep I relive old memories. I let Ivennie die, pull the trigger on Hort, feel the impact of my fist hitting Apollo's jaw a hundred times over.

Other times, a black cloud spreads to envelop Titan. General Altair's accusatory eyes meet mine as it consumes him. I stand helpless while my team crumples to the floor, Magda using her last breath to call me a traitor before falling facedown in a puddle of black goo.

Others still, my hands are wrapped around Momma's neck. As she dies, she uses the last of her strength to reach out and touch my face, her eyes smiling as the light fades from them. *"I'm so proud of you"* echoes in my ears.

Regardless of the nightmare, I wake up with a scream building in my throat more often than not. As the days go on, my reflection grows more haunted and haggard. Shadows pool beneath my bloodshot eyes and in the hollows of my cheeks, and my beard grows bristly and unkempt. I should take care of myself more. I should take care of my siblings, be strong for them. But I can't. Not anymore. I've lost too much.

When I left the army, I felt cracks forming beneath my surface. Now, I fear that I'm on the verge of breaking. And this would be a terrible time to shatter.

CHAPTER TWENTY-SEVEN

The Golden City

Scorpia

I squint at the mirror in my palm, an eyeliner pencil trembling in my other hand. No matter how hard I try, I never seem to get this shit right. Devans make it look easy, but this is the only place where I bother with cosmetics, and I've never been fond of them.

If we were traveling to one of the small villages nestled in the Devan jungle, our usual planet-side getup would work just fine. But we're not traveling to some simple little village barely keeping the plants at bay; we're headed to Zi Vi, the Golden City, Deva's capital and crown jewel. In a city where appearances are everything, the only way to blend in is to look like we're trying as hard as everyone else to stand out.

"Lyre!" I call out across the cargo bay, lowering the pencil. "Help me out, will you?"

"Busy." I glance over to find her standing on her tiptoes, preoccupied with painting Drom's eyes and lips. "Drom, stop fidgeting."

"I will when you stop poking me in the fucking eye."

I sigh and glance over at Corvus. He's barely spoken to me, or any of us, on the trip from Titan, though I've heard him crying out in his sleep. I wasn't sure what to expect from him today, but he seems as ready to go as the rest of us. He's already adorned his eyes with dramatic black rings and contoured his cheeks with sharp lines of glittering highlighter. Rather than making him look ridiculous, as it rightfully should, it suits his glower. Of course he's as good at this as he is at everything else, and here I am struggling to line my eyes. I take some petty satisfaction in the fact that his beard is still unkempt and his clothes don't sit quite right on his shoulders anymore. He looks deeply uncomfortable in his Devan outfit, which exposes a generous amount of his stomach.

Lyre, of course, looks amazing. She always goes all out for her home-planet. She insists it's a matter of practicality and keeping a good reputation here, but I suspect she enjoys it more than she lets on. Her face is painted with decadent gold, her body wrapped in a complicated dress made from multiple pieces of colorful fabric.

"So do we have a plan?" Drom asks, once Lyre is done with her makeup. She reaches a hand up to itch her face, only for Lyre to slap it down again.

I swallow, trying to shake off my nerves. Though my siblings support me, and I've taken charge of the family for now, my grip on leadership is precarious at best. Worse yet, I'm nowhere near as confident in this plan as I'm trying to pretend I am. Part of me fears that Corvus is right, and getting involved with Leonis will only result in disaster.

She's a monster that manipulated us into killing an entire planet. The thought of making a deal with her turns my stomach, too. But as I tried to explain to him, we don't have any other options. And if Momma were here, she'd find a way to save our family, no matter what it took. No one ever ended up dead or infected with some alien disease on her watch. Now taking care of my siblings is my job, and I'm not going to let them down, even if it means making choices that rip me apart inside.

So I'll make a deal with a monster if I must. I'm not going to let my conscience get in the way this time, like it did with Ives. If I hadn't failed then, we might have more options now.

"We're heading to an off-worlder-friendly bar Momma used to frequent," I say. "We'll watch the council meeting there, see how it goes, pay attention to what any other interplanetary visitors have to say. If suspicion falls on Leonis, she'll get desperate. Make our job easier." Or it might make Corvus's plan more viable, but I hurry on before he gets a chance to speak up. "After that, we look for an opportunity to speak to Leonis alone. If we don't get one, we'll have to force something. Then we threaten her with what we have."

Including the alien vial. I'm all too aware of the devastating power we brought to Deva. I'm leaving it on *Fortuna*, since no one has any reason to search our ship as long as we avoid too much attention, and I'm not too keen on carrying it around when we have no idea how this will go. But we can't afford to let anyone stay to watch it. Lyre's our ticket on-planet, Drom's muscle is a necessity in a place like this, and—as much as it pains me to admit—I just don't trust Corvus with it. He seems like a ticking time bomb lately, and I want to keep an eye on him.

Once Lyre helps me with some half-assed makeup, we open the ramp, letting in a wave of heat and moisture. The landing zone is lined with freshly cut jungle, its edges expanded to allow for many more ships than usual for the Interplanetary Council. The thick black foliage surrounding the area seems hungry, like it's waiting for its chance to retake the clearing.

It's hard not to gawk as we step into the landing zone. I don't think I've ever seen so many ships in one place. Scarce as travelers like us are these days, it's easy to forget how impressive spacecrafts can get. There are enough to outnumber the drones. Even aside from the official government vessels, I suspect anyone with any way to access Deva is eager to be here for the show. The landing zone holds everything from a transport ship so blocky and angular it must be Gaian, to a flat, disklike vessel I suspect is of Nibiran design. Thankfully, I don't spot the familiar ungainly bulk of the *Red Baron* anywhere among them. We have more than enough on our plate without the pirates interfering.

The landing zone has extra security patrols, and the customs agents seem tense. But they relax once Lyre shows them her proof of citizenship and the ship's registration. While she talks to them, my eyes snag on a television screen in one corner of the room. I frown as I read the words scrolling across it: *Record-breaking storm on Gaia leads to multiple casualties. President Leonis remains silent on third fatal weather event this week.*

Shock fills me as the words sink in. Gaia's weather is usually mild, and I can't imagine a storm intense enough to kill people on such an organized, high-tech planet. What the hell is happening over there? I think about everything I've already put together about Leonis's plan. Is it all linked somehow? Intuition tells me yes, but how could natural disasters be related to everything else? There was strange weather on Gaia while I was there, too, but nothing like this. Perhaps the storms are what ruined the crop fields, making Leonis desperate enough to attack Titan...

My attention returns to the Devan agents as the time comes to renew my work visa and the registry on my blaster, which is legal to carry openly in Zi Vi. Once that's settled, we head into the Golden City.

Glittering buildings stand tall against the cloudy sky. Between them stretch twisting metal walkways crowded with people. In a place where time has little meaning, the city is always busy. Some Devans are finishing their workdays, others just beginning, still more stumbling drunk or sleeping in the tiny, jammed-together apartments that line the streets. The near-constant drizzle of rain provides ample breeding grounds for rust and plant overgrowth even in such an overpopulated area. Despite the nonstop efforts of city workers to keep the jungle at bay, vines crawl over the walkways, and weeds sprout in the narrow cracks between buildings, stark black against the otherwise-colorful city.

We pass by neon signs and billboards, each of them screaming promises in bold letters, endorsed by the plastic smiles of gorgeous celebrities: SPICIEST FOOD ON DEVA! BEST LIVE SHOWS IN ZI VI! PUREST SANITA IN THE CITY!

Like most beautiful things here, it's best to assume they're all lies. The truth of Deva is far uglier: a drunk vomiting off the curving pathway onto the head of an unsuspecting man on the crossing below; a hovercraft racing by so quickly that several people skin their knees diving out of its way; a thin child begging for food on the steps of a luxury apartment complex. And occasionally, when the pathway takes us high enough, we get a look at the dark jungles closing like a noose around the city. They serve both as a constant threat and a reminder of the less fortunate living in tiny, overgrown villages in its depths, dreaming of the neon city that will never be more than a speck of light glimpsed through tangled foliage.

By the time we make it near the center of the city, my clothes are sticking to my skin, and I'm choking on the humidity and the smell of so many warm bodies pressed together. The first walkway we try is closed off for clearing. Beyond the glowing, bright green cones stretched across the path, quarantine-suited workers spray the intruding strangle-vines with chemicals. Even in Deva's most developed city, the jungle constantly grapples for control.

We're stopped again halfway down the next walkway, this time by a line of police wearing all black. Law enforcement is a rare sight anywhere on Deva; they must be in place just for the Interplanetary Council, to keep the crowd under control. People still press as close as they can get, snapping pictures with their comms though the Hall is barely visible from here.

Corvus's expression is dark as his eyes land on City Hall. When a passerby trying to snag a picture bumps into him, he shoves her and sends her stumbling.

"Hey, watch it," I tell him, but he doesn't even look at me. I sigh. Zi Vi is notoriously chaotic and difficult to navigate even without roadblocks like these, so it'll be damn near impossible to find a way there now. For me, that is. "Lyre, do you know another route?" I was hoping to project some false confidence by taking us there myself, but this place is giving me a headache.

"Of course," Lyre says with a smile, and leads us there with ease.

The bar, which a neon-blue sign declares THE SALTY BASTARD, looks like an especially good place to get stabbed, even considering we're on a planet where public dueling is legal. It also has a sign boasting THE CHEAPEST WHISKEY IN ZI VI. I took only a couple swigs of rum to find my courage earlier, intending to stay sober enough to focus on the mission, but I didn't plan on that. I can practically taste the corn whiskey.

"We're going to miss the broadcast," Corvus presses me when I pause.

"Yeah, yeah, yeah." No helping it now; hesitating further will make me look weak.

The bar is stuffed with a wild assortment of patrons, all wearing the same over-the-top cosmetics and clothing we've put on ourselves. Despite the general reek of spilled liquor, Sanita smoke, and piss, not to mention the sorry state of the furniture, the place contains no fewer than three huge screens playing the broadcast. One especially rowdy table seems to have turned it into a drinking game, though most of the crowd is watching with a seriousness that doesn't fit the locale.

I push through the crowd toward the closest screen, my siblings close on my heels. The sight of Leonis standing with her hands folded behind her back and an expression of polite solemnity makes me grit my teeth in anger. Beside her stand two reps from among the seven who make up the Nibiran Council, both wearing the planet's colorful, floor-sweeping robes. Ennia Heikki, a bronze-toned, matronly woman with a head of wild silver curls, is the oldest of their council; Iri Oshiro, fair-skinned and agender with long, straight black hair, is the youngest. The Paxians have sent a lean, middle-aged woman with a rich brown complexion, who the screen identifies as Representative Silvania Azenari. I'm not sure who she is, given that Pax has no formal leader. When she turns to the side, I shudder at the electronic device implanted in the back of her head. Wires extend down beneath the back of her black suit. I guess even Pax's elite are into those crazy modifications of theirs.

The council is only waiting on Jai Misha, the Devan prime minister, who is now ten minutes late to a meeting on his own planet.

"Misha's still in office?" Corvus asks, surprised. Devan politicians aren't known for their longevity. "People must love him."

"He's a joke," I say. The sight of Leonis has my throat itching, so I give in and snatch a shot from a nearby table too drunk and focused on the broadcast to notice. "But I guess a well-received one, since nobody's put a knife in his back yet." I shrug and down it, sighing in contentment afterward. Damn, even cheap whiskey on Deva is alarmingly good.

"Well, look what we have here! Our good friends, the Kaisers."

I tense, whirling guiltily to face the approaching bar patrons and hiding the empty shot glass behind my back. My nerves recede as I recognize them, and I break into a relieved smile.

"Well, if it isn't Eri and Halon. Been a while, huh?" *Friends* is a stretch, but the pair of arms dealers are old contacts of my mother's. They aren't enemies, at least, so I happily give them each a warm Devan greeting, clasping their hands and kissing them on both cheeks. Eridanus Vasquez is a fair, freckled man with a bristling beard and a hint of a Paxian lilt to his speech. His Devan husband is slim and dark-skinned, with clever eyes and a warm smile.

"It has, it has," Eri says with a nod. He embraces each of my siblings in turn, including a rather reluctant Drom. "And the soldier's returned, I see. Glad to find you well. But where are Apollo and Auriga?"

My smile turns fragile and strained. I've known Eri and Halon since childhood. If I let them know that Momma's dead and Pol's in danger, they might help us out with our situation. On the other hand, they might see it as a vulnerability to exploit. How am I supposed to decide the best course of action? I pause, my silence lasting a beat too long, and wonder—what would Momma do?

"Pol's watching the ship," I lie. "And, well...Momma decided it was high time for her to enjoy her retirement."

So many times, Momma told us to trust only one another. That's more important now than ever.

"Retirement?" Eri asks, so shocked for a moment that I worry he won't believe me. "I can't blame her for it, but what a shame! She was a great businesswoman. Though I suppose we should be glad to lose some competition." He lets out a booming laugh. "Well, with Auriga out of the picture, it's a good thing you have Corvus back to take care of you all."

My smile fractures. I'm saved from having to respond by a cheer from the crowd around us. I turn to see that the beloved Devan prime minister has finally made an appearance at the council, and now beams from every screen in the room.

Jai Misha is a slender man in his midforties, but if not for the hints of silver creeping into his dark hair and carefully groomed beard, the spring in his step would make him seem much younger. There's a sense of barely contained urgency about him, from the sharpness in his small, dark eyes to the wild gesticulations he makes even when speaking quietly. Today he wears a cream-colored suit with a pattern of flowers that glint metallic in the light, a perfect complement to his brown skin. He clomps his way into the meeting room in a pair of platform boots with dramatic heels.

The Paxian rep is the only one who appears unruffled by his late entrance. In fact, she favors him with a smile that seems surprisingly friendly. The two Nibiran council members exchange uncertain looks, though neither seems eager to speak up. When the camera shifts to Leonis once more, my stomach goes cold with hatred at the sight of her face, the emotion intense enough that I can't savor how thoroughly annoyed she seems with this whole ordeal.

Leonis used us as her tools. Tried to kill us. And right now, I can't even hope that this council will punish her for it—both because I doubt it will ever happen, and because, as I told Corvus, we need her.

Then the camera view shifts, and I freeze. There, on the screen, is a very familiar face among the small Gaian delegation waiting on the council's sidelines. Shey Leonis is here. On Deva.

And now I have an inkling of a plan.

But it's a plan dangerous enough that my siblings don't need to be involved. I glance around, and find all of their eyes locked on the screen as the council begins. Corvus's expression is stormy, Lyre's pensive, and Drom is fighting her way to the bar for a drink. I take a deep breath and head for the door, stealing two more shots along the way. Right now, I can use all the courage I can get.

CHAPTER TWENTY-EIGHT

Diplomacy

Corvus

In a crowded bar full of drunken revelry, I watch foreign politicians judge my people. The chatter of the Devans around me fades into background noise as I strain to follow the conversation on the screen. In cold, clinical voices, the representatives discuss how they initially learned of the destruction. Leonis noticed it first, she says, when an unmanned delivery drone to Titan was never received by local officials. She sent word to the other planets, who sent their own drones to investigate.

They all reported back the same thing. The icy tundra is untouched; the underground cities and armored forts still stand. The Paxian representative even reports finding signs of animal life and untouched greenhouses, sparse as they were on Titan to begin with.

But the people are dead. Millions of bodies lying in the snow with black goo frozen on their stiff faces. In the cities, in the forts, in the tunneled-cave villages and all the open space in between. Some ran, and some hid, and all of them died. There's no sign of a single human being left alive on Titan.

I shut my eyes, thinking of Magda, Daniil, Sverre, Altair. Momma. Pol, frozen and still. All the people I've lost. Now Scorpia wants to make a deal with the woman who did it. I've stayed quiet, let her believe I'm willing to go along with it. But there's still time for another option. Scorpia was right—going forward with our information will implicate us. I won't force my siblings to do that. But if I can drag Leonis down with me, I'll gladly turn myself in. All I need is some suspicion to fall on Leonis. Once it does, my information will have more weight.

"So whatever this was, it targeted humans specifically," Misha muses, sipping a glass of shimmering fireberry wine as he listens to descriptions of genocide. "Perhaps intentionally. A weapon of some sort."

"Are we really meant to believe the Titans had the technology to create something like this?" Leonis's voice floods my chest with hot anger—and shock that she would be the first one to imply blame rests on one of the other planets. But I see her intent as Misha and the Nibirans immediately cast glances in the direction of the Paxian representative. Anyway, given Leonis's history of distrust toward the other planets, I suppose it would be stranger if she didn't make accusations.

Eri makes a disgruntled noise beside me, folding his arms over his chest. His home-world, Pax, is well-known for manufacturing the majority of the system's laser weapons and playing a bit too hard with genetic engineering—an easy scapegoat.

"If we had a weapon of such power, I assure you we would not place it in the hands of the Titans," Azenari says coolly. "Nor would they have the means to pay for it."

"A very fair point," Halon says with a nod. I grit my teeth. But as much as the arms dealers rub me the wrong way, it's important for me to listen to their comments. Public opinion is the best way for me to gauge whether or not the council will believe my story.

I'm surprised Scorpia isn't here listening in as well—but maybe she's already so set on her plan that she doesn't care. She must be at the bar getting herself a drink.

"Perhaps it was not a weapon at all, then," Leonis says. She seems eager to drive the conversation, keep suspicion off herself. "Maybe it was a disease, and we are seeing the aftermath." Now she looks pointedly at the Nibiran council members. Oshiro's pale face splotches with anger.

"How dare you once again accuse—"

"Now, now," Misha says, flapping his hands. "Let us not dredge up old grudges. The last council meeting already put the matter of the plague to rest."

"Yes, I do recall that your planets all agreed," Leonis says icily. "But if such an *accident* could happen once, why not again? Nibiru sells algae rations to Titan, does it not? A drone shipment could have carried a disease."

"We have no evidence that any algae harvests have been tainted. I'll provide the necessary records to prove it," Heikki says, resting a hand on Oshiro's shoulder. I study Oshiro's face, hoping to find a potential ally, but their expression is unreadable now. "Regardless, given how quickly this happened, it seems ridiculous to blame it on a simple disease. But, on the other hand, Gaia is the closest to Titan. I'm sure you had dealings. And with your love for that wicked alien technology—"

"You believe we would let such a precious resource fall into Titan hands?" Leonis asks, her voice loud and furious. I'm sure she doesn't have to fake it when that accusation drifted so close to the truth. I lean forward, hope surging up. This is it. Someone needs to see through her lies. "Gaia would never have a hand in such barbarism. And why would we give them a weapon that they could use against us? The Titans were always jealous of our world."

"I'm almost offended that no one has accused me yet," Misha says.

A group of drunkards in the corner laughs, and I grimace at the derailing of the conversation. This must be how the man has maintained a foothold in the dangerous world of Devan politics. He's more of an entertainer than a leader, and Devans do love their entertainment. The other planetary leaders, on the other hand, are less than amused by Misha's antics.

"Your comments help no one, Prime Minister," Heikki says.

"Perhaps he does have a point," says Azenari. "Deva has always struggled to harvest natural minerals, with those plants overtaking the mines. It could have been easier to use Titan as a resource."

"Such extreme lengths to avoid paying a pittance for raw materials? I think not," Misha says, looking rather pleased at having successfully taken the spotlight. The Paxian scrutinizes him while the two Nibirans murmur among themselves. Leonis clears her throat.

"It is possible I spoke too hastily," she says. "In reality, we all know Titan was a difficult planet. There would be little strategic value for any of us to take it. And, with that horrible war, the Titans have seemed on the path to this end for a while now."

There is a long pause. I wait, holding my breath, hoping that someone—anyone—will call Leonis out on her lies, or at least speak up for my people. Let them give us the benefit of the doubt, see us as more than a planet hell-bent on self-destruction. If a single person believes there's more to the story, it will give me a chance to go forward with the truth.

"The Titans have always been creative about finding ways to kill each other," the Paxian says. "Perhaps they finally became too good at it."

The two Nibirans confer briefly. I keep my eyes on Oshiro, who seems the most likely to go against the grain after that earlier outburst against Leonis.

"The most obvious answer is often the most correct one," Oshiro says, though they sound reluctant. My heart sinks.

"We will discuss further, of course, but unless new evidence surfaces, I see no reason to suspect one another," Misha says with a shrug. "Now, moving forward..."

I turn away in disgust. Not one of them defended Titan. So quick to accuse one another, to place blame—but where is the grief? The regret? The sympathy? There's a heat in my chest and a buzzing in my ears that have been growing ever since we arrived here—no, ever since Scorpia decided that she would rather make a deal with Leonis than make her pay. Damn Leonis, and all those other smiling politicians so eager to pass Titan off as a planet of barbarism, as an inevitable conclusion rather than a horrible tragedy. Damn Scorpia. Damn them all. I'm the only one left in this system to know how much was lost. I'm the sole mourner for good people like General Altair, and my team, and so many innocent lives.

Maybe Scorpia was right. Even if we told the truth, there was never a chance that anyone would believe us. Just like the Titans, no one has ever given my family the benefit of the doubt. They'll never trust us. But I'm not going to be part of a deal with Leonis. I can't. Not even for Pol. If bringing the truth to the council isn't an option, then I'll find another one.

Such as killing Leonis. The moment the thought occurs to me, it feels right. Even if the world doesn't know what she did, I can make her suffer for it. If I can get close enough, it will be simple. It's what I'm good at. What I've been trained to do. Afterward I'll be imprisoned or killed myself, of course, but a death to avenge my people wouldn't be such a terrible thing. And my family doesn't need me anymore; they have Scorpia now.

"So sad," Eridanus says, tugging on his beard and dragging my thoughts back to the bar. "With Titan off the market, we may have to reconsider our profession."

"Not if this ends in war," Halon says. Catching my glance, he hastily adds, "Not that I would ever hope for such a thing. God forbid." He shudders. "Things are looking quite bleak, though. Did you see how quickly they went for one another's throats? And on an interplanetary broadcast, no less."

Their conversation shifts into lowered tones, and I turn to my sisters. Lyre is standing with her arms folded over her chest, and Drom is nursing a beer in silence.

"We need to get out of here," I say. "Before—" Before I do something stupid. "Before the representatives head back to their ships. Maybe we can catch Leonis on her way there." And make her pay, regardless of what Scorpia wants. My brow furrows as I realize I don't see her anywhere. I crane my neck to look at the bar.

"Looks like Scorpia is a couple steps ahead of you," Lyre says.

"What?" My head snaps back toward her.

"She left right after the meeting started. Without a word." She looks none too pleased about that. I'm not sure what she expected when she started supporting Scorpia.

"I was focused on the broadcast. Isn't that why we came here?" I let out a frustrated sigh. Leave it to Scorpia to wander astray from her own plan…Unless she's already moving forward without us. My chest tightens. I need to stop her. "So where the hell did she go?"

"She seemed stressed out," Drom offers. "Maybe she went to sample the wares."

"What wares?"

My sisters exchange a look.

"She's talking about prostitutes," Lyre says. Seeing the look on my face, she adds more defensively, "Perfectly legal here. There's nothing wrong with it."

"There is when we have a very important, very time-sensitive purpose," I say through gritted teeth. Time is running out. "Stop joking around."

"You can be real Gaian about these things sometimes," Drom says.

"Must be those Gaian sensibilities of yours," Magda teases in my memory.

I lunge toward her without thinking, without considering what I plan to do. Lyre steps in between us and grabs my arm; Drom's eyes go wide. The look on her face, more than Lyre's grip, holds me in place.

"What the hell is wrong with you?" Lyre snaps.

"You don't get it." My heart drums an angry beat in my chest. It's all too much. Those drunks, the arms dealers—now not even my family is taking this seriously. The crowded bar presses in on me from all sides. "None of you fucking get it." I look at Drom, who is feigning indifference as she sips her beer. "Never call me Gaian again."

"Yeah, yeah," Drom mutters, avoiding eye contact. She rubs one thumb over a scar on her arm. "Just a joke."

Lyre releases me to pull out her comm and frown at it.

"Scorpia messaged me," she says. "She wants us to meet her in an apartment building near the landing zone. Says it's urgent." She sighs. "What has she done now?"

"Let's go find out," I say, and head for the door with them on my heels, shoving my way through the crowd. The rising chatter is making my head pound; the heat of bodies is stifling. But most of all, I'm thinking of what Scorpia could be doing right now. Of course she would move ahead by herself. Take away any chance I have at a better option. It might already be too late for me to stop her. Too late for all of us.

As I pass by the table of drunks, one of them breaks into a botched version of the Titan planetary anthem, peppered with a generous amount of profanity.

My feet come to a stop. All thoughts flee my head. I move by instinct.

I grab a fistful of the closest man's hair and slam his face into the wooden table. Twice, and a third time, and just as there's a satisfying crack of his nose breaking, his friends overcome their shock and lunge at me.

The first one trips over his own feet in a drunken stupor, but the second manages to entangle himself with me, and we go down in a heap at Drom's feet. She steps back, her face impassive, and leaves me to my own mess.

Not that I have any problems handling it on my own. These men are Devans, made soft by the decadent Zi Vi lifestyle, and so drunk they can barely keep track of their own fists. They're lucky I decide not to pull my weapon. Instead, I leave one howling on the ground with a broken wrist, and rise to my feet before the other one manages to stand. I seize him by the collar the moment he does, and throw him across the nearest table, sending glasses shattering to the floor and patrons scattering. He lies still on his back, groaning, beer dripping off the table beneath him. The last member of the group is still sitting at the table, clutching his bloodied face.

But now the owners of that spilled beer are standing to meet me, and other furious eyes watch from the rest of the suddenly quiet bar. Too late, I remember a lesson Momma taught me on our first visit to Deva: *"You won't get arrested for something as mundane as a bar fight, but you will get your ass kicked for ruining someone's good time."*

I glance over my shoulder for support, stomach sinking as I realize I just sabotaged my own plan without even thinking about it. Drom is doing her best to pretend not to know me, and the arms dealers are slipping out the door. Lyre stands with her comm in her hand and a resigned look on her face.

"I'll tell Scorpia we're going to be late," she says.

CHAPTER TWENTY-NINE

Blood Ties

Scorpia

Five, ten, fifteen minutes pass in an increasingly tense quiet. The apartment complex I told Shey to meet me in is empty except for a few homeless Devans camped out in the floors below. It was easy enough to find an abandoned building on the outskirts of the city, where struggling against the jungle is an everyday occurrence. This complex was initially shut down for dolor-tree infestation, and the city must have seized the property, likely because the owner couldn't pay to handle the issue. Now, the tall building is acquiring dust and waiting for someone to buy it. Knowing Zi Vi, it won't take too long. I shift and check my comm, receiving nothing, barely resisting the urge to message Shey again or check in with my siblings. The shots I took in that bar are hitting me harder than I expected—Devans certainly like their shit *strong*—and my spinning head isn't doing me any favors as I wait. Finally, I hear footsteps on the stairs.

Even knowing what I have planned, seeing Shey again makes my heart jump against my ribs. She's wearing her usual stiff Gaian clothing and gloves, her thick hair frizzing in the humidity. Her look is beyond understated on a planet like this, yet I know I'd pick her face out of any crowd.

She steps forward and holds her gloved hands out toward me, palms facing the sky and fingers spread. The gesture sends a jolt of surprise through me. I know that gesture—a traditional Gaian greeting, but unlike the crossed arms she gave me last time, this one is informal, familiar. It's a greeting for your family and friends—your "in-group," as Gaians think of it. No one has ever greeted me like that before. I've never been accepted in such a way by a Gaian.

When she sees my shock, Shey closes her hands into fists and crosses her arms in a smooth transition to the more formal greeting, mistaking my surprise for a rejection. I quickly hold my hands out, mirroring the gesture she first performed. It feels strange and alien, as if I must be doing something wrong, but Shey's dazzling smile soothes my worry. I force a smile of my own as we both let our arms fall to our sides.

"Well," she says, looking me over in a way that really shouldn't make my pulse race, given the situation. "This Devan style suits you."

"You should've tried it yourself," I say with a half smile. "Though I imagine the Devans are jealous of all the attention that outfit brings. A Gaian on Deva. Never thought I'd see the day."

"Me neither," she admits. "I doubt my mother would have ever brought me here if not for..." She halts as if realizing she's saying something she shouldn't.

"The storms on Gaia? Yeah, I saw the newscast." I search her face for any hints about what might be happening, but she only nods, her expression guarded.

"What in the world is a 'dolor-tree,' by the way?" she asks, in an obvious attempt to change the subject. "Should I be concerned about this infestation?"

"Just don't touch any of those curly leaves along the stairwell. Very painful, very toxic. The rash can last over a year."

"Stars above," Shey murmurs, with a wary glance around the area. "I wish I could say that's the worst thing I've heard of on this planet. And their food is also...quite something. Everything is either sickeningly sweet or painfully spicy."

"Devans aren't fond of subtlety," I say with a laugh. As soon as I realize how easily I'm smiling, guilt curls in my belly. I'm not here for small talk. As much as I wish it weren't so, I have bigger things to focus on than the attention of a beautiful woman. And unfortunately for both of us, my plans involve ruining any slim chance I had for a friendship—or more—forever.

But there's no time for guilt. This is about my family, and nothing is more important than my blood. Not my moral compass, and certainly not my heart.

"I was so glad to get your message," Shey says, pulling my attention back to her. "I wasn't sure I'd ever see you again, after... last time." She takes a breath, pushing a strand of hair behind her ear. "I hope you know that I immediately went to my mother to beg for your release. But at that point, you had already...well."

"Broken out of jail and caused mass panic?"

I catch a brief glimpse of a smile on Shey's face before she covers it with one hand and clears her throat.

"Yes. That." Her tone manages to be serious, but when she lowers her hand, there's still a ghost of a smile on her lips. My heart flutters.

Damn. Damn. A million times, *damn*. If only things were different.

"I'm hoping you took extra precautions not to be trailed this time?" I ask, arching my eyebrows at her.

"Of course. As you can imagine, my mother is too preoccupied to keep many eyes on me," Shey says. "And it's important that we aren't interrupted. There's something very important I need to talk to you about."

"Yeah. Me too."

I step forward. While she looks up at me, face full of curiosity and not a hint of suspicion, I pull the blaster out from the back of my pants and push the barrel into her stomach. I'm close enough to hear her let out a soft gasp, and read every line of the betrayal written on her face when she looks down to see the gun. She stares at me, her eyes wide and her lips slightly parted. I swallow my guilt and lean forward, putting my mouth right next to her ear. "The moment your mother is out of that meeting, tell her to come here. Alone."

I pace back and forth as I wait for Leonis to show, keeping my blaster trained on Shey. She's remained frozen in place ever since I pulled my gun on her, but the threat of the weapon doesn't keep her from glaring at me.

"I don't understand why you won't simply *talk* to me," she says. "I believe we can help each other—"

"Don't make me gag you." I avoid looking directly at her, knowing it will only make me feel guilty. My conscience won't stop me now like it did with Ives. If I hadn't failed then, we wouldn't be forced to turn to Leonis in our time of need. But now, I have no choice but to make this risky move.

"I thought we were allies. Now you're using me as bait for my mother?"

"*I'm* using *you*?" I whirl around, anger overwhelming my guilt, and advance on her. "What, like you weren't doing the same to me on Gaia? The only reason you ever talked to me is because of what I could do for you. And the second things went sideways, you were willing to let me pay for your mistakes. So quit the bullshit." Before she can respond, I yank off my scarf and shove it into her mouth, pressing the blaster to the side of her head. She doesn't try to fight me, and I try to ignore the hurt on her face.

I tear my eyes away from her as footsteps approach. Keeping the gun pressed to her head, I step behind Shey. My hands are shaking, my stomach churning. This is it. I'm risking everything right now. But this is the only option I have—the only way to save my brother.

Leonis steps into the warehouse alone, like I asked, but I don't lower my weapon. The president is a smart woman, and I don't doubt that she has some sort of trick up her sleeve, plus at least a dozen of her officers ready to barge in on a moment's notice. My own family should be here any minute now, too.

Hands clasped behind her back, Leonis stops in the middle of the room and regards me with thinly veiled distaste—like I'm a minor inconvenience rather than a real threat.

"I suppose your mother didn't survive, or there would be no need for all this," she says in her smooth politician's voice, empty of emotion. "Last I checked, you were running a job for me. If you wanted to speak, a comm call would have sufficed."

I resist the urge to roll my eyes and instead nod at the blaster.

"Let's call it insurance."

Leonis scrutinizes me, her eyes narrowing.

"Stars above, you're *drunk*, aren't you?" she asks, her voice heavy with contempt. "This is ridiculous. If I wanted you dead, my guards would have taken you out before you saw them coming. Put the gun down and let's talk."

"Not that easy, though, is it? You're not going to kill me. Not unless you want the whole system hearing what my family knows." I glance at Shey, wondering if she's aware of her mother's plan. She keeps her eyes downcast, and her expression betrays nothing. Would she have condoned the massacre on Titan? I hope not—but that's not what I should be worrying about right now. "And not unless you want us handing over the evidence."

"Evidence?" Leonis asks.

"Oh, you know, those pretty little vials? Sending five was a bit excessive. We've still got one—"

An elbow to the stomach steals the rest of my breath. I stumble backward. Shey doesn't even give me time to consider pulling the trigger of my blaster before she hits me in the jaw and follows it up with a swift disarming. I gape at her, winded and stinging, as she aims my own gun at my face.

"Wow," I mutter, head spinning, unable to help but be impressed. She gives me a smug look, annoyingly similar to the one her mother is wearing, and yanks the scarf out of her mouth with her free hand.

"Hands behind your head," she orders, and I slowly move to obey.

"Well done, honey," Leonis says to her daughter in a surprisingly warm voice. "Are you all right?"

"I'm fine," Shey says. They share a brief, affectionate look that makes me uncomfortable to witness. Leonis may be a monster, but she genuinely loves her daughter, and Shey loves her back. Maybe that'll be useful, I tell myself, trying to push away my discomfort.

"Now pat her down, will you?" Leonis asks.

Shey keeps the gun trained on me with one hand and uses the other to give me a thorough once-over. I stay perfectly still, my hands folded behind my neck and my head reeling. I didn't plan for this. If I wasn't drunk, Shey never would have caught me off guard—and my siblings are supposed to be here, backing me up. Where are they? Did Lyre not get my message?

"She doesn't have anything," Shey says, retreating to her mother's side. "What is this about, Mom?"

"I thought the two of you were close," I say, turning my attention to her. "She didn't tell you about her plans for Titan?"

"Shey." Leonis's voice is patient, but strained. She looks directly at her daughter instead of me. "There's a lot happening right now that you don't understand. I promise I will explain everything to you, but for now, please hand me the gun and leave."

Panic swells inside me. Leonis may not be able to kill me straight-away, but if she holds me hostage, she can use me as a weapon against my family. That can't happen. I won't let my screwup put them all in danger again.

"You didn't find it a little surprising that your mother let me and my family leave Gaia after what I did?" I talk as quickly as possible, trying to hold on to Shey's attention before her mother can steal her ear. "It's because she needed us. She made a deal with my mother, gave us these Primus vials. Then she sent us to Titan and—"

"Don't listen to this criminal. She's only trying to save herself." Leonis speaks above me, trying to drown me out. Shey looks back and forth between us, brow creased.

"Perhaps I should call the authorities. Let the Devans handle this—"

"*No*," Leonis and I say at the same time. The room is abruptly silent afterward. Shey stares at her mother, her uncertainty and suspicion evident. I hold my tongue. I've already planted the seed of doubt I needed to.

"My dear," Leonis says gently. "As I said, I will explain every-thing to you when I can. But for now, please hand the gun over and let me handle this. Tell Yvette and the others to stand down."

Shey gives her a long look. After a moment, she turns and walks toward the stairwell. But when Leonis holds out her hand for the weapon, Shey passes by without a glance at her, holding on to the gun. As her footsteps recede, the two of us are left alone and unarmed. Leonis takes a deep breath and turns to face me.

"Let us be honest with each other," she says. "If you truly think the council will believe your word against mine, why aren't you speaking with the other leaders right now? Why go through such great lengths to speak to me alone?"

I fold my arms over my chest and try to ignore my pounding heart. My bullshit got me to this point, but it'll get me no further. Now, I need to figure out if this trip was worth all the trouble, or if I just doomed what's left of my family by coming here.

But Leonis seems more confident than I expected. I didn't catch much of that broadcast, but I'm guessing it went well for her. She doesn't seem too concerned about me potentially sharing information with the council. Maybe blackmail isn't enough. And if I'm going to put my brother into her hands, I need to know we have a solid arrangement. I need to offer her something.

Part of me rebels at the thought of what I'm about to do, but I crush it down. My conscience foiled me once, back on Titan, and I'm not going to let it happen again. I'll protect my family, save Pol, no matter how much of myself I have to sacrifice to do so.

"I'm not here to have you arrested," I say. "I'm here to make a deal."

Leonis's eyebrows rise, but she says nothing.

"Look, I'm well aware you didn't intend for us to make it off that planet. You underestimated us, and that's not a mistake you want to make again." I take a deep breath and continue. "And I've figured out why you're doing this, too. Your last cycle of crops failed. The other planets already distrust you. Maybe they're pushing the price of food higher. So you're getting desperate. You promised your people Gaian independence, and you failed. If drone trade ends now, Gaia will starve." I study her expression while I talk. A flicker in her confidence makes me pretty sure I'm on the right track. "So you went after Titan for their resources—"

"What are you trying to do?" she cuts me off. "Impress me with your wild guesses?" Despite her apparent disdain, I suspect I was getting too close for comfort.

"But building a fleet takes time," I continue, emboldened. "And now... now you've got those natural disasters happening on Gaia, and suspicion from the other planets. So you need to move up your timetable. You need to secure access to a planet that can feed your people. And you need help to do it." She scoffs, but I keep going. "Titan proved you don't need a whole fleet if no one sees you coming. You just need one ship with access to the planet. And as it so happens...we're looking for work."

Leonis's eyebrows rise a fraction farther before she draws them back down.

"You came all the way to Deva, kidnapped my daughter, and threatened me...so you could ask for a *job*?"

I clear my throat and shrug. It does sound a little ridiculous when she puts it like that.

"Well...yeah." I force a smile, trying to pretend that nerves aren't turning my knees to rubber, and that merely asking such a thing doesn't make me hate myself. I'll learn to live with it if I can pull this off. "My family has contacts, business savviness, and the unique advantage of legal access to wherever we need to go, assuming your business isn't on that shithole Pax. We can do whatever you need us to do. Quickly, quietly, and efficiently." I pause. There's no use pretending I don't suspect exactly what she'll ask of us, and I need her to know we'll do whatever it takes. "And I wasn't lying earlier. We've still got one of those vials."

Leonis's face is completely neutral.

"And in return?"

"Twice what you paid us for Titan." I pause to gather myself, refusing to let my voice falter. "And a cure for my brother."

"A cure?" the president repeats. I say nothing, and watch understanding dawn on her. "You don't mean to tell me..."

"He was infected by the bio-weapon. He's in cryosleep on our ship now."

Leonis takes a step back.

"You shouldn't have brought him here," she says. "You've endangered millions of people on this planet by doing so. And all for—"

"For you to save him. I know you can." Though I aim for conviction, the words come out desperate, like a zealot defending her cause. I take a deep breath, try to focus on logic. "He's not contagious as long as he's in cryosleep, or else my entire family would be dead by now. He can be transported safely."

"Simply bringing him back from cryosleep would be a risky gamble," Leonis says, slowly, as if breaking bad news to a child. "And the bio-weapon must have already taken a toll on him. To handle both at once would be—"

"No." I stop her before the word *impossible* can come out of her mouth. My heart can't take it. "You really expect me to believe you unleashed that weapon without some kind of countermeasure planned in case it was turned back against you? With all of Gaia's resources, all of its research on the Primus? There has to be a way." I take a moment to breathe and suppress the emotion threatening to overwhelm my reasoning. I have to remember I'm trying to strike a deal, and desperation doesn't play well in dealmaking. "We can help each other. Save him, and you will have more than our ship and our unique services."

I pause, sick to my stomach at the mere thought of what I'm saying. My conscience rears its head, just like it did back on Titan—but I shove it down. I have to do this. Leonis is the only one with a chance at saving my brother.

"You will have our loyalty." I take a step closer, lowering my voice. "And you need as many allies as you can get in the times ahead. I know you don't want to make your planet the scourge of Nova Vita, Madam President. You don't want to make enemies of the entire system." I splay a hand across my chest. "So we'll do it for you. We'll be your weapons, and your villains."

The moment I finish, self-loathing rises in the back of my throat like bile, but I swallow it down. I couldn't believe that Momma made a deal with Leonis, but now I understand why she did it.

Now that I'm in charge of the family, I need to protect them, keep us all together, like she always did. If this makes me a terrible person, if I hate myself for the rest of my life for making this deal, it will be worth it as long as my family is safe. I'll do what I have to do. Become worse than Momma if I must.

Leonis studies my face. The silence lasts so long that it takes all of my self-control not to break it myself.

"If we try to treat your brother, the methods will be highly unconventional," she says. "Experimental, and extremely expensive, with no guarantee of success."

Despite her words, it's all I can do not to grin, because she's no longer trying to tell me it's impossible.

"The expenses can be subtracted from our payment. Do whatever you have to," I say. "Do what you would if it were your own daughter."

She goes quiet for long enough that I believe I actually got through to her.

"You know, when my family fell ill with the Nibiran plague, I held on to hope for a very long time," she says. "I was furious when my aunt made the decision to pull the plug on my parents and sister. I never forgave her, all the way until her own death. It took me many years to realize that sometimes death is the kinder option. If it was my own daughter now... I would make the same choice that my aunt did." She doesn't say it coldly—no, her words hold the sting of an emotional but honest truth. "Even if we salvage his life, your brother will never be the same again. I want to make sure you understand that."

My mind flashes unwillingly to Corvus. The change in him since his return, the physical and mental scars, the unshakable feeling that he is a stranger wearing my brother's flesh as a disguise.

"No matter what, he'll still be my brother," I say.

CHAPTER THIRTY

A New Job

Corvus

Despair hangs over me like a cloud as I limp back toward the ship. Every bruise and jolt of pain reminds me how severe of a mistake I've made. I'm lucky to emerge without anything broken, but the physical pain is nothing compared to the overwhelming sense of my failure. This was my chance to avenge my people, bring Scorpia and the rest of my family back from the point of no return, and instead I let my emotions get the better of me.

"I cannot believe you," Lyre says. By the time the fighting was over, Scorpia had sent us all a curt message ordering us to meet her at *Fortuna* rather than the apartment building she initially indicated. "A bar fight? Seriously? After all your talk about our 'very important, very time-sensitive' purpose?"

"It was kind of badass, though," Drom says begrudgingly. She still won't look directly at me ever since I lunged at her. Whatever rift I created when I hurt Pol, I've torn it open more now.

I stay silent. Not only did I fail today, but everything I've done has only pushed me further to the outside of the family. Over and over, I'm proving to myself that I don't belong here. All I know how to do is hurt people. If I had pulled off my plan, sacrificed myself to take out Leonis, we would all be better off.

As we enter the landing zone, we pass by a group of Nibirans who seem in a rush to leave the planet. Given the hostility of that interplanetary meeting, I can't say I blame them. The peacekeepers around the delegates eye us warily as we draw near, though the two robed council members don't spare us so much as a glance, caught up in what seems to be a quiet but heated argument among themselves. I recognize Oshiro, who looks as angry as they did during the meeting. I could try to approach them now, but I don't have the energy. And I suspect it's too late anyway. Scorpia has already done whatever she decided to do. I've failed.

Back at the ship, Scorpia waits on the open ramp, her face stony. The emotionless mask flickers for a moment when she sees my bruised face, but it quickly returns. We pause at the bottom of the ramp, and I stare up at her. There's something different. Something cold and shut-off in her expression.

"What the hell happened?" she asks, looking from me, to Lyre, to Drom. To my surprise, neither of them offer an answer. I glance sideways at Lyre, who was so glad to berate me on the entire trip over, but she stares down at the ground with her lips pressed together. Scorpia sighs. "Whatever. It doesn't matter. I handled everything on my own."

"Handled?" I ask. A moment later, a small group of people approach from behind us and head into the cargo bay, carrying heavy metal crates. I stand up straighter, bristling as I recognize the white uniforms they're wearing. Gaians. Bringing cargo on board our ship. "What's going on?"

I start to head up the ramp, but Scorpia blocks my path.

"As I said, I handled everything." She glances behind me at our sisters. "Great news, everyone," she says, though her tone remains flat and hollow. "We've got a job."

My stomach drops. It can't be. She couldn't have done what I think she did. The thought of her blackmailing Leonis to cooperate was bad enough, but surely she didn't stoop so low as to work for her.

"What do you mean, a job?" Lyre asks. Even she looks hesitant.

Before Scorpia can respond, Drom shoves past us, bounding up the ramp and into the cargo bay.

"What the fuck do you think you're doing?" she shouts. I step forward as I see the group of Gaians wheeling the cryosleep chamber toward the ramp. Drom gets in their way, her hands clenched into fists and her face twisted in fury.

"Whoa, whoa," Scorpia says, rushing over to get between her and the Gaians, who have all taken a step back. "Hey, it's okay, Drom. We talked about this. They're going to help Pol. They're going to take him to Gaia and save him, all right?"

"Alone?" Drom asks. "They're taking him alone? I thought we'd go with him."

Scorpia's face shatters, but she quickly composes herself again.

"We can't," she says. "I'm sorry. We'll pick him up as soon as we can."

Drom stares at her. For a split second, it looks like she's going to burst into tears. Then she whirls around and stomps up the stairs to the middle deck without another word.

Scorpia takes a deep breath and looks at the Gaians.

"Go on," she says, addressing a tall woman at the head of the group. "You look after my brother, Commander Zinne."

"Of course, Captain Kaiser," the woman says, her expression tightening in clear displeasure.

Momma's title attached to my sister gives me a jolt, but Scorpia only smiles. I turn to watch the Gaians roll the chamber containing our little brother down the ramp and resist the urge to stop them. Scorpia and I disagree on many things, but I know his best chance is with the Gaians. If Scorpia's made a deal for him, I have to trust that they'll do what they can. But I can't celebrate the news.

"What kind of job did you take?" I ask, turning back to Scorpia. "We're working for the president again?"

"I know, it's a miracle, you're very welcome for saving our brother," Scorpia deadpans. "So glad you know what's important here."

Damn her and her question dodging. As she pulls away from me, I reach forward and grab her arm. I search her face, but she won't look me in the eye. Something about this feels wrong. What has she done?

"Of course I'm grateful about Pol," I say in a low voice. "I just want to make sure we didn't sell our souls to save his."

Scorpia snorts out a laugh and yanks free from my grip.

"You and your dramatics."

"Scorpia." I wait until she grudgingly meets my eyes. "If this job involves waging a war on Leonis's behalf, I want no part in it." I steel myself. I won't be made into a weapon again. If that means being alone, so be it. "Leave me here, if that's the case."

Scorpia is silent for a moment. She looks past me at Lyre, and nods her head toward the ship.

"Lyre, get on board and leave us alone for a sec," she says. Lyre does as she says, shooting a nervous glance at us as she passes.

Once we're alone, part of me is suddenly, devastatingly certain she's going to say, *To hell with it, then, stay here on Deva*—but after a moment, she sighs and throws up her hands.

"Okay, okay. I was going to do a big announcement for everyone, but since you're so concerned about our *souls*, I'll tell you." She steps closer to me, lowering her voice. "You were right. There's a war brewing in the system." My stomach plummets. Maybe this is her way of telling me to fuck off after all. "But this is a diplomatic mission." She pauses. Something flickers across her face so quickly I can't be certain I really saw it. "To Nibiru."

Suspicion overshadows my relief.

"Why would Leonis be interested in diplomacy with Nibiru?" Nibiru is a quiet planet without much military value, and the Gaians despise them.

"Food supply, obviously. Leonis is willing to trade some tech to secure a big deal for dried algae. It'll last forever, even if the trade drones are grounded as things progress."

I frown. It makes some amount of sense...but still, if food is the goal, Nibiru isn't the best option.

"Why don't they secure a deal with Deva instead?"

"Come on, do I really have to spell everything out for you?"

"They're going to war with Deva?"

Scorpia holds a finger to her lips, glancing pointedly in the direction of the customs building and then the Gaian officers still milling outside their ship. My frown deepens. Things are starting to click together now. If Leonis is still keeping this quiet, even from her own people, it makes sense that she's sending us to do her business rather than an official diplomatic mission. But a war with Deva, of all planets, brings up a new issue.

"Gaia will never win." I don't care how much advanced alien technology Gaia has on their side, Deva is the wealthiest planet in the system by far. They have abundant food and a strong standing military, though they're mostly used to fight the jungle. Gaia doesn't have the resources to outlast them, even if they secure a ludicrous deal with Nibiru.

"Not our problem," Scorpia says, waving a hand dismissively. "This deal is gonna make us rich, and as soon as Pol is back with us, we'll find a way to settle down wherever's safest. Pax, maybe. Unless that also offends your delicate sensibilities?" When I don't answer, she nods and heads into the cargo bay. "Good, then let's go."

I sigh. Another damn war, when I've just escaped one. It never ends. But if I'm not forced to fight, maybe I can find a way to live with it. And at least this time I won't be alone.

Still, my heart feels heavy as I step inside *Fortuna*.

Later I toss and turn in the dark, unable to sleep. I know the moment my eyes close I'll see Momma—or Pol, or Daniil, or Magda, or one of the other hundred faces that wait for me in my nightmares. There are so many now, a bottomless well of memories I'm not ready to confront. There's so much blood on my hands.

Eventually I give up and drag myself out of bed. I splash water on my face and stare at my reflection in the mirror as the water slides off. One droplet follows the length of my scar before falling. I let my head drop toward my chest, and trace the black warbrand on my wrist with a finger.

I've escaped one war only to find a worse one. Now, the entire system is at stake, not merely some desolate planet on the outer reaches. Millions of lives hang in the balance. Will this war crowd my nightmares with more faces, more silent planets hanging in the darkness?

Scorpia said this is a diplomatic mission, but it's still for the purpose of war, and we're still working for the woman who massacred the people of Titan. Leonis is a warmonger, and we're furthering her agenda. But she's also the one person who can save Pol, and he's in her hands now. So what choice do we have?

No. It's wrong to think like that. I've let myself fall into that trap too many times before. I let the war on Titan turn me into someone I hated because *I didn't have a choice*. But that's never true. Sometimes it's just one I don't want to face.

And as much as I want to trust Scorpia, I have to be sure. If everyone else plans on following her as blindly as they followed Momma, it's up to me to ensure we aren't made pawns again.

The ship is silent and empty as I make my way down to the cargo bay. But halfway down the stairs, the sound of whistling floats up from below. I pause before continuing downward.

Scorpia sits atop one of the cargo crates, her boots resting on another, a bottle of whiskey in her hands. She pauses her whistling to take a long swig, and nearly spits it up again as she notices me. She coughs, wipes the back of her mouth with one hand, and sets down the bottle.

"Oh, fancy seeing you here," she says, her tone full of fake levity. She's drunk—the kind of drunk where her eyes won't open more than halfway and her smile keeps tilting sideways. I haven't seen her get this bad since Titan. If I question her now, she might not be able to keep her lies straight...But merely thinking that makes me feel guilty. I've always hated to see Scorpia like this. This isn't a happy drunkenness, but a desperate one. The worst part is that I'm not sure she can tell the difference.

"You need some sleep," I say.

"I'm the captain," she proclaims, pointing the bottle at me and swaying a little. "Which means I can do whatever the hell I please."

I suppress a grimace. I guess she's fully embraced the title now.

"Suit yourself, Captain."

She laughs as if I made a joke, and holds out the bottle in offering.

"You want? It's good Devan shit, I just picked it up."

I almost take it just to stop her from having more but stop as I notice her hand shaking. My suspicion rekindles; I can't forget why I'm here.

"No. Thanks."

"You sure? Might kill those nightmares."

I stare at her as she shrugs and takes another drink, humming to herself.

"How do you know about the nightmares?"

Scorpia laughs, spraying whiskey as she does, and claps a hand over her mouth.

"Oops." She lowers the hand. "You, uh, didn't know? I can hear you. We can all hear you. Crying out and talking and...who is Magda, by the way?"

My face heats up. Rather than answer, I snatch the bottle from her hand and take a long drink, letting the fire burn away my humiliation. I thought I had a decent handle on my emotions, at least enough to keep my siblings from noticing. But if Scorpia and the others have heard me, no wonder they all look at me like I'm on the verge of exploding.

"I know why you're here," Scorpia says, holding her hand out for the bottle. It's steady now. "You think I lied to you about the cargo. You want to see it."

I take another swig before handing it over, and say nothing. She sighs.

"I guess I can't blame you. If I was you, I wouldn't trust me, either." She looks down at the bottle, swirling liquor around, her eyes distant. After a moment, her gaze snaps up to meet my own. "How'd things get so bad?"

While I consider my answer, she takes another drink before passing the bottle over to me.

"Between us, or in general?" I drink and pass as well.

"Both. It's shit. It's all shit. I don't want it to be like this anymore." Her voice quavers, and she drinks rather than continuing. I sigh as the bottle passes back into my hands.

"It doesn't have to be." It's hard to say it, hard to open myself up again when all she's done since my return is hurt me over and over again. But she's drunk, and she probably won't remember the details of this conversation in the morning, and I can't stop myself from trying. "I miss the way things were. I want to fix them. But I have to know that you're telling the truth."

Scorpia takes a long time to respond, chewing her lip and staring at the bottle still in my hands.

"See, this is how broken we are. Here I am trying to fix shit, and you accuse me of being a liar." She snatches the bottle from my hand. "Go to bed, Corvus. That's an order."

With the harshness of her tone and the dim lighting of the cargo bay, for a brief flicker in time it feels like I'm staring at Momma's ghost.

CHAPTER THIRTY-ONE

Trust

Scorpia

My dreams bring me back to Nibiru. Vivid recollections of floating on my back in an endless ocean and watching clouds roll across a red sky; of the twins laughing and splashing each other while Corvus taught Lyre how to clean a fish; of peaceful days blurring into quiet nights, all of us stuffed together on a ratty mattress inside our little houseboat.

But inevitably, the dreams turn to screams and panicked crowds, to an alien shimmer in the air, to stillness and silence blanketing an entire planet. I wake up soaked in sweat, and bite my knuckles to hold back a sob.

What have I agreed to? Why does it have to be Nibiru? Leonis never explained, and I wasn't in a place to question. I suppose it doesn't matter anyway. It's not like it would change anything. I told Leonis we were willing to do whatever she asked, and now it's time to prove it, for the sake of my brother.

By the time I roll out of bed, I'm more exhausted than I was when I fell into it, and my head pounds with a dawning hangover.

I grab the alien vial from my nightstand and place it in my pocket, unwilling to let the thing out of my sight for a single second.

In the kitchen, I make myself a strong cup of coffee topped off with a generous pour of whiskey. Once I finish it, the pounding in my head has receded to a dull ache. I lean back in my chair, stretching and yawning, when I notice Corvus watching me from the doorway to Apollo's room, claimed as his own for now. I finish my yawn and dump my empty mug in the sink.

"You need something?" I ask, parsing through fuzzy memories of our conversation last night. It was a bad idea to talk to him while I was so drunk, but I think I did a decent job of throwing him off my trail. If I don't want him getting suspicious, it's better to play nice, and pretend the mere sight of him doesn't feel like ripping off a freshly formed scab. I still can't believe he and the rest of my siblings left me to fend for myself on Deva, and *then* he had the audacity to question me when he finally showed up.

For a moment, Corvus looks like he's about to say something. But then Lyre comes out of her room, rubbing the sleep from her eyes on her way to the kitchen. She pours herself a cup of coffee and leans against the counter, lingering in the space between me and Corvus, watching him.

He shakes his head and moves toward the cockpit for his shift at the wheel. As soon as he's gone, Lyre looks at me, lifting her eyebrows. I turn away and search the pantry for something to settle my stomach.

"What was that about?" she asks.

"What was what about?"

Rather than respond to the question, Lyre narrows her eyes at me while I tear into a sheet of algae.

"I think we need to talk about Corvus," she says. "Can we trust him? Because I'm starting to think he might be dangerous." Before I can interrupt, she hurries onward. "To himself most of all."

"What the hell are you talking about?"

She hesitates.

"I didn't want you to be angry with him," she says, "but he got into this bar fight on Deva. You've seen how he's been acting. It's like he doesn't care what happens to him, and—"

"Stop." My head is starting to pound again, and I have enough to worry about right now. "Let me deal with Corvus. It's not your problem."

"It's a problem for all of us." Lyre folds her arms over her chest. "He's our brother."

"Well, we've got worse issues to deal with," I say, and hold up a hand to silence any further argument. "Enough. I don't want to hear anything more about it. Go tend to the engine or whatever it is you do."

Unexpected hurt flashes across Lyre's face. It clears quickly, though, and before I can say anything else, she nods and heads for the engine room. I remain where I am, tapping my fingers on the counter, and realize uneasily how my words imitated phrases Momma often said to me. *Shut up, Scorpia. We'll talk about it later. Mind your own business.* I think of Lyre helping me to my room when I was stumbling drunk, supporting me when I made a grab at leadership, and sigh, pressing my fingers into my forehead.

By the time this is over, I'm going to have a lot of explanations and apologies to make to my siblings. But until then, I'll do what I have to do to keep the family together. We can't afford to break apart right now, and sometimes it feels like I'm the only one trying to stop it from happening. Corvus certainly isn't stepping up. All he does is brood or pick fights with me, like he's determined to keep a wall up between himself and the rest of the family.

I pass the day drinking and trying not to think of the planet we're headed toward and what I'm going to do when we reach it. Luckily for me, none of my siblings are eager to dig into our cargo or inquire about details…except for Corvus, of course. But he's busy with a long shift at the wheel I assigned to him.

Once the day is gone and I'm sufficiently drunk, I fold myself into bed. My thoughts still plague me. Lyre's words replay in my head. *"Can we trust him?"* The truth is, I don't know. Thus far, I've had to remain content that he isn't trying to steal my title as captain. Corvus might be broken, but he hasn't seemed to be the kind of broken that endangers us. Just the kind that makes him mope around and make snippy comments.

And apparently get into a Devan bar fight when I needed him to back me up. Maybe Lyre is right—maybe he could be dangerous, to himself and to the rest of us. He does seem to be getting worse. Are my own feelings about my brother preventing me from seeing the threat he poses? I think on that, chewing my thumbnail. Damn Lyre and her suspicions, putting all these doubts in my head. Now, I won't be able to sleep unless I check on the cargo.

As I reach the cargo bay, my heart nearly stops. Corvus sits on top of a crate. A knife rests in one of his hands, its blade the sleek, glossy black of Primus material. The crates are gutted, and the floor is strewn with the scrap metal and other junk that filled them. They've been exposed for the diversions they are, and I'm sure Corvus has figured out that our only real cargo is the vial I've had this whole time.

For several long moments, we only stare at each other. Then I clear my throat and take another step forward.

"I really didn't think you'd do it." I didn't realize he had a Primus blade—those can cut through almost anything—but more than that, I didn't think he'd distrust me so much, especially not after our conversation last night. I could try to talk my way out of this, stack further lies on top of the ones I've already told, but the look on Corvus's face tells me it isn't going to work this time. There's something defeated in his expression. It scares me.

"Funny. I was about to say the same." Corvus's voice is completely flat. He stands up, the knife still in his hand. "I guess we don't know each other as well as we thought."

I swallow hard. It's true. Because right now, I have no idea what Corvus is going to do next. I find myself keeping an eye on his knife, and wishing I carried a weapon myself.

"How the hell did it come to this?" he asks, his voice strained, his words mirroring my own thoughts.

"I'm doing what I have to do."

"Including lying to us all?"

"Absolutely." The word is barely a breath. "You think telling the truth would have made it better? This way, the burden is mine alone." I tap my hand to my heart. His gaze hardens, and I realize too late how close the gesture is to his home-planet's salute. "None of you needed to know until…until it was done. I was trying to protect you. You've all been through enough."

"No. You lied for the same reason you always do: because it's the easy way out."

"None of this is easy!" My voice rises to a shrill peak. "Least of all for me! But I guess everything looks different from your stars-damned moral high ground, huh?"

"You want to talk about morality?" Despite my anger, when Corvus takes a step toward me, my feet automatically propel me back. He stops, and follows my gaze to the knife in his hand. Something dark flashes across his face as he slides the weapon back into the sheath at his waist. "You're the ones who brought that abomination to Titan and killed my home-world. And you're the one who was trying to do the same to Nibiru." Pain and anger pierce his tone. "*Nibiru*. We used to live there. How could you even think about doing this?"

"I'm doing what I have to do," I say again, more firmly this time. "I'm taking care of the family, like Momma always did. So don't you dare judge me."

"This isn't just some job!" Corvus smashes a fist into the nearby wall, and the bang of metal makes me jump. "You're going to get millions of people killed."

For a moment I'm frozen in shock, half-worried that the noise will bring someone running, half-hoping that it will so I won't have to be alone with him anymore. I take a deep breath and lower my voice.

"The war's already started. Those people are going to die, with or without our involvement." Just like on Titan. Backing out of the deal with Ives didn't save anybody, it only screwed me. "You think we're the only ones on Leonis's payroll? There's always gonna be someone with less scruples. At least this way, we get to choose the winning side."

"Winning side?" Corvus repeats incredulously. "You saw the weapon Leonis used on Titan. It's a world-ender. There will be no *winning side* to this war. It won't be over until everyone's dead." He shakes his head. "We don't have to be like her, you know. Just because Momma ran this ship one way doesn't mean you have to be the same. You can be better than her. Better than this."

For a moment it grates on me that my thought process is so transparent to him—but that's followed by fresh annoyance over his words. All this, from Momma's precious little golden boy? Even after she abandoned him on Titan, he still followed every order she gave, without a moment's hesitation. I'll never forget him standing outside of Altair's office and telling me to leave. He never would have spoken like this when Momma was alive, and he shouldn't be saying it now.

"Momma kept us alive through some of the worst shit imaginable," I say. "She was rich. Successful. She protected us all."

"That doesn't excuse everything she did," Corvus says. "You know that most of all. You were the one who rebelled against her when I was too afraid to. Why are you defending her now?" I stare at

338

him, at a loss for words for a moment, and he presses onward. "You're so quick to forget the worst parts of her. Momma was cruel. She was killed by her own greed. Not to mention universally despised."

I brush off my doubt. Things were different back then. I was childish, weak. I can't afford to be that person now, not with all the responsibility resting on my shoulders.

"We're already despised. We're smugglers, remember? Off-worlders wherever we go. Scourge of the system, and all. Nobody cares which lines we cross and which we don't. They can't tell the difference." Anger surges up as I think of the Titans fighting in their endless war, and the Gaians digging up alien weaponry; of Devans crossbreeding plants capable of destroying entire ecosystems, and Paxians selling weapons throughout the system. All of them treating us like we're the criminals. Me especially, merely for the crime of existing. "We owe these people nothing. They treat us like shit. They think we're scum. And why should we be anything else? Why should we try to be anything better than what they expect us to be?"

"To show them we can be more than what we were!" Corvus shouts, and I flinch back at the unexpected boom of his voice, the way he steps forward like he's ready to throw a fist in my face. But he doesn't. He stops, and lowers both his eyes and his volume. "To show them they can do the same." He searches my face. "Don't you remember what I used to say? That when I'm in charge, we could be whoever we want to be. Now that's in your hands. Is this who you want to be, Scorpia? Is this who you want all of us to become?"

"That..." A lump forms in my throat. "That was a long time ago. We were stupid. Ignorant. Being in charge isn't about who you want to be at all." I shake my head. "It's about becoming who you have to be. Being willing to get your hands dirty for the sake of everyone else. Like on Gaia, when I had to lie and steal because you couldn't. Now all of you are counting on me."

"I know exactly what that's like," he says, his voice rising again. "I was a sergeant on Titan. Did you ever stop to think about what that means? To think about the things I had to do in order to survive there? The choices I had to make? You think I got through three years keeping my hands clean?" He's shouting again, too loud for me to even think about interrupting. "I did horrible things for the good of my people. And they died anyway." His voice cracks, the anger dissolving into despair. I'm shocked to see his eyes wet with tears. "I'm never going to be able to come back from that. I'm never going to be able to sit with you and the others ever again without thinking of all the people who died for me to get there." He sucks in a shaky breath. "I know I don't deserve forgiveness for any of it. But I am doing everything I can to redeem myself. And that includes trying to keep you from making the same mistakes I did."

My resolve is crumbling despite my best efforts, my shoulders starting to tremble.

"But you came back to us," I say. "You survived Titan. What if becoming like that is the only way to keep going?" As much as I try to keep it down, an uncomfortable truth fights its way free of my mouth. "I don't want to be like this. I don't want to be like Momma, after everything she did to us. But the person I was before this wasn't good enough to lead us. If I have to become someone I hate to take care of you all..." I've spent so long telling myself that becoming like Momma was the only way to save my family. I didn't admit to myself until now how much that idea terrifies me. "I—I can feel all of you slipping away from me. I can feel myself fading away. I'm so fucking scared that's the price of getting through this. But if that's really the only way for us to survive, then what choice do I have?"

"I let myself think that way for too long," Corvus says. "The truth is that there's always a choice." He takes a step toward me, hesitantly reaching out with one hand. "And you don't have to shoulder the burden alone."

I throw my arms around his neck and squeeze him against me. He wraps his arms around me, and I press my face into his shoulder to muffle my sob. Stars, it's a relief to lean against someone rather than standing on my own. We hold each other until both of our tears die down. I pull back, ducking my head and wiping a hand under my eyes, my shoulders slumping. As meaningful as it is to begin to mend things with Corvus, it doesn't change the fact that we're completely screwed.

Before all of this happened, I couldn't believe that Momma would work for the president she hated. On Titan, I backed out of my deal with General Ives because I knew it was wrong. Now, I've made my own agreement with Leonis, though I know exactly how terrible it is. Ever since Momma's been gone, everything has fallen apart. First we lost her, and then Pol, and now we're wrapped up in this mess with no way out. I'm afraid it's too late to stop the war we've helped start.

"I'm scared, Corvus," I say, my voice hoarse. "I don't want to be a part of this. I don't want to be this person. But I think it's too late to turn back."

"We'll figure something out." Corvus presses his forehead to mine and clasps the back of my head. "We've always been stronger together. That's probably why Momma did her damnedest to keep us apart. But you need to come clean with everyone."

"Yeah. I know." I clear my throat as something else occurs to me. No more secrets. "Oh, and, uh... while we're doing the whole honesty thing, I guess I should let you know that Momma wanted to leave *Fortuna* to you. She told us on the way to Titan."

Corvus blinks at me, one corner of his mouth creeping into something close to a smile.

"She's all yours, Scorpia. I was never going to take that away from you."

Before I can respond, a clattering from the supply closet interrupts us. I jerk away from Corvus, who has his knife in his hand before I see him reach for it. We exchange a nervous glance.

"Someone there?" I call out, my stomach dropping. Shit, shit. I really hope that isn't one of my sisters eavesdropping. This wasn't the kind of explanation I wanted to give them.

"Lyre?" Corvus asks the darkness, which seems like the most reasonable guess, but no one responds.

"Maybe something just...fell?" I suggest half-heartedly, but Corvus is already pressing forward, his knife raised and ready. Gnawing my lip, I follow him toward the supply closet. The bay is silent as we approach, and I hold my breath and step lightly, afraid to make any sound.

Corvus shoves the door open with one shoulder and steps in at the same time.

"Hands up, now!"

Shit. He found someone. Someone who's clearly not one of our siblings, if he's threatening them. I hang back, heart pounding, unsure what to expect. How could someone have snuck on board the ship? I was distracted during the exchange with the Gaians. Could Leonis have sent someone? Did she plan to sabotage us from the start?

"W-wait, please. Where is Scorpia?"

My brain grinds to a halt at the sound of that voice. I *know* that voice. But there's no way.

"Corvus, hold up."

I push forward, grabbing his hand and jerking the knife's point down. Standing in the supply closet, wide-eyed and wild-haired but still the same pretty face I remember, is—

"Shey? What the *hell* are you doing on my ship?"

CHAPTER THIRTY-TWO

The Stowaway

Corvus

As soon as my sister explains who the stowaway is, I want to tie up the Gaian and demand that she talks. Instead, Scorpia insists on bringing her to the kitchen to get something to eat and drink.

We sit across from her while Shey scarfs down an inhuman amount of water and dried algae. Scorpia still hasn't deigned to explain how or why she's acquainted with the daughter of the Gaian president and what exactly the nature of their relationship is, but it's not difficult to guess why she's going easy on her.

Even after a couple of days spent hiding in the cargo bay, with unwashed hair and bags beneath her eyes and algae crumbs sticking to her lips, Shey is unmistakably beautiful. And as hard as Scorpia is trying to put on a threatening face, her gaze is softer than it should be and lingering in places where it doesn't belong. I keep catching her staring at Shey when she thinks I'm not looking, and then shooting me guilty looks when she realizes I am.

After Shey tears through her third packet of algae, I snatch the rest away and level her with a glare.

"That's enough." My annoyance makes it very easy to layer threat into my tone. "Time to talk. First things first: How the hell did you get on our ship?"

Scorpia folds her arms across her chest and says nothing. Either she trusts me to take point on this, or she doesn't trust herself enough to handle it. Works for me.

Shey wipes the crumbs off her face and folds her hands primly in her lap. Even if I didn't know who her mother was, it would be easy to see the Gaian manner in her straight posture and gloved, neatly folded hands. I suppress a sigh. Of course Scorpia had to get entangled with the worst person possible: not only a Gaian, but the daughter of the treacherous, xenophobic president who hired us to start a war. Scorpia always has to make everything as difficult as possible.

No matter how my sister feels, considering that this woman's mother made the call to wipe out my entire home-planet and everyone I've known and loved over the past three years, I'm not inclined to be gentle or forgiving with her.

"If you would give me a few minutes to freshen up," Shey says. "I would—"

"You're a stowaway, not a guest. You're not in a position to be making demands. Answer the question."

Shey's eyebrows rise. She glances at Scorpia. "Well, isn't he charming," she says.

Scorpia puts a closed hand to her mouth to hide a grin, and clears her throat when I glare at her.

"I have to say, I didn't take you for the stowaway type," she says, looking at Shey. "Tell us what's going on."

Shey sighs, her hands tightening on her lap.

"I already had some suspicions, but I knew something was wrong after that conversation with my mother," she says. "I couldn't return to Gaia with her, knowing what I know. So, instead I came to your ship, waited for you to unlock it for the cargo, and found the emergency escape hatch near the engine room." She shrugs at Scorpia's surprised look. "Every ship has one, of course. While you were all distracted making the exchange with my mother's people, I snuck on board and hid. I wanted to make sure we were far enough out that you wouldn't turn back and drop me on Deva."

"Okay," Scorpia says, while I stare at the Gaian with narrowed eyes. "That explains the how. But why?"

"I'm trying to stop you from making a very serious mistake."

"Skip the cryptic shit and get to the point." I drum my fingers on the table. Shey frowns, eyes darting to Scorpia again. My sister gestures for her to go on, and I resist the urge to snap at her for coddling the woman.

"Give me a moment, I'm trying to get my thoughts in order," Shey says. She shuts her eyes and takes a deep breath. As much as I want to think she's putting on an act, she does look genuinely exhausted, so I wait. "I suppose I should start with the obvious: My mother lied to you."

"Shocking," Scorpia says dryly.

"That doesn't explain why you're here," I say.

"I'm here because I don't want you to start a war based off my mother's lies," Shey says, her voice surprisingly fierce. She takes a deep breath and flicks hair out of her face, collecting herself again. "I don't want you to start a war at all. I believe there's another way."

"Another way to do what?" I ask, glancing at Scorpia. Even after our heart-to-heart, I feel a flicker of doubt, wondering if she still hasn't told me the whole truth—but she looks as confused as I am.

"Your mother didn't tell us anything about what she's doing," Scorpia says. "Though I assumed this is part of her crazy plan for

Gaian independence, sped up because of the storms and shit on your planet. Wiping out only the people so she can have Titan's resources, Nibiru's food supply."

I think again of Titan, of the rapid updates flooding my phone. Whole forts wiped out, entire cities gone. I set my jaw, leaning forward to speak to Shey again.

"Talk faster."

"I'll be frank, then." Shey raises her eyes to meet mine, lifting her chin as if to show she's not afraid of me. "Gaia is dying."

I blink, and scrutinize Shey's expression for some sign that she's lying, but find nothing.

"Dying?" Scorpia repeats, and then her confusion seems to clear. "The crop fields, the sanitation checks, now the storms...It *is* all connected somehow."

Shey gives a small, miserable nod.

"Gaia is no longer the home I knew, and it's only getting worse. That's why my mother brought me to Deva in the first place."

Unease prickles on the back of my neck. I thought a blossoming war was bad enough, but it seems the situation is even more complicated than we thought.

"When did it start?" The moment I ask the question, Shey's eyes drop, and she bites her lip.

"I'm not supposed to know the details. My mother—"

"Your mother already wiped out Titan and is trying to use us to kill Nibiru. You owe us a full explanation."

Shey shuts her eyes for a moment, takes a deep breath, and opens them again.

"I suppose I'm already committing treason," she says. "As Scorpia knows, I work in Gaia's alien research department. We discovered a new Primus technology. Something we found buried deep in the earth, beneath the statues. It—"

"Hold up, beneath the statues?" Scorpia butts in, sitting up straighter.

"Yes. There's a whole network of Primus-made tunnels below them. We haven't even finished mapping them out."

"Knew there was something weird about those things," Scorpia mutters.

"Keep talking," I tell Shey.

"We found a vial of blue liquid that evaporated into mist when released. We tested it in the labs, and it seemed . . . miraculous, for lack of a better word." Her eyes get a faraway look, as if reliving that sight. "With the help of the mist, plants grew—no, *thrived*—even in Gaia's barren soil. They grew at three times the rate one would expect, lush and fruitful and . . ." She trails off with a sigh. "Of course, my mother was overjoyed. All of us were. It seemed like a blessing from the Primus, an answer to all of Gaia's problems. We could finally sustain our people without relying on ever-shakier drone deliveries. We had lived so long in fear, watching the food prices climb, knowing that if we refused trade with Nibiru and Deva the people of Gaia would starve in less than a year." She glances at us. "Though you know that, of course. People like you profited off it."

"Yeah, yeah," Scorpia says. "We're smugglers, your mom committed genocide. I think the time for discussing ethics is long past. Go on."

Guilt flashes across Shey's face, and she continues.

"My mother was so excited that she signed an order to rush through testing," she says. "We were enthusiastic enough that no one second-guessed her. We were optimistic . . . and foolish." Her shoulders slump with the words. I can see where this story is going, but I stay quiet to hear it anyway, shaking my head. The Gaians always had far too much faith in aliens. "We used it on all of our

347

crop fields. We thought that, at the worst, we would lose one harvest," she says. "We weren't able to grow much as it was, so it wasn't a terrible price to pay, and such a high reward if it worked. And it seemed to at first. The crops grew, and flourished. And then, when they were about to be ready for harvest, they withered and died. Not only that, but the soil became completely sterile, unusable. The thing we used was not a miracle."

"It was a weapon." I let out a dry laugh. "So much for the virtuous Primus you Gaians liked to imagine. They were designing bio-weapons. Bio-weapons masquerading as helpful tools. They probably used it to trick their enemies…Make false deals." Just like Leonis did. I fight off a flash of anger at that, and fold my arms across my chest, mulling over this information. It all seems to check out. The whole system knew of Gaia's tendency to search for knowledge that was better left buried, the way they practically worshipped the Primus civilization they inherited the planet from.

"But this wasn't too long ago, right?" Scorpia asks. "So, what, you lose one season of crops, and your mother decides the best solution is to start a war? That seems extreme."

"The loss of our limited crop fields was a huge blow, but since we were already relying on the other planets for food, it wasn't unrecoverable," Shey says. "But that was only the beginning." She lowers her eyes, hesitating for a moment before continuing. "First it started to spread. Soil that was nowhere near places we used the growth stimulant became similarly unusable. Then people started getting sick." She draws a shaky breath. "It didn't make any sense. They hadn't consumed any tainted food, weren't near the fields. At first we thought they weren't connected, but…then came the storms. Huge ones that appeared out of nowhere. Impossible to detect with our weather radars. And the starting point for the storms was always—"

"Let me guess," Scorpia says. "The statues?"

Shey nods. A chill runs down my spine as I think of the storms on Titan, the Primus statues buried beneath the ice. It's eerie how the situation Gaia faces mirrors the conditions there in some ways. But what's the connection?

"And you're certain all of this is connected to the technology you used?" I ask, trying to pull my thoughts away from my home-planet.

"We're not positive, but it started directly afterward. Perhaps it's a part two to the weapon we accidentally unleashed on ourselves, a chain reaction, or…" She trails off.

"What?" I urge.

"Or we awakened something else," she says softly, meeting my eyes. I suppress a shiver as Scorpia shudders openly beside me. As alarming as that thought is, and as strange as the parallels to Titan are, all of this information about Gaia is merely background. We need to focus on what's happening now, and what it means for the future.

"So, essentially, Gaia is no longer habitable," I say, trying to ignore Scorpia's mutterings about "creepy-ass alien shit." "That's why your mother is doing this? The war-waging, the population-destroying weapon, is meant to…"

"Clear a path for us. More people die on Gaia every day, and the situation is escalating rapidly. We don't have enough ships to transport everyone at once, nor the resources or time to build more, which is why she must have chosen Nibiru. It's the closest. I assume she means to begin relocating our people there once the Nibirans are dead." She bites her lip. "This weapon was carefully chosen, if it affects only humans. The weapons department must have discovered another buried alien biological weapon. Altered the design so that it targets human DNA."

"But why release it on Titan?" I ask, trying to keep my voice neutral. "We thought you wanted to build a fleet, but it sounds like Gaia never had the time for that." My mind flashes to the alien power source I brought Altair, the one he was going to hand over to Leonis. Even if she needed that, though, she didn't need to kill the entire population to get it.

"I can't be certain," she says haltingly. "But I suspect Titan was…" Her eyes drop. "A test. After what happened with the previous technology, my mother must have wanted to ensure the weapon would work as expected. As the council reported, it was confirmed that only humans were wiped out, with no other adverse effects on the planet, unlike the one we accidentally unleashed on ourselves. And it dissipates fast enough that it would be safe to settle quite quickly."

Anger floods my body so fast and hot that I can barely breathe. I push myself away from the table and turn my back before I lash out, moving away from the conversation to lean against a counter in the kitchen. My head hangs, my breath coming in bursts.

A test. My entire home-planet dead, and that's all it was to them.

"*Fuck.*" I slam a fist down on the counter.

"Maybe we should continue this conversation later," Scorpia says.

I want to hit this counter until my knuckles bleed, smash every piece of glass in the kitchen, ruin that pretty Gaian woman's face with my fists.

"All my mother really wants is a safe place for our people," Shey says pleadingly. "But her mistrust runs so deeply. She still believes the plague that killed her family was a deliberate move by the Nibirans, and that the rest of the planets conspired against us in the council that followed. She must think the only way to find a new home is to force her way into one. But I believe there's another way."

"Damn right there's another way," I say, whirling around to face them again. As I stalk toward the table, Scorpia rises from her seat and blocks me from Shey. I glare at her over my sister's shoulder. "We can turn around and dump this alien weapon on Gaia. They brought it upon themselves."

"Whoa, whoa," Scorpia says, placing a hand against my chest. "He doesn't mean it," she says over her shoulder to Shey. "He's from Titan, he fought in the war, it's..." She stops talking to renew her efforts to hold me back.

"My people have nothing to do with this," Shey says, her expression remarkably composed as she meets my gaze. "I agree that those who engineered the plague should be punished, along with any government officials who sanctioned the attacks, including my mother. But most Gaians have no idea what my mother's done, or what she plans to do. They're innocent."

"People on Titan were innocent, too," I spit at her, trying to push past Scorpia.

"Apollo's still on Gaia," she murmurs in my ear. That gives me pause. I take a deep breath, and slowly the anger subsides, leaving me hollow and helpless.

"Okay," Scorpia says, looking back and forth between Shey and me. She waits for me to slump back into my chair before she takes a seat herself. "So...since bombing Gaia is *clearly* off the table"— she pauses to shoot me a look—"what are you proposing that we do, Shey?"

"I believe that if the Nibirans knew the truth, and they knew the plight the Gaians face, they would help us," Shey says. To her credit, she's still calm and collected, though she now avoids making eye contact with me and instead speaks directly to Scorpia. "I think we could find a way to coexist on their planet. Given our resources, it wouldn't be too difficult to create new islands."

My mouth twists in a grimace. It's ridiculous idealism. From what I've seen in my interplanetary travels, I can't say that Leonis has the wrong idea. The planets have spent so many years viewing each other as enemies that it's hard to imagine them welcoming

Gaians with open arms. Two peoples mingling on one planet is unheard of, and these two peoples have a particularly uneasy history as well. It's not difficult to imagine it turning into a situation like on Titan: people turning against each other, fighting over resources, tearing their own planet apart in the conflict.

But earlier today, I argued to Scorpia that we could prevent the war. I told her that people can be better. Perhaps the world Shey paints is possible.

"So what's your plan, exactly?" I ask. Shey glances in my direction but still doesn't look me in the eye.

"I think we should be honest," she says. "I think we should talk to the Nibiran Council, tell them what happened on my planet, and ask for safe haven."

"Talk to them," Scorpia repeats, and laughs dryly. Shey's cheeks flare red. "That's your grand plan? Sneak on board a smuggler ship and then just...talk to the Nibirans?"

"Well I haven't figured everything out yet," Shey snaps. "My relation to the Gaian president should be enough to gain us an audience with the Nibiran Council. And then I was thinking..." She bites her lip. "I was hoping you all would help me."

A headache is already building in my skull. Just when I thought this situation couldn't get any more complicated, along comes another wrench.

"Ugh," Scorpia mumbles. She drags a hand across her face and leans back, letting out a dramatic sigh. "How does this keep getting more convoluted?"

Shey's eyebrows rise.

"Is that all you have to say?" she asks. "After everything I explained to you—"

"I'm a little bit drunk and very emotionally compromised right now, so forgive me if I'm not eager to risk my life and save the universe or whatever." Despite the joke, there's strain beneath

Scorpia's voice. I know she must be thinking the same thing I am: Even if we want to be noble, even if Shey's plan for peace is possible, Leonis holds our brother hostage.

"We have a lot to talk about," I say, and stand up. "And we'll discuss it further in the morning. For now, we all could use some sleep...and you need to find out how we deal with stowaways on this ship."

In all reality, *Fortuna* has only had one stowaway in all the time I've been on board, and Momma dealt with her by promptly flushing her out the air lock while she begged and screamed for mercy. It wasn't a grand affair, just a quick, no-nonsense disposal before the woman could finish telling the sob story she started spewing when Momma found her crouched in the cargo bay.

"There's no time for mercy out here," she said, while Scorpia and I looked on in horror.

I don't deal with Shey in the same way, partially because she's Leonis's daughter and could be helpful for us, partially because Scorpia has been making puppy eyes at her the whole time and would surely hate me for it. But that doesn't stop me from tying Shey up and locking her in the supply closet. It's important to maintain some semblance of order on this ship. Scorpia seems to agree, since she doesn't voice any complaints throughout the process, though she does murmur an apology before shutting her inside.

"So?" I ask Scorpia in a low voice as we walk up the stairs, not eager to be overheard by either our prisoner or our siblings. "What do you think of all this?"

Scorpia rakes her fingers through her hair.

"I don't know. I really don't. I believe Shey is telling the truth, but I'm not sure if it's possible to turn back at this point." She lets out a long sigh, her shoulders slumping. "But...I know you're right. Either way, I need to tell everyone the truth before we go any further. The whole truth. We need to be together on this."

We stop outside her doorway. Scorpia looks nervous, and I don't blame her. But as much as I feel an urge to comfort her, I hold my tongue. This is all on her shoulders now.

"So, family meeting in the morning?"

"Family meeting in the morning," she repeats with another sigh. She hesitates, and then a faint smile breaks through her gloomy expression. "Hey, at least I've got you on my side, right?"

"Something like that," I say, but smile wryly despite myself. "Good night, Scorpia."

"Night."

Even with all the problems still ahead of us, when my head hits the pillow, I fall into a dreamless sleep for the first time in months.

CHAPTER THIRTY-THREE

The Vote

Scorpia

Talking to Corvus may have been the hardest part, but dealing with my sisters won't be easy, either. He and I sit across from each other at the table the next morning, me fidgeting and him perfectly still, as we wait for Drom to finish showering and Lyre to wrap up some supposedly vital chores in the engine room. I untied Shey this morning, though I told her to stay down in the cargo bay until I'm ready for her to step into the conversation. For now, this is a family affair.

"If Drom punches me in the face, it's all your fault, you know," I grumble, pouring myself a second glass of whiskey in an attempt to quell my nerves. Corvus snatches the bottle out of my hand before I can fill it more than halfway. When I glare up at him, I'm surprised to see a rare smile lighting his face. It's a pale imitation of his old grins, but it's enough for me to smile back despite my anxiety.

"You'd deserve it," he says, taking a pull from the bottle himself before corking it.

"A normal punch, maybe. A Drom punch will ruin my face forever." I lean back in my chair and sip my drink.

"Tragic."

"I know. It's one of my best qualities."

"Are you claiming to have other good ones?"

"Oh, fuck off."

Corvus looks up. I follow his gaze to find Lyre waiting in the doorway, a wrinkle between her brows, looking back and forth between us in clear confusion. It takes me a moment to realize how strange this must look to her: Corvus and I sharing a drink and smiling together. It's hard to believe that just last night, he and I had what felt like a gaping abyss between us. Now, we may not be back to the way things were, but we're on our way there.

Still, this conversation is serious, and I can't have any of my siblings thinking I'm taking it too lightly. So I wipe the smile off my face and set down my glass to wave Lyre forward.

"What is this about?" she asks, tentatively taking a seat at the end of the table. She folds her hands, her thumbs twitching nervously. "Is it...have we heard from Gaia?"

"Not exactly," I say, at the same time Corvus answers:

"It's not about Apollo."

We pause, exchanging a look.

"Right," I say, after a moment. "Pol is—" As soon as I start to speak, I realize I have no clue how he is. We haven't heard anything from Leonis since leaving Deva...and if he isn't dead already, potentially going forward with Shey's plan could get him killed. "He's fine," I finish after an uncomfortable pause, and take another long drink. "Let's wait for Drom," I say as I lower the glass, and the table descends into silence.

It remains until Drom emerges from her room, hair still damp from the shower and face stony. She sits at the opposite head of the table from Lyre, folds her arms over her chest, and waits.

With everyone seated—and two seats left glaringly unfilled—panic swells inside me. This is it: the moment I have to come clean with everyone, and the moment my sisters lose their faith in me forever. I'm guessing I can say goodbye to my hope of being the captain, though at this point I'm not even sure that I want it anymore.

I meet Corvus's eyes across the table and he inclines his head in a small nod. It gives me enough courage to stand and clear my throat.

"Okay," I say, and take a deep breath. "I called this meeting because I have something to tell you all." Lyre scrutinizes me, while Drom looks deeply unimpressed. "I lied to you." No one looks remotely surprised. "And I'm sorry." Their eyebrows rise slightly. "And I'm going to tell you the truth about everything."

Now I have their attention. Lyre leans forward in her chair, head tilted toward me.

"That could take a while," Drom deadpans, her expression unchanging. "Get on with it, then."

"When we left Deva, I told you all this would be a diplomatic mission. That was a lie." I drop my gaze, unable to look anyone in the eye now. "Leonis sent us to do the same thing to Nibiru that she manipulated us into doing on Titan. Our cargo is junk. The real delivery is the last vial of the bio-weapon we watched destroy people there."

Just speaking of it conjures up a memory of Pol writhing on the cargo bay floor, his mouth frothing black. The others look queasy, their thoughts likely following the same path. I take a deep breath and force myself to continue.

"I agreed to do this because I thought it was the only way to save Pol and protect the rest of the family. And I lied to you because I wanted to save you from the burden of guilt." I look around at them. "Now I understand how awful it would be to deny you a choice. But Leonis has our brother."

Drom and Lyre exchange a glance, both faces holding a silent question. I hurry on before either one of them feels the need to make that decision without all the information.

"Furthermore, on board we have someone who thinks there may be a better way to do this. I'd like to introduce you all to someone."

At my gesture, Corvus goes to bring Shey upstairs. Lyre gasps when she emerges. Drom shoots me a knowing look.

"You smuggled your girlfriend off-planet, huh?"

"Wha—no! That's not...she's not..."

"That's the Gaian president's daughter, idiot," Lyre stage-whispers at her.

"Exactly," I say. "Her name is Shey Leonis. She's—"

"Way out of Scorpia's league," Lyre supplies.

I sputter for a moment before heaving a sigh.

"Just listen to what the lady has to say, all right?"

I step aside and gesture for Shey to speak. If my sisters' words bothered her, she doesn't show it. She stands tall, hands clasped behind her back, in the same composed position I've seen her mother take before she makes a speech.

The room is silent as Shey explains what she already told me. I squirm in my seat, eyes darting around, wondering what's going through everyone's heads as they listen. Will they take a chance on this, or will they do whatever it takes to save our brother? I can't be sure. I'm not even sure what I want.

By the time Shey is done, Lyre is covering her mouth with one hand, and Drom's head is lowered, her expression obscured. Corvus keeps glancing at me, waiting for me to speak, but I'm not sure what's left to say at this point. I let them think.

After a moment, Drom sighs and raises her head, pushing damp hair out of her face. Shey looks at her expectantly, face full of unabashed hope, while everyone else in the room braces themselves.

"Damn," she says. "Why couldn't it be Pax? Nobody likes Pax."

Shey blinks rapidly at her. She opens and closes her mouth, but nothing comes out.

"What she means is that Nibiru has a special significance to us," I say hurriedly. "The twins were born there. But none of us are Paxian, and we've only been there once. Good years."

"I see," Shey says.

"I mean, not that it matters. Killing any of the planets would be terrible. Obviously."

"Except for Pax," Drom says. "Shitty-ass desert planet and its creepy mutant cows."

"She's kidding."

Drom shrugs.

"Please," Corvus speaks up, his tone full of barely restrained annoyance. "Let's focus on the issue at hand. We have an important decision to make."

Both Drom and I go silent at that.

"What decision is there?" Lyre pipes up from the end of the table. She sits with both hands in her lap, chewing her lower lip. "If we go against Leonis's wishes, she'll have Pol killed."

"No," Shey says. "All my mother really wants is a home. If we provide that through another way—a more peaceful way—she will honor your agreement and be grateful to you."

"You can't be certain of that," Lyre says. "Especially when we don't know if a peaceful method is possible. And if it fails, we won't have another chance to try. We have one shot at this." She takes a deep breath and looks down at her lap. "I appreciate your honesty, Scorpia, I really do. But I don't think we can risk deviating from the original plan."

"These are innocent people we're talking about," Corvus says, his voice getting heated already. I tense, worried he's going to explode like he did last night. Seeing him like that—talking about things like bombing Gaia—frightened me. "Millions of innocent lives."

"If we don't do this, Leonis will find someone else," Lyre says quietly, without looking up. "This way, at least we'll be alive, and we'll have our brother back."

"I would do almost anything to have Apollo back, same as any of you, but this is too much," Corvus says. "We have to believe that Shey is right, and her mother won't harm him. This is a chance to stop the war here and now, before it consumes the rest of the system. Our *one* chance to stop it. We have to take it."

He and Lyre both turn to me, each of them clearly seeking support. Drom stares down at the table. Shey has her eyes shut and her hands clasped to her chest. I swallow a lump in my throat and shake my head.

"I'm the one who got us into this mess," I say. "I think I've made more than enough decisions for the family. This one is for the three of you to decide."

All eyes turn to Drom now. She sighs and rubs the bridge of her nose with one hand.

"You're asking me to choose between my twin and my homeplanet?" she asks. "Well. That's a shitty choice if I ever heard one." Though she aims to adopt her usual devil-may-care drawl, her voice trembles. "Seriously, why couldn't it have just been Pax?"

"Think of all those people," Corvus says in a low, urgent voice, leaning toward her. "The fishers, the storytellers, the children playing tag in the market every morning. You remember them all, don't you? They welcomed us when no one else would."

"Ugh, shut up." She grimaces, covering her face with her hand.

"Think of Pol," Lyre butts in quickly. "Think of never seeing him again. He needs us. He—"

"I can't think about a damn thing with both of you talking!" Drom slams a fist on the table hard enough to make it rattle. She takes a deep breath, jaw clenched, and jabs a finger in Shey's direction. "Prissy Gaian lady. Walk me through the plan if we do this your way."

Shey's eyes open, and she looks at Drom in shock. I have to admit I'm surprised as well. Of all of them, I wouldn't have expected her to try to approach this from a reasonable viewpoint rather than let her emotions rule her.

"As Leonis's daughter and a public figure in my own right, I have enough political pull to secure a hearing with the Nibiran Council," Shey says, gazing at Drom with hesitant, rekindled hope. "Once there, I can explain the situation on Gaia and beg for refuge. I expect they'll want something in return, and I'm sure Gaia will be willing to give up anything for a peaceful solution. Once we reach an agreement, I will contact my mother to make it official."

"And you're sure your mother will agree?" I ask. As much as I want to remain impartial, that part of the plan is difficult for me to believe, and we have to think of Pol's safety. But Shey nods, her face full of complete confidence.

"My mother is only doing this because she believes there's no other way. If there's a peaceful alternative, she'll take it."

"You *think* she'll take it," Lyre says. "And that's assuming that the Nibirans will agree to the plan in the first place."

"You really believe they would turn away someone in need?" Shey asks. Her voice is full of honest confusion—but I can't help it. I burst out laughing. My other siblings laugh as well, except for Corvus, who grimaces and shakes his head. Shey looks around at us, bewildered by the response.

"Your own planet isn't exactly kind to people in need," I explain to her, once I manage to stop my laughter. "Especially outsiders."

Shey's cheeks flush at my response, whether in guilt or embarrassment, but she doesn't back down.

"I have faith they'll make the right decision," she says. "We're human, just like them."

"We can't have a plan that hinges on *faith*," Lyre says.

"Should we have left Pol for dead then?" Corvus asks. Lyre glares at him, two pinpricks of red rising in her cheeks.

"Of course not!"

"Both of you need to shut up," I say, raising a hand to silence them as Lyre opens her mouth again. To my surprise, they listen, though they continue glaring at one another. "You've each said your piece. This is Drom's call." I turn to look at her. She's rubbing the bridge of her nose again. "Drom, we need a decision. We'll arrive at Nibiru in under twenty-four hours, and we have to know what to plan for. But no matter what you choose, we're all in this together."

I glance around the table. After a moment's silence, Lyre murmurs her assent. Corvus stays quiet, his expression pained, but gives a small nod of agreement. Shey has her head bowed, awaiting judgment.

Drom lets out a long, low sigh and leans back in her chair.

"I never really liked Nibiru. Real dull place," she says, her eyes distant, her mind somewhere other than this room. "But Pol loved it. He always said all his best memories were there. He'd talk about how we should both retire there one day." She pauses, lips twisting into a wry grin. "I always argued for Deva, myself. But..." She shrugs. "When I see him again, I don't wanna have to break the news that we killed everything he loved about the place." She looks up at Shey and nods. "So let's try your political shit."

As much as I was trying to remain neutral on the issue, a knot in my chest relaxes at her final words, and I can't help but smile. Shey breaks into a dazzling grin herself, extending her hands in a Gaian gesture of gratitude that makes Drom roll her eyes and look deeply uncomfortable.

"Don't make me regret this," she grumbles.

Meanwhile, Lyre mutters some excuse before fleeing down the stairs to the engine room. Corvus looks at Drom like he can hardly believe what he heard. He walks over and grips her shoulder.

"Thank you," he says, the words coming out thick. Drom, looking supremely embarrassed at this point, shakes him off.

"If anyone starts crying, I will punch them," she warns, and then half smiles. "Anyway, don't thank me. Thank Pol when you see him again."

Still smiling, I nod at her, and then at Shey, who is doing her best to blink away the tears in her eyes.

"All right," I say. "Let's figure out how to stop this war."

CHAPTER THIRTY-FOUR

Something Worth Fighting For

Corvus

wanted redemption, a reason that I survived Titan when so many others didn't. Now here it is: a chance for peace. Drom's shocking decision to negotiate with the Nibirans fills me with hope. The others seem similarly enthusiastic, because Shey and Scorpia immediately launch into discussion of the plan, while Drom begins some celebratory drinking. But as time goes on, doubt creeps into me.

I agree with the idea of this plan. It's the only way to stop the war, and as shamefully as I reacted last night, I realize Shey is right: The average Gaian is entirely innocent in this. They don't deserve to be punished for their leader's mistakes any more than the people of Titan deserved to die for Altair's hubris. The more I think of them, trapped on that dying planet with no idea what was going to happen, the more sympathy I have for the people of Gaia. The storms Shey spoke of, the food supply that must be dwindling after the failure of their crops... it reminds me of the harsh climate my own people suffered in. If no one helps them, I know they will follow the same path Titan did while the rest of the planets watched from afar: starvation, war, and an eventual, tragic end.

I couldn't fight to save my own people, but I am prepared to fight for the Gaians. Never again will I be silent and helpless while government officials decide the fate of innocents.

But Shey is no average Gaian. She's the president's daughter, and a scientist specializing in Primus research as well. Are we really supposed to believe she's as innocent as she claims to be, or that her reasons for being here are entirely benevolent? It all seems too convenient; she snuck onto our ship, laid out this plan for us, assured us her mother would agree, and now seems eager to take the lead. What does she stand to gain from this? If her mother sent her after all, what is the goal?

I watch as she discusses the logistics of scheduling an emergency council meeting with Scorpia, trying to figure her out. Perhaps she's here to keep an eye on us, but she does seem determined not to follow her mother's plan. Maybe Leonis really does want one final attempt for peace, without sacrificing her pride by asking for help herself... but knowing the woman's policies, I find that unlikely. If only I had five minutes alone with Shey, I would find a way to get her to spill her true intentions. But with the way Scorpia fawns over her, I doubt she's going to grant me that chance.

"I don't think you'll have any problem securing a meeting," Scorpia says. "Off-worlders are rare, and you've got political clout. They'll listen. But whether or not they'll make a decision with any haste is a different matter."

"I never did understand how seven people are supposed to agree on something," Shey says, sighing.

"Well, personally, I don't understand how a single person is supposed to be a figurehead for a whole planet," Scorpia says. "But...yeah, they're notoriously slow when it comes to big choices like this."

"We have to force them to decide quickly," I say. Both women look up at me like they'd half forgotten I was here, and Shey with no small amount of trepidation. She hides it well, but I can tell she's scared of me. Good. I want her to be. "You told us more Gaians are dying every day. We'll have to make sure they understand the stakes," I clarify, since she looks like I'm suggesting we shoot the lot of them.

"Of course," Shey says, and turns back to Scorpia. "I'll need a crash course on Nibiran manners, if you don't mind? I learned the basics in school, but it's been many years, and of course, I've had no practical application for them."

"Oh, yeah, sure." Scorpia pauses. "Maybe, uh...somewhere quieter?"

Shey glances quickly at me, and at Drom, and then nods. The two of them exit, Scorpia mouthing *sorry* at me on the way out, leaving Drom and me alone. I glower at the table, still musing over what Shey's real goal is. Drom sips her beer and shrugs.

"Scorpia and a Gaian. Who would've thought?"

I look up at her, torn from my thoughts by shock that she's actually speaking to me.

"She certainly does have the worst taste," I say. Perhaps our agreement in the argument has softened things between us...then again, exasperation at Scorpia's decisions has always been something for our family to bond over. She's always seemed utterly determined to make everything as difficult as possible, and her love life is no exception. I still haven't decided if the Gaian president's daughter is better or worse than her fling with the *Red Baron*'s pilot. At least Shey has never tried to kill us, I suppose. Yet. Perhaps that's what she's really here for—taking us out of the picture somehow...

"Yeah. Gaia has some weird STIs floating around," Drom says, immediately derailing my train of thought once more.

"That's . . . not what I was concerned about."

"Well, it's true." Drom sips her drink again. "Don't ask me how I know."

"I really, truly was not planning on it."

"Then again, I'm sure you had some equally weird shit going around Titan. What's that saying they have there? 'Fuck like the world is ending'?"

"Yeah, no, we're not talking about this." I push up from my chair. "I'm going to check on Lyre."

Drom, still chuckling to herself, salutes with her fingers to her brow as I leave the room.

As much as I was looking for an excuse to get away from that particular conversation, I have been meaning to speak with Lyre. I still vividly remember how painful it was when the rest of the family voted against me to negotiate with Leonis. Though I disagreed with her about Nibiru, I know she had good intentions at heart. And I also know how lonely it is to be on the outside.

As usual, Lyre is hard at work in the noisy engine room, her hands moving to do a million tasks at once. She must notice me standing in the doorway, but she doesn't acknowledge my presence. I am content to wait, looking around the engine room as I do. This is my first time down here since my return to the family, and I'm surprised how little it's changed. *Fortuna*, at least, is a steadfast presence in our tumultuous lives. When Lyre finishes her latest job and strips off her gloves to wipe the sweat from her forehead, I step forward.

"I was thinking we could play some dice later," I say, a shameless attempt at coaxing her out of this room. She gives a disdainful sniff without looking at me.

"I'm busy."

"I think the engine can survive an hour or two without you."

Her face creases in irritation.

"Well, it won't survive a landing on Nibiru unless I finish this," she snaps. "Water landings aren't a simple process. And I wasn't prepared to stay there long. I thought it would be..."

"A hit and run?" I try to keep my voice mild, but it only seems to make her angrier.

"Don't you dare judge me. As if you kept your hands clean in Titan's war."

"That's what I'm trying to make up for." I fold my arms over my chest and lean back against the wall, studying her face. This isn't like Lyre—not this conversation, not the argument to bomb Nibiru, not anything about the way she's been acting since I returned to the family. When she was younger, we were always the two rational ones amid the craziness of our family. Scorpia's bitterness I can understand, and forgive. But Lyre's resentment is still a mystery to me, and I have no idea what to say to calm her down.

Even when my siblings were little terrors, Lyre was never the one who needed calming. She was always quiet, independent. And she's never appreciated sugarcoating, so I decide to go with a straightforward approach.

"Why are you so angry with me?"

For a split second, guilt flashes across Lyre's features.

"I'm not," she says, and turns back to face the main fan, slipping her gloves back on. "As I told you, I have work to do."

"Talk to me, Lyre."

When she turns around, I'm surprised to see tears trekking clean paths through the dirt and grease smeared on her face. She wipes at them with one hand, looking frustrated, and takes a deep breath. She stands up straighter and collects herself before she speaks.

"I'm just so tired," she says. "So tired of trying to be the logical one. Tired of trying to do the smart thing for the sake of everyone."

"No one blames you for voting for what you believe in."

"But I don't believe in it. Not really." She winces as she makes the admission, looking away. "You think I want to bomb Nibiru? You think the guilt wouldn't have killed me if we did? But since no one else was going to be the voice of reason, it had to be me." She wipes her eyes again. "Just like it had to be me to push Scorpia to take charge, even though I knew it would hurt you. And look where that almost led us." She pauses, but it's clear she wants to say more, so I wait. "Just like I let everyone believe you willingly went to Titan, even though I knew it was a lie."

That catches me completely off guard. Familiar anger flares inside me—but it sputters out just as quickly, drowned by a wave of hurt. If this was anyone else, I would be furious. Perhaps murderously so. But this is Lyre, my baby sister who always seemed so small compared to all the rest.

"At least, I suspected as much," she says softly. "And once I began to suspect, it was easy to figure out an explanation that made more sense than the one Momma told us."

As much as I struggle for words, only one makes it out of my mouth:

"Why?"

"What good would it have done to tell everyone the truth?" Fresh tears spill over. She gives up the effort to wipe them off. "It's not like knowing would have given us a way to get you back. And it would have torn the family apart, even more than the lie already did."

I can see how that might make sense to her. But... "What about Scorpia?" Scorpia was nearly broken beyond repair by this. She spent years thinking that her worst fear had come true, and the person she trusted the most had abandoned her. She fell so hard into her drinking habit that I'm not sure she's going to ever claw her way back out again.

"It gave her purpose, at least." She sniffles, wiping her nose with the back of one hand. "To take your place. She was still a mess, but at least she was trying. Knowing the truth would have made her give up completely. Either that, or she would've done something stupid enough to get herself kicked off the ship and left somewhere."

As much as it tears at me, I can understand what she's saying.

"This still doesn't explain why you're upset with me."

"I'm mad because..." Lyre cuts off in a hollow laugh. "Because you coming back made me the odd one out again. The twins always had each other, and you and Scorpia were even closer than the two of them," she says. "And then there was me. Alone."

I'm immediately ready to argue, but stop myself. I think back to years past, to memories of Lyre holed up with a book or sleeping in the engine room.

"It always seemed like you preferred to be alone."

"Because the twins treated me like a naggy older sister, and you and Scorpia treated me like I was a child." Her eyes dart up to me before dropping again. "And that's when anybody noticed me at all. Most of the time, I might as well have been a ghost." She twists her fingers together. "And just as well, I suppose. I never really fit in with the rest of you." She swallows, and then more words rush out, faster and faster. "Momma always knew it, too. Do you know how many times she tried to get me to stay behind on Deva? She said I would do well there, said I...I wasn't stuck on the ship like Scorpia. I knew she was trying to get rid of me. And nothing I ever did was enough to prove I belonged here."

I stare at her while she struggles not to let more tears overflow. I'm not sure how I never noticed she felt like this. Lyre was always aloof, but I thought it was because she wasn't as horribly codependent as me and Scorpia or the twins. Now, I think of all the times I found her curled up on the engine room floor with a blanket and a pillow, and my heart aches.

"You must think of me as the weakest link," she says, and I shake my head, finally finding words.

"You always seemed like the strongest of us, Lyre. The one who didn't need me."

"I tried to be you when you were gone," Lyre continues, like she didn't hear me. "I tried to take care of everybody. But nobody listens to me unless I trick them into it somehow. So all I did was make them hate me. It's not fair, they loved *you*. Everyone loves you so damn much. Even Momma did, and she hardly loved anyone."

"Momma left me on Titan to die," I remind her gently. "That wasn't love. She only favored me because—" I pause before forcing out the truth that part of me has always known. "Because I was the most obedient. But you were too smart to believe the lies she fed us." I catch her gaze and hold it, making sure she hears this next part. Really hears it. "Plus, no one else in this stars-damned system is qualified to do the job that you do. None of us could keep this thing running for a single day. This is your *home*, and exactly where you belong. You don't have to try to be like me, or Momma, or anyone else—you're one of us. Fuck anything that Momma ever said or did to make you believe otherwise."

Another tear breaks free and slides down her cheek.

"Stars, Corvus, I'm sorry for everything," Lyre whispers. "I'm so, so sorry."

Without thinking, I reach to clasp her arm, but stop at the last moment as I remember my siblings aren't used to such contact. To my surprise, she reaches out a hesitant hand and meets me halfway.

"It's a Titan thing, right? All the touching?" she asks, squeezing my arm.

I swallow a lump in my throat.

"Yeah."

"I don't mind it."

She leans forward and wraps her arms around me in a tentative hug. I put an arm around her shoulders. I almost forgot what this feels like—this closeness. Now, it's like a knot inside me is unraveling, letting me breathe deeply for the first time in a long while. For now, I'm able to forget about the coming war, my concerns regarding Shey, all of it, and focus on this moment. This is what matters, I remind myself. This is what I'm fighting for.

CHAPTER THIRTY-FIVE

The Heroine

Scorpia

I sink to the floor with a groan. All the times I've imagined spending a day alone with Shey, I never thought it would involve endless bowing practice. I never thought I'd be the one giving her lessons in manners, either, but it turns out Shey knows very little about Nibiran culture and what she does "know" is mostly wrong. Given how much I've traveled between the planets, sometimes it's easy to forget that they hardly interact with each other at all.

"Okay, that's enough," I say, letting my head fall back against the wall.

Shey, frozen halfway through a deep, formal Nibiran bow, frowns at me.

"What do you mean?" She straightens up. "We still haven't been over the proper bow for an apology, or asking forgiveness—"

"Wait, there's a difference?"

"Of course. Subtle, perhaps, but on Gaia they're done like so." She performs two gestures with her hands held out, palms facing upward. As far as I can tell, they're completely identical. I roll my eyes.

"Look, not everyone makes politeness as pointlessly complicated as Gaians do. Trust me, you'll be fine with what I showed you already." Shey opens her mouth to protest, but I hold up a hand and she stops. "We'll run through it one more time tomorrow morning before we land. But that's enough for tonight."

"It's not pointless," she says.

"What?"

"Gaian etiquette isn't just about being polite. It's a matter of achieving harmony."

"Ri-ight. Harmony." While I was willing to give Shey this lesson in Nibiran social protocol, I'm really not interested in discussing theory about proper manners with a Gaian. "Well, I promise Nibirans don't take it quite so seriously."

"Traditions are a way of binding people together," Shey says stubbornly. "It's a way for complete strangers to find common ground. And that's what I have to do with the Nibirans. I need to connect with not only one person, but all seven of the council members. So it's...it's important."

I rub my temples, fighting the urge to roll my eyes.

"You're overthinking it," I say. "Honestly, you'd have a much harder time dealing with Deva or Pax or..." I swallow back the word *Titan* and hurry onward. "Everyone on Deva wants to be rich and famous, and people on Pax don't think about much beyond their own backyard. But the Nibirans will listen to you."

"What makes you say that?" Shey asks. "I've heard that Nibiran values are completely different. They're against the use of Primus technology, for example."

"For good reason, obviously. Gaians will hate it, too, once they find out it killed their planet," I point out, and Shey nods reluctantly.

"Fair enough...but I've also heard that they're selfish, and overly ambitious, and it creates dissonance in their communities."

"Is that what your mother told you?" I ask—perhaps a bit too sharply, because Shey goes quiet. "Look, that kind of surface stuff doesn't matter. People are more similar than you think. It's like... you talked about harmony, right? On Gaia, creating harmony means finding similarities, like doing the same stupid gestures and shit, right?" Shey's lips tighten, but she doesn't say anything. "So being part of a community means acting as much like everyone else as possible. It means knowing your place in society so everything moves like clockwork." Which is probably why I never seem to fit in there. "Harmony is important on Nibiru, too. But there, being a good member of a community means having something unique to contribute to it. Your strengths cover up someone else's drawbacks, so there are no weak spots left in the whole."

"Strength in difference rather than strength in unity," Shey says, tapping a finger against her lips. "That's why they have seven leaders instead of one figurehead."

"But you're not really convincing seven individuals. You're convincing one community." I shrug. "There you go. Much more important than learning to bow. Now can we relax for five minutes?"

Shey looks like she wants to prod me more about it, but after a moment she reluctantly nods.

"Thank you for the lesson," she says. "I do appreciate it."

"Ask Lyre next time, she's much more knowledgeable about this stuff."

"Oh, I think you know more than you think," she says with a smile. "You have something much better than book smarts. You understand people."

"Eh, Gaians still seem to hate me."

"*Most* Gaians, perhaps," she says, which draws a grin out of me. I watch her as she walks along the cargo crates, trailing a finger over the tops of the tall metal boxes. She pauses at the last one, eyeing the hole carved in its side by Corvus's knife, but doesn't ask. At least someone, likely Lyre, has taken the time to clean up all the scrap metal that was strewn across the floor.

"This must've been a big couple weeks for you," I say. "First Deva, now a smuggler ship, and tomorrow Nibiru. It's a lot for a sheltered Gaian to handle, huh?"

"It's all very strange to me," she confesses. "Certainly overwhelming, but not bad. It's like something out of a romance novel, really."

"Huh?" I sit up a little straighter.

"You know. A woman with a crew of smugglers, off on an adventure across the system, all sorts of political intrigue…"

"Sure," I say, scrutinizing her. "But you didn't say an adventure novel. You said romance."

Shey shoots me a coy smile before disappearing around the back of the crates. I can't help myself; like a marionette dragged by its strings, I follow. On the other side, she rests her back against one of the crates. I lean against the one beside her, close enough that our shoulders brush.

"And would this story of yours feature a very dashing pilot?" I ask.

"You mean a very loudmouthed and occasionally charming pilot who used the heroine as a hostage?"

I wince at the reminder, but lift my shoulders in a shrug.

"Only after your 'heroine' left the pilot to die, as I recall."

Now it's her turn to look uncomfortable.

"But the pilot didn't die."

"And she decided to go along with the heroine's crazy plan."

"So in the end I suppose the two are—"

"Even?"

Shey nods. I smile.

"All right, then." I lean closer to her. "So, tell me more about the 'romance' part of the story."

Shey smiles, but she turns her face away, not meeting my eyes.

"It doesn't end well, I'm afraid. These things rarely do, especially when the two come from completely different worlds."

"But they can still be nice and steamy for a while, right?" I ask, still holding on to a thin thread of hope.

"Scorpia," she says, her voice more serious now, the playfulness from before gone. "If things were different..." She hesitates, stops, starts again. "But they're not. We have so much else to worry about right now. I don't think either of us could afford such a..." Her eyes flicker over me, and she bites her lip. "Distraction."

I hold her gaze for a moment before folding my arms behind my head and looking up at the ceiling.

"Well, you know, they have this saying on Titan—"

"Scorpia!"

I jump at the sound of my name called down the stairs, abruptly straightening and brushing off the front of my jumpsuit as if I was caught doing something wrong. Shey presses a gloved hand to her lips to stifle a laugh, and I step around the cargo crates to look up at Lyre at the top of the stairs.

"What?" I ask, unable to hide my annoyance at the interruption.

"Corvus is making dinner," she says. Her eyes shift past me to Shey as she steps out from the crates, and she frowns. "It'll be ready in thirty minutes. Don't be late."

She disappears. Rubbing the back of my neck, I glance at Shey.

"She didn't seem happy," she says.

"She rarely is." I shrug. "So. Thirty minutes. You want to go somewhere more private? Such as...my room?"

"You said there wasn't enough room in there to practice bowing."

"No, but there's room for plenty of other things."

She glances up at me in a way that makes my heart race with hope.

"Actually," she says. "I have a better idea."

I suppress a sigh, hope withering.

"And that is?"

She drops her eyes to the floor. All at once she becomes almost shy.

"Well...I've never seen Nibiru before," she says, as though it's an embarrassing admittance. "Aside from pictures, and the sky, I mean, but that hardly counts."

I can't help but grin despite the still-lingering disappointment.

"Ah, yes, the sheltered Gaian." She shoots me an unimpressed look, and I shrug and smile. "I didn't get a real education, but I've seen every planet in the system up close and personal. Pretty sure that counts for more."

Shey sighs.

"Stop bragging and show me Nibiru already," she says, the corners of her mouth lifting.

Shit, I think, though I keep the smile plastered on. There's only one place in the ship where you can see much of open space, and that's the viewing panel in the cockpit. I'm not usually keen on bringing people into my personal space...especially people I'm looking to impress. Because, as much as I love the cockpit, years of spilled drinks and long, sweaty shifts at the wheel have taken their toll on the cramped little room. It's not exactly a good spot to woo someone.

"All right," I say, trying to muster up swagger despite the awkward pause. "The cockpit has the best view. Let me get it set up." I back away from her, holding up a hand. "Five minutes."

Thankfully, Shey doesn't question what "setting up the cockpit" actually means. I'm grateful that she's not experienced with spacecrafts, because anyone more familiar with one would instantly smell the bullshit on that statement. She follows me to the middle deck, where the smell of the meal Corvus is cooking makes my stomach rumble impatiently. If it smells this good, he must have started at least an hour ago, while I was busy practicing with Shey.

I scoot past the kitchen with her, ignoring Corvus's displeased look, and duck into the cockpit while Shey waits at the end of the hallway outside.

There isn't much I can do to spruce up the space in five minutes, but at least it gives me some time to spray it down with compressed air, pick up shards of glass I must have missed in my last cleaning, and scrub at some of the worst stains with a wet rag. I make sure the bottle strapped under my chair is secure and well hidden, take a deep breath, and go to fetch Shey.

"It's ready," I say. "Time for your first Nibiran experience. Shut your eyes."

She rolls her eyes at my theatrics before obediently shutting them. I take both of her gloved hands and lead her to the cockpit, my pulse rising as we approach. It's ridiculous, really; I feel like a teenager bringing her crush to her room for the first time. But the cockpit, cramped and reeking of old whiskey though it may be, is a part of me, much more than the tiny bunk I spend my nights in. It's the place I feel the most at home . . . and the most myself. Letting her in feels like I'm baring a part of my soul to her—and, worst of all, I'm not sure if she really understands how much it means to me. What if she laughs? Makes a flippant comment? Will my heart be able to take it?

I'm not sure, but it's too late to turn back now. I gently pull Shey into the cockpit and shut the door behind us, closing us off alone with the wheel and the screens and the view of brilliant blue Nibiru out the front panel.

"Okay," I say softly, letting go of her hands. "Take a look."

Shey opens her eyes and looks around. She must be used to luxury far greater than this, and I expect her to scrutinize the cockpit with a wrinkled nose and puckered lips. Instead, her eyes are as full of wonder as they always were when I brought her off-world goods. She runs a delicate finger up the back of my chair, and

379

then across the control panel, her gaze traveling across the blinking screens and colorful buttons and levers. Finally, she's drawn to the panel, and the sight of blue Nibiru through it, and brings a hand to her mouth to stifle a gasp. I grin, leaning against the back of my chair.

"It's sure something, huh?" I ask, though I'm staring at her instead.

"It's beautiful," Shey says, lowering her hand from her lips. Her eyes shine in the light. "If the people of Gaia could only know...if my mother could see it for herself..." She lapses into silence, leaving the thought half-finished. But I know exactly what she means. Though Gaia is particularly bad, I've seen it everywhere in the system: Nobody thinks of the other planets as real, of the people on them as really *human*. They don't understand that no matter how different they look on the surface, it's all the same shit beneath. Would Leonis be willing to wipe this planet out if she had ever been here? If she had come face-to-face with crowds of people who looked and acted much the same as her?

I don't know. Maybe she would. I was just about willing to do it myself, even after seeing everything the system has to offer. The thought makes a lump of guilt rise in my throat.

"And you haven't even been on the surface yet," I say, trying to steer the conversation back in a lighthearted direction. "It's completely different from your home." I grin at the thought of her stepping off the ramp and onto one of the islands, staring around with the same unabashed awe she gives everything new. But when she glances at me now, there's a hint of nervousness I've never seen in her before. I lift my eyebrows. "Oh," I say. "Are you afraid, Shey Leonis? Never thought I'd see the day."

"Well, of course it's daunting," she says, and toys with her hair, lowering her eyes. "Deva was my first time off-planet, and this is...this is different. You know our history with Nibiru. You heard what the schools on Gaia teach about it. And...there's so much at stake." She bites her lip. After a moment, she raises her eyes to me again, and I try to pretend I wasn't staring at her mouth. "You really think they'll listen to us? To me? A Gaian?"

I run a hand through my hair and look out at Nibiru again.

"Yes," I say, and mean it. "Like I told you, I think you'll find them more similar to you than you expect. I mean, overall, people are pretty much the same wherever you go." I shrug. "There are wonderful ones who will give you the clothes off their back if you need them, and terrible ones who will take everything you have merely because they don't want you to have it, and all kinds in between. We're all just people, you know? Nothing worse and nothing better." I nod, not sure if I'm trying to reassure her or myself. "All you need to do is remind them of that."

Shey is silent. When I look at her, I find her smiling up at me in a way that makes warmth curl in my stomach.

"My, my. An awfully philosophical statement for a smuggler..."

"Why shouldn't I be philosophical? I've seen more of Nova Vita than any of those scholars back on your planet. Probably more than ninety-nine percent of people anywhere in this system." I spread my hands out toward the expanse of space through the panel and shoot her a grin just as wide. "I'm bound to have some big thoughts."

I'm hoping to make her laugh, but the look she gives me is thoughtful.

"I suppose that's true," she says, and once again gazes out at the planet we're approaching. I study her face as she turns toward it: the delicate swoop of her nose, the wistful look in her eyes, the long lashes fanning out around them. "Have you been to Nibiru many times?" she asks without looking away from it. I'm grateful, as it gives me a chance to stare a little longer.

"Uh, yeah. We spent a few years there when I was a kid." I tear my gaze away from her and look out at Nibiru instead, playing back those memories, so different than my earlier childhood on Gaia. My mind wanders to the waves, the salt-tinged wind, the smell of fresh fish roasting over a fire, and the sound of laughter in the marketplace.

"You loved it there," Shey says, and I blink, turning to find her looking at me.

"I guess I did." I had my own problems on Nibiru, but at least me and my siblings were all together, and safe. "It was never the same as *Fortuna*, but… it was as close to a home as someone like me could find planet-side."

Shey is silent. When I glance at her again, her eyes are distant and misty. I realize, with a jolt of guilt, that she must be thinking of home as well. While Gaia might have been hell for me growing up, it's the only place she's ever known. It must be as important to her as *Fortuna* is to me, and no doubt as full of good memories as my years on Nibiru. Thanks to her mother's mistakes, it will never be the same again.

With a sigh, I put an arm around her shoulders and pull her closer. She bites her lower lip and leans into me, her eyes on the increasingly closer planet out the viewing panel. I stare out at Nibiru alongside her.

The weight of what we're about to do is heavy on my shoulders. Who the hell do I think I am, trying to pull off something as enormous as this? And risking the lives of my whole family to do it? I swallow hard, resting my chin against the top of Shey's head and letting my fingers curl against her arm, seeking comfort as equally as I'm giving it.

"Tell me this isn't a fool's gamble," I say, my voice coming out rough.

"It's not," she says quietly. "We're going to save them. We're going to save them all."

When it comes out of her mouth, I can almost believe it.

CHAPTER THIRTY-SIX

Hereditary Guilt

Corvus

I t's been a long time since I've been in a kitchen, you know," I say, adding a generous dose of salt to the meal bubbling on the stove. "And I don't have much to work with." We haven't had time to restock in quite a while, so I have to rely on freeze-dried vegetables and potatoes from Deva and frozen synthetic meat cubes from Pax. At least I found a variety of dried spices hidden in Momma's closet.

"Oh, shut up," Drom says. She leans against the counter next to where Lyre sits atop it, both watching me as I cook. "We all know it's going to be amazing."

"I just want you to temper your expectations."

"My expectation is that it will be better than Scorpia's cooking," Lyre says. "Which isn't a very high bar."

"What about me?" Scorpia asks, walking into the kitchen to peer at the meal. On the other side of the main deck, her little Gaian slips into my sister's room. I clench my jaw, avoiding the impulse to tell someone to keep an eye on her. Everyone seems to have forgotten awfully fast that she's an outsider we have no reason to trust.

"We're discussing your terrible life decisions," Lyre says all-so-innocently. She pauses long enough for Scorpia's cheeks to flush before clarifying, "I mean the time you tried to cook, of course."

"Right. Yeah." Scorpia coughs and shrugs. "I mean, I did my best. No one else stepped up."

"Stars," Drom groans. "I almost managed to forget about that." She clutches her stomach in mock pain while Scorpia flips her off and reaches into the cabinet for a bottle of whiskey.

"Scorpia? Cooking?" I glance at her, eyebrows raised.

"Only once," Lyre says. "Once was enough. She lit the rice on fire."

"On *fire*?" I ask, while Lyre and Drom nod somberly, and Scorpia takes a long swig. "How...?"

"And the curry was so spicy it was physically painful," Drom says. "Not even Pol would eat it."

"Momma threw hers in the trash after one bite," Lyre says, giggling at Scorpia's sour expression.

"Okay," I say. "I'll concede that my cooking is likely better than that."

"In my defense, I was very drunk," Scorpia says.

I laugh, shaking my head as I turn back to stir the stew. When I turn around again, all three of them are staring at me.

"What?" I ask, glancing down to check if I spilled something on myself.

"Holy shit," Drom says. "I think that's the first time."

"The first what?"

"It is," Lyre says, with a small smile. Baffled, I look at Scorpia.

"The first time you laughed since you got back," she says.

I stare at her, confused for a second as it sinks in. A moment later, my contentment melts away into guilt. Who am I, to be laughing and enjoying myself as if the last couple of months never happened? I don't deserve moments like this. Not anymore.

"Well, there hasn't been much to laugh about," I mumble, and turn back to the stove. Behind me, Drom groans, and I hear a quiet *whap* of contact followed by a whine from Scorpia.

"Aw, see what you did? Now he's got that broody-ass look back again," Drom says.

"All right, get out of here and let me finish dinner," I say, their presence starting to grate on me now.

While the other two wander off, Lyre slips off the counter and stands behind me, putting one arm around me in a hug and resting her cheek against my back. I stay as I am, staring down into the bubbling stew and trying to fight the guilt still gnawing at my insides.

"You doing okay?" Lyre asks, her voice muffled.

"I'm fine." It's not quite the truth, but I don't think I could put the feeling gnawing at me into words even if I wanted to. I wish I could be fully present in this moment, enjoying the company of my family, but I can't. Guilt from the past and fear for the future sit too heavily on my shoulders.

If Lyre had intended to pry more, she's stopped by the arrival of Shey to dinner. The Gaian seems to have washed up and dressed in what must be one of Scorpia's jumpsuits. It's huge on her, but that doesn't stop Scorpia from letting out a wolf whistle when she walks into the room. Shey sighs, and Drom makes a gagging motion behind Scorpia's back as she goes to meet her. I turn back to dinner, trying to ignore the irritation that burns inside of me the moment I see the Gaian. I never considered that she'd be joining us for dinner as well.

When I announce the stew is ready, Scorpia leads Shey by the hand and seats her in her old chair, left of the head of the table, where she sits now. I take my seat at her right, beside Pol's empty place. Whether it was a slip of the mind or an intentional gesture, someone put an empty bowl at his spot at the table. Everyone's eyes slide toward it as we pass the serving bowl around.

When the stew reaches Drom's end of the table, she fills her bowl nearly to the point of overflowing and plops a spoonful into her twin's as well.

"There," she says. "Now, let's eat."

As if a spell is broken, dinner descends into its usual chaos. The room fills with the sound of silverware clanking and mouths slurping and sounds of appreciation, casual conversation through half-full mouths, demands for Scorpia to stop hogging the whiskey. Shey looks a little lost among it all, but doesn't comment on what must be abhorrent manners from her point of view. I eat my own portion quietly, savoring the warm meal and the sense of togetherness. The food's not my best, but it's not bad, either.

Before I'm halfway done with my serving, the fight for seconds begins. Drom leans over to take another too-big helping, and Lyre leans in to nab a roll off her plate while she's distracted. Drom spills a ladleful of soup in her haste to try to stop her, and Scorpia yells at them both to stop wasting food in between shoveling spoonfuls into her mouth. Knowing how this usually goes, I move my own bowl onto my lap to keep it safe, trying to finish my first serving in peace while my sisters argue.

Shey ducks with her spoon halfway to her mouth when Scorpia leans over her to fight Drom away from the stew. She glances at me, and moves her own bowl onto her lap.

"Corvus," she says, trying to speak above the clamor of the others. "This is delightful. Where did you get the—hey!" Her mouth drops open in shock as Scorpia scoops a potato off her plate, and she abandons the attempt at conversation in favor of defending her food.

The familiar commotion almost makes me smile. I didn't realize until now that this is the first time we've eaten dinner together since my return to the family…and also the very first Kaiser family dinner without Momma. My beginnings of a smile dissolve at that, and I stare down at my almost-empty bowl, my chest suddenly hollow. Though Pol's seat is the most visible difference, Momma's absence hangs above us like a storm cloud.

Now that the thought's occurred to me, it's impossible to sit at this table and not think of her teaching me how to cook at this very stove, smacking away thieving hands with her spoon and giving me those rare, valuable nods of approval when I made something to her liking. Momma rarely smiled, but when she did, it was usually during times like those. Dinners like this one, when we were all together. When our family was whole.

I wonder what she would think if she could see us now: Scorpia sitting in her chair, an outsider among us, celebrating before our job is done while our brother rests in the enemy's hands. She would be furious. Worse—she would be disappointed. I wish that thought didn't still make me ache.

Something hits me in the face and yanks me out of my thoughts. My head jerks to the side, and I raise my hand to my cheek just before the mystery object drops to the table. I consider the still-steaming potato, and then slowly turn in the direction it came from. Lyre has both hands to her mouth in shock, and Drom is grinning.

"No brooding at the dinner table," she proclaims, hefting another potato in her spoon as a threat. I shake my head and finish my bowl, refusing to rise to the bait and start what would no doubt escalate into an all-out food fight.

By the end of dinner, even Shey is smiling and laughing about it all. When Scorpia slings an arm around her shoulder, she leans into her without a moment's hesitation.

I can't deny that it rankles me. This outsider—this *Gaian*, of all things—waltzes into our family and seems to fit right in within a matter of days. Meanwhile, I'm shoved to the outskirts. I've mended some of the wounds between us, but I'm still trying to figure out my place here...if I have one.

Before anyone can notice my consternation, I stand and gather as many dirty plates as I can to bring to the sink. Scorpia jumps up from her seat and accompanies me, bumping a shoulder against mine.

"Cheer up before Drom throws another potato at you," she murmurs. When I give no response, she asks more loudly, "Who's ready for some dice?"

"Hell yeah," Drom cheers from the table. I grimace. As eager as I was to have some family time earlier, at this point I'm feeling drained enough. I forgot how it gets here—too loud to think. And I have a lot to think about before we arrive on Nibiru.

"Maybe not tonight," I say. "I'm tired."

"Corvus!" I don't notice Lyre beside me until she speaks, frowning as she lets her plate clatter into the sink. "You promised."

I sigh. I never have been able to say no to her pouting face.

"Fine. As long as I don't have to do the dishes."

Lyre rushes to help, enlisting a grumbling Drom, while Scorpia darts off to find the dice bag. I move around to the other side of the counter and lean against it, trying to work up the energy for the game. After a moment, Shey comes to my side.

"Dice?" she asks.

"Gambling." I'm not in the mood to talk to anyone, let alone her, so I keep my answer crisp.

"Ah. That's illegal on Gaia."

"Of course it is."

Silence falls. Shey laces her fingers in front of her, looking as uncomfortable as I feel. But there's no easy way to disengage from a conversation when we're both waiting for Scorpia's return. Shey hesitates, glancing up at me.

"Corvus," she says, and I grimace at her serious tone. This is exactly what I've been wanting to avoid with her. I don't want empty apologies from a woman who contributed to the destruction of my home-planet, the daughter of our enemy, who very well may be our enemy herself. "I wanted to say—"

"Don't bother," I say flatly, and she pauses, face reddening. I expect her to shut up, but instead she continues, more firmly.

"I hope you know that I had no idea what my mother was doing, and I never would have made the same choice. Regardless, I'm sorry about what happened on your home-planet." When I say nothing, she frowns. "If guilt is hereditary, then I suppose we both share the blame."

I turn to face her then, holding her gaze, my grip on the counter tightening enough that my knuckles turn white. Regardless, she lifts her chin and doesn't look away.

"At least I don't pretend otherwise," I say, my voice soft despite my anger. I don't want the others overhearing this, but it needs to be said. "I'm trying to make up for her mistakes."

"And why do you think I'm here?" Shey asks, her voice lowering to meet mine.

"I don't know. You shouldn't be." I study her face. "You may have the others fooled, but I know you're up to something. And I intend to find out what it is."

Shey's eyes flash, returning my glare with a strength that surprises me.

"You think—"

"Found 'em!" Scorpia shouts, bursting back into the room with the bag of dice held triumphantly aloft. Shey cuts off whatever she was about to say, and I take a step back as I realize how close we are. Scorpia lowers the bag, lifting a questioning eyebrow at Shey and then me. "Did I miss something?"

"He was explaining this game to me," Shey says smoothly, moving to take her seat. "It sounds rather confusing, I must admit."

Scorpia pauses, her eyes still on me, but I let my expression reveal nothing. After a moment, she shrugs and moves over to sit in her chair, spilling the dice out in the middle of the table.

"It's easy," she says. "Here, these dice are yours..."

We play for hours. Hours full of laughter and drinking and conversation, until the combination of alcohol and good company is enough to melt the ball of ice in my stomach. For a few blissful hours, I'm able to forget about Shey, and everything else. I'm able to feel like we're a family again.

But of course, it can't last forever. At some point Scorpia walks Shey to her room, and then, looking distinctly disappointed, retires to Momma's empty bedroom for the night. Drom stumbles off to her own bed to sleep, and Lyre passes out with her head on the table and dice still clutched in one hand. I finish my drink and carry her to her bed; she's so tired she barely stirs.

When I return to the main deck, the ship is silent. It's hard to believe how full of life it was merely a few minutes ago. I sit at the table again, pour myself another drink, and listen to the creaks and groans of the ship as the loneliness seeps back in. After a moment, I pour another glass, and push it over to Momma's empty place at the table.

"Here's to you," I murmur, lifting my cup. "And everything you left behind." Shey's words from before echo through my head: *"If guilt is hereditary, then I suppose we both share the blame."* I sip from my cup, thinking of the risk we're taking tomorrow, and our fragile plan that *must* succeed. If I can't trust Shey to see it through, perhaps it's up to me to ensure it works. No matter what it takes. "Debts included," I whisper, as an idea starts to form in my mind.

CHAPTER THIRTY-SEVEN

Nibiru

Scorpia

The moment the ramp opens, a salty Nibiran breeze floats into the ship. Normally, that ocean smell means the start of a nice vacation. But now, I can't afford to relax. There are a million ways this plan could go awry, and any one of them ends with my family—and probably the whole planet—dead.

Lyre is staying on board with the alien vial in case anything goes wrong. The rest of us are dressed in casual, knee-length Nibiran robes, which are both comfortable and conveniently fitted with a number of hidden pockets in the sleeves. Shey, wearing an ill-fitting one borrowed from my own closet, steps up next to me and stares out at the ocean with wide and wondering eyes. Taking in the hovercrafts skimming over the surface and the traditional boats bobbing along with the waves, the island and the docks and the crowds of people who must seem so different than the ones on her own planet, and yet so similar at the same time. She takes a deep breath, and I shut my eyes and breathe with her, trying to imagine what it must be like to taste Nibiru's clear air for the first time.

"Wait," Corvus says, and my eyes snap open. He nods toward Shey. "We need to check her for weapons."

"What?" I stare at him. "You've got to be kidding me." But, of course, Corvus is never one for jokes.

"She could be plotting an assassination attempt on the council," he says. "Trying to pin it on us."

I groan. "Corvus—"

"It's fine," Shey says, surprisingly calm. She lifts her chin and meets Corvus's eyes. "It's a rational thought. I understand."

"Scorpia can do it, if you're more comfortable with that," my brother says. I grit my teeth, resisting the urge to argue on Shey's behalf. She can handle herself.

"If this is what's necessary to put your mind at ease, I quite insist you do it yourself."

Arms folded over my chest, I glare at him as he checks her. Damn him for ruining what should have been a beautiful moment.

"Are you satisfied?" Shey asks mildly, once he's finished with a thorough pat-down. He steps back and, after a moment's pause, dips his chin in a brief nod. "Good. Let's continue, then."

Corvus sets off without another word, and doesn't so much as pause to look out at the ocean as he heads down the dock toward the city. I roll my eyes and step up to Shey, nudging her with an elbow.

"Sorry. Someone's got a stick up his ass today."

Shey shoots me a thin-lipped look of disapproval.

"I don't blame him. This is serious, Scorpia. The fates of two planets are at stake."

"Oh, no." I gasp dramatically and press a hand to my chest. "It's contagious!"

Shey mutters something unintelligible and follows my brother onto the island. All dumb jokes aside, my heart is pounding so hard I'm half-afraid it will leap out of my body. It seems impossible to walk down this dock and step onto an island where I've spent so many happy days, knowing we almost unleashed an alien weapon on everyone here. But Drom follows after the others, her face turned out to the endless ocean, so I force myself to keep up.

It also seems impossible that we should be able to stroll to the end of the docks and greet customs agents like we would any other day, and yet that's exactly what we do. Drom shows them proof of her citizenship here and the ship's registry under her name, and the rest of us already have business visas established here as her crew. Same as on Deva, customs agents here aren't too wary of a citizen's ship arriving, especially given that we're not taking any cargo. They wave us on after a step through a scanner.

Just when I think we're about to get past without any trouble, the official frowns and gestures for us to wait.

"Hold on," she says, looking down at her computer and then up at Shey. "I'm not seeing this one in the database. Did you send over a transmission?"

"Er." I didn't know anything about a transmission. "We can do that here, can't we?"

"Of course not." The official seems affronted at the mere thought. "It takes at least a month to process." She gestures at Shey to step back. "No visa, no entry. She'll have to stay on the ship."

Shit. Our whole plan hinges on Shey speaking with the council.

"What I mean is, the transmission should be there," I blurt out, thinking as I talk. "From Gaia?"

"Gaia?" Now the officer looks more confused, verging on hostile. "What does Gaia have to do with it?"

"This is..." I look at Shey, who seems unsure about what to say, and then back at the customs agent. "This is the new Gaian ambassador! You should've gotten the file."

"There is no Gaian ambassador on Nibiru." The officer squints at me as if she suspects I'm trying to pull a joke on her.

"Yes, hence the *new*." I lean forward, tapping a finger on the counter and molding my face into a look of impatience. "I mean, come on, lady, don't you recognize her?"

The officer's gaze swivels between me and an obviously embarrassed Shey. The latter clears her throat and clasps her hands behind her back in an attempt at regaining her poise.

"My name is Shey Leonis," Shey says, lifting her chin. "Daughter of Talulah Leonis, the president of Gaia. And, as my escort has already told you, the new Gaian ambassador. My presence here is a matter of utmost importance."

The officer's eyes widen as she makes the connection. She stares at Shey, some of the color draining from her face, and I resist the urge to grin.

"I'd hate to tell the president her daughter was turned away because of a transmission error on your end, Miss..." I reach forward, flicking her name tag. "Miss Ahlu. Wouldn't you?"

She turns quickly to her computer, hands flying across the keyboard, face going whiter still as she no doubt verifies Shey's identity.

"My mistake, of course. I'm so sorry, Ambassador Leonis, ma'am. Let me just—May I have twenty minutes to work something up for you, please?"

"Of course," Shey says with a pleasant-but-strained smile, one I'm sure she doesn't have to work too hard to fake. "Though I do have an appointment with the council to make, unless that transmission failed to arrive as well?"

"Yeah, time is of the essence," I say, with a meaningful glance at Shey. She only frowns at me, so I lean closer and whisper, "Give her some credits." She raises her eyebrows. "It's normal here," I add.

Still frowning, Shey taps at the slim device wrapped around her wrist and extends it toward the woman. The clerk holds out her own comm, silently accepting the bribe, and smiles at us.

"I will contact them immediately," she says, her fingers already moving rapidly across her keyboard. "Five minutes."

True to her word, the woman has us out of the customs office and stepping onto the grassy island five minutes later. We're docked on Vil Hava, the largest of Nibiru's seven human-made isles, and the seat of the council. Standing on its surface, it's hard to tell the difference between this constructed island and the natural land on other planets. The buildings here are rounded, shaped like either broad domes or tall cylinders, all standing on stilts or platforms. The buildings are rife with stained plexiglass windows and other colorful decorations.

But the permanent structures are all government offices and other official buildings. The common people of Nibiru favor a more nomadic life, especially after issues with islands flooding in the past. The streets are lined with tents and pop-up stalls selling anything from food to medicine to clothing, and most people prefer to live in floating houseboats docked at the edges of the island rather than on its surface.

On the island, life carries on as normal. It's midday, and the merchants' booths are busy. Sunburned fisherfolk shout out about their catches of the day, holding up huge, glistening fish with gaping mouths. A storyteller sits with a drum in his lap, weaving a tale of distant planet Earth for a crowd of fascinated children. The air is full of scents fried and sweet, the weather sunny and gorgeous.

I lag behind the rest of my family, drinking it all in, my chest heavy as I think of how close I came to destroying it all. I never should have taken this job in the first place. I'll carry the shame of it for the rest of my life—but maybe today we can make up for it, at least partially. If all goes well, we can save not only this planet, but the citizens of Gaia as well.

I'm so caught up in my thoughts that I don't notice Shey has stopped until I run right into her. I catch her by the shoulder as she stumbles. For a moment I think all the noise and sun has made her dizzy.

"All these people..." she murmurs, and I know that her thoughts have followed the same path mine did. Her mother ordered this entire planet dead, and Shey must feel the weight of that as much as I do. Trying to stifle my own guilt, I squeeze an arm around her shoulders and pull her along down the street.

"Right," I say, instilling my voice with as much false cheer as I can manage despite my own dark mood. "I completely forgot to give you the Nibiran tour! This is Vil Hava, Isle of Flowers, seat of the council."

"Scorpia," Shey says crossly, but I carry on.

"Honestly, not the best vacation spot, but it is what it is. Maybe one day I'll take you to Kitaya—now *that's* a view, and less crowded. But this place does have its perks. Like..." I crane my head and pull Shey closer to the side of the street and a food vendor there. When the vendor turns the other way to shout about her wares, I dart in and steal one of the pastries off her booth. By the time she turns around, it's already tucked into one of the hidden pockets in my robe's sleeve, and I give her a grin and a wave.

"Did you just—" Shey protests, as I steer us away.

"Of course not." Once we're out of the vendor's sight, I pull out the pastry and split it in half. "Anyway, as I was saying. This is one of the island's specialties. Fish pastries. Usually, I prefer Devan food. But this... this is an exception." I stuff half of the salty-and-sweet treat into my mouth in two big bites and offer the rest to her, wiggling it tantalizingly under her nose when she doesn't take it immediately. She eyes me, her nose wrinkled, though I know the smell of curried fish and fresh-baked dough must be making her mouth water.

"I'm not going to eat stolen goods," she says.

"Oh?" I ask through a half-full mouth before swallowing. "Too bad. Everything tastes better when it's free. But, in that case…" I slowly move the pastry toward my mouth, maintaining eye contact with Shey the whole time. She watches me, eyes narrowed. Just before my lips can close over it, she snatches the pastry and shoves the entire thing into her mouth at once. I burst into surprised laughter while she chews.

"Well?" I prompt. "What do you think?"

Shey swallows and wipes her lips with one delicate hand.

"I think I never want Gaian food again," she says, and I laugh again.

"Next time we end up on Deva, I'll have to show you around. They have the best desserts, if you know where to look."

"Already making plans to tour the system with me, hm?"

"You saying you'd be opposed?"

She searches my face for a moment, as if actually considering the question, and my heart skips a beat. For a moment it's all too easy to imagine: me and Shey and my family, touring a peaceful system together once all of this is over.

"I'm saying…" She trails off as she looks ahead. I follow her gaze to find my family waiting outside of the Council Hall, a very tall and narrow cylindrical building that is covered almost entirely with stained-glass windows. Drom is leaning against the building and eyeing nearby food vendors with interest, but Corvus has his arms folded over his chest and looks none too amused by the delay.

I sigh, removing my arm from around Shey's shoulders and letting it fall to my side as we approach. For a few blissful minutes, I almost managed to forget the reason we're here. At least Shey is looking less wan and more herself. She pulls away from my side and brushes off the front of her robe.

"All right, all right," I say loudly, deciding to take charge of the situation before Corvus gets a chance to scold me. "As Shey and

I were just going over, the plan is for her to go in alone first. Her political connections and fancy words should be enough for her to grab an emergency hearing today. Then she'll get us, and we'll all come in, verify her story, et cetera, et cetera. Everyone understand?"

"It's really not that complicated," Drom says.

"Yeah, well, we tend to be bad at plans, so I'm just making sure." I glance at Shey. She clasps her hands in front of her, staring up at the tall building with obvious trepidation. "You've got this," I say, and she glances at me and gives a small nod. Without further prompting, she strides into the Council Hall alone.

I watch her go, tapping my fingers against my leg and trying to pretend my pulse isn't rising with every passing second. After a moment, I sigh, shove my hands into my pockets, and lean against the side of the building next to Drom. Around us, life on Nibiru carries on as normal. The crowds pass us without a second glance, more interested in the nearby sweet stands and passing boats than the small collection of off-worlders waiting outside the Council Hall.

At least thirty minutes pass, at which point I'm getting seriously antsy thinking of all the ways the plan could have gone astray. Maybe Shey can't arrange a council meeting after all, or they'll refuse to see her for six months. The council is notoriously slow and fussy. Or maybe they'll call her bluff about being an ambassador in the first place. Is impersonating an ambassador a crime? Probably. Guess that's a new one to add to the list after today.

But Shey finally emerges from the building looking triumphant.

"They cleared their schedule for the next few hours. They'll see us now," she says, gesturing for me to join her. "Councillors Heikki and Oshiro have just arrived from Deva. The timing is perfect."

"Knew you could get us in."

"I merely emphasized that it was a matter of national security. And gave the clerk some credits to speed the process along."

My eyebrows rise, and I break into a delighted grin.

FORTUNA

"Wow, look at you," I say. "I'll make a criminal of you yet."

Shey blinks at me.

"You said bribes were normal here," she says, forehead pinched in confusion.

"Well, yeah. Still technically illegal, though." I nudge her with a shoulder. "Which still makes you technically a criminal."

Shey's face blanches.

"You could have specified that!" she sputters, looking utterly mortified, as I laugh my way past her and into the building. The rest of my siblings follow.

The lobby is a small, simple room. Wide windows ring the walls near the ceiling, flooding it with light. The furniture is sparse, lending the building a quietly refined look without any of the extravagance so commonly found on places like Gaia and Deva.

The clerk, a curvy young woman with tattoos around her wrists, waits in the center of the room. She goes wide-eyed at the sight of us. I fake a cough to hide my grin, imagining what we must look like through her eyes, when she's so used to dealing with politicians all day. Even cleaned up and dressed in our Nibiran getup, we're still an odd collection. She looks especially nervous at the sight of Corvus, with his scarred face and hard eyes, though at least his long sleeves hide his war-brand.

"Are... all of you going in?" She glances at Shey for confirmation, her eyes practically pleading for her to say no.

"Of course." Shey raises one brow as if she can't imagine why she's being questioned. "This is my entourage. Is there a problem?"

The clerk struggles for words for a moment before bowing her head respectfully.

"Not at all," she says. "Right this way."

She leads us down a long hallway that curves into the interior of the building and gradually upward in a spiral. After passing through scanners and past a number of security guards, we enter

399

the Nibiran council room. Several more guards stand at the doors, each of them eyeing us suspiciously as we pass.

The chamber is huge and circular, with high ceilings and especially intricate stained-glass windows. The colorful designs dye the light different hues as it filters into the room, painting the white tile in rainbow light. The council members sit in a raised half circle of seats. Each is dressed in uniform silk robes belted at the waist, the deep blue fabric pooling around wrists and ankles. It's silent when we enter, but the air is laden with the quiet tension of a conversation abruptly ended.

Seven people sit on the Nibiran Council, each representing one of the islands of Nibiru. Each representative holds equal weight on the council, though the largest island, Vil Hava, holds three times the population of the smallest, Lan Iroh. The council does not make decisions unless at least five of its seven members vote in accordance. But in especially important matters, it will often postpone its final decision until a unanimous agreement is reached. For an issue as colossal as the one we're bringing to the chamber, I'm sure that will be the case today. Which means we have to convince not most, but *all* of these officials that they should provide refuge to a planet whose people have been their enemy for half a century. Even among the many disagreements between planets, Nibiru and Gaia have a particularly complicated history, considering their disagreements over Primus tech and the whole issue of the plague.

Bringing Gaian refugees to this planet will cause civil unrest at best, and at worst, endanger innocent Nibiran citizens. But Nibiru is the only planet close enough to be viable for a swift evacuation, and even so, it will take a week to travel here. According to Shey, the Gaians lose more lives every day, so they need to begin evacuations as soon as possible. At the very least, the Gaians will need to use this planet as a temporary stop before moving onward. So the Nibirans have to agree on this. We have to *make* them agree.

As I look up at the seven stony faces passing judgment on us, doubt gnaws at me. The council members vary wildly in age and appearance, but each regards us with the same naked suspicion. They clearly are not used to welcoming outsiders into their chambers, especially ones who didn't announce their presence until today. But at least they've agreed to see us. That has to mean something, even if it's merely a courtesy extended to the Gaian president's daughter.

Shey stands in the middle of the chamber, her hands clasped behind her back and her chin raised, without a hint of self-consciousness or doubt. Even in her ill-fitting, borrowed clothes, standing in the seat of power of her people's historical enemy, the sole representative of her entire planet, she looks fearless. For a moment, a surge of affection nearly overwhelms me as I think of her risking everything to be here. Defying her mother, sneaking on board our ship, asking for mercy from people who have every reason to hate her...she did all this, with her head held high, for a chance at peace.

Damn, I sure picked a terrible time to start falling for someone. I swallow hard and tear my eyes away from Shey as the council rises.

"Welcome," says Councillor Oshiro, who I recognize from Gaia. Their voice is light and airy as it floats through the open chamber. "While this is an unusual occurrence for us, the council is, of course, pleased to entertain visitors from our neighboring worlds. Tell us, off-worlders, what is it that you seek?"

For all her confidence, when the moment comes for Shey to speak, she hesitates. Uncertainty flashes across her features, and her mouth stays glued shut. When the silence lingers a moment too long, and Oshiro raises questioning eyebrows, I clear my throat and step forward.

"Esteemed council members," I say, a little too loudly, my voice booming dramatically around the small chamber. I pause briefly, trying to determine where the hell the rest of this sentence is going. "I would like to introduce you all to Shey Leonis, the daughter of Talulah Leonis, president of Gaia. Shey sought passage on our ship and a hearing in this chamber for…" I hesitate, realizing I should probably leave the general explaining to Shey. "For a very important reason. So, please, I implore you…take this shit seriously."

I wince at the awkward closing. Silence falls. A mustached man whose nameplate reads Nikhil Acharya covers a smile with a cough.

"We're already well aware of who she is," he says, not unkindly. "Otherwise we would have never granted her an audience."

Someone titters. I smile in the face of their derision. I expected as much, but it was the best stalling I could manage on a moment's notice. If making myself look like a bumbling idiot buys Shey the time she needs to seem prepared, then I'd do it a hundred times over.

"Right, yeah," I say, bowing and stepping back. "Of course. Please excuse my terrible off-worlder manners." Hopefully they don't hear the edge of amusement to my voice, or the snort Drom lets out in response. Once I'm done, I glance sideways at Shey and say, more quietly, "That's your cue, darling."

Shey shoots me a grateful look and takes a deep breath before beginning to speak.

"Esteemed council members of Nibiru," she says, "I know that there has been a long history of hurt between our planets. I come to you today hoping that we can begin to mend the divide between us. And I come asking for you to save my people."

There's no hint of her former hesitation now. The words pour out of her. She is both humble and regal, both plaintive and strong. She paints a picture of her home-world in disrepair, of innocent people in need, of her mother's desire to help them. Then she builds up a new image: an image of a new age where the planets are allies rather than enemies, where they work together as a united humankind and forgive each other for past mistakes to move toward a better future.

Of course, her pretty words leave out the fact that it was President Leonis who originally brought this upon her people, and that the president was hell-bent on wiping out the entire population of Nibiru to get what she wanted. Still, even knowing that, I find myself inspired. Hopeful.

"In the past, we have too often let our differences come between us," she says as her speech winds to a close. "When, in reality, I believe our differences should work to balance one another within the larger community of the system. I also believe that, if we work together, we have so much to teach one another. If we share our traditions and experiences, if we learn to help each other and find harmony between our peoples, both Gaia and Nibiru will be stronger for it. And together, we can pave a new path for our system's future—one in which the planets come together, just as the many nations of Earth did when their world was threatened. Like them, I believe we can use our strengths to make up for one another's weaknesses and become a unified whole."

I bite back a smile as I recognize some of my own words in her speech. As silence falls, I glance around at the half circle of council members. Some of them look as moved as I felt during Shey's speech. Some even more so—the mustached Councilman Acharya discreetly wipes his eyes with a handkerchief. But others, like silver-haired Heikki, look completely unaffected. Oshiro looks almost angry. I resist the urge to break the silence, since this is no place for stupid jokes and quips.

After some murmured, private exchanges among the council members, Heikki stands and looks down at us.

"We thank you for your speech," she says, and glances to her left and right as if seeking silent agreement. "Of course, an issue of this magnitude will require great thought and care. After the recent tragedy of Titan, we must be especially careful in how we choose to deal with our planetary neighbors." She pauses, and I chew my lower lip. Perhaps the fall of Titan will make them more sympathetic to Gaia's plight... or perhaps it will only make them more wary. I'm sure that hostile Interplanetary Council meeting didn't help their relationship with Gaia. "The council will ruminate in private, and reconvene to make our final decision."

Shey stands with her hands clasped and her expression mild.

"How long, may I ask, do you expect a decision will take?" she asks, her voice as calm as if she's inquiring about the weather, though I know the fate of her people must weigh heavily on her mind.

"In order to make a careful decision, we must continue to look into Titan, as well as better understand the circumstances on Gaia," the councilwoman responds. "I expect the investigation and discussion will take us at least one month's time."

My stomach drops. A month? We have no idea what will happen on Gaia during that time period. And that's a month minimum. Knowing how this shit works on Nibiru, it will likely be longer. By the time the council decides, there could be no more Gaians left to save.

"I beg you to reconsider," Shey says, her voice trembling slightly. "Gaia cannot begin to evacuate our citizens until we are sure we have a safe place to go. And even if we start immediately, we do not have the ships to transport our population all at once. If each trip takes a week to arrive here from Gaia, and another to travel back..." She trails off, shaking her head. "We can't afford to wait so long."

"We sympathize with your plight," Acharya says, his expression genuinely regretful. "But for the sake of our own people, we will not rush such a choice."

"Sorry, but that's not going to work for us," I burst out before I can stop myself. Heikki raises her eyebrows in clear shock of my lack of protocol, but I keep going. "With all due respect, more people die every day on Gaia, and we don't know how much worse this thing is going to get."

"I understand the dire situation, but a decision like this could place our people in just as much danger as the Gaians," Heikki says, holding out her hands. "We cannot afford to be hasty."

"And the Gaians can't afford for you to wait," Corvus snaps. A number of alarmed faces from the council turn toward him at his tone. The sight of him—hands clenched into fists, rage threatening to boil over—does little to soothe them. I'm surprised to see him rush to the defense of the Gaians—but then again, I'm sure he must be thinking of his own people. He knows exactly how bad this could get, and understands the loss it would bring. I step toward him and place a hand on his shoulder, giving him a gentle squeeze. He lowers his head. "Leonis isn't going to wait a month," he murmurs, quiet enough that only I can hear him. "Even with a peaceful solution potentially on the table, she'll make her move before then."

As much as I want to believe that Leonis is more reasonable than that, I fear that he's right. The president has already proven she is willing to take drastic measures to save Gaian lives. But how do we make the Nibirans understand that without revealing Leonis's treachery?

"My people are human, no different than you," Shey says, her voice taking on an edge of desperation, her cheeks flushing. "They're dying every day waiting for an answer that won't come until you make a decision. Nibiru is their only hope. Please, I ask that you find a way to decide more swiftly. If you could at least indicate whether or not you're open to negotiations, we can connect you to the president and see what we can offer one another."

"You come to us asking for help," says the regal, dark-skinned Councilwoman Govender, "and, as you say, we are your sole option. I do not believe you are in a position to be making further demands."

Corvus's eyes flash toward her. I squeeze his shoulder again, but he shrugs me off and steps forward several paces, until he's within spitting range of the council. Shey, barely containing her emotions over the council's words, shoots me a questioning look, but even I'm not sure what he's planning to do.

He takes a deep breath and pushes up his sleeve, holding out his wrist so that the council can see the black war-brand on his wrist.

"My name is Corvus Kaiser," he says, "and I am, as far as I know, the last surviving Titan."

Shit. What the hell is he doing? I shoot him a panicked look, but his focus is entirely on the council, whose eyes are all on him. My breath catches as I remember the argument we had before arriving on Deva, when he was so eager to inform the Interplanetary Council of the truth and get justice for his people. Surely he doesn't mean to tell the Nibirans now, when it could ruin our entire plan. They will never allow the Gaians to settle here if they know that President Leonis was responsible for Titan.

"You bring up Titan as a tragedy now," he says. "And its end was tragic. But long before the massacre there, the people of Titan suffered. They struggled to survive in a harsh world, as the Gaians are struggling now. You, along with the rest of the system, ignored Titan when they needed you. You watched from afar while they froze and starved and grew so desperate that they began to kill one another. Now you intend to ignore Gaia in the same way? Are you willing to let them meet the same fate? Watch them succumb to hunger and in-fighting as my people did?"

The council murmurs uneasily among themselves. Oshiro stands, leaning forward with a spark of excitement in their eyes.

"If you are truly a survivor of Titan, does that mean you know what happened there?"

Corvus hesitates. I take a step toward him, but stop. Surely, he won't let the people of Gaia suffer for the sake of his own revenge.

"Yes," Corvus says. I shut my eyes, bracing myself, but open them again as I hear him rustling in one of the hidden pockets in his sleeve. The mere motion is enough for the security at the doors to step forward, raising their weapons, but Oshiro halts them with a hand. The councillor's eyes remain on Corvus as he pulls a vial out of his pocket.

"Oh, no," Shey whispers, while I let out a long string of curses under my breath. So much for keeping the incredibly dangerous alien weapon safe on the ship. Lyre must have agreed to this, little schemer that she is.

"What is this?" Councilwoman Govender asks.

"If the scanners didn't catch anything"—another council member—"then it's—"

"Primus technology. Correct." Corvus holds it up for them to see. "This is an extremely powerful biological weapon. It wiped out the entire population of Titan in less than twenty-four hours. It's airborne, fatal, and entirely unstoppable."

A few of the council members rise to their feet in immediate panic. The security guards rush toward us, shouting frantic commands at Corvus. I hurriedly step between him and the nearest one, terrified that one will shoot and make him drop it.

"Hold your fire," Heikki yells at them, likely making the same realization about what a very bad idea that would be.

"He's just informed us of what this vial does," Oshiro says, surprisingly calm. "I would suggest we give him some space."

The guards retreat at the council's command, though they keep their weapons trained on my brother.

"I really hope you know what you're doing," I mutter to him.

"You put our entire planet at risk by bringing that abomination here," Heikki says, the fury in her voice barely controlled. "You must know that Primus technology is banned here, let alone such a powerful weapon."

"I do," Corvus says. "But I have to make sure you understand how dire this situation is." He lowers the vial, though he keeps it gripped tightly in hand. "Titan has fallen. Gaia is dying. I don't know the cause of either, or if they are linked. But I do know that the system needs to start finding peaceful solutions for its problems, and it needs to do it now, before the situation worsens." He scrutinizes the members of the council one after another. Few of them meet his steely gaze. "Gaia does not have time to wait. Whatever your decision may be, you need to make it today, so that they can decide how to proceed if shelter here is not an option." He turns the vial over in his hand. "Until you decide, I will remain on Nibiru with this weapon, to serve as a reminder of everything at stake."

"This was not the plan," Shey hisses at me, while the council erupts in outrage. I give her an apologetic shrug.

"We've never been very good at plans," I mutter, and step forward to stand at my brother's side. "Well, you heard the man," I say, loudly enough to be heard above the clamor. "As we've tried to make clear to you, the Gaians don't have time to spare. So we're going to skip all of the bullshit and the time-wasting and get right to it. Now you need to decide if you're willing to help out your fellow humans, or if you're going to turn them away in their time of need."

I lower the upper half of my body in a proper Nibiran bow to hide my grin.

"So I suggest you get to the decision-making," I say, and step back as the council begins to shout again.

CHAPTER THIRTY-EIGHT

The Decision

Corvus

I sit in the lobby of the Council Hall, the alien vial gripped tightly in my hand, trying not to think about how terribly wrong that situation could have gone. I know I should have told my siblings about what I had planned, but it was impossible to steal a moment with Scorpia without that Gaian woman around. The only person I could confide in was Lyre, who agreed to hand over the vial this morning before I left the ship.

But all things considered, this desperate ploy is working well so far. The council promised us a decision in no more than five hours. If they hold to it, it will be an unprecedentedly swift decision for the Nibiran rulers. They are clearly eager to get this alien weapon off their planet.

The hours pass rapidly. I hardly notice the council's time is up until the clerk—along with several armed security guards—comes to inform Shey that the council has reached a decision. The rest of us wordlessly accompany her. Other than a nervous glance from the clerk and an icy look from Shey herself, no one dares try to stop us.

"You really should have warned me, but I gotta say, this is a pretty good plan," Scorpia says as we walk up the winding hallway. "I'm loving the VIP treatment."

"I believe the goal is to treat us like terrorists," I mutter to her, noting how the clerk looks back at us and quickly looks away again.

"Very important terrorists."

I fight an absurd urge to smile, and instead give her a disapproving look.

"Maybe we should see if we end up in a jail cell before deciding if this was a good plan."

"Aw, c'mon, they're not gonna arrest us. This is for a good cause."

"Terrorism for a good cause? Not sure they'll buy that."

Scorpia's laugh echoes around the hallway, drawing another nervous glance from the clerk leading us. Her laughter goes on too long, the sound too high-pitched, like it always does when she's trying not to act scared. She stifles it as we reach the council chamber. The guards glare at us as we enter, their hands on their weapons and their eyes on the vial in my hand, but they let us pass.

Shey takes her place in the center of the room, with the rest of us flanking her. Scorpia shifts from foot to foot, while Drom yawns and rests her hands behind her head. I fold my arms across my chest and sweep my eyes over the council, trying to gauge their reactions. Their expressions are stony and unreadable, their hands folded and backs straight, in their usual picture-perfect image of a completely uniform and united front.

For all the jokes Scorpia and I made, I have no idea how this is going to go. If the Nibirans decide not to take in the Gaians, we'll surely be arrested, and all of this will have been for nothing. And even if they do agree, I doubt they're going to let us walk so easily after I brought a class-one contraband item into the council chamber. No matter how this goes, it's hard to see how it will end well for us.

Acharya rises to speak for the council. One voice for one unanimous decision, as is traditional.

"Normally, I would begin this judgment by thanking you for bringing this matter to our attention," he says, nervously smoothing out his mustache. "But given the circumstances, I believe we can skip directly to our decision."

Drom chuckles behind me.

"The council has heard your plea and considered this grave matter with as much care as our time constraints allowed," the councilman continues. "After deliberation, we have decided that we do not have the space nor the resources to host the population of Gaia."

My stomach drops, a cold feeling spreading throughout my limbs. Did we really come so far, do so much, all for nothing? Despair grips me at the thought—but the man continues.

"We cannot offer our planet as a permanent solution to the Gaians' problem. However, we also cannot turn our back on a neighbor in need."

A thin sliver of hope breaks through—but still, it's not clear what that means. I glance at Scorpia, who looks as confused as I do.

"C'mon, spit it out already," she blurts out. "What did you decide?"

The man clears his throat.

"The Gaians will be welcome here for a temporary stay," he says, his voice stiff. "In return for full disclosure about the circumstances of Gaia's decline, and proper compensation to ensure our own people will not suffer. They may remain on Nibiru for three months, during which time we will do our best to assist them in finding a permanent solution." He looks directly at Shey now. "Will the terms of this agreement be acceptable, Ambassador Leonis?"

Shey, standing at the front of the room, is frozen in place for a moment. She takes a breath. Her hands start to extend in the Gaian expression of gratitude, but she stills it halfway through and inclines her body in a deep Nibiran bow instead.

"Your generosity is boundless, as is our debt to you," she says, her voice little more than a whisper.

The man gestures for her to rise, his expression softening.

"We will discuss the specifics directly with the president."

"Yes. Of course. I will contact her immediately."

I glance around at the other council members. Surely it can't be that easy. They couldn't have reached a unanimous consensus in such a short, stressful amount of time. I expected that when they reached a decision, there would be dissenters—I expected a chamber full of arguments and resentment. But instead, each member of the council is quiet. Is it really possible? Under pressure, did each of them decide that they would grant refuge to their longtime enemies?

"That's it?" I murmur to Scorpia, while Shey steps forward to talk in low tones with the council, arranging a conversation with her mother.

"Stars, I hope so," she mutters back. "I could really use a drink."

"We're on the same page for once."

Scorpia clears her throat loudly, gaining the attention of the council again, whose faces are quite a bit less serene when they're looking at us instead of at Shey.

"So, uh, thanks and good luck and all that," Scorpia says, either not noticing or not caring about the looks she's getting. "If you need us, we'll be at...what's the nearest pub?"

Acharya continues his conversation with Shey as if Scorpia had never spoken, but Heikki looks directly at her and forces a strained smile.

"Actually, I'm afraid we aren't quite done with you yet," she says.

"Meaning?" My hand snakes toward my hip, reaching for a blaster that isn't there, before I remember the vial in my hand and tighten my grip on that. But though they kept their distance earlier, the security guards approach now at Heikki's nod, warily closing in on us. Beyond them, a large force of Nibiran peacekeepers floods into the room.

"What were you saying about not getting arrested?" I ask Scorpia, who sighs and flips me off with one raised hand.

CHAPTER THIRTY-NINE

A Tangled Web

Scorpia

As it turns out, we're not actually being arrested, for once. The peacekeepers, as the council explains, are here to escort us to our ship, which we will then be expected to board immediately. If we're not off-planet within the hour, *then* we'll be arrested.

All things considered, it seems like a fair judgment, and nobody—certainly not Shey—tries to argue in our defense. Even Drom is quiet as they usher us out the door.

Shey doesn't say goodbye. She doesn't even turn to watch us leave. I guess I deserve that, too, though I can't deny it stings. I cast one last look at her as I'm herded out of the chamber, catching a glimpse of her profile as she discusses specifics with the Nibiran council members. Then she's gone.

It didn't occur to me until now that it's probably the end for the two of us. There's little reason for us to ever come face-to-face again. For a moment I have a mad desire to run back into the room and kiss her, without giving a single damn for anyone who's watching—but the moment passes. She'd only be pissed at me for making her look bad in front of the council, and anyway, I'll probably get shot if I try to go back in there.

"So that's it, I guess," I say, and glance around at my siblings. Drom looks exhausted. But Corvus, even with guns pointed our way, looks more relaxed than I've seen him since he returned to the family. He doesn't look happy, per se—there's still no sign of his old smile—but he looks as though a weight's been lifted off his shoulders. He nods at me and says nothing.

The peacekeepers rush us back to the ship, making only a brief stop at the customs office on the way out. A whole lot of words are exchanged that I can barely keep up with, but I get the gist of it: We're no longer welcome on Nibiru. Ever. Not even Drom, who's being stripped of her citizenship. I didn't know that was possible, but I guess we're a special case.

"Seems fair," I mutter, glancing over at her to see if she's upset about the new development. But she shrugs, looking completely unsurprised.

"Never liked this place much anyway," she says loudly, for the benefit of the customs agents.

The peacekeepers leave us on the dock, but they hover near the customs checkpoint, their eyes still on us. We make our slow way toward the ship. Despite Drom's words, she doesn't appear in a rush to say goodbye to Nibiru for the last time.

I lag behind the rest of my siblings, taking deep breaths of the cool, salty air, drinking in the smell and the sight of the ocean stretched out all around us. In the distance, a slim hoverboat carves across the water, kicking up a spray of mist; back on the island, I still hear the cries of the street vendors advertising their fresh fish and other goods. I wish I had stopped to taste a pastry one last time.

That thought, of all things, sends a pang of heartbreak through me. I stop where I am, sucking in a shaky breath, and try not to think about childhood memories spent drifting on the water, or roasting fish over the fire with my siblings, or sharing that pastry with Shey a few hours ago.

Of all the prices to pay in this situation, I never thought of this one. And it's worth it—it will be worth it—but that doesn't make it hurt any less. I take a deep breath, trying to steady myself and ward off tears. The rest of my siblings are already on board, waiting for me, though their eyes are all on the ocean.

As I take my first step onto the ramp, a frantic cry cuts through the general harbor noise.

"Scorpia!"

I turn around, surprised to see Shey running up the dock toward me, pushing through the crowd of officers, who give her suspicious looks but make no move to stop her.

I grin. Guess she wasn't ready to let me leave without a goodbye after all. I stop at the edge of *Fortuna* and head down the dock to meet her halfway. But my grin dies as I get close enough to see her. She's out of breath, her robe in disarray and beads of sweat running down her face. Her eyes are wide and wild.

"Wow, miss me that bad already?" I ask, trying to push down a wave of worry. With everything we've been through, I've never seen Shey in a state like this. Not even being kidnapped with a gun to her head made her look so frantic. She clings to my arm, chest heaving as she struggles to catch her breath and get the words out. I glance over my shoulder at my siblings, crowded just inside the cargo bay and peering out at us, and draw Shey a few steps away for some semblance of privacy. I take the hand that rests on my arm and squeeze it. "What's going on, Shey?"

"My mother," she gasps out. Tears fill her eyes before she can continue. I wait, icy fear already spreading through my stomach. "She . . . she lied."

"Not surprised, but you're gonna need to give me details," I say, trying not to jump to the absolute worst conclusion before she says it. Shey gulps air, her hand trembling beneath my fingers.

"She agreed to the council's plan. Made a deal with them. But then she contacted me privately." She finally regains enough breath to start forming coherent sentences. "I swear, I never thought she would do this. I really thought we could achieve peace. But she doesn't believe that the Nibirans will take us in. She's convinced it's a trap."

"Shit." Damn Leonis and her paranoia. All this work for peace, and she has to ruin it. "What is she going to do?"

"She already did it," she says. "The bio-weapon she gave you… you weren't the only ones. There's another ship headed here now."

"*Shit.*" Now that really is the worst-case scenario. "How long do we have?"

Shey's face is stricken.

"Less than five hours," she says, her voice barely audible. I stare at her, and then the island behind her, teeming with people and life and laughter, as fear paralyzes my body.

Five hours. So little time. Even if we warned the council, even if we warned the entire planet, there wouldn't be enough time to intercept them before they hit the atmosphere.

"Get on the ship," I say, breaking through the fear holding me in place. "We need to get as far away from here as possible."

I tug on Shey's arm, but she yanks out of my grip, taking a step back and shaking her head.

"Shey, we tried," I say, taking a step forward as she pulls away. "We really tried. We almost did it. But there's nothing more we can do here. We have to save ourselves."

"No." She takes a deep breath and raises her chin, her fear melting away in an instant. "I've already told my mother: I'm staying with the people of Nibiru. I'll share their fate."

"What the hell is the point of that?" I ask, my voice rising. A few heads from nearby boats turn to us, and I lower it again. "Forget about your pride, Shey. This is stupid."

"I gave these people my word. It's not about pride. It's about principle."

"Is there a difference?" I'm struck with an urge to grab her and drag her on board the ship, but I can't bring myself to step forward. I can't do that to her. My stars-damned conscience sure has a habit of showing up at the worst possible times.

"I know you don't understand." Shey smiles at me, the expression muted and sorrowful. "But this is my choice. I've spent far too long being complicit in my mother's actions. I've let others pay for my mistakes while I stayed safe. You said as much to me on Deva, and you were right."

"Now's not the time to make a point," I say. "We'll find a way to make sure your mother pays for this. We'll find a way to make things better. We have a ship, and..." I trail off as the realization hits me. "We have a ship," I say again. A much faster ship than anything the low-tech Nibirans have on hand.

There could still be time to intercept the incoming vessel. We might just be the only people in the entire system who have a chance to stop this from happening. And yet, the thought fills me with dread instead of hope. Haven't we done enough? Sacrificed enough? I can't make another choice like this.

Not even for an entire planet? a small voice in the back of my head whispers. As much as I try to push it away, I know what the right thing to do is... but how can I ask that of my siblings? We've been through so much already.

Shey moves closer, her face gentle. She reaches up to grab the back of my neck and pull my lips down to meet hers. One brief kiss, and she steps away again.

"I understand," she says, but slips her hand out of my grip

when I try to hold on to her. "No matter what choice you make, I understand. None of this is your responsibility."

"It's not yours, either. Come with us."

"It is my responsibility. As I said, I gave them my word." She steps back farther. "Goodbye, Scorpia. I..." She hesitates. "Words aren't enough. But...thank you."

"Don't do this." The words come out so softly that I'm not sure she hears them. But even if she does, she turns away from me and heads down the dock toward the doomed island. Despite knowing the clock is ticking, I watch her go until she's no longer in sight, not trusting myself not to follow her until she's really gone. I suck in a deep breath, digging my nails into my hand in an effort to stop myself from breaking into tears. Once I manage to get my emotions under control, I turn and race down the dock to the ship.

I'm surprised that my siblings aren't waiting impatiently on the ramp or trying to spy on me and Shey. Instead, I find them huddled around Lyre in the cargo bay, murmuring among themselves. She's staring down at her comm, while Drom has her arms wrapped around herself and her head lowered. Corvus looks up at me, his expression troubled. My steps slow, my rush to tell them the news stopped by sudden dread as the realization hits me. Leonis clearly isn't happy about our interference in her plans...and she has our brother at her mercy.

I can't bring myself to ask, so instead I stare at Lyre, waiting for the news.

"We just received two messages from Gaia," she says. "They're labeled with your name."

"Okay." The word comes out little more than a breath. "Show me." I step closer and put an arm around Corvus, hugging him close to me as we watch the bar finish loading. Lyre silently hits the play button.

I take in a shaky breath as Pol's familiar gap-toothed smile fills the screen. Drom lets out a strangled noise. My heart surges at the sight of him alive and awake, a sight I wasn't sure I'd ever see again—and swiftly plummets once more. The message only shows his face, but even so it's easy to see the toll the disease has taken on him. He's paler than I remember, his cheeks hollowed out in a way that makes me almost grateful I can't see the rest of him right now. His usually shaggy hair is shaved down to fuzz, and his eyes wander somewhere behind the camera rather than looking directly into it.

"Hi, everyone," he says, his voice quiet and croaky. "I wanted to send a message, let you all know I'm feeling…" He pauses, swallows. "I'm feeling, uh, all right, I guess? They say I'm making good progress, but it's…" He trails off into silence, as if he's lost the train of thought. "I miss you all. Come get me soon, please?" His eyes focus on something offscreen, and the message ends.

My siblings are silent. I don't trust myself to speak, either.

"Man, he looks like shit." Drom's voice trembles.

"He's alive," Lyre says gently. "That's what matters." She pauses, biting her lip. "And there's one more message."

Corvus's face is cloudy.

"Play it," he says.

I nod my agreement. We need to know if that message was as much of a threat as I'm thinking it was. Lyre meets my eyes briefly before hitting the button.

This time, Leonis's face appears on the screen, as smooth and composed as always.

"This is a message for Captain Scorpia Kaiser," she says, her eyes boring into me through the screen. "As you can see, Captain, I've fulfilled my end of the deal, though at this point it's clear you have not done the same." She pauses to smooth down her dress. In the long moments of silence, my heartbeat becomes an increasingly erratic drum in my ears. "I will give you one more chance. Bring me my daughter, unharmed and without delay, and we will welcome you back to collect your brother. I'll be expecting you soon."

The screen goes dark.

"Shit," I say.

"What do you mean *shit*?" Drom asks. "This is easy enough. Get the prissy Gaian over here, and let's drag her home to her mommy, get Pol, and be done with this."

Despite her words, it's easy to see she's been shaken by the messages—and I'm about to make it worse. But I can't hold my tongue on this. No more lying or omissions or making decisions by myself. It's time to lay everything on the table.

"Unfortunately," I begin, "it's not that simple."

CHAPTER FORTY

All or Nothing

Corvus

By the time Scorpia finishes her explanation, my stomach feels like a ball of ice. I can see in the defeated slump of her shoulders and the tired grief in her eyes that Scorpia feels the same way I do—that she thought our fight was over, and the idea of doing more seems impossible. We're already running on fumes. After all that we've been through, it only seems to get worse and worse, and the stakes higher and higher. To go against this ship now would mean risking everything. It would mean risking Pol. And we've gambled our lives too many times already. But do we really have a choice? If we turn our backs on Nibiru now, what was the point of everything else that got us here?

"We're the only ones who can do anything to prevent this," I say. Though I try to channel conviction into the words, they come out tired and flat. "We have a responsibility."

"No, we don't," Lyre says almost apologetically. "This isn't our fight. These aren't our people. We can still run."

"You don't have to be the voice of reason," I tell her, thinking back to our conversation in the engine room. "You don't have to believe something is logical to believe that it's right."

She looks away, hesitating. "I..."

"What about Pol?" Drom interrupts before she can finish. "We all saw that message. Leonis still has him." Her eyes are on Scorpia. "You said Leonis would forgive us if we struck a deal for peace. You told us she wouldn't do anything. But now—"

Scorpia holds her hands up as if in surrender, her expression pained.

"I wasn't lying. I really thought that was true." She drops her hands, expression growing bitter. "Shey seemed so convinced."

Drom looks like she wants to say more, but I shoot her a look and shake my head. She grimaces. After a moment of silence, Scorpia looks up at us again.

"We have only one ship," she says, her voice stronger than before. "And this isn't a decision I'm going to make for everyone. We'll do it like last time. We vote. Either we run together, or we fight together."

A somber silence falls. As eager as everyone was to share their opinions before, now that they know their words really matter, everyone is quiet. I drop my eyes and resist the urge to study their faces or argue for my own point. Scorpia is right. This is a decision we all need to make for ourselves. We need to decide what we're willing to risk, and what we're willing to live with.

"This isn't like the last time we voted," Scorpia says, gazing around the circle, her face uncharacteristically serious. Even with all the other emotions flooding through me right now, I feel a burst of pride in my sister; she really was meant to lead. She's doing a far better job than I ever would have in her position. It wouldn't have occurred to me to bring the issue to a vote, though it should have. "The situation has changed. This time, if we decide to act, our lives will be in very real danger." She pauses, licking her lips. "And even if we succeed...we'd be deliberately acting against Leonis."

"And Leonis has Pol," Drom says. Scorpia nods.

"We don't know what the president could do to him in retaliation," she says. "Even if we stop her now, the president seems hell-bent on starting a war to save her people. Doing this will place us on the other side of the conflict, and Pol is effectively her hostage."

Drom bows her head and says nothing. Scorpia runs a hand through her hair and takes a deep breath before continuing.

"And aside from that...I think I know exactly which ship we're going to meet out there," she says. It takes me a moment to realize what she means.

"Of course," I mutter. The *Red Baron* always shows up at the worst possible moments.

"Last time we fought them, Orion hinted they were out near Titan for a reason. He called it 'legitimate business,'" Scorpia says. Before I can question why she was speaking to the old fling she notoriously hates, she continues, "And...I never mentioned it, but as we were leaving Titan, we passed a ship heading there."

"Leonis must have wanted something," I say. "Maybe confirming how soon the Gaians would be able to move in after the bio-weapon was used..." Or maybe she needed them to retrieve something for her. I think of Altair setting that power source on the table. That's what Leonis was meant to gain from the deal with Titan, after all.

"Right," Scorpia says. "We were never supposed to make it out alive. So she needed another ship working for her, and there are only so many ships that can cross borders nowadays."

"Well, at least we know what we're up against," Drom says.

"Yes. And we know the *Red Baron*'s crew is nothing to scoff at.

Plus, this time we can't pull off some quick gimmicks and escape. We'll have to find a way to fight our way through them without setting off the weapon and killing us all."

Her words spark another thought in my head. Technically, that isn't true. If we manage to set off the bio-weapon in space, it's possible the effects wouldn't reach the planet below. If other options run out, we may end up having to sacrifice ourselves to save Nibiru. Scorpia's eyes flicker to mine as if overhearing my thoughts.

"But if we run, everyone on this planet will die," I say. "And we still have no guarantee that Leonis will give Pol back unharmed. We've defied her once, she may have already decided we're her enemies."

"We have her daughter," Lyre says, looking thoughtful. "Perhaps we can use that."

My stomach lurches with fear, all of my worries about Shey coming to the forefront again.

"Maybe this was her plan the whole time," I say. "The supposed deal with the council could have been a distraction. Now, if Leonis gets her daughter back—"

"Shey isn't coming with us," Scorpia says flatly, interrupting me. "She's decided that she'll meet the same fate as the Nibirans, no matter what we decide. She already informed her mother."

The rest of my words die in my throat. I stare at Scorpia, and she meets my gaze levelly. She's not rubbing it in, but it's clear what the look means: I was wrong. Shey was never trying to sabotage us. She wanted peace as badly as we did. I lower my eyes, shame sinking my stomach.

"Which means Leonis would *definitely* be grateful if we dragged her darling daughter back," Drom says. When everyone glances at her, she shrugs. "Just saying."

"That would solve many of our problems," Lyre says.

"No," I say, glaring at each of them. I can't believe it's even up for discussion. "Shey gets to make her own choice." After how much I doubted her, at least I can give her that dignity.

"Anyway, it's pointless debating that now," Scorpia says. "First things first. We need to decide whether or not we're going to try to stop the ship."

An uncomfortable silence settles. Lyre and Drom both stare at the ground, while I study Scorpia's face, trying to determine what she's thinking. Last time it came to a choice like this, she abstained from the vote. I never had a chance to find out what she would have done. Even after mending our relationship, I still find it impossible to tell what her real feelings are.

"Are you voting this time?" I ask her. She hesitates, and then nods.

"This time will be different," she says. "Like I said, we only have one ship, and I'm not asking anyone to die for something they don't believe in. So we're doing this Nibiran style."

It takes me a moment to realize what she's saying.

"A unanimous vote," I clarify.

"Yep," Scorpia says. "Either way, we're all in this together. Unless we each agree to go after the *Red Baron*, we'll leave together and figure it out from there."

My stomach sinks, but I can't bring myself to argue against her. I know that she's right—we can't force our siblings to risk their lives. They deserve a choice. Yet Lyre already voted once against trying to save Nibiru, and Drom was hard enough to convince before she knew the decision would certainly put her twin at risk. And I have no idea what Scorpia will vote for. Any one of them could sink this plan before it begins.

And if they do, will I be able to bring myself to follow them? They're my family, my blood... but I'm not sure I could forgive them for abandoning Nibiru. I'm not sure I could ever forgive myself. As soon as I think it, I resolve myself to the thought: If they vote to run, I'll make the same choice as Shey and go down with Nibiru. I won't bear the responsibility of any more lost lives.

But saying as much wouldn't be fair to my family. Scorpia is right: Everyone deserves a chance to decide for themselves, including her. And as much as I hope that Scorpia would make the right choice regardless, I know that hearing I'll stay behind will sway her opinion more than the millions of lives at risk on this planet.

"We should do this anonymously," I say, as difficult as it is to force the words out. I clear my throat. "That's the fairest way to do it. We each make the decision for ourselves."

Scorpia nods. "We'll all write them down and I'll read them out," she says, and looks at Lyre. Our little sister retrieves paper and a handful of pens from the supply closet, and hands out the writing utensils and strips of paper.

"So, one of two options," Scorpia says. "We either run, or we stop the *Red Baron*. No getting clever with this, make sure your vote is clear."

Once each of us holds a scrap of paper and pen in hand, there's an uncomfortable pause. Despite my decision being secret, it feels strange to make the choice in the view of the others. My siblings seem to have the same thought, because one by one we turn our backs to one another, carving out spots of solitude to make this final choice.

I clutch my pen in one hand and press the paper against the wall to hold it flat. Now that I'm making the decision, a sliver of doubt cuts its way into my heart. Is fighting the *Red Baron* really the best option here? As Scorpia said, even if we succeed, Leonis may kill Pol in retaliation. Am I willing to let that happen? Am I willing to never see my brother again, to let my last memory of him before he was infected be the one time I ever raised a hand against him? Am I willing to give up my chance to ever apologize for that mistake?

And yet, if I don't, I'll be choosing to sacrifice an entire planet's worth of people. People who welcomed us when we were young, sheltered us when so many others turned us away. If I do that, there's no turning back from becoming the person Titan nearly turned me into.

Either way, I will be giving up a piece of myself. My decision will haunt me for the rest of my days. One more in the string of impossible, terrible choices I've been forced to make. I take a deep breath, close my eyes for a moment, and open them again. I write.

Scorpia gathers the papers and unfurls the first. She licks her lips, hesitating briefly before reading it out loud.

"Save Nibiru," she reads. Hope fills me—but as she lets the paper flutter to the table, I see my own neat handwriting printed on the paper. Scorpia grabs the next one. "Stop them," she says, and drops that one as well. I recognize the blocky handwriting as Drom's, and faint hope blossoms inside me, though I try to keep it contained. She squints at the next one. "Stop *Red Baron*," she reads, and drops it. The writing is shaky, confusing me for a moment before I realize it must have been written left-handed. It has to belong to Lyre, the only one clever enough to try to conceal her handwriting. I resist the urge to glance at her, though pride surges in my heart. It seems she finally decided to follow what she believes in.

So that leaves Scorpia. I stare at her, wondering if the others have figured out that the last vote is hers as well, wondering what's running through her head. She takes her time unfurling the last piece of paper and pretending to read it, though she already knows what the answer will be.

Rather than reading it out loud, she looks up at me, a hint of a smile on her lips though there's worry in her eyes.

"It's settled," she says. "We stop them."

Rather than a celebratory cheer, the response to her statement is a tense silence. I wonder if any of the others expected this, or if, like me, everyone thought that one of the others would make the decision to run for all of us. I wonder if anyone is already regretting their choice.

Our fate is sealed. For better or for worse, we're doing this. If we die, we die together. If we win, we all share the burden of whatever that victory means.

"All right then," Scorpia says. "Let's go take these bastards down."

CHAPTER FORTY-ONE

Chaos

Scorpia

The radar lets us know that the *Red Baron* is coming in to Nibiru fast. We need to hit them before they're close enough that we'll all crash down onto the planet, which means we have a scarce fifteen minutes until impact. Fifteen minutes to gear up and strategize about how the hell we're going to win the most important battle of our lives.

Everyone on Nibiru is counting on us. Shey is counting on us. And my family is counting on me. We may have all made this decision together, but I'm still the captain. Right now, that responsibility is making me want to vomit. My hands shake as I set a course for the autopilot, and I can't stop thinking about Pol and Nibiru and everyone else who will suffer if we fail. Even beyond the death of an entire planet, if we don't pull this off, Leonis's actions will incite a system-wide war.

I know that we're doing the right thing, but as much as the thought fortifies me, it doesn't mean I'm not absolutely terrified. I'm not much of a fighter on my best days, and now, I desperately need to find some confidence before going in against the pirates. But when I reach down under my chair, my fingers find empty space. Fresh fear spikes through my heart. I quickly search the cockpit, but there's no sign of my bottle here. My *last* bottle. It's been a long while since I was able to properly restock, and with the stress of the last few weeks, my supply has been quickly dwindling—but I know I didn't finish my last bottle of whiskey yet. I rush out to the middle deck to search.

The moment I step into the kitchen, I find my bottle clutched in Drom's hand.

"What the hell are you doing?" I snap, anger bubbling up to replace the fear twisting my guts into knots.

"What's it look like?" Drom takes a long swig. "Should be pretty familiar to you, of all people."

I grab for the bottle, but she easily lifts it out of my reach.

"Don't be a fucking idiot," I say. "We need you sharp for the fight. You and Corvus are our front line right now."

"As if you weren't planning on doing the same thing?"

"I'm serious, Drom! This is important!"

"You really need me to keep pointing out your hypocritical bullshit?"

I grit my teeth. Responses flit through my head—angry, threatening, wheedling, pleading—before I settle for telling the pathetic truth.

"I just need a little bit of courage, all right? I'm scared shitless right now."

Drom scoffs, lifts the bottle to her mouth, and takes another swig. But after lowering it, she hands it over to me. Only when I grip it do I realize how badly her hand is trembling. Startled, I raise my eyes to hers, as wide and bloodshot as my own must be.

"Is that why you're drinking?" I ask, taken aback by the prospect. Her lips twist to the side, and I expect her to deny it.

Instead, she says, "Seems to work well enough for you."

She releases the bottle, leaving it suddenly heavy in my hand.

"But you…" My thoughts tumble around one another, unable to wrap around the idea. Drom scared of a fight? Drom imitating *my* behavior? I'm not sure which of the two is more baffling. "You're never scared," I say, finding that one easier to grasp on to. "You're always the first one in the fight and the last one out. You're…*you*."

She averts her eyes, teeth grinding against each other. Her thumb rubs against the scar on her left arm.

"It was easy to be brave when I had to," she says. "Pol always counts on me to be the strong one. I have to protect him." Her voice grows shaky, her words speeding up. "The only reason I voted to save Nibiru is because I know that's what he'd want. But…now I can't stop thinking about how he looked in that message. And how I can't protect him. Just like I couldn't protect him from Corvus, or that alien bullshit. And I'm starting to realize maybe I'm not as strong as I thought I was. Nowhere near as strong as *he* thought I was. Maybe I was pretending the whole time, but it took until now to realize it." She pauses for a few seconds, while I struggle to find words. An uncomfortable laugh escapes her. "This was a whole lot easier when Momma was telling me what to do all the time."

"Yeah," I say softly. "It was easier for me, too. But it's okay to be scared. We're all scared. Corvus spent three years in the war on Titan, and I guarantee you he is still on the verge of shitting his pants right now." I manage a weak smile. "Fear only makes us weak if we let it stop us. But as long as we still get our jobs done, then we win, yeah?"

I thought it was pretty good for an on-the-spot speech, but Drom's face doesn't change. She rubs her fingers over her scar again.

"Easy for you to say; you're drunk all the time."

"That's not—" I pause, let out a breath. "I'm not drunk *all* the time." She fixes me with an irritated look, and I brush hair out of my face, avoiding her eyes. "Look, this shit isn't easy for me. I've never been a fighter. Not like—" Not like *you*, I almost say, but that's not going to help with the conversation we're having right now. "—like Corvus. I need to take the edge off to get through moments like this."

"So why the hell are you trying to stop me from doing the same?"

I stare at her as she holds out a hand for the bottle. It's difficult to wrangle my thoughts into something logical, try to find the words to explain why the idea of her imitating me—growing up to be like me—makes me feel sick to my stomach. Because she is still growing up, as hard as it is to remember sometimes. She may be tough as nails, but she's still barely nineteen, too young to drink legally on Gaia, though a handful of years older than when I started. She's still deciding who she is. It took me until now to realize that she's taking cues from people like me.

And I don't want her to deal with the same shit I deal with. I don't want to look at her one day, see my flaws reflected back at me, and learn to hate her for it. Maybe like Momma did with me. Because I'm finally starting to realize that maybe that's what she was trying to tell me during our conversation about why I couldn't be captain. Not that she hated me because I was her failure, but that I reminded her of all the most terrible parts of herself.

I made some of the worst decisions of my life trying to be like Momma. If Drom does the same in imitation of me, the cycle will go on and on, causing more pain for everyone involved. But as Corvus has reminded me, it's not too late for me to change. I get to choose who I want to be.

"Damn it," I mutter, my stomach already sinking at the mere thought of what I have to do. "I really hate this responsible-older-sibling bullshit." Drom raises her eyebrows at me, taken aback by the sudden turn in the conversation. "Why couldn't you all just take after Corvus, huh? He's clearly the smart one."

"The fuck are you talking about?"

Ignoring her, I march over to the sink, clutching the bottle so tightly that my fingers hurt. My heart is pounding like I'm staring down the barrel of a blaster.

"Have it your way," I say. "We're both going in sober."

"Wait—"

I upend the bottle. The sight of the last of my liquor pouring down the sink makes bile rise in the back of my throat, so I shut my eyes until it's done. Even then, the sharp smell makes me thirsty. I swallow hard and turn to look at Drom, who is staring at me in utter bafflement.

"There's no way that was really the last of it," she says.

"It was." The croak in my voice makes it clear it's the truth. Realizing I'm still clutching the bottle, I let it drop to clatter in the bottom of the sink.

"Shit, Scor."

"Yeah."

"I can't believe you just did that."

"Me neither." I take a deep breath. "Stars damn. Let's get to the cargo bay before the regret kicks in."

In the cargo bay, Lyre doles out our entire supply of weapons while everyone else outfits themselves in combat gear. Everyone looks grim and determined. Though Corvus, surprisingly, is looking a little green around the edges. Part of me aches at having to send my still-suffering brother into combat—but we don't have a choice.

If we succeed here, we'll finally have the peace Corvus has been wanting. And if we fail . . . well, if we fail, we won't be alive to suffer the consequences. And at least the universe will know that we tried.

Lyre hands me my equipment, including the last of the body

armor, which will mean leaving herself exposed. As she leans close, she pauses, giving an exaggerated sniff.

"You don't smell like alcohol," she says, almost accusingly.

"Yeah? What about it?"

"Did you take something?"

"What? No." I start to gear up, layering protective armor and pads on top of my jumpsuit. "I'm completely sober."

Corvus shoots me a surprised look and then nods. "Good."

I roll my eyes, trying to hide how embarrassed I am by their scrutiny. It never really occurred to me how closely my siblings watch my drinking.

"Hm." Lyre's eyebrows rise. "Yes, good for you, but… you do realize you have only a few hours until withdrawal kicks in?"

"Uh, shit, right." I clear my throat, rubbing the back of my neck. That didn't occur to me while I was busy focused on making a dramatic statement, but there's no helping it now. "Well, let's get this done fast, then. We don't have much time as it is, so listen up good." Nobody pauses what they're doing—no time for that—but all eyes remain on me. "We're going to be outnumbered on there. More than usual, I mean." The *Red Baron*'s crew has always been bigger than ours, but we've never gone against them with such small numbers. And never without Momma, the planner of the family, and the one who knew their ship almost as well as ours. Without her, we'll be half-blind.

And yet, when I think back to the last time we fought the pirates, and how willing Momma was to put us all in danger to protect the cargo… for the first time, I feel a glimmer of relief that she's not here. If Momma was still our captain, we never would've had this chance to save Nibiru and prevent the war. We would be long gone already, safe but likely hating ourselves for it. Now, we have a chance to do things our own way and redeem ourselves for all the wrong we've done. A chance to save the system.

435

Just knowing that we're trying, that we all chose to be here of our own free will, fills me with pride. But still, panic prickles in my chest as I think of the odds stacked against us. I clear my throat and turn to Corvus. "You know I've never been much of a fighter," I say, and leave the not-question hanging in the air. As badly as I want to, I can't bring myself to ask outright—not when I know exactly how much I'd be asking. I can't deny we could use Corvus's expertise, but I can't ask that of him after everything we've been through.

Corvus meets my eyes. He's silent for a long moment, his face stony. Finally, he nods.

"I'll take it from here."

I want to ask if he's sure, to give him an out if he wants it, but the rush of relief chokes the words off in my throat. Stars, am I glad this responsibility isn't mine. I've fucked things up enough lately.

"Like Scorpia was saying, we're outnumbered, and also likely out-equipped. We'll also be fighting on their territory, and sans the element of surprise, since they'll see us coming before we hit."

"Last time we got lucky with the night-vision trick, but we can't pull the same shit again," I say when he pauses, deep in thought.

"They'll also know what we came for. They'll be organized and ready."

I was hoping that passing the reins to Corvus meant he would have some grand solution that I didn't see, not that he was going to repeat all the bad news I've already thought of. Lyre and Drom are both glancing back and forth between us, so I try not to look as dismayed as I feel. Corvus frowns down at the floor, arms folded over his chest.

"So we need a plan," I say, trying to prompt Corvus into speaking again when the silence gets too nerve-racking.

"Right." He clears his throat. "We have one advantage here,

and one advantage only," he says, looking up at us. "Like I said, they're organized. Disciplined. They're used to having orders and sticking to them. And we…are not."

There's a brief pause. I try not to wince. Corvus really isn't much help with motivation.

"Yeah, we're historically terrible with plans. Which is an advantage because…" I gesture at him to continue.

"It's not, usually. But it is if we make it one. It is if we fuck up their plans and their organization." One corner of his lips curls. "Our plan is simple. We bring the chaos." He looks around at us. "Drom and I will be the main fighting force," he says, while she nods at him. "We'll work together, harass their forces, try not to get ourselves in deeper than we can handle. Scorpia—"

"I have an idea," I interrupt. "I want to talk to Orion."

"Orion?" Corvus asks, his nose wrinkling in distaste. "Why?"

"Well…he might be able to help us out," I say with a shrug. "I'm guessing he might not know the full truth about what they have on the ship."

"Don't you and Orion hate each other?" Drom asks, her brow furrowed.

"Yeah, about that…" I grin uncomfortably, and bend down to tie my boots, struggling to find an explanation that glazes over the fact I've been lying to my whole family for years. "It's a little more complicated than that."

"I knew it," Lyre says matter-of-factly.

"Wait, you two are fucking?" Drom asks, while Corvus's displeased expression grows even more so. "I mean, I knew it happened once, but jeez—"

"Hold on," I say. "That's not the important—"

"—a Gaian *and* a pirate? You really have the worst—"

"Enough," Corvus snaps, loud enough to speak over both of us. We fall silent and stare at him like guilty children. "We don't have time for this," he says. "If you think that's the best move, Scorpia, then do it. I trust you."

The words give me pause. Damn, when's the last time I heard *that*? I shake it off and nod.

"I won't let you down," I say. "So, uh, I guess Lyre will come with me?"

"Unless you have any other ideas, Lyre," he says, and she pauses, clearly caught off guard by the question.

"Well…I…that's, um…"

"Why wouldn't she come with me?" I ask, dumbfounded. Lyre hates being put on the spot like that—she's much more the type to follow along with orders. But Corvus's eyes never leave our younger sister as she stutters and hesitates. I scowl at the dismissal, while Drom feigns an exaggerated yawn at the delay.

"Lyre?" Corvus prompts gently. "We don't have much time."

She pauses, takes a deep breath, and says:

"Air ducts."

I exchange an exasperated look with Drom.

"That's not a plan," I blurt out, and Lyre glares at me.

"I can climb through them," she snaps, as if it was obvious.

"And?"

"And get to the systems room."

"*And?*"

"And then…you name it." She gestures vaguely. "If I get in, I can…I can shut down their communications system, set off the emergency alarms, screw with the gravity drive. Give me a few minutes uninterrupted, and I can create all sorts of chaos."

By the time she's finished, a grin is spreading across my face despite my earlier lack of confidence.

"You're a genius," I say. But Lyre doesn't seem to hear me, looking at Corvus for approval.

"They'll be expecting us to sabotage their systems after you did it last time," he says. But instead of backing down, Lyre lifts her head, her face determined.

"Not this kind of sabotage. All I need is a distraction," she says. "Three minutes alone with their systems. That's it."

"So Drom and I will have to pull their forces away from that area," Corvus says.

"And you're gonna do it all by yourself, Lyre?" As eager as I am to believe this plan will work, my little sister is usually the type to crumble under pressure. She seems to deflate at the mere question, glancing at Corvus as if expecting him to defend her, but he waits along with the rest of us to hear her response.

"Even if we pull off a distraction, some of their security might remain in the room," he tells her.

"And they won't see me coming until it's too late," she says. "I'm perfectly capable of handling a pirate or two on my own."

Corvus nods.

"If she says she can, then she can," he says, and looks pointedly at me and Drom. "Remember, we're not doing this their way. And we're not doing it Momma's way. We each make our own decisions. We know our own strengths and our own limits. That's why this is going to work."

Before I can respond, the lights flash green, drawing all of our gazes upward. When I look back at my siblings again, they're all staring at me. I swallow my nerves.

"Two minutes till we hit," I say.

This is it, then. That's as much of a plan as we have time to make. We're all going to have to believe that Lyre can follow through on her part, and that I can follow through on mine, and that Drom and Corvus can handle all the rest.

We're just going to have to trust in ourselves and each other.

"Strap in and brace for impact," Corvus says, and I run for the cockpit.

*   *   *

We may not have any weapons, but we've always been the faster ship. With *Fortuna* heading straight for them in a collision course, the *Red Baron* has no chance to dodge us. Their only options are to let us ram into them and likely kill us all, or—

Or the option they decide on. At the last second, they launch their grappling hooks.

I let out a triumphant whoop as they start to drag us in. They took the bait.

But once they have us in their clutches, even with *Fortuna*'s engine working at full speed to pull us in the opposite direction, we are both dragged slowly, inevitably toward the planet ahead. It's just a matter of time before we hit Nibiru, or at least get close enough that it will be impossible to escape from the pull of the planet's gravity.

The clock is ticking.

As we breach the *Red Baron*—using our never-before-used, "just-in-case" adjustable bridge, and a couple of rarely utilized space suits—it's impossible not to think about our previous encounter with the pirates. Last time there was so much smoke and confusion, blasters blazing on both sides, Momma's pulse rifle punching through enemy ranks. Now, the ship is silent and eerily still. The only sound is the steady hum of the engine. Corvus was right: The pirates will wait for us to come to them. They have all the time in the world, after all, and just about every advantage imaginable.

While the others split off to do their own jobs, I go deeper into the ship, heading away from the cargo bay and straight toward the cockpit. If most of the pirates are off defending their haul, I should have a clear path to find Orion. My unlikely friend may be a pirate, and not exactly morally scrupulous, but I can't bring myself to believe he'd support wiping out an entire planet. And as long as I can get to him, I'm confident I can talk some sense into him. He might be a little pissed off after I embarrassed him in front of his father and nearly got him shot last time, but surely I can make him see reason.

But when I round the corner to the cockpit, it's not Orion I find waiting outside. Izra peels herself away from the wall she was leaning against, a cruel grin cutting across her face.

"Well, if it isn't the most cowardly Kaiser of them all," she says. The alien gun on her arm whirs to life, and I swallow hard. "I've been waiting for a good opportunity to kill you."

I step back, spitting a curse. Of all the people to run into, it had to be the stars-damned Titan deserter with the alien weapon built into her arm. Anyone else I could try to talk to, use either reason or a trick to prevent them from killing me right away. But this woman? Forget it. She has a fucking *gun* in her arm.

But I can't run, either. My siblings need me. So I take my weapon, try to muster up some bravery, and meet her eyes.

"Look, I'm really not a fan of killing people," I say, making an effort not to sound terrified. "But I'm gonna need you to get out of my way."

Izra's smile is cold and humorless. Rather than speak, she aims her weapon.

I shoot first, aiming for her shoulder to disarm her, but she doesn't even flinch. The shot tears through the outer layer of her clothing to reveal skintight black armor underneath, which is barely scorched. I take a step back. Apparently, working for Leonis allowed them to pick up some fancy new tech. Maybe if I hadn't pissed the president off quite so badly, we could've geared up more, too.

I fire another shot at Izra, mostly trying to stall. She blocks it with her weapon. Before I can think of a cleverer ploy, she returns fire, forcing me to dodge sideways. The projectile glances off my arm harmlessly. But when I look down, I find that it cleaved straight through my own body armor as if it was nothing but cloth.

"Shit," I say, looking up at the woman with wide eyes. She grins and levels the weapon at me again.

So much for bravery. I turn tail and run.

Dodging another shot from Izra, I sprint as fast as I can down the hall and duck into the mess hall. I dive across the nearest table to avoid another shot and hide behind a chair. She stands in the doorway, looking my way with a bored expression.

"This is pointless," she says while I creep farther away, ducking around furniture to stop her from getting a clear shot at me. "You're outmatched. Your whole family is. You know this. What do you really think you're going to accomplish here?"

"I just want to talk," I call out, and immediately duck behind the shelter of a chair again when she looks my way.

"Then come out and talk." She advances. I retreat toward a doorway that must lead to the kitchen. This room is nearly empty, but maybe I could find something useful there—if I could make it through the doorway without getting shot.

"I think it's better if we talk from a distance," I say, peeking out again. "And maybe with Orion present? Where is he?"

"You got him in quite a bit of trouble last time," Izra says. "He's not going to go easy on you again."

"You'd be surprised. I can be very convincing. Just let me—" I cut off with a yelp as a shot whizzes right past my ear.

I'm scared shitless by the close call, my breath coming in short bursts, but this is the opportunity I was looking for. I jump to my feet and run for the kitchen as Izra reloads. It seems the pirates were in the middle of making dinner when we hit them, and the kitchen is an absolute mess. Cutting boards and half-prepared ingredients are strewn across the floor, along with dangerously sharp-looking knives. A pot of thick broth bubbles on the stove.

I almost reach for one of the knives, but stop at a striking mental image of Izra stabbing me to death with my own weapon. Instead, I grab the pot of broth by both handles and heave it toward the door. Steaming liquid splashes all over Izra the moment she steps inside. She recoils with a hiss. I back away while she's distracted, retreating to the other side of the island counter and trying to find something else useful.

"Running and hiding isn't much of a plan," Izra says, shaking soup off herself and glowering across the room at me.

She's right, of course. My actual plan of finding Orion is seeming more impossible by the second. At this point, I guess the best thing I can hope for is distracting Izra until Lyre pulls off her job. But I can't keep this up for long, especially not when I'm trapped in this kitchen. And now I'm starting to realize I made a critical error: This room has a single exit, and Izra is standing right in front of it.

Shit. I need a distraction. Thinking fast, I raise one hand and extend my middle finger.

"Running and hiding seems to be working pretty well for you, deserter," I say, and tap my finger to my heart in a crude mockery of a Titan salute.

Izra's face contorts in rage. She raises her gun and fires off a shot—wild and wide, as I hoped for. I dive forward and slide across the soup-coated floor, right beside her, out the doorway.

I scramble to my feet, slipping and sliding, and head for the hallway. If I can make it out, I can buy myself more time. Just a little more time and then—

There's a *plink* as Izra's weapon releases another shot. A hiss of air. Pain sears me as it spears through the flesh of my shoulder. The sharp tip protrudes through me, just below my left collarbone.

My vision goes dark, a scream ripping free from my throat as I stumble and fall to my knees. The alien blade pulses in my shoulder, vibrating down to my bones and sending fresh waves of agony through my body. I try to drag myself to my feet, but my legs give out as it pulses again, sending me crashing back to the floor with a sob. The most I can manage is turning to face Izra as she advances, her steps unhurried, a triumphant smile on her face.

"There we are." She crouches in front of me. "Now, let's *talk*, hm?" She grabs the blade stuck through my shoulder, not seeming to care as an edge slices into her palm, and twists.

The pain is blinding. I scream, tears pouring down my face.

"Shit," I whimper. "Shit, shit, shit, *wait*."

To my surprise, she does, head cocked to one side and a grin on her lips.

"Going to beg for your life?" she asks. "I'd like to hear it."

"No." I take a deep breath, try to think through the pain. My bastardization of the Titan salute offended her more than I expected—which means, deserter or not, Izra still has some attachment to her home-world's ideals. I could beg, I could lie. I'm sure the latter is what Momma would've done in this instance, considering how she went on and on about how we can never trust anyone other than each other. And yet, when I look at Izra, I can't help but think she might not be so very different than us. She scares the shit out of me, but people look at Corvus like he's a monster, too, just because of his scarred face and the brand on his wrist. Gun arm aside, maybe she's no more a mindless killer than he is. So maybe the best thing I can say right now is the truth. "I want to tell you what happened on Titan."

Izra gives me an unimpressed look and flicks the blade puncturing my shoulder. The tiny motion is enough to tear another scream out of me.

"We saw what happened on Titan. They wiped each other out, like we always knew they would," she says…but for a moment, her face flickers with something like grief.

I fight through the pain, gasping for air—and force out a hoarse laugh.

"That what Leonis told you?" I ask. "You really believe that shit?" I think of Corvus's anger, his sorrow, the way he adopted Titan customs and cared for the people he left behind. The loss of the planet nearly broke him. Perhaps I didn't know Titan as well as I should've, but it's clear the place was far more than its war. "You think so little of your own people?"

I manage an actual laugh at the look on Izra's face. She reaches forward to twist the blade again, but instead lets her fingers come to a rest on the tip of it.

"Talk," she says.

Finally. Something I'm good at.

Izra marches me to the cockpit with her gun arm pressed against my spine. It's really not necessary, given the blade still stuck in my shoulder making every step utter agony; I wouldn't make it far if I tried to run. But I suspect she's enjoying herself.

She forces me into the cockpit. If not for the excruciating pain and the situation, I would probably take a moment to admire the *Red Baron*'s awe-inspiring expanse of screens and buttons. Orion is seated in one of the two pilot's chairs. He whirls to face us, and I catch a flash of worry before he schools his face into neutrality.

"What the hell is she doing here?" he asks, standing. His eyes linger on the blade through my shoulder. "And what'd you do? Didn't I make it clear I want to handle her myself?"

Izra shoves me forward. I stumble two steps before my knees buckle beneath me. Orion catches me before I hit the floor, his arms holding me up as I sag against him. Izra makes a low sound of disgust.

"I should have known," she says.

"It's not what you think." Despite the words, Orion doesn't let go of me—so I both hear and feel the way his breath hitches. I turn my head to see Izra's gun now leveled at him. Her eye shimmers with unshed tears.

"I trusted you," she says through gritted teeth. "You and your father."

"Izra," Orion says slowly, "I'm not sure what my father has to do with it, but I had no idea you would take this so personally. Honestly, she means nothing."

"Not *her*, you idiot!" Izra shouts, before I can figure out what the hell is happening right now. "I'm talking about the cargo."

"Oh?" Orion sounds almost disappointed. "What about the cargo?"

"Orion," I butt in, desperate to save this mess of a conversation. Stars, these pirates are even worse at communication than my family is. "Do you know what you're transporting?" I raise my eyes to his, silently begging him to say no, even if it's not the truth. I'd really rather not have this end with both of us getting shot.

Orion looks down at me, his forehead creased.

"Those little shimmering vials? Some sort of alien tech, I assume. I mean, my dad showed them to me, but…" He frowns. "What is this about?"

Izra's gun is still aimed at him, her scarred face contorted with rage. I almost speak up, but her finger twitches and I hold my tongue.

"And did he tell you what happened on Titan?" she asks.

"Doesn't everyone know? They all killed each other. What am I missing here?"

"You lied about her." Izra swings her gun at me, and I flinch, sending new waves of pain through my shoulder. "How am I supposed to trust you now?"

"Okay, okay." Trying to ignore the throbbing wound, I push myself up to my feet and stand between the two pirates. "Seems like you both got played here. Same as me and my family." I look at Izra long enough to reassure myself she isn't about to shoot anyone, and swivel to Orion. "Those vials? The ones you got from President Leonis?" Surprise flickers across his face. "Yeah, she gave us some, too. They're what really happened to Titan." I take a deep breath; I haven't told this next bit to Izra yet, so I turn to her, trying not to cringe. "We're the ones who brought them there. Just like you, we didn't know what we were transporting. President Leonis lied to us. It was a horrible mistake I'm going to regret for the rest of my life, and I'm trying to prevent you from doing the same."

Izra looks over my shoulder at Orion.

"Stars," he says, his voice rough. "I would never want to be a part of something like that. I had no idea. I swear, Izra, I didn't. My dad told me nothing about this. Maybe he doesn't even know."

I highly doubt that, but I keep my mouth shut. I remember being desperate to believe the same about my own mother, though now I suspect she knew exactly what she was getting into. Maybe, when Momma went with the general alone to test the weapon, she was trying to do one last good thing for the rest of us. Or maybe that's just what I want to believe. I'll never know for sure.

"I told your father when I joined," Izra says. "No more wars, no more bombs. No more murdering innocents. This isn't what I signed up for."

"Okay, good, we're all on the same page then," I say, pushing away thoughts of my mother. "Now can someone get this stars-damned thing out of my shoulder so we can do something about it?"

CHAPTER FORTY-TWO

Redemption

Corvus

Once we near the cargo bay, Drom and I fight our way through what feels like a never-ending flood of pirates. There's a veritable army of them blocking each route we try. For every enemy we dispatch by laser-fire or grav-grenade or my black Primus knife, two more pop up to take their place. And they're not easy to get rid of, either. Each of them is clad in top-notch body armor that would've made my comrades on Titan green with envy. Nothing other than my blade and direct headshots are able to do any damage. Soon enough, we're each left with a single emergency grenade, and my pulse rifle is starting to overheat.

"It doesn't make any sense," Drom pants when we retreat into a side corridor to recover. She leans against the wall, catching her breath, while I clean my knife. "Why the hell are there so many of them?"

She's right. The *Red Baron*'s crew is bigger than ours, but nowhere near this big. We've tried three separate approaches now, and each one was swarming with unfamiliar faces. They must have picked up new recruits.

"We can't fight them all," I say. My hand roams to the pocket on the inside of my jacket, touching the Primus vial nestled there—my last resort. If we're going to lose—if my family is going to die anyway—then the pirates and these alien weapons will go down with us. As I pull my hand away, I glance at Drom to see if she noticed anything, but she's watching the entrance to the corridor.

"So what do we do?" she asks.

The question makes my nerves flare up. After everything that happened on Titan, I never thought combat would scare me again. But being here reminds me of the war—the crushing responsibly of being in charge of other peoples' lives, the losses I suffered because of my choices. Uwe, who died to defend me. Ivennie, who I let die for the sake of the objective. And so many more, an endless parade of faces to populate my nightmares. I won't let my siblings join them.

Once more my thoughts return to the vial in my pocket, and the last grenade I kept to detonate it and the other vials all at once if necessary. It reassures me. If all else fails, at least I won't have to live long with my mistakes.

"Corvus?" Drom asks, dragging me from my thoughts. "What the hell do we do? We need to pull enough heat that Lyre can get to the systems room."

"Let me think." I need to come up with something other than using the vials, but my mind returns to them again and again, as if already resigned to that end.

"We don't have time," Drom snaps. "We need to—"

She cuts off as we both spy movement at the entrance. Two armored pirates on patrol, both with weapons raised and ready.

Drom fires immediately, dropping one of them, but I fumble with my weapon in my distraction.

The man fires. I sidestep in front of Drom as I raise my gun. A half second later, my own shot singes a hole through the middle of his forehead, and he crumples to the floor. I suck in a deep breath and look down at the smoking wound near my knee, a moment before my leg wavers beneath me.

"You fucking idiot," Drom says behind me. "What the hell did you just do?" She catches me as I stumble and eases me to the floor, pressing one hand to the wound. I let out a grunt of pain and she grits her teeth as if she feels the injury herself. "Why did you do that?"

"Can't you shut up and be grateful?" I ask through gritted teeth, trying to think through the pain and Drom's muttered curses. This isn't a terrible wound, not the kind that will kill me, but it will certainly slow us down. And we can't afford that. "You're going to have to leave me."

Drom's head whips up.

"Don't say that."

"Listen." I clasp her arm with as much strength as I can manage, make sure she looks me in the eye. "Lyre needs a distraction. She needs you."

"No." A hint of panic shows through on her face. She's never been the type to hide from a fight before—but she's also never fought by herself. "There's too many of them. This is pointless. We need to get back to *Fortuna* and—"

"Drom." My tone silences her. "I know it's hard to be alone. Believe me, I know. But you're the only one who can do this."

She's quiet for a long moment. She must feel Pol's absence as keenly as I do. But finally, she nods. I hand her my pulse rifle, keeping merely a simple blaster, and she takes it without hesitation.

"What do you want me to do?"

"Get to the engine room." I was trying to avoid a plan this drastic, but it's becoming clear we don't have any other options. "That's the only thing that will draw enough of them away. Blow up their engine."

"We're too close to Nibiru," she says. "If the *Red Baron* crashes with those vials on board, this will all be for nothing."

"We'll figure that out later. You need to get those pirates away from here. All right?"

Drom nods. She starts to stand, but then pauses.

"Corvus," she says, her voice thick and uncertain. "I..."

"I know." I force a slight smile. "Me too."

She straightens up.

"Don't do anything stupid," she tells me.

"Trust me, I'm not going anywhere fast."

The moment she turns the corner, I plant one hand against the wall for support and drag myself to my feet.

"I'm sorry," I murmur, and limp down the hall.

I hide out near the closest entrance to the cargo bay, trying to ignore the dull pain radiating from my leg and my growing concern for my sisters. Each of them is alone now. I hope they can handle their roles in this fight—but our chances were bleak from the start, and getting bleaker by the second. I need to make sure that if we fail here, Nibiru won't suffer for it. No matter what it takes, I'll ensure those vials are taken care of.

"C'mon, Drom," I mutter, waiting for her distraction to come. But I have no reason to worry. For all her flaws, no one can ever say Drom doesn't know how to pull off a good explosion.

The sound rumbles throughout the entire ship. Green lights flare in the hallways, and a siren wails. Panicked shouts come from the engine room. A few moments later, the smell of smoke hits us, and the majority of the pirates guarding the cargo bay take off down the hall. Not all of them, but it has to be enough.

The moment they're out of sight, I turn the corner and open fire on the three remaining pirates. One hits the floor immediately, and another stumbles back from the force of the shots hitting her chest. I jump on the third, dropping my gun to rip my knife out of its sheath and sink it deep into his stomach. He lets out a choked gasp, and I pull the knife free and whirl, using his body as a shield when his companion opens fire. I shove him into her, and jam the knife into the side of her neck when she stumbles.

The emergency alarm shuts off, and silence falls in the corridor. I breathe heavily and spare one last glance for the fallen bodies before grabbing my gun and heading down the stairs to the cargo bay. The ache in my leg has deepened. Pushing onward could do permanent damage to it, but I need to finish this.

I find Captain Murdock alone in the cargo bay, speaking in a low voice into a comm. The sound of his voice freezes me in place for a moment. Despite how many times we've faced off against the *Red Baron*, I've only seen their infamous captain once before, during a brutal fight with the pirates when I was almost killed. He seems smaller than in my memory, but I remember his heavy-lidded eyes and thick, dark hair. I also vividly recall him dragging me half-dead back to *Fortuna* after Momma's surrender, and the way he laughed when he threw me at her feet. *"A gift for old times' sake,"* he'd said.

But I'm a lot stronger than I was back then. I'm no longer anyone's tool or bargaining chip. I step forward, raising my gun.

When he sees me, the captain pauses, surprise flickering across his face. I keep the gun aimed at him, but I know I can't shoot; I need him to tell me where the vials are. He's a private man, not the type to share information with his crew.

"Drop the comm," I say. Too late, I realize how foolish my hesitation is—he could call for help and have the whole pirate crew descend on us in moments. But instead, he clicks the device off and lowers it to the floor. Good. If Drom blowing up the engine wasn't enough of a distraction for Lyre, the abrupt loss of their captain's orders should plant more confusion among the pirates. Perhaps the silence will bring them here to me, but if that's the case, so be it.

"The weapon, too," I say, noting the blaster on his hip. He obeys, moving very slowly. Still, I remain on guard. It doesn't make sense that he's being so compliant.

"Ah, if it isn't Auriga's eldest," he says as he straightens, his gaze hovering on my wounded leg before flicking up to meet my eyes. "Made it through the war, then, Corvus? I thought of you when I heard the news about Titan."

I frown but stay silent, stepping forward and waiting for him to reach for a weapon or pull some trick. Surely he must have something up his sleeve. Yet he merely remains with both hands in the air, his dark eyes tracking me.

"I'm sorry to hear about her, by the way," he says, and I scowl. Bringing Momma into this is too much.

"Shut your mouth. You two hated each other."

He chuckles.

"It was a fair bit more complicated than that," he says. The words bring me back to Scorpia saying something similar about Orion, and Drom's crude response to it. I grimace. "Your mother was a spirited woman," he continues, while I try not to let my thoughts follow the path he's trying to lure them down.

"I'm not interested in talking about her. Where's your cargo? The vials?"

"You've got a lot of her in you. More than your siblings, I reckon." He studies my face and smiles. "Though I guess you're all pretty damn brave, trying to steal our cargo like this when you know it's hopeless."

"Answer the question." I can't let him get into my head.

"Your mother ever tell you about her time serving on my ship?" He seems completely unruffled by my tone or the weapon in my hands. I grit my teeth, fighting the urge to shoot him and be done with it. I don't know what he's trying to do here, but maybe getting him talking is a good thing. It's possible he'll slip up and reveal something useful. Or maybe some part of him truly means what he's saying about my mother, and I can take a note from Scorpia's book and talk my way through this.

"Of course she did. But I'm guessing that won't stop you from telling me again."

He barks a laugh.

"Fine, I'll spare you," he says. "Here's a better question: Did she tell you why she left?"

Again, I feel a flare of anger when I really shouldn't. Momma's gone now, and the past he speaks of was so very long ago anyway. Still, it irks me to hear him speak of it in such a way.

"She didn't leave. You abandoned her to die on Titan."

"Ah, is that how she put it?" Again comes that annoying grin. "Truth is, the two of us agreed it was time for her to go. As I'm sure your unfortunate sister would tell you, space isn't a great place for a child to be born, and a ship is no good place for a pregnant woman." His grin drops. "You were supposed to provide access to Titan for the both of us, but that backstabbing bitch decided to cut me off and go out on her own."

Even as I will my mind to ignore what he's saying, the pieces click into place. Momma never mentioned that she was already pregnant when she left the *Red Baron*, only that I was born on Titan. And she never offered an answer to the question I was bold enough to ask only once. I remember again the sting of her hand on my cheek, the taste of blood. *"The blood you share is the only thing that matters."*

My emotions claw and tear at each other—grief and uncertainty and red-hot fury tumbling over one another in my head. Fury wins. I step right up to Captain Murdock, jamming the barrel of my gun against his chest.

"The fuck is this supposed to be? Some misguided attempt to get mercy?" I growl in his face. "Enough. Tell me where the cargo is or I'll rip that stars-damned tongue out of your mouth."

Murdock's lips stretch in a satisfied smile that's even more infuriating up close.

"Mercy from a Titan vet? Unlikely. Just wanted you to get close enough."

I see his hand moving, and fire my weapon as pain erupts in my side. The captain stumbles back with a grunt as I gasp and bend over. My eyes travel from the red-soaked knife in his hands to the gaping gash in my side. Blood gushes out around the fingers I press against it. I don't need a close look to know that it's bad. I've seen enough of these kinds of wounds. On Titan we called them "countdowns." They might not kill you right away, but once you have one, it's only a matter of time.

Captain Murdock wheezes, coughs, then laughs. He rubs at the scorch mark my shot left on his body armor, already fading.

"Damn, this Gaian tech is *nice*," he says appreciatively.

I raise my gun, but he lunges at me and slashes the knife, forcing me back. My shot pings off the metal hull, and his boot slams into my wounded side. My gun drops as pain blackens the edges of my vision. I stumble back while he keeps advancing on me.

"Maybe not so much of Auriga in you after all," he says. "You're far too emotional."

While he's busy gloating, I slide my own knife out of its sheath on my leg, Primus blade glinting in the light. He hesitates, less certain now that I have a weapon in hand—so I strike first.

No point conserving energy when my one hope is a short fight. I pour every ounce of myself into attacking: a thrust at his ribs, a slash toward his neck, a flurry of jabs toward his stomach. He blocks and deflects the first few, but he can't keep up. I shred through his vest and sometimes cut deep enough to draw blood beneath it. After one attack cuts a shallow gash across his torso, he lets out a hiss of pain and frustration and makes a predictable thrust toward me.

Dodging to the side, I grab his arm at the elbow and twist it hard enough to send his knife clattering to the floor. We end up face-to-face. Despite being in control now, cold sweat breaks out on my forehead; he's barely winded, his wounds insubstantial, his expression more angry than defeated. I'm gasping for air, barely able to hold him when he struggles.

"The cargo—" I pant out, and he grits his teeth and shoves the fingers of his free hand deep into the wound at my side. Darkness consumes my vision. Next thing I know, I'm on the floor with him on top of me, my knife gone.

He pins me down with both hands wrapped around my neck. I thrash against him, claw at his face—but my strength is waning, and his weight holds me down. My struggles gradually weaken, and he leans harder into me, his teeth gritted and the tendons in his neck standing out with the effort. His thumbs press deep into my skin, cutting off my airflow entirely. I gape, helpless, vision fading.

"You put up a good fight," he says grimly, his voice distant to my ears. "There's no shame in this."

My eyes close. Rapid images shutter across the darkness behind my lids: Daniil and Magda with drinks in hand and smiles on their faces, Pol's gap-toothed grin when he saw me for the first time in three years, Momma's face as she said, *"I'm so proud of you.*" Then—a memory of Nibiru, of stretching out on a hover-boat and gazing up at the sky with my siblings all around me. The clouds parting to let the sun shine down on my face.

I've fought so hard, so long, for so little. Maybe some peace won't be so bad. Maybe this is what I've wanted all along. I cease my struggles, let myself drift in memory.

But the pressure on my neck disappears. Despite my readiness to give up, my body struggles to live, sucking in a desperate gasp of air to fill my empty lungs. My eyes flutter open, and I realize the weight on top of me has lifted. Captain Murdock's face swims into my vision. He looks around, baffled, apparently not realizing he didn't quite manage to kill me yet.

And both of us are floating. Even with my lungs desperately heaving for air and my heart pounding as I realize how close to death I just came, I grin viciously as I realize what it means.

Chaos.

A moment later, Captain Murdock lets out a surprised shout as the ceiling rushes toward us. I wrench myself free of his grip on my neck and twist my body midair. When we slam into the ceiling, the reversed-gravity momentum slams my elbow into his stomach. His mouth expels air and a spray of blood. The room is turned upside down, furniture banging into the ceiling all around us, but I ignore it and focus on my opponent as the emergency alarm starts to wail. The lights dye the room deep green.

We tussle our way across the floor, banging into toppled furniture and crates, clawing and punching at each other. Any semblance of a real fight is gone. This is a pure mess of a brawl, both of us waning and desperate. His nails dig gouges in my cheek, a thumb digging into one of my eyes—but a second later I secure a grip on the side of his head and slam it into the nearby wall. I move blindly, banging him into it again and again until he falls off me.

And then we're floating again. I curse under my breath, knowing what comes next and how badly it's going to hurt, and push off from the ceiling as hard as I can. For a moment I dangle in suspension— and crash to the floor along with everything else in the bay. I hit with a thump that knocks the wind out of me, but a sickening thud of flesh on the other side of the room tells me Captain Murdock landed even harder. As we both lay still, the emergency lights shut off. The green dye fades from the room, and all I see is red, red, red, smeared across the floor and splattered all over the ceiling. Too much of it is my own blood.

My first attempt to push myself off the cold metal floor fails. So does the second. My body is weak. Dying. But I'm not done yet. I can't be.

"Get up," I rasp, hauling my face up and grabbing a nearby crate for support. "Come on." Agonizingly slowly, I drag myself to my feet. I'm dizzy and breathless from the effort, my injured leg barely holding my weight. I limp across the room to grab my fallen blaster, and then over to Captain Murdock. He still hasn't moved. His face is bloody and swollen, his breath comes in wheezes, and one of his legs is bent at an unnatural angle, but he's still conscious.

He smiles at me, his teeth red, his face triumphant despite the fact that I have him at my mercy.

"You hear that?" he wheezes, tilting his head. Against my better judgment, I pause to listen. There's only one thing to be heard: silence. Captain Murdock's grin widens at the confusion on my face. "So fast," he says. "Battles aren't so quickly won by underdogs."

As much as I want to deny them, his words ring true. This silence is wrong, just like the shift back to normal gravity. The battle should still be raging on. We knew that winning this fight would be a long, bloody process. My siblings should be finding ways to fight, however they can. They should be buying me time, buying Lyre time. But if the gravity already swapped back, and the fighting is over, then...

Cold splinters throughout my chest, making it hard to breathe. *No.* It can't be.

"That silence can only mean one thing," Captain Murdock says. "It's too late. Your siblings are dead, or they will be soon."

"No." The denial comes out weak. I sway on my feet. "They could still be—"

I cut off, and we both look upward at the sound of unintelligible words and heavy footfalls on the main deck above us. The sound of one pair of boots, then two, three, then...too many. I shut my eyes, fighting off a wave of pain. The captain was right. No weapons are being fired. The fight is over.

We lost.

"If you spare me, I'm sure we can arrange a deal," the captain says, his words barely audible through the growing buzz in my head. "Now that your mother is gone, we don't have to be enemies, you know. My crew will be here any minute, and—"

"And I don't have a single stars-damned thing to lose." I bend to press the blaster to his forehead. "Now tell me where the vials are."

He lets out a gurgling wheeze of a laugh. My finger twitches toward the trigger. I'd like nothing more than to put a hole in this man's head. But at the last moment, something stops me. Killing Captain Murdock will solve nothing, nor make me feel any better.

"Mercy from a Titan vet? Unlikely."

"Fuck you," I mutter, and smash the gun into his temple. He goes limp, out cold.

So that leaves me, bleeding out alone in the enemy cargo bay. I scour the room for the vials, limping through the mess of upturned furniture and empty crates. I find nothing, and only add more blood to the splatters all over the room. I lean heavily against the wall beside Captain Murdock to catch my breath and think, one hand pressed to my side. Then I hear footsteps descending toward me.

I whirl toward the stairs, raising my gun just as Orion Murdock steps into the room. The pilot freezes at the sight of me. His eyes glance around to take in the situation—my weapon, my wound, the sprawl of furniture and gore—before stopping on the unconscious body of his adoptive father.

"Is he—"

"Alive," I say. "For now. Tell me where the vials are and maybe I'll—"

"They're in the quarantine section of the med bay," Orion blurts out before I can finish. I stop, hesitating for a moment.

"If you're lying to me, I'll come back here and kill you both."

"Yeah, yeah, I believe you." Hands held up in surrender, he slowly moves toward his father and nods his head toward a door on the other side of the cargo bay. "It's right through there. In the cabinet. Go see for yourself."

I back toward the door, still expecting some kind of trick, but all Orion does is crouch at the side of his fallen father and check his pulse.

The *Red Baron*'s medical wing, like most things about their ship, is far more impressive than our own. As Orion said, there's even a pressure-sealed quarantine room. Smart, especially given what they're transporting. I limp past the medical beds and supplies and hit the pressure pad to open the quarantine area, leaving a bloody handprint behind. Once the door shuts behind me, it's like I'm in my own cramped and sterile little world. The room holds a single metal bed and a small cabinet.

Inside, I find five familiar vials. Orion was telling the truth.

My lips curl slightly. Clever of Captain Murdock to hide these in plain sight. His crew would have had no reason to search for them here. And if I didn't know what to look for, I never would have found these even if I glanced in the cabinet. I remove them carefully now, setting each out on the counter. Five tiny vials with barely visible, shimmering content—and so much potential destruction. But it ends here and now. Maybe the quarantine room won't be enough to hold the alien weapons' destruction, and the pirates will go down as well. But if they don't, at least the weapons will be destroyed. And I will die with them.

It's better than what I imagined. No—it's perfect. The perfect ending for me, though I didn't realize how desperately I was searching for one until this very moment.

I take my own family's vial out of my pocket and set it alongside the others. Next, I pull out the photograph I took from Momma's cabinet and unfold it, placing it on the counter. And one last object: an energy grenade. Simple but effective.

I study the photograph before shutting my eyes, trying to fill my mind with the memories I saw before. I reach for another glimpse of the clouds parting to reveal the sun on Nibiru—but I see only darkness. Perhaps that's all I deserve. I take a breath and move my thumb over to the grenade's pin.

A body slams into me, and my wounded leg gives out. My forehead thuds against the floor, along with my chest, knocking the air out of me and sending the grenade skittering. I scramble to grab it as my head spins and my ears ring, but a hand clamps down on my wrist and pins it there.

"Corvus, you stars-damned moron," my captor shouts in my ear, and I go still as I realize who's pinning me. Scorpia's lanky body presses against my back, her hand holding my wrist trapped. "Wanna explain to me exactly what you're doing?"

I go limp. Part of me is overwhelmed with relief that she's still alive... but part of me is also horribly, crushingly disappointed that she stopped me. The promise of redemption was so close I could nearly taste it. I just want it to be over. I'm tired of fighting. But someone has to end this.

"Get out of here," I say, reaching for the grenade again. "Go back to *Fortuna* while you still can, Scorpia. Let me do this."

461

Scorpia grabs the back of my head with her free hand and slams it into the floor, hard. I gasp at the unexpected violence, stars blossoming across my vision.

"*No*, you idiot. You absolute idiot. I can't believe you almost…" My sister's grip on the back of my skull loosens as her sentence trembles and fades. She presses her face into my back, but I shove her off with as much strength as I can muster. As she crashes to the floor, I raise myself up, pressing one arm across her neck to hold her down. Her face is streaked with tears, her combat gear stained with gore. One of her shoulders is wrapped in sloppy bandages already soaked through with blood.

"Leave and let me finish it," I say, my voice coming out a plea. "You know we're outmatched. And we can't let those vials get into anyone else's hands. Just let me do this one last thing. Let me prove that I'm more than the terrible things I've done."

Scorpia struggles, gasps for air. I release some of the pressure on her neck, but not enough to let her up.

"Corvus." She coughs, her voice strained. "You already are more than that. You don't need to prove anything. And…and you…"

She stops as her shoulders start to tremble—and bursts into laughter. Gasping, half-choked, hopeless laughter. I'm so stunned that I recoil from her and sit back. She sits up as well, still laughing, hard enough that fresh tears well up in her eyes.

"You tragic, heroic moron," she says, gasping for air between chuckles. I tense up, anger flickering through me—how can she make a joke even of this?—but cold shock douses it at her next words. "We've already won."

I blink, uncomprehending, while she continues to laugh, pressing one hand to her mouth as if trying to hold it in.

"What?"

"The battle is over, you dumbass! Izra and Orion and a bunch of other crew members turned to our side, Lyre's ploy worked, it looks like you took out the captain, so…" She holds her hands out, still giggling helplessly. "We won! We fucking did it!"

"So it…we…" I fumble with my words, unable to process it. Some part of me whispers that she's tricking me, just trying to talk me out of sacrificing myself in whatever way she can…but through that paranoia, a delicate hope blooms. "It's over?" I ask, my voice hoarse.

"It's over," Scorpia says. She reaches to grab one of my hands and squeeze—and then abruptly drops it and punches me in the shoulder. "And even if it wasn't, what the *hell* were you thinking? Don't you ever try to do that again, you bastard!"

I grimace as the impact of her punch sends fresh waves of pain through my wounded side. Getting tackled and slapped around by Scorpia really hasn't helped my injuries. Though I say nothing, my sister's face creases in worry when she sees my expression, and her eyes find the wound on my side. She gasps.

"Oh, stars, you got stabbed."

"Yeah. I realize." I grit my teeth, pressing a hand to the wound.

"Shit, sorry. I'm sorry. Let's clean you up." She stands and carefully helps me to my feet, then slips one arm around my shoulders to help support me. Putting any amount of weight on my injured leg nearly makes me crumple again, so I lean gratefully into her.

"No," I say, shaking my head to chase off the blackness threatening to close in on the edges of my vision. "Not until it's really over. Take me to the cockpit and get the ship away from Nibiru. I want to see this through."

"All right." She squeezes my shoulders and begins to help me along. "Let's finish this."

CHAPTER FORTY-THREE

Countdown

Scorpia

By the time I get Corvus out to the cargo bay, Drom and Lyre are waiting for us. Drom is scuffed and singed, blood running down her face and one arm dangling limply at her side, but she's still grinning wide enough that it's hard to worry too much. Lyre leans against her for support, but though she looks exhausted and covered in dust from the air ducts, she seems unharmed. Both of their expressions light up as they see us emerge from the quarantine room but dim with concern as they see Corvus in such bad shape. I'm not in the greatest condition myself, with my hastily bandaged shoulder, but it's obvious he's much worse off.

"He all right?" Drom asks, stepping closer to help me support his weight with her good arm. I breathe a sigh of relief at the reprieve.

"I'm fine," Corvus says, his voice weak and rasping.

"He's hanging in there," I say. My eyes find Orion's form slumped next to his father's, and I gasp. "Who the hell hurt Orion?"

"Relax," Drom says. "He's just unconscious."

"He helped us, you know! He's on our side!"

Drom shrugs unapologetically. "Whatever. Help me get Corvus to the cockpit."

We struggle toward the stairs in an awkward, shuffling procession, Lyre trailing along behind us.

Getting to the cockpit is more easily said than done. As hard as Corvus is trying to put on a tough face, it becomes progressively clearer that he's hurt worse than he initially let on. Merely helping him from the cargo bay to the main deck has him breathing raggedly and leaning heavily on our shoulders. Progress is terribly slow, especially when I'm so eager to find out what's going on in the rest of the ship.

We pass a number of bodies both dead and unconscious on the way up, which I assume is Corvus's handiwork. But just as many of the *Red Baron*'s crew are still standing. They nod to us as we pass by. I'm still stunned at how readily Izra agreed to our cause. Once she and Orion were on our side and started spreading the truth about what they were transporting, many of the others joined us as well. Some refused, of course—whether because of loyalty, old grudges, or anger over the fact that Corvus and Drom had already carved their way through a chunk of their crew—but between the mutiny and Lyre sowing discord by screwing with the gravity drive, we soon overwhelmed them. In the end, most of those who stayed loyal to Captain Murdock were the mercs they hired on Gaia, not his own crew.

"You holding up?" I ask Corvus as we enter the last hallway. I try not to sound overly concerned, but it's impossible not to notice how much he's slowing down.

"Fine." Despite his words, his face is pale and sweaty. "Just get me there."

So I do.

Once we reach the cockpit, I stop in the doorway, letting out a low whistle now that I'm able to properly appreciate it. Even for an experienced pilot like me, the vast array of machinery is a little dizzying to look at. Beyond that, Nibiru looms larger than I expected through the viewing panel.

"Mind setting me down before you admire the view?" Corvus asks through gritted teeth.

Drom and I help him over to the copilot's chair. I take what must be Orion's usual chair, and my two sisters stand in the back of the room.

"Okay..." I eye the shiny buttons and displays, all unfamiliar. "So... let's start with..." I tap my way through the basic functions, but it soon becomes clear that something is very, very wrong. "What the hell? Where are the damn diagnostics...?"

"Oh," Drom says. "I guess I should probably mention I blew up some shit in the engine room."

"You *what*?" The color drains from my face as I finally pull up the ship's diagnostics. A small hologram of the ship appears above the dashboard, and all over it is the green, green, green of system failure. "Oh, stars." I let out a half-hysterical laugh. This is bad. Really bad.

"My fault," Corvus murmurs next to me.

"Hey, don't you steal all the credit. I set off the explosion," Drom says.

"Scorpia?" Lyre is hovering behind me now, staring at the hologram with her face pinched in worry. "We're awfully close to Nibiru. I think we're already getting pulled in."

"Stars damn it." I take a deep breath, try to steady myself. "You're right. The engine's fucked, we don't have enough thrust to escape."

The battle may be won, but it'll all be for nothing if we crash onto Nibiru with the weapons on board. They'll likely be unleashed on impact—or, best-case scenario, they fall into the hands of the Nibirans. And I don't want them in *anyone's* hands at this point.

"We'll have to get onto *Fortuna* instead. And fast."

"How much time do we have?" Lyre asks. "We'll have to bring the *Red Baron's* crew aboard. I'm not sure we even have enough launch chairs to secure everyone. And *Fortuna's* likely damaged from the impact as well. By the time we get there..."

Swallowing back panic, I tap on the nearest computer, looking for a destination timer of some kind. My stomach drops.

"We're entering Nibiru's atmosphere in ten minutes."

All of us fall into a stunned silence.

"There's not enough time. It's not possible," I say as the realization hits.

Which means we have to prioritize. Even if we're doomed to crash and burn on a failing ship, maybe there's something we can do to stop the entire planet from dying along with us. That means getting rid of the Primus bombs. If we were a little farther away, we could toss them out the air lock and hope for the best. But this close to Nibiru, we can't risk it.

As much as I hate to admit it, there's only one option left.

I try not to think too hard about the alien weapons I'm handling, or Corvus still bleeding in the cockpit, or the planet we're careening closer to every minute and the millions of lives depending on us down there. It's a whole lot to avoid thinking about. But luckily, the simple job of transporting all the alien vials over to *Fortuna's* cargo bay takes enough concentration to distract me. I'm all too aware of how much damage any one of these little vials could do, and I'm handling six of them now.

An extra set of hands would be helpful, but I've already set every other conscious body I found—including Lyre, Drom, and some of the pirates—to the task of making sure all the nonconscious bodies are strapped into chairs and secure. Thankfully, nobody asked too many questions. It seems everyone was able to assume the truth.

Once I transport the last of the alien vials over, I head to *Fortuna*'s cockpit, set a course on autopilot, and type in the command code I never thought I'd have to use. My heart aches as my hands slide across the familiar controls for the last time. I want to savor every step on this ship and every moment in the cockpit that's always been my favorite place in the world, but there's no time for sentiment. Seems there rarely is, nowadays.

I settle for kissing my palm and smacking it against the dashboard. For once, I'm glad to be sober. If I can savor nothing else, I'll savor the hurt of this moment, the pure unfiltered pain of letting go. I want to remember every last second of it.

On the way back to the *Red Baron*'s cockpit, I pass a number of unconscious mercs and pirates strapped into launch chairs. Captain Murdock is one of them, covered almost head to toe in duct tape, which makes me laugh despite the circumstances. If he survives this crash, he's not going to be happy when he wakes up. But that's assuming any of us survive, I guess.

My family waits in the cockpit. Thankfully, the size of the room means there are enough chairs for us all to be together. Lyre is already strapped in and waiting, while Drom is making sure a now-unconscious Corvus is secured to the copilot's chair I left him in. His breathing is even, though weak, and his face is peaceful.

Somehow, I find myself smiling as I take my own seat. I buckle the straps and click through the ship's external cameras just in time to watch *Fortuna* launch away from us. She's clearly struggling against Nibiru's pull, but gradually, the space between us widens. My throat is tight, my chest constricted, but I fight off tears. I want to see this clearly.

"Wow," Lyre murmurs. "I never realized she looked so..."

"Small?" Drom suggests, seating herself now that she's done with Corvus. I flip her off without turning around.

"She's not small. She's majestic as fuck." A tremor worms into my voice despite my attempt at levity. I swallow hard and try to pull myself together. If nothing else, *Fortuna* deserves a dignified end. I look again at the only home I've ever known, the place that contains so many of my memories and so much of myself, the clunky little ship that so recently became my own. She gradually travels farther and farther away, until she's no more than a speck on the screen. Knowing what comes next, I bite my lip and wipe away the tears starting to blur my vision.

I want to say something, but sometimes words fail. Everyone is silent as *Fortuna* erupts in a dazzling array of shimmering light.

For a moment, an awed hush blankets the ship. It's as though the entire universe is holding its breath to witness the spectacle of *Fortuna*'s end. The sight of my ship, my home, breaking into pieces. A gleam of alien light leaks through the cracks, shining faintly in the emptiness of space. I suck in a breath, imagining that deadly glimmer traveling over to engulf us—but then that too fades into nothingness, leaving only chunks of metal floating out into the void.

There's a moment's pause. A moment's peace.

And then the emergency alarm begins to blare, and the entire cockpit is bathed in sickly green light. I squeeze Corvus's limp hand before biting my mouth-guard and grabbing the wheel, using the last of the *Red Baron*'s failing power in an attempt to make the crash a little more graceful.

CHAPTER FORTY-FOUR

Touchdown

The arrival of a spacecraft is rare enough on Nibiru, but never before has one crashed into the ocean.

A crowd gathers on the docks to watch, raised fingers and hushed voices pointing out the ship dropping toward the water. A few observant folk noticed the odd flash and shimmer in the sky not too long ago, and wonder if the two are connected.

One such witness is a young woman standing at the very edge of the dock. She has been watching the sky since long before the ship began to careen toward the planet's surface. If anyone were paying attention to her rather than to the spacecraft falling out of the sky, they might notice something strange about her—an unfamiliarity in the way she carries herself, a certain alienness in the way she clasps her gloved hands. One might almost think she were praying, if such a thing happened on this planet. But regardless of the difference, she is here with the crowd now, watching and waiting and hoping as the ship struggles to stop itself. Though it slows, its struggling engine loses the fight. So far out in the ocean that it's barely visible, the ship hits.

Unlike those around her, the woman does not flinch or gasp as the ship strikes the water, skidding and sliding toward the island and kicking up a mighty spray of ocean. She does not falter as the resulting wave makes the dock shiver and sway beneath her feet, and she does not retreat when most of the crowd flees inland to safer ground. She holds steady, though she alone knows of the doom the ship might have brought to Nibiru.

But no death or danger comes from the fallen ship. No life does, either. The ship—*Red Baron*, as crimson letters slashed across one dented and scuffed side declare—bobs silently on the ocean's surface after coming to its dramatic stop.

Soon the peacekeepers' hoverboats approach, first circling the ship like curious birds, then closing in to investigate. They attach long ropes to the craft and climb aboard, a couple dozen of them stepping carefully across the wet and damaged metal. One finds an emergency hatch on the side, and two more use a laser device to cut it open.

Smoke billows out from within. A thick cloud gathers in the air, riding the wind toward the island. Most members of the remaining crowd cover their noses and murmur uneasily to their neighbors— except for the strange woman, who leans toward the smoke rather than away, straining to get a better look as the peacekeepers slip on protective masks and drop down into the ship.

Minutes later, the first few occupants are brought out in tightly sealed body bags, and the crowd bows their heads and murmurs in mourning. But their heads soon snap up again as new faces— living faces—are brought out into the sunlight. The peacekeepers parade a motley assortment of people across the hull of the floating ship: a pale Titan woman with a black rectangle on her arm, a handsome man with a head of curls and a lump on the side of his head, a grizzled and bloody old pirate with a broken leg and bits of duct tape stuck to his outfit, and more. Each of them is brought aboard a rescue ship and promptly put in handcuffs.

The crowd gawks and murmurs at the sight. Rumors swirl and spread. But the strange woman at the end of the dock does not move or speak, not even when time slides past and the crowd around her thins, many of the onlookers assuming that the show is over.

But the show, as it turns out, is not quite done. The hatch opens once more—this time surprising even the peacekeepers, who shout orders and rush to surround it. The first to emerge is a tiny young woman with a head of wild curls and a fierce scowl. Then comes a mountain of a woman, broad-shouldered and tough, who reaches down to help up the wounded man behind her and slips an arm around his waist to help him stand.

The bearded man stands on the hull, unsteady on his feet and blinking in the sunlight like someone freshly awoken. He tilts back his head, gazing out at the sky and the ocean and the red sun, and he smiles. It is the kind of smile that transforms his whole face, even after it fades. It leaves him looking gentler.

Despite the man's wounds, and despite the peacekeepers shouting at them from the nearby boats, the three of them wait.

Finally, one last survivor climbs out of the crashed ship. She sways with the movement of the water, one foot slipping on the damp hull. Then, with an exuberant yell, she stretches both arms wide as if she means to embrace the whole world in front of her. She is still grinning when the authorities slap the handcuffs on her.

That look of elation is mirrored by the strange woman standing on the end of the dock, even as tears start to roll down her cheeks.

CHAPTER FORTY-FIVE

Missing Pieces

Corvus

The ocean is calm today. The hoverboat barely rocks beneath me as I stretch out on my back, and the salt-touched breeze is a soothing reprieve from the sun overhead. I'm not sure how long I've been here. With one arm over my eyes and my wounded leg soaking up the warm rays, I could spend all day in this boat. I often have, in the week since the Nibiran Council decided to release my family from jail, declaring us heroes instead of criminals. They even gave us medals, which Scorpia found unreasonably hilarious. I keep mine on the nightstand beside my bed, and look at it often.

My comm beeps at my side. I pick it up, holding a hand up against the sun and squinting at the screen. The time surprises me; only one more hour until the Gaian Arrival Ceremony. I've been trying to keep myself from thinking too much about it all day, but now my heart surges with a simultaneous rush of nerves and excitement. Today the first wave of Gaian refugees arrives on Nibiru—and I will see my brother again. I still haven't decided what to say to him. I've relived our fight a thousand times since that day, and I have no idea how I can even begin to make it up to him, but I'm prepared to try for the rest of my life.

My leg twinges as I stand, and I grab onto the edge of the craft to steady myself, waiting out the wave of pain. The Nibiran doctors did what they could, but both my leg and my side were thoroughly ruined after that fight with Murdock, and the subsequent crash didn't do my body any favors. The wounds would have been easy to fix on Titan. Deva or Pax would likely be able to do more for me—for an exorbitant price, no doubt—but without a ship, we're in no position to travel off-world anytime soon.

Most days the pain is a near-constant plague, making it difficult to sleep or fish or do any number of things I took for granted, but today it's also a reminder of everything I've done to get here. I wait for it to recede before taking the wheel and heading for home.

Soon I pull up alongside the houseboat, a two-story, oblong structure granted to us by the Nibiran Council. It's a bit showy for my tastes, but we weren't about to decline, especially when the last of our savings were barely enough to buy this hoverboat. The main rooms are inside the dome-like structure in the middle, but at the moment both Drom and Lyre are waiting out on the flat deck that surrounds it, Drom sprawled out on her back and Lyre's bare feet hanging in the water.

It's rare to see both of them home at the same time. We've all been changed in our own way by everything that happened, and I suspect my siblings, like me, are eager to spend some time alone and figure out who they are now. Drom restlessly prowls the islands, usually in the company of one pretty-faced boy or another. Stars know what Lyre is ever doing, but she seems quite busy with it. Today, though, is a special occasion.

Which is why we're parked near Vil Hava, rather than the

smaller and less crowded island of Kitaya. It's strange to look out and see so many other floating homes crammed near the edge of the island, all tied together in neighborhood clusters. Ours is the only one that floats alone.

As I pull in, Drom stands with a grumble and helps me secure the hoverboat to its station. She hangs back as I carefully stretch out the kinks in my scarred leg and test my weight on it before stepping onto the deck.

"We're gonna be late," she complains the moment I'm on board.

"We have an hour. We're fine." I glance around. "Where's Scorpia?" Hopefully she's not at a bar somewhere, pining over that Gaian woman again. For the most part, Scorpia's drinking has been much better than it was before, but she still slips up occasionally, and Shey Leonis is yet another bad habit of hers. The council said that the Gaian ambassador spoke passionately for the release and pardon of our entire family, but she wasn't around to see us when we were set free. That's for the best, I think. As much as my respect for Shey has grown, she's no good for my sister. Scorpia's heart can get the better of her sometimes.

"Why should I know?" Drom asks.

"She's visiting Ca Sineh again," Lyre says, splashing one foot through the water. Drom shudders, and I grimace. Speaking of Scorpia's heart, that option isn't any better.

"I don't know how she can spend so much time in that place," Drom says. "An underwater prison? No fuckin' thank you."

Nibiru has no death penalty, but its famous super-maximum-security prison has to be one of the worst fates in the system. Still, I can understand why Scorpia visits so frequently. I feel the weight of the guilt, too. We knew the Nibirans never would have gone through with their agreement with Gaia if they knew that Leonis had tried to betray them. We couldn't let innocent Gaians suffer for her choice, so we twisted the truth—and the *Red Baron* crew was blamed entirely for the attack on Nibiru, with Leonis's name left out of the official record despite Captain Murdock's insistence she was involved. The pirates will be imprisoned beneath the ocean for the rest of their lives.

We all pleaded for mercy for Orion and Izra and the others who helped us, argued that they didn't know what they were transporting, but the Nibirans weren't willing to grant reprieve to anyone involved in the plot. And no matter how much Scorpia keeps arguing for their release, I know it's unlikely that the council will change their minds.

"Have you been keeping tabs on her, then?" I ask Lyre.

She shrugs noncommittally. "I just think someone should make sure she isn't doing anything stupid."

I nod. If Lyre is watching her, that's one less thing I have to worry about.

"Thanks for keeping an eye out." I turn to Drom and gesture at the hoverboat. "Help me take today's catch in."

"We're going to be *late*," she grumbles again, but helps me nonetheless. I take my time bringing the fish inside and packing it in the fridge, hoping Scorpia will arrive by the time we're done. But as we head back out to the deck, Drom is practically growling with impatience, and Scorpia still isn't here. I check the time on my comm. We really are going to be late if she doesn't get here soon.

"Maybe she forgot," Drom says.

"Maybe she's going to meet us there?" Lyre suggests.

I shake my head at both of them and settle down on the deck to wait.

"She'll show up," I say. "She always does."

CHAPTER FORTY-SIX

The Underwater Prison

Scorpia

've scrutinized every angle of Ca Sineh, but there is only one way in or out: a single, sturdy elevator, which needs to be activated by prison staff. Two guards accompany me on the descent from the disk-shaped entry building above. We travel down a vertical shaft to the larger disk of the main building, down below the waves. When the elevator stops again, I feel uncomfortably aware of the weight of the ocean above us. One guard steps out and gestures for me to follow. As usual, I have to fight the urge to flee back to the surface as fast as possible, and instead swallow hard and follow her to the visitor's room.

I've never seen any part of the main building aside from that room and this narrow hallway leading there, lined with windows of thick plexiglass that serve as a sobering reminder of the dark water outside. It's all I've been allowed to see, but I've researched as much as I can about what lies beyond: the cafeteria, the recreation room, and the one hundred oval-shaped, modular cells that ring the outside of the building, each equipped with its own air lock. Ca Sineh is a small prison, reserved for criminals who are considered especially dangerous, like those who threaten the lives of the entire planet. Had things gone a little differently, my family would have ended up here, too.

For all of its security, the truly ingenious part of Ca Sineh's design is how it makes attempting escape seem not only impossible, but incredibly dangerous. One wrong move, and you'll die a slow death by drowning. I can tell that Orion has already given up hope that he'll ever leave this place, but I haven't.

My escort leaves me in the visitor's room, where two others wait to supervise. Early on I considered bribing or overpowering the guards, but it soon became clear that was a foolish plan—there are too many of them, and too many moving parts and handoffs that make sure compromising one or two or even three guards won't make the whole security system grind to a halt.

Shaking off thoughts of escape for now, I put on a smile and head to the table where Orion is already waiting. He never talks about it, but I can see the toll the prison is taking on him. He's growing pale and thin and hollow-eyed, drained of his usual energy. He wraps his arms around himself like he can't get warm. This is a cold and dark and miserable place. No place for someone who helped us.

"Hi, friend," I say, sliding into the uncomfortable metal chair across from him. He smiles at me, but the expression doesn't make his eyes crinkle like it used to. "How's it going?" A stupid question, but I never know what to say to him.

"Oh, you know, fabulous as always." His voice scratches like he hasn't used it in a while. Pain pulses in my heart.

"I'm going to the council in person again tomorrow," I say. "I've been writing every day, arguing for your release. Shey's trying to help, too. I'm not gonna let them do this to you, okay?"

Another bland smile that doesn't reach his eyes. He believes me a little less every time I say it.

"Oh, it's not so bad, really." His tone aims for flippant but falls flat. "My dad is already practically running this place. And I have a solar lamp in my cell now, for Vitamin D deficiency and such. Izra got a surface trip for nitrogen narcosis, so fingers crossed I'll get that next." He forces a small laugh and shrugs. I can't bring myself to respond, and after a moment he clears his throat. "But I don't want to talk about that. Tell me about the outside."

"Right. Yeah. Uh, I'm sure you've already heard, but the Gaians are arriving today. Which means Pol will be with them." I swallow. "We haven't gotten much word on how he's doing, so we're not really sure what to expect."

"That boy's a force of nature. He'll be fine."

I manage a laugh. "Yeah, you're right. I should probably be more concerned about how the Gaians and Nibirans are going to mesh."

"I'm not sure Gaians mesh well with anyone except other Gaians."

"You never know. Maybe they'll surprise us," I say, thinking of Shey with another painful twist of my heart. I know she must be busy as the acting Gaian ambassador, preparing for the arrival of her people, but…after I heard that she spoke for my family in front of the council, I can't deny that I came out of jail expecting to find her waiting. She wasn't, and she still hasn't sent so much as a word to me.

Though he speaks haltingly at first, conversation soon flows easily with Orion, as it always does. We talk about everything from how Nibiran food is going to change the Gaians' lives, to what the Nibirans will think of the Primus worshippers, to where the Gaians will go after their time in Nibiru is up, which is still very much up in the air.

"Personally, I say we send them all to Titan as soon as we're sure the planet is safe to settle on again," I say. "Let them see how they like all that ice." I glance out of the corner of my eye at the clock, and then do a double take. "Shit, I gotta go. I'm gonna be late for the ceremony."

I stand, and he follows. The disappointment on his face makes my chest ache. Two guards are already heading over to collect him, but before I can second-guess myself, I pull him against me in a tight hug. "If the council doesn't agree, I'll break you out myself," I whisper, more fiercely than my last promises.

"Hey, hey, no touching," one of the guards says. If not for my status as a local hero, I'm sure they'd be prying me off already, but my reputation won't get me too far. I give Orion's shoulder a last squeeze as I pull back, searching his eyes. Finally, I see that spark of hope I've been waiting for. He dips his head at me before the guards lead him away.

As soon as they disappear through the security door, I walk as quickly as I can without alarming the guards escorting me, cursing under my breath. If I'm really late for this, my siblings will never let me hear the end of it. I tap my foot impatiently on my way back up the elevator, squirm my way through the exit pat-down by a guard, and race out of Ca Sineh and down the walkway to Vil Hava. The biggest island of Nibiru is even busier than usual today, with a huge crowd gathering around the landing harbor to watch the arrival of the "aliens" from Gaia. I shove my way through the crowd, hoping nobody notices that it's the so-called hero who saved their planet elbowing past, and run for home.

By the time I arrive, Drom and Lyre are already sitting on the hoverboat and awaiting departure. Only Corvus is still standing on the deck, waiting for me.

"Get your ass in here already," Drom yells as she sees me.

I run past Corvus and jump into the boat, drawing a squeak of complaint from Lyre as the vessel rocks wildly from side to side, water spraying over the edges.

"Come on," I say, grinning up at my brother. "We're gonna be late."

CHAPTER FORTY-SEVEN

The Arrival

Corvus

Once we find a decent spot in the harbor, I halt and lower the boat so it rests on the surface of the water, rocking gently with the movement of the waves.

The docks are crowded with eager, upturned faces and the ocean is dotted with vessels like ours. I was worried there would be tension in the air, uncertainty about these new arrivals and what they'll mean for the planet, but instead people are drunk and dancing and happy. The steady beat of music and a variety of mouth-watering scents drift over the waters, along with excited whispers about the arrival of the "aliens," as the Nibirans are calling them.

Despite the atmosphere, my heart is hammering in my chest now that we're here. I'm nervous about what the arrival of the Gaians will mean for this planet, how the system's first intermingling of two cultures will turn out after so many years of distrust and hatred—but mostly, I'm afraid to see Pol again. A few days ago, a note from Shey informed us that he would be arriving with the first wave of Gaians today. Though she didn't say as much, I suspect she fought her mother for it.

"Not sure what they're so excited about," Lyre murmurs, though she looks to the sky along with all the Nibirans on the shore. "Gaians aren't really all that thrilling."

"Scorpia might disagree," Drom mumbles, the joke coming out half-hearted at best.

Half-hearted or not, it hits home enough for Scorpia to flip her off from the boat's floor. Drom doesn't notice; she's leaning over the side to skim her fingers along the water, her eyes distant.

"Rumors have been passing among the fisherfolk that the Gaians have webbed feet, or green-tinted skin." I gaze out at the crowds of eager people. "Think they'll be disappointed when they find out the 'aliens' look the same as them?"

"To be fair," Scorpia says, speaking up for the first time since we left home, "if anyone in the system can be called aliens, it's the Gaians."

I laugh, and she grins up at me. Whatever mood's been hanging over her seems to have lightened, at least for now. And she's sober, as far as I can tell.

"Mostly I'm disappointed I don't get to witness how scared the Gaians on that ship must be," I say. "So many off-worlders waiting on the other side . . . it's their worst nightmare."

"They must be shaking in their boots," Scorpia says, and then sits up with a gasp. "Holy shit. I never realized it. They're the off-worlders now. *Forever.*" She cackles. "Sweet, sweet justice."

While she continues to laugh, I glance over at Drom, my smile fading. She's sitting quietly on the side of the boat, her face tilted upward with the same unabashed expectancy of so many Nibiran children on the docks. I nudge her with one foot, and she lets out an annoyed grunt without looking at me.

"He'll be here soon," I say. "Staring won't make it happen any sooner."

"I'm not a fucking idiot," she grumbles back. Still, her eyes never leave the sky, even for a second.

I give up on trying to distract her. Truthfully, I think what I want most is to distract myself. If it weren't disrespectful to Scorpia, I would have sanded down the edges of my feelings with alcohol before coming here. Right now, my anxiety is raw and sharp. Even with Shey seemingly calling in favors with her mother on our account, we've seen nothing of Pol since that initial message, and the only news we've received is that he's alive, awake, and "steadily improving." I'm not surprised, though. We've heard Gaia has been in chaos in preparation for the big migration, and I'm sure one ill off-worlder wasn't anyone's priority other than ours.

Still, as much as logic tells me that must be the reason behind the lack of news, I can't help but worry that Leonis did something to him as one last, cruel twist of the knife. For the sake of peace, my siblings and I all agreed to keep our mouths shut about Leonis's final attempted betrayal of the Nibirans, which is why the deal went through in the first place . . . but I know she must be furious with us.

Not wanting to worry my siblings, I haven't told anyone of this concern—except once, in a message to Shey, when I grew particularly desperate. Her curt reply assured me that her mother would never do such a thing, and Apollo would be returned to us safely.

Shey has been wrong before. But maybe I shouldn't be so focused on that, regardless. Maybe I should be more worried that even if Pol comes back to us safe and sound and boisterous as always, that he'll never forgive me for what I did before he was infected.

Drom gasps. Even distracted, I know what that gasp must mean, and turn my eyes skyward.

The conversation in the boat, the whispers drifting over the water, the music on the docks—all of it falls silent at once as the Gaian ship enters the atmosphere.

It's hard to look directly at the craft. That's enough of a hint in itself. But as the glossy, shimmering vessel draws closer, it becomes even more obvious that the ship isn't of human origin. The sight of it brings back a flash of the ship buried beneath the ice on Titan— but this vessel is even stranger, and much, much larger.

The spaceship is huge enough that it would dwarf even the *Red Baron*, which is already a much bigger ship than *Fortuna* was. Rather than metal, it's made of an iridescent black material that seems to ripple as the ship descends. Its shape is nothing like the hard angles and logical proportions of every other ship I've seen. Instead, it is bulbous and softly rounded, its shape nonsensical for flight. And, perhaps most disconcerting of all, the ship is completely silent as it lands in the water before the dock.

Once again my mind returns to the buried ship—and the pulsing, glowing power source at the heart of it. I remember Altair placing it on the table to trade for the bio-weapon—a false deal set up by Leonis—and the *Red Baron* returning to Titan after the destruction to retrieve something for her. All of it led up to this moment.

There is clear hesitation before one of the council members gestures, and the peacekeeper boats drift out to help secure the ship to the dock, tying metal chains around whatever protuberances they can find. At each touch, the spaceship's surface shivers like the flesh of some living thing, and many of the peacekeepers reel back in terror.

A lackluster wave of smaller ships trickles in behind the huge alien vessel. Small merchant vessels and luxury ships, many of them so clunky and outdated it's clear they were designed long before the borders closed down, drift down to land in Nibiru's ocean. The Gaians must have sent everything they had in order to transport as many people as possible, though even so, it's not nearly enough. This is the first of at least three waves that will arrive. At the very least, Leonis had enough sense not to send any ships with weapons—though that alien spaceship is surely even more offensive to the Nibirans.

I realize, after a moment, that Scorpia is gripping my arm hard enough that her nails dig into my skin. She lets go and looks at me.

"What the hell are they thinking?" she asks, voice trembling.

"I was wondering how the Gaians could possibly have enough ships to transport their citizens," I murmur, troubled. "Hopefully the council approved it."

Scorpia's fear is nothing compared to that of the Nibirans, so notoriously averse to alien technology. The council stands steady on the dock, though they murmur among themselves; they either knew what was coming, or are doing an incredible job of holding it together for the sake of their people. But the average Nibirans are not reassured by their leaders. Most of the waiting boats peel away from the area as fast as they can, and the crowd on shore backs up with panicked shouts. Soon, few remain other than us to await the new guests.

"What are you waiting for?" Drom snaps, turning away from the ship to look at us. She seems completely oblivious to the cause for shock. Despite the harshness in her tone, her eyes are brighter than I've seen them in weeks. She leans as far over the edge of the boat as she can get without falling into the water, as if half tempted to swim to shore herself. "Get to the docks!"

I steer us there.

The seven members of the Nibiran Council stand alone on the docks, with a half circle of peacekeepers at their backs. What's left of the crowd is being dispersed by another group of peacekeepers, likely in expectation of trouble arising. My heart sinks at the sight of the perimeter they're establishing. There's no way we'll be able to get up there and greet Pol. Once the Gaian refugees begin to emerge, we'll be lucky if we can find him before morning. Just as I'm wondering if I have enough credits saved up to bribe our way onto the docks, one of the men at the front shifts, and reveals a familiar face that was hidden among the councillors.

Shey looks up at the same time I glance at her, and our eyes meet. Among the long robes of the Nibiran Council, she wears a stiff-shouldered, pale blue dress. The hood and the shoulders are Gaian fashion, though it flows long around her ankles and is cinched at the waist in the way Nibirans favor. She looks surprised, and not particularly pleased, to see me—but then her eyes slide past me to Scorpia, who still hasn't noticed her. Her expression softens, and she tugs on the arm of a nearby councilman, standing up on her tiptoes to whisper into his ear. He looks over at us and, after a brief hesitation, gestures for us to join them.

Hardly believing our luck, I steer us close and tie us to the dock. "Oh, what's this?" Scorpia asks, noticing what's happening when a councilwoman reaches down to help us up—Ennia Heikki, if I remember correctly. "VIP treatment again?" Scorpia jokes, and then catches sight of Shey standing a couple of yards away. Shock spasms across her face, followed by a splash of hurt, before she manages to clear it again. "Well, well," she says, as if she's setting up for another statement, but she says nothing more.

A few of the council members, recognizing us, step forward to help us onto the docks. Regardless of our shaky past with the council, we're now hailed as heroes on Nibiru for what we did to stop the *Red Baron*. If any of them hold reservations about us after being held hostage in the council chamber, they hide it well, and shower us in generosity despite it. For public appearance's sake, if nothing else.

I go first, grimacing slightly as I step up and my leg wobbles. Heikki steps forward as if to steady me, but I stop her with a glare.

As people shift on the already-crowded dock to make room for my family, I end up next to Shey. I pretend not to notice her, but the next wave of movement through the crowd shoves me right into her. I step back, muttering an apology. She gives me a cool look and says nothing. We stand in silence while the rest of the gathering whispers around us, awaiting the opening of the Gaian ship. But after an agonizing few minutes of quiet, I clear my throat. I've avoided this conversation for long enough.

"I was wrong about you," I say, glancing down at her. She looks up at me, the mask of her face betraying nothing, and I sigh. "You're… much more than I thought you were, and you've done so much for my family. I'd like to apologize."

Shey's lips purse. "Then apologize."

I suppress another sigh. Scorpia never did go for the easy ones. After struggling with my pride for a moment, I hold out both hands and bow my head in the Gaian gesture of requesting forgiveness. Shey lets me linger there for a few moments before tapping each of my palms and letting me rise. With a jolt, I realize she's not wearing gloves—a gesture that will not go unnoticed by either the Nibirans or the Gaians.

All other things aside, the woman is brave. I can see why Scorpia is so taken with her.

"I forgive you," Shey says with a nod. A smile flashes across her formerly guarded face. "As long as you move and let me stand beside your sister, that is." She glances past me. I follow her gaze to see Scorpia standing nearby, separated from us by a willowy councilwoman. My sister glances away as Shey and I look at her, doing a poor job of pretending she wasn't eavesdropping.

"Very well," I say, and turn to the councilwoman. "May I?"

She looks vaguely irritated as I try to push through the crowded dock past her, but acquiesces as she catches a glimpse of the tattoo on my forearm. Her eyes go wide, and dart from the mark to my face.

"As you wish," she says, and I'm surprised to see respect rather than fear on her face as she lets me shuffle past. Scorpia waggles her eyebrows at me as she scoots by to take my place, though it's easy to see the nerves beneath the veil of humor.

"Good luck," I murmur, and take my place on the edge of the dock just in time for the Gaian ship's ramp to open.

At least, logic says it's a ramp, but it's impossible not to imagine it as the gaping jaws of some great beast falling open. The revealed interior of the ship is black and damp in appearance, and the air that rolls out of the opening is warm and humid. The council-woman beside me presses the sleeve of her robe to her face as if loath to breathe it in. The gathered Nibirans are silent as the Gaian officials emerge, their shoes leaving behind faint imprints in the spongy material of the ramp.

President Leonis is at the head of the procession. Behind her stands a broad-shouldered, dark-skinned man I recognize as her husband. They're flanked by a variety of other politicians and offi-cials I'm not well-informed enough to recognize, along with a small handful of uniformed guards who must be the president's personal security team. Each is dressed in starched, hooded Gaian formal wear and long gloves, so very different from loose Nibiran clothing. As both feet touch down on the dock, Leonis pauses and takes her first deep breath of Nibiran air. There's an uncomfortable pause as neither side appears eager to close the gap between the two peoples.

Iri Oshiro, the young council member who participated in the Interplanetary Council, is the first to step forward. They cross both arms over their chest in a smooth, practiced rendition of the traditional Gaian greeting. Leonis returns the gesture, and then transitions into a respectful Nibiran bow. The ice in the air melts at that, and soon there are bows and crossed arms being exchanged on both sides. Some are clearly more comfortable with the foreign gestures than others, and a minor few refuse to display anything other than their own planet's greetings. Still, the Gaians come forward to meet their new allies, and soon the two groups are thoroughly intermingled.

I let out a sigh of relief, glad to see the tension fading, and scan the Gaian procession for any sign of my brother. But these are all higher-ups, no common folk among them, let alone a criminal off-worlder. He must still be on the ship. I press forward, past the officials exchanging pleasantries. Halfway to the ramp, the shifting crowd brings me face-to-face with President Leonis.

My feet go still and my mind blank as our eyes meet. I've never met Leonis in person—and never been close enough that I could kill her before anyone noticed what was happening. This is the woman who got my mother killed, and very nearly did the same to my brother; the woman who erased the people of my home-planet, wiped an entire civilization out from history. If she's surprised to see me, or feels any shred of guilt about meeting one of the last surviving members of the people she destroyed, she doesn't show it. Instead she smiles, an expression that manages to be outwardly pleasant but cruel at the same time.

"You must be…" She pauses, her eyes flickering to the brand on my wrist as if noticing it for the first time. Her nose wrinkles in distaste. "Sergeant Kaiser, is it?"

I fight back a tempting mental image of my hands around her neck.

"Not anymore."

"Ah, yes. I suppose not. My apologies." Now I know I'm not imagining the cold tinge to her smile; there's not a hint of remorse in her expression, making her words mocking.

Another image surges in my mind, this time of her body sinking deep beneath the ocean's waves. It would be so easy to throw her over…but no. I wrench my thoughts away. I can't let revenge be more important than peace. And I can't fuel her belief that Titans are the violent people she imagined us to be. I can't let her think for one second that she was justified in what she did. So I suppress my rage, though I can't bring myself to imitate her callous smile.

"It's just Corvus now," I say, and step closer. She stiffens up at the nearness, though she doesn't step back, even when I bend low enough that my face is mere inches from her ear, my hands within grasping range of her neck. "Remember the name. I will remember yours."

As I straighten, I turn and catch Councillor Oshiro's eye. They step away from the crowd and stop beside me.

"President Leonis. I'm going to have to ask you to head for the end of the dock, if you will?"

Leonis draws herself up, indignant. I wait, eager for an excuse to force her to comply.

"What is this about?" she asks. "Don't tell me these dramatics are about the ship. I did warn you it was our only option for transporting such a large amount of people."

"It's about a matter I expect you aren't eager for the rest of your retinue to overhear," Oshiro says. "Though it's your choice, of course. We can speak here if you truly prefer it."

After a moment, Leonis nods stiffly, and begins to move through the crowd toward the island. We follow closely behind. At Oshiro's gesture, a group of peacekeepers approaches us. Leonis tries to step back, but I move into her way and prevent her from retreating.

"What is going on here?" she asks, glaring first at me and then at Oshiro. "We have a deal, Councillor. You plan to betray me now, after bringing us all the way here?" Though the rest of her remains still and composed, her eyes flash with anger. "I knew I shouldn't have trusted Nibirans."

"Your deal still holds, Madam President." Oshiro's smile is

mild, calm. "Your people are welcome here. But you, I'm afraid, are under arrest due to a unanimous agreement from the Interplanetary Council."

"On what grounds?" Leonis remains remarkably dignified, to my disappointment. I want to see her rage and seethe, but she stands with her head held high.

"You stand accused of the destruction of Titan," I say, before Oshiro can speak. The council member glances at me and nods.

"You will be held in custody here pending your trial by the Interplanetary Council," Oshiro says.

Leonis's eyes shift to me. I hold them, relish the look on her face as she realizes what's happened. We knew we couldn't tell the truth about her involvement in the *Red Baron*'s plot and risk innocent Gaians paying the price... but she will see justice for what she did to my home-planet.

"I suggest not making a scene," I tell her. "Think of your people."

For a moment, she looks so furious I'm sure she won't heed my advice. But eventually she presses her lips into a thin line and bows her head.

"I always do," she says, her eyes never leaving me. "And if this is the price I pay for their safety, so be it." She turns her back to us, facing the peacekeepers. "No restraints. I don't wish to alarm anyone. You have my full cooperation."

At Oshiro's nod, the officers lead her away.

"There were others," I murmur to Oshiro. "She didn't engineer that weapon on her own."

"We'll find them," the council member says. "I assure you, Titan will have justice."

And that will have to be enough. After a grateful bow, I make my way into the crowd again.

I thought having Leonis arrested would soothe the anger still simmering in my chest. It doesn't. Maybe nothing will. Even if I find personal peace, the loss of my people will always remain with me. My throat is still tight with rage after facing her, my lungs hot. Even now, Leonis believes her choices were justifiable.

But when I look up and see my brother coming down the ramp with a Gaian officer at his side, it douses the fire inside me.

Pol's skin is pale and clammy, his muscles wasted away to the point where he leans on metal crutches for support. He looks like his former self was split in two, and the smaller half remained—as if he's been wasting away for years rather than gone for a matter of weeks. Whether it's a result of the sickness or the cryosleep or whatever cure the Gaians gave him, I'm not sure, but the combination has taken a substantial toll on his body.

Still, when he looks up and sees me, his gap-toothed smile is familiar and heartbreaking all at once. I pause, uncertain despite my eagerness to see him. The Gaian officer respectfully retreats to give us our privacy, but still the words stick in my throat. Before I can find the right thing to say, Pol lets his crutches fall and throws his arms around my neck in a hug. I wrap an arm around him. Relief and guilt flood me in equal measure.

"It's good to have you back." I finally force some words out. They aren't enough—what could be?—but at least it's a start. Pol squeezes me tighter. Once, an embrace like this from him would have been chest-crushingly painful. Now, his arms are so thin, shaking while they grip me. More words stick in my throat before tumbling free. "I...I haven't been able to stop thinking about what happened back on Titan, how I never got a chance to apologize. I'm sorry that I hurt you. I'll never do it again."

Pol pulls back, and I grab his arm to steady him. His eyebrows draw together, his eyes distant.

"What happened on Titan..." he says, and stops.

"Yes. When you and I—" I pause at the blank look on his face. "You don't remember?"

During all of this, I almost forgot the side effects that cryo-sleep often has. No one wakes up quite the same, in the event they wake up at all. I told Daniil as much back on Titan, and yet somehow it never crossed my mind.

"I...I don't..." A shadow passes over Pol's face, and he licks his lips uncertainly, his expression strained. "Titan—"

Whatever he was about to say is cut off by Drom's arrival. She sweeps her twin up in a bear hug and spins him around. I almost warn her to be careful with him, but he's laughing, his earlier consternation gone, so I let it rest. Soon Lyre and Scorpia arrive as well, complaining at Drom to let them have a turn with him, while Drom spins him around and around and murmurs words too quiet for us to hear into his ear.

Calm settles over me. We're together at last. I smile at the thought, standing back to watch my sisters pry Drom off of Pol and give him their own greetings. Scorpia is as enthusiastic as always, Lyre a little more subdued, though she splits into a wide grin when Pol reaches down to ruffle her hair.

Yet somehow, there's still a pit in my stomach I can't quite identify, a subtle fear hanging over my head. Maybe it's Momma's absence I feel looming over me, or the lack of true absolution for what I did to Pol. Or maybe it's the fear that this can never last. No matter what it is, the others don't seem to feel the same. It only serves to remind me that a space remains between us.

Still, I manage to quiet the fear in my heart and smile when the others look my way. At least now I feel ready to step forward and start to cross that gap. At least now I feel that it's possible. And for the first time, I feel that I deserve it.

CHAPTER FORTY-EIGHT

Together

Scorpia

As the council members step forward to greet the Gaian retinue, Shey and I are squeezed together. I murmur an apology, struggling to find a way to give her space without stepping on any council members' toes. But to my surprise, Shey leans into me rather than recoiling from my touch. When I hesitate, she glances up at me, and one of her hands moves to grasp mine. I'm shocked to feel bare skin against my own—the first time I've felt or even seen her hands without gloves. I wrap my fingers around hers.

"I'm nervous," she whispers. Her hand is warm, her mouth so close that her breath on my skin makes me shiver. Which is weird, given that we haven't spoken in weeks and are currently surrounded by old people in robes, but not weird enough that I plan on pulling away anytime soon. Sad as it is, I'm eager for as much time with Shey as I can steal—especially given that we're about to face down her powerful mother, who must hate me even more than the last time we met. Then again, I'm not too nervous about it, knowing the peacekeepers intend to take her in the moment she steps away from the crowd. I know Corvus wants a chance to confront her, but personally, I'm hoping to watch from afar. I've had enough of dealing with Leonis.

"About which part? The meeting, or...?" I ask, and she shoots me an annoyed look.

"The meeting. The rest pales in comparison. Though I can't believe my mother traveled over in a Primus ship." She huffs quietly. "She did warn the council—a few days ago, when it was too late to say no. They agreed, as long as the ship returns to Gaia once everyone is here, but still...it's not a good start."

"Yeah, that thing is incredibly creepy," I say, eyeing the ship. I can't fight the impression that it will come to life and swallow us at any moment.

"I'm not sure why she's so insistent on making everything more difficult. I just want..." She pauses and takes a deep breath. "I want this to go well. A visit of this scope between planets is unprecedented. History in the making. And if it goes smoothly..."

"It could change everything," I say, understanding.

She nods. "It could pave a new path for our system's future." Her voice is so small and so full of hope that I only resist pulling her against me because of a half-curious, half-disapproving glance from a councilman to my right. I settle for squeezing Shey's hand as the ramp of the alien ship opens and the Gaian officials emerge.

I'm not close enough to get a good look at the ship, which I can't help but be grateful for. Even from a distance, the alien craft freaks me out as much as those Primus statues back on Gaia. I shudder as a wave of air from the ship reaches me, oddly warm and moist like an exhaled breath. The one reason I manage not to physically recoil from the ship is that Shey's grip on my hand holds me at her side.

I follow her gaze to see President Leonis stepping out of the ship. When I glance at Shey again, her expression is tight and nervous. It's strange to see her so strongly affected by the sight of her own mother, knowing that she's been brave enough to sneak aboard a ship of criminals and stay upon a potentially doomed planet for the sake of her ideals. But I can't pretend that I don't understand. Facing down family is an entirely different beast.

"Hey, you can do this," I murmur to her. Her cheeks flush, and she shoots me an embarrassed smile.

"I know it's ridiculous to be scared, but…" She takes a deep breath. "She'll never forgive me."

"I get it." I rub a thumb over her hand, thinking of Momma, and all the things I never got to hear from her. "But she's a fool if she's not proud of you. And it doesn't matter what she thinks. You did good. You saved people. You know that, right?"

She smiles, squeezes my hand, and releases it.

"I do," she says with a tilt of her chin, summoning up her confidence once more. "I'm going to go talk to her before the peacekeepers come, and find my father." She swallows hard as she says it, but shows no other reaction. We both know what fate awaits the president here. I can't imagine what complicated feelings Shey is experiencing right now. She takes a step forward, but hesitates, glancing back at me. "Meet me on the beach in half an hour?"

My pulse stutters. I can't seem to manage a response, but she doesn't wait for one before slipping through the crowd to face her mother.

"Ah, stars," I mutter, running a hand through my hair and trying to calm my racing heart. I could really use a drink right now, but I've been doing my best to avoid being inebriated in front of my family. They have enough to worry about without realizing I still haven't quite shaken off that habit.

I glance around, wondering if anyone would notice if I wandered off to find some alcohol, and whether or not I'd be back in time to meet Pol as he comes out of the ship. None of the common citizens have emerged yet. If I run now, maybe—

"Captain Kaiser."

For one disorienting moment I half expect my mother to answer, but finally I remember the title refers to me. I turn toward the speaker, eyebrows lifting as I see a uniformed Gaian officer coming toward me. It takes me a moment to recognize the tall woman: Yvette Zinne, head of President Leonis's security, and the woman who arrested me and dragged me to jail back on Gaia. It feels like a lifetime ago, but I definitely remember her face. I throw on a strained smile as she stops a few feet in front of me. For a moment, she studies me, her expression difficult to read. And then, slowly, she holds her arms out, palms up, and bows her head to me.

I'm too shocked to react for a moment. I honestly might not have recognized this gesture if Shey hadn't shown it to me back on the ship. This grim-faced Gaian officer, part of the president's personal security, is formally apologizing to me. Or asking forgiveness. I've already forgotten the difference between the gestures, if there even really is one.

"I wish to express my deep gratitude and respect for saving my people and bringing peace to us all," she says, not breaking the pose. "And to apologize for underestimating you."

"I, uh..." I glance around, seeking Shey or someone else who can help me respond in a proper manner, but no one comes to my aid. I clear my throat, rubbing the back of my neck with one hand. "Thanks? I don't know how to, uh, do this, but...I accept."

Zinne lowers her hands and straightens up, meeting my eyes again.

"I've been looking after your brother personally," she says. "Both at Shey's request and out of personal gratitude."

My breath catches in my throat.

"Is he...?" I start, not even sure where the sentence is going. "Where?"

She smiles.

"Wait here," she says, and heads back to the ship.

I stay exactly where I am, shifting from foot to foot and craning my neck to see past the sea of Gaian politicians and Nibiran council members crowding around me on the dock. My heart thuds painfully.

I would hardly recognize Pol if not for the fact that Zinne is escorting him. He leans heavily on a pair of crutches as he moves toward us, sweat beading on his forehead and arms shaking from the effort. He pauses on the edge of the dock to catch his breath while Zinne waits patiently at his side. A moment later, he looks up and breaks into a grin. I follow his gaze to see Corvus standing a few yards away from him.

I push through the crowd until I find Drom, and tug on her arm. She's still searching the crowd, her brow furrowed, no doubt looking for someone quite a bit larger.

"What, what?" she asks, brushing my hand off. "Quit yanking at me."

"Look, idiot."

Drom follows my gaze, and her eyes go round.

"Don't break him!" I yell when she takes off in his direction. I make my way through the crowd as it splits in her wake. Halfway through, I become aware of Lyre at my elbow. Corvus is already at Pol's side, and they embrace and exchange a few words before Drom arrives and sweeps her twin up in a tight bear hug. For a moment I think I see something dark cross Corvus's face, but by the time I arrive he's smiling again and Pol is erupting in riotous laughter familiar enough to make my heart ache.

"Okay, okay, my turn!" I say, attempting to pull Drom away from her twin for a few seconds, but she's not so eager to give him up now that she has him back. It takes a few minutes of arguing for her to let go, releasing a breathless and stumbling Pol. I put an arm around him to steady him, and press my forehead to his. "Missed you, little brother."

He grins his broad grin at me. "Missed you, too."

"How was your vacation on Gaia?" I ask, a weak attempt at a joke, and his smile immediately fades and leaves something unreadable in its wake.

"It was loud," he says. "So many voices."

"What?"

"Here is quieter." He looks out over the waves beside us, and his brow furrows. The next words come out a mumble. "But... not silent."

Unsure what to make of that, I glance around to see if the others heard the odd words. But Corvus seems lost in thought, and Drom is saying something about pastries, and Lyre is still hanging back. When I look at her, she steps up to Pol with a hesitant smile. The darkness on Pol's face breaks as he reaches over to ruffle her curls.

"Hi, sis."

"Hi, Apollo." She takes his hand and presses it to her cheek. "Welcome back."

"Thanks." He looks around. "Can we, uh, get something to eat? Gaian food is—" He cuts off and grins as Drom produces no less than three slightly squished fish pastries from her pockets and shoves them at him.

I shake off the strangeness from earlier. We were prepared for Pol to be suffering from some aftereffects, and I'm sure it's nothing to be concerned about. No matter what comes next, we'll be strong enough to face it. We're together now.

I'm so caught up in the reunion with Pol that it takes me a while to remember Shey wanted to see me. A thrill of excitement goes through me at the thought of being alone with her again, after so much time.

"I'm gonna go find a bottle of something to celebrate with," I tell the others.

"Scorpia," Corvus says in a warning tone, and I hold up my hands in surrender.

"For you, I mean! Not for me. Jeez, have a little faith." I flash him a grin, though he looks unconvinced. "Be back soon." I squeeze Pol's shoulder one last time before slipping away.

The official meeting between the planets seems to be going well, and beyond the officials on the dock, a cautious but curious crowd of Nibirans is starting to form again. Despite their initial terror over the ship, more are daring to draw near now, craning their necks for a glimpse at the foreigners. Some of them are even carrying food or drink or other small gifts, and signs welcoming the newcomers, which makes my heart surge with hope. Leonis may be a liar and a vicious warmonger, but her people deserve a warm reception to their temporary new home.

The beach is quiet and empty but for a single figure standing just beyond the edge of the lapping water. Shey's face is turned toward the ocean, features lit by the red sun.

"Have to say, I'm a fan of this new Nibiran style of yours," I say as I walk closer, hands in my pockets, admiring the curves of her body beneath the rippling silk gown. The shoulders are still squared-off and Gaian, so the dress is a marriage of the two styles, but it's still a huge improvement. "Fits you much better than stuffy Gaian clothes."

As she turns to face me, no doubt with some prim retort ready on her tongue, I catch her face in my hands and kiss her. Her lips press eagerly against mine.

This time, there's no race against the clock, no impending danger. This isn't a single, stolen moment. This time, I kiss her like I have all the time in the world and am willing to give every second of it to her. I kiss her like she deserves to be kissed, like I've always wanted to do it. Quiet and patient, reveling in every moment. Shey's lips are soft against mine, her hand gentle as it brushes my cheek. But when she pulls away, her eyes are dewy with tears. My heart sinks as I realize why she really called me here. I pull my head back and stare at her. After a moment I sigh, brushing a tear away with one thumb.

"Shit," I murmur. "This is goodbye, isn't it? You're saying goodbye."

I always knew, deep down, that this moment would come. So why does it hurt so much?

"I'm sorry," Shey says. She speaks quietly, but sounds as composed as ever despite the tears. "I have my people to look after, and they certainly need looking after right now. And you have your family." She takes a deep, shaky breath. "I am truly grateful for the time we spent together, Scorpia. I will always remember it, and I will always be grateful that fate brought our paths together. But...we always knew they would separate again, didn't we? Our walks of life are too different."

I know she's right. This was inevitable. Still, the hurt wells up inside me, prickling the backs of my eyes. I push it down and force a half-hearted laugh.

"That's the most Gaian breakup line I've ever heard." I sigh and pull her toward me. She leans against me while I wrap my arms around her. "I care about you. You care about me. Why can't that be enough?"

"I wish it was." She rests her forehead against my shoulder. "Truly, I do. But it's never that simple."

"Well, it's bullshit." I lay my cheek on the top of her head.

A few minutes pass like that, while Shey's tears dry and I try to commit the feeling of her in my arms to memory. Then, with a quiet sigh, she pulls away. As much as it hurts, I let her go.

"They'll be expecting me back at the reception," she says. "I'm doing my best to smooth over relations between the council and the other officials, now that my mother's been taken into custody."

"You and your politics," I say, half smiling even as my heart twists. "Well, I've got a lot to do myself, anyway. Plenty of drinking to be done, maybe some petty theft. You know how it is."

"You and your debauchery," she teases back, her eyes crinkling at the corners. She takes my hand and gives it one final squeeze before releasing it. "You're a good person, Scorpia Kaiser," she says. "Safe travels."

For once, I can't bring myself to speak. She gives me one last, warm smile before leaving me alone.

The closer I get to the harbor, the more apparent it becomes that the reception is turning into a full-fledged celebration. The Gaian refugees are leaving the ship now, and the crowd of Nibirans has swelled. Though the Gaians seem timid, the Nibirans are eager to make them feel as welcome as possible—which, in their planet's terms, means lots of drinking and music and gifts. I half smile, thinking of how appalled the Gaians must be by it all, though I hope they can see that it's well-meaning.

But well-meaning or not, I'm no longer in the mood for celebrations. So I move past the party, sipping from the bottle I picked up after I left the beach, and head for the quiet docks on the other side.

To my surprise, I'm not alone there. I find Corvus sitting by himself at the end of a dock, far enough from the Gaian ship that the Nibirans have all abandoned it in favor of better spectator spots. He takes a long drink from a bottle and tilts his head back, staring up at the stars. The moment he notices me, he starts to move the bottle out of sight, but stops as he sees the one I'm already carrying. I settle down beside him with a sigh, and take another sip of my whiskey.

"Scorpia..." he starts, his voice more weary than angry.

"Don't. Please." He gives me a look, and I groan. "Look, I know, all right? I do. You can be mad at me tomorrow. For now, let's just...let's just not."

He's silent for a long moment.

"Tomorrow," he says, but caps his own bottle nonetheless. I glance at it and make a face.

"Vodka? Ugh."

"One of those nights."

"Yeah. Me too."

I don't ask, and neither does he. I don't bother inquiring about our younger siblings, either. They have each other, and they'll be fine for a night without us. Corvus and I sit shoulder-to-shoulder and enjoy the quiet, listening to the distant sounds of the continued celebration over at the harbor. My boots dangle off the edge of the dock and skim the water's surface.

It's been a long time since I had a moment like this. I thought it would be peaceful. Instead, the silence makes me more aware of the dull ache deep in my bones and the weight of all my losses on my shoulders. Now, I guess I have to add Shey to the list. I expected as much given the last few weeks, but that doesn't lessen the hurt.

"Wonder what Momma would think if she could see us now," I say, and smile wryly. I hold out my bottle and pour a bit of it into the ocean as I think of her. After a moment, Corvus uncaps his vodka to do the same. "Her kids being heroes. With medals and shit. Who would've thought?"

Corvus laughs, and I grin. The sound isn't as rare as it used to be, but still infrequent enough that every time reminds me how much I missed hearing it.

"She'd hate it," he says. "Stopping a war wasn't a very profitable decision."

"Who knows? With all of those Gaians to be transported and settled, maybe business will be booming." I pause, sigh, and lay back on the dock. "Would be booming, I mean. If we had a ship."

"We'll get a ship," Corvus says, more confidently than he has any right to be, considering the rareness of spacecrafts—let alone on Nibiru, of all places. I'm about to argue, but his smile stops me. "We always figure something out," he says.

"Yeah, yeah, yeah." I kick my feet restlessly, looking up at the stars and wishing I was up there rather than stuck down here. I'm already getting the itch. "Even if we do, it won't be the same as *Fortuna*."

"True." He glances down at me. "I'm sorry about that, by the way. We all loved that ship, but I know how much she meant to you."

"And she was finally mine," I sigh out. But after a moment, I shrug. "Whatever. Too many bad memories. Maybe it's for the best." I chew my bottom lip. "It was never really about the ship, anyway."

Corvus's eyebrows rise as he looks down at me.

"Huh. That was going to be my line."

"Gross, look what spending time with you does to me. Making me all introspective and shit." I groan and sit up, nudging his shoulder with mine. "Is *this* what all your brooding feels like? This is terrible. Why do you do this to yourself?"

"Better habit than drinking," he says.

"Agree to disagree."

I laugh. But as the sound fades away into silence, a somber mood settles over us. In the distance, the Gaians' alien ship slowly rises into the sky once more, hurrying off to shuttle the next wave of refugees over. I watch it disappear, quiet for a long while, until I can no longer keep down the question that's been eating away at me all night.

"What if we made things worse?" I can't meet Corvus's eyes, so I stare out at the water instead. "Lying about Leonis? Letting the Gaians come here? We still don't know what's really happening on their planet."

We tried so hard to be good, to help people, but I can't fight off the doubt that we haven't really made anything better. I can't help but feel that some huge, terrible thing has been set in motion, and everything we've done has only slowed it down...or maybe even done the opposite.

Whatever happened back on Gaia, I doubt Leonis is telling the full truth. She never does, and we know how dangerous she can be. What if we put the Nibirans in danger by letting the Gaians come here? What if we lost *Fortuna* and endangered our brother's life for nothing? What if the lives we saved will mean greater loss in the future? I let out a gusty sigh, splashing the toe of my boot across the water. So many questions, but only one really matters.

"Do you think we did the right thing?" I ask.

Corvus is silent for so long that I'm not sure he's ever going to answer.

"I don't know," he says, finally. "But we did our best."

I sigh and take another long swig. I want to drink more, or crack a joke, or do something to break this silence. But instead I set the bottle aside, lay my head against my brother's shoulder, and soak in the quiet.

We sit for a long while, him staring out at the rolling sea, me staring up at the stars that are out of my reach—for now. I don't know what comes next, but I do know that right now there's a celebration raging on a world that wouldn't exist without us, and whatever the future brings, we'll face it together. However long this peace may last, that's enough for me.

The story continues in . . .

The Nova Vita Protocol:
Book Two

Acknowledgments

Many thanks to:

My agent, Emmanuelle Morgen, who was enthusiastic about *Fortuna* from the very start and helped bring the heart of the story to the forefront. Thanks as well to Sanaa Ali-Virani for the insightful feedback, and the rest of the team at Stonesong.

My editor, Bradley Englert, who made the initial brilliant suggestion to add Corvus's POV and never stopped pushing for this to be the best book it could be; Lisa Marie Pompilio for the incredible cover design; and the rest of the ever-amazing Orbit team for all of their hard work.

Michelle Chaves, for giving incisive notes and talking me through my first-draft panic.

And, of course, my family. I love you all and am so grateful to have you in my life. Gramma: Thank you for always thinking of me despite the distance between us. Mama and Papa: Thank you for your constant support and excitement for my work. I promise that one day I'll write a book featuring parental figures who aren't terrible and/or dead! And lastly, Todd and Lucas: No matter how far apart we end up, I know we'll always find our way back together. This one's for you.

extras

orbit

meet the author

Photo Credit: SunStreet Photo

KRISTYN MERBETH is obsessed with SFF, food, video games, and her dog, and she resides in Tucson, Arizona.

interview

Where did the initial idea and plot for **Fortuna** *come from, and how did the story begin to take shape in your mind?*

The world came together first when I saw NASA's announcement about the discovery of potentially habitable planets in the TRAPPIST-1 system. Much of the basic details of Nova Vita are based off that system, including the red dwarf star and five planets in the habitable zone, which are close enough to see each other in the sky. The graphics NASA made, including a super cool fake travel poster about "planet hopping," really sparked my imagination. I started to imagine a water planet, an ice planet, a world overtaken by jungle, and more. But that universe remained in the back of my brain, interesting but unpopulated, for about a year. Until one day, when I was watching the show *Animal Kingdom* and thought: I would love to write about a family of criminals. When I mashed the two ideas together and came up with the concept of a family smuggling contraband between the close-together planets, *Fortuna* was born.

What were the challenges in developing this new system where humanity has found its home?

It was definitely challenging coming up with five different planets with distinct cultures and geographical traits, and making sure that they each come through clearly on the page.

In terms of the overall system, it was difficult at times to keep a clear image of a universe so different from the one I'm used to. The fact that the planets are tidally locked and it's always daytime tripped me up in the first draft; I kept envisioning scenes taking place at night, and had to remind myself it was always light out for Nova Vitans.

Did you do any specific research to build the technology and universe?

Lots of it! Though it's not my usual process, I put in quite a lot of research before I even began to write. Much of my early research revolved around what life would potentially look like in a system like TRAPPIST-1, including a red dwarf star and tidally locked planets. One of my favorite details was plants being black to absorb as much light as possible. When developing Devan flora, I researched strange plants that exist in our own world: for example, touch-me-nots, which have explosive seed pods, and the stinging tree that can cause painful rashes lasting upward of a year. And, while it only shows up briefly in this book, figuring out how an underwater prison would work was a bit headache inducing. I eventually based its structure off the designs for Dubai's Water Discus Underwater Hotel, and looked into the effects on divers of extended periods underwater.

Scorpia and Corvus have such vivid voices. How did you tackle making each of them sound so drastically different, especially using a first-person voice? Was one of them more difficult to write?

When I'm using a first-person POV, I want to get as deep into the character's head as possible and let them tell their own story. I approach it the same way I write dialogue, having the character's background and personality inform their distinct voices and verbal tendencies. For example, with Corvus's formal education and military background, he's more proper and favors short, straightforward sentences. Scorpia, on the other hand, is much more casual, can be occasionally rambling, and often peppers her narration with colloquialisms and profanity. Also, since Corvus's POV was a later addition to the manuscript (based on my editor's suggestion), I ended up having to swap some scenes from Scorpia's POV to his, which turned into a fun narrative exercise as I thought about how the two characters would view and describe the same set of events differently.

Scorpia's voice came to me more naturally, and her narration was also a part of the story's concept from the beginning. Corvus was more difficult to get the hang of writing, especially because I added him later in the drafting process. His early chapters on Titan were the last scenes I wrote in the first draft, but once I finally completed them, it gave me a much better grasp of what was going on inside his head.

How did you develop the dynamic between the Kaiser family? They all have their own important role on* Fortuna, *but they still have to navigate being a family. What was your process like while writing their relationship?

I'm a messy drafter and write quite a lot of material that doesn't make it into the end product. Here, I think, that really helped with fleshing out the various relationships in the family. I wrote pages of backstory that ended up distilled into flashbacks lasting only a few lines, one-on-one scenes between characters that didn't fit into the final narrative, long conversations that had to be cut short to keep the pacing even. Rather than being wasted words, it all contributed to building those family relationships. It was important to me to make sure each pair of siblings had their own unique dynamic, and that the relationships felt real and complex, since these characters have known each other for their entire lives.

Do you have a favorite scene in Fortuna? *If so, why?*

There were a lot of scenes I really loved writing. Scorpia's opening chapter, Corvus discovering the alien ship, the two of them meeting for the first time in three years, the final fight scenes... But I think my number one favorite scene is when the siblings return to *Fortuna* after the evacuation of Drev Dravaask. I loved writing the delicate balance of power between Scorpia and Corvus during those moments, before either one of them is "officially" in charge, and the stress as the twins race back to the ship. The scene has so many layers of tension, and it's also the first moment where Scorpia makes a big decision for the family. Everything that happens afterward is really the result of what happens there.

Who are some of your favorite writers, and how have they influenced your work?

Two of my favorite authors right now are Kameron Hurley and V. E. / Victoria Schwab. Both are incredible, unique, bold writers who taught me the importance of fully embracing your own personal brand of "weird" and injecting it into everything you write. I'm also a big fan of Paul Tremblay, whose deeply unsettling horror provides great examples of how to write tension and dread. Maggie Stiefvater and Holly Black both have such great characterization and dialogue, and influenced me to keep a good balance of darkness and fun. Margaret Atwood, Philip K. Dick, and Haruki Murakami are other old favorites of mine.

extras

When you're not writing, what do you like to do in your spare time?

Aside from reading a ton, I spend a lot of time playing video games and board games, and I have a weekly Dungeons & Dragons group that has been meeting for about two years now. I also love cooking, especially when I get to make big meals for my friends or family. I've also recently taken an interest in gardening and baking, though my attempts at both so far have had...well...mixed results at best. But I'm working on that!

Fortuna *is the first book in a trilogy. Without giving too much away, can you tell us what we can expect in the upcoming novels?*

Now that the Kaisers have garnered the attention of various planetary governments, they're going to find it's not so simple to return to the life of relative leisure (and casual crime) they're used to. The choices the Kaisers made throughout *Fortuna* have really shaken up both their family dynamic and the system at large, and they're going to have to deal with the consequences of that. There will also be plenty more of what I loved about this book: big fight scenes, family drama, and tough moral decisions. Plus, a deeper dive into the Primus and what exactly happened to them.

Finally, we have to ask, if you had the choice to visit any of the planets, which would it be?

Ooh, I'm going to have to go with Deva, as long as I get to stay in the Golden City and avoid the jungle. Nibiru would probably be a safer choice, but the food and whiskey call to me!

if you enjoyed

FORTUNA

look out for

A BIG SHIP AT THE EDGE OF THE UNIVERSE

The Salvagers: Book One

by

Alex White

A crew of outcasts tries to find a legendary ship before it falls into the hands of those who would use it as a weapon in this science fiction adventure series for fans of **The Expanse** *and* **Firefly.**

A washed-up treasure hunter, a hotshot racer, and a deadly secret society.

They're all on a race against time to hunt down the greatest warship ever built. Some think the ship is lost forever, some think it's been destroyed, and some think it's only a legend, but one thing's for certain: whoever finds it will hold the fate of the universe in their hands. And treasure that valuable can never stay hidden for long. . . .

Read the book that V. E. Schwab called "a clever fusion of magic and sci-fi. I was hooked from page one."

CHAPTER ONE

D.N.F.

The straight opened before the two race cars: an oily river, speckled yellow by the evening sun. They shot down the tarmac in succession like sapphire fish, streamers of wild magic billowing from their exhausts. They roared toward the turn, precision movements bringing them within centimeters of one another.

The following car veered to the inside. The leader attempted the same.

Their tires only touched for a moment. They interlocked, and sheer torque threw the leader into the air. Jagged chunks of duraplast glittered in the dusk as the follower's car passed underneath, unharmed but for a fractured front wing. The lead race car came down hard, twisting eruptions of elemental magic spewing from its wounded power unit. One of its tires exploded into a hail of spinning cords, whipping the road.

In the background, the other blue car slipped away down the chicane—Nilah's car.

The replay lost focus and reset.

The crash played out again and again on the holoprojection in front of them, and Nilah Brio tried not to sigh. She had seen plenty of wrecks before and caused more than her share of them.

"Crashes happen," she said.

"Not when the cars are on the same bloody team, Nilah!"

Claire Asby, the Lang Autosport team principal, stood at her mahogany desk, hands folded behind her back. The office looked less like the sort of ultramodern workspace Nilah had seen on other teams and more like one of the mansions of Origin, replete with antique furniture, incandescent lighting, stuffed big-game heads (which Nilah hated), and gargantuan landscapes from planets she had never seen. She supposed the decor favored a pale woman like Claire, but it did nothing for Nilah's dark brown complexion. The office didn't have any of the bright, human-centric design and ergonomic beauty of her home, but team bosses had to be forgiven their eccentricities—especially when that boss had led them to as many victories as Claire had.

Her teammate, Kristof Kater, chuckled and rocked back on his heels. Nilah rolled her eyes at the pretty boy's pleasure. They should've been checking in with the pit crews, not wasting precious time at a last-minute dressing down.

The cars hovering over Claire's desk reset and moved through their slow-motion calamity. Claire had already made them watch the footage a few dozen times after the incident: Nilah's car dove for the inside and Kristof moved to block. The incident had cost her half her front wing, but Kristof's track weekend had ended right there.

"I want you both to run a clean race today. I am begging you to bring those cars home intact at all costs."

Nilah shrugged and smiled. "That'll be fine, provided Kristof follows a decent racing line."

"We were racing! I made a legal play and the stewards sided with me!"

Nilah loved riling him up; it was far too easy. "You were slow, and you got what you deserved: a broken axle and a bucket of tears. I got a five-second penalty"—she winked before continuing—"which cut into my thirty-three-second win considerably."

Claire rubbed the bridge of her nose. "Please stop acting like children. Just get out there and do your jobs."

Nilah held back another jab; it wouldn't do to piss off the team boss right before a drive. Her job was to win races, not meetings. Silently she and Kristof made their way to the door, and he flung it open in a rare display of petulance. She hadn't seen him so angry in months, and she reveled in it. After all, a frazzled teammate posed no threat to her championship standings.

They made their way through the halls from Claire's exotic wood paneling to the bright white and anodized blues of Lang Autosport's portable palace. Crew and support staff rushed to and fro, barely acknowledging the racers as they moved through the crowds. Kristof was stopped by his sports psychologist, and Nilah muscled past them both as she stepped out into the dry heat of Gantry Station's Galica Speedway.

Nilah had fired her own psychologist when she'd taken the lead in this year's Driver's Crown.

She crossed onto the busy parking lot, surrounded by the bustle of scooter bots and crews from a dozen teams. The bracing rattle of air hammers and the roar of distant crowds in the grandstands were all the therapy she'd need to win. The Driver's Crown was so close—she could clinch it in two races, especially if Kristof went flying off the track again.

"Do you think this is a game?" Claire's voice startled her. She'd come jogging up from behind, a dozen infograms swimming around her head, blinking with reports on track conditions and pit strategy.

"Do I think racing is a game? I believe that's the very definition of sport."

Claire's vinegar scowl was considerably less entertaining than Kristof's anger. Nilah had been racing for Claire since the junior leagues. She'd probably spent more of her teenage years with her principal than her own parents. She didn't want to disappoint Claire, but she wouldn't be cowed, either. In truth, the incident galled her—the crash was nothing more than a callow attempt by Kristof to hold her off for another lap. If she'd lost the podium, she would've called for his head, but he got what he deserved.

They were a dysfunctional family. Nilah and Kristof had been racing together since childhood, and she could remember plenty of happy days trackside with him. She'd been ecstatic when they both joined Lang; it felt like a sign that they were destined to win.

But there could be only one Driver's Crown, and they'd learned the hard way the word "team" meant nothing among the strongest drivers in the Pan-Galactic Racing Federation. Her friendship with Kristof was long dead. At least her fondness for Claire had survived the transition.

"If you play dirty with him today, I'll have no choice but to create some consequences," said Claire, struggling to keep up with Nilah in heels.

Oh, please. Nilah rounded the corner of the pit lane and marched straight through the center of the racing complex, past the offices of the race director and news teams. She glanced back at Claire, who, for all her posturing, couldn't hide her worry.

"I never play dirty. I win because I'm better," said Nilah. "I'm not sure what your problem is."

"That's not the point. You watch for him today, and mind yourself. This isn't any old track."

Nilah got to the pit wall and pushed through the gate onto the starting grid. The familiar grip of race-graded asphalt on her shoes sent a spark of pleasure up her spine. "Oh, I know all about Galica."

The track sprawled before Nilah: a classic, a legend, a warrior's track that had tested the mettle of racers for a hundred years. It showed its age in the narrow roadways, rendering overtaking difficult and resulting in wrecks and safety cars—and increased race time. Because of its starside position on Gantry Station, ambient temperatures could turn sweltering. Those factors together meant she'd spend the next two hours slow-roasting in her cockpit at three hundred kilometers per hour, making thousands of split-second, high-stakes decisions.

This year brought a new third sector with more intricate corners and a tricky elevation change. It was an unopened present, a new toy to play with. Nilah longed to be on the grid already.

If she took the podium here, the rest of the season would be an easy downhill battle. There were a few more races, but the smart money knew this was the only one that mattered. The harmonic chimes of StarSport FN's jingle filled the stadium, the unofficial sign that the race was about to get underway.

She headed for the cockpit of her pearlescent-blue car. Claire fell in behind her, rattling off some figures about Nilah's chances that were supposed to scare her into behaving.

"Remember your contract," said Claire as the pit crew boosted Nilah into her car. "Do what you must to take gold, but any scratch you put on Kristof is going to take a million off your check. I mean it this time."

"Good thing I'm getting twenty mil more than him, then. More scratches for me!" Nilah pulled on her helmet. "You keep Kristof out of my way, and I'll keep his precious car intact."

She flipped down her visor and traced her mechanist's mark across the confined space, whispering light flowing from her fingertips. Once her spell cemented in place, she wrapped her fingers around the wheel. The system read out the stats of her sigil: good V's, not great on the Xi, but a healthy cast.

Her magic flowed into the car, sliding around the finely tuned ports, wending through channels to latch onto gears. Through the power of her mechanist's mark, she felt the grip of the tires and spring of the rods as though they were her own legs and feet. She joined with the central computer of her car, gaining psychic access to radio, actuation, and telemetry. The Lang Hyper 8, a motorsport classic, had achieved phenomenal performance all season in Nilah's hands.

Her psychic connection to the computer stabilized, and she searched the radio channels for her engineer, Ash. They ran through the checklist: power, fuel flow, sigil circuits, eidolon core. Nilah felt through each part with her magic, ensuring all functioned properly. Finally, she landed on the clunky Arclight Booster.

It was an awful little PGRF-required piece of tech, with high output but terrible efficiency. Nilah's mechanist side absolutely despised the magic-belching beast. It was as ugly and inelegant as it was expensive. Some fans claimed to like the little light show when it boosted drivers up the straights, but it was less than perfect, and anything less than perfect had to go.

"Let's start her up, Nilah."

"Roger that."

Every time that car thrummed to life, Nilah fell in love all over again. She adored the Hyper 8 in spite of the stonking flaw on his backside. Her grip tightened about the wheel and she took a deep breath.

The lights signaled a formation lap and the cars took off, weaving across the tarmac to keep the heat in their tires. They slipped around the track in slow motion, and Nilah's eyes traveled the third sector. She would crush this new track design. At the end of the formation lap, she pulled into her grid space, the scents of hot rubber and oil smoke sweet in her nose.

Game time.

The pole's leftmost set of lights came on: five seconds until the last light.

Three cars ahead of her, eighteen behind: Kristof in first, then the two Makina drivers, Bonnie and Jin. Nilah stared down the Makina R-27s, their metallic livery a blazing crimson.

The next pair of lights ignited: four seconds.

The other drivers revved their engines, feeling the tuning of their cars. Nilah echoed their rumbling engines with a shout of her own and gave a heated sigh, savoring the fire in her belly.

Three seconds.

Don't think. Just see.

The last light came on, signaling the director was ready to start the race.

Now, it was all about reflexes. All the engines fell to near silence.

One second.

The lights clicked off.

Banshee wails filled the air as the cars' power units screamed to life. Nilah roared forward, her eyes darting over the competition. Who was it going to be? Bonnie lagged by just a hair, and Jin made a picture-perfect launch, surging up beside Kristof.

Nilah wanted to make a dive for it but found herself forced in behind the two lead drivers.

They shot down the straight toward turn one, a double apex. Turn one was always the most dangerous, because the idiots fighting for the inside were most likely to brake too late. She swept out for a perfect parabola, hoping not to see some fool about to crash into her.

The back of the pack was brought up by slow, pathetic Cyril Clowe. He would be her barometer of race success. If she could lap him in a third of the race, it would be a perfect run.

"Tell race control I'm lapping Clowe in twenty-five," Nilah grunted, straining against the g-force of her own acceleration. "I want those blue flags ready."

"He might not like that."

"If he tries anything, I'll leave him pasted to the tarmac."

"You're still in the pack," came Ash's response. "Focus on the race."

Got ten seconds on the Arclight. Four-car gap to Jin. Turn three is coming up too fast.

Bonnie Hayes loomed large in the rearview, dodging left and right along the straight. The telltale flash of an Arclight Booster erupted on the right side, and Bonnie shot forward toward the turn. Nilah made no moves to block, and the R-27 overtook her. It'd been a foolish ploy, and faced with too much speed, Bonnie needed to brake too hard. She'd flat-spot her tires.

Right on cue, brake dust and polymer smoke erupted from Bonnie's wheels, and Nilah danced to the outside, sliding within mere inches of the crimson paint. Nilah popped through the gears and the car thrummed with her magic, rewarding her with a pristine turn. The rest of the pack was not so lucky.

Shredded fibron and elemental magic filled Nilah's rearview as the cars piled up into turn three like an avalanche. She had to keep her eyes on the track, but she spotted Guillaume's, Anantha's, and Bonnie's cars in the wreck.

"Nicely done," said Ash.

"All in a day's work, babes."

Nilah weaved through the next five turns, taking them exactly as practiced. Her car was water, flowing through the track along the swiftest route. However, Kristof and Jin weren't making things easy for her. She watched with hawkish intent and prayed for a slip, a momentary lockup, or anything less than the perfect combination of gear shifts.

Thirty degrees right, shift up two, boost... boost. Follow your prey until it makes a mistake.

Nilah's earpiece chirped as Ash said, "Kater's side of the garage just went crazy. He just edged Jin off the road and picked up half a second in sector one."

She grimaced. "Half a second?"

"Yeah. It's going to be a long battle, I'm afraid."

Her magic reached into the gearbox, tuning it for low revs. "Not at all. He's gambling. Watch what happens next."

She kept her focus on the track, reciting her practiced motions with little variance. The crowd might be thrilled by a half-second purple sector, but she knew to keep it even. With the increased tire wear, his car would become unpredictable.

"Kristof is in the run-off! Repeat: He's out in the kitty litter," came Ash.

"Well, that was quick."

She crested the hill to find her teammate's car spinning into the gravel along the run of the curve. She only hazarded a minor glance before continuing on.

"Switch to strat one," said Ash, barely able to contain herself. "Push! Push!"

"Tell Clowe he's mine in ten laps."

530

Nilah sliced through the chicane, screaming out of the turn with her booster aflame. She was a polychromatic comet, completely in her element. This race would be her masterpiece. She held the record for the most poles for her age, and she was about to get it for the most overtakes.

The next nine laps went well. Nilah handily widened the gap between herself and Kristof to over ten seconds. She sensed fraying in her tires, but she couldn't pit just yet. If she did, she'd never catch Clowe by the end of the race. His fiery orange livery flashed at every turn, tantalizingly close to overtake range.

"Put out the blue flags. I'm on Cyril."

"Roger that," said Ash. "Race control, requesting blue flags for Cyril Clowe."

His Arclight flashed as he burned it out along the straightaway, and she glided through the rippling sparks. The booster was a piece of garbage, but it had its uses, and Clowe didn't understand any of them. He wasn't even trying anymore, just blowing through his boost at random times. What was the point?

Nilah cycled through her radio frequencies until she found Cyril's. Best to tease him a bit for the viewers at home. "Okay, Cyril, a lesson: use the booster to make the car go faster."

He snorted on his end. "Go to hell, Nilah."

"Being stuck behind your slow ass is as close as I've gotten."

"Get used to it," he snapped, his whiny voice grating on her ears. "I'm not letting you past."

She downshifted, her transmission roaring like a tiger. "I hope you're ready to get flattened then."

Galica's iconic Paige Tunnel loomed large ahead, with its blazing row of lights and disorienting reflective tiles. Most racers would avoid an overtake there, but Nilah had been given an opportunity, and she wouldn't squander it. The outside stadium vanished as she slipped into the tunnel, hot on the Hambley's wing.

She fired her booster, and as she came alongside Clowe, the world's colors began to melt from their surfaces, leaving only drab black and white. Her car stopped altogether—gone from almost two hundred kilometers per hour to zero in the blink of an eye.

Nilah's head darkened with a realization: she was caught in someone's spell as surely as a fly in a spiderweb.

The force of such a stop should have powdered her bones and liquefied her internal organs instantly, but she felt no change in her body, save that she could barely breathe.

The world had taken on a deathly shade. The body of the Hyper 8, normally a lovely blue, had become an ashen gray. The fluorescent magenta accents along her white jumpsuit had also faded, and all had taken on a blurry, shifting turbulence.

Her neck wouldn't move, so she couldn't look around. Her fingers barely worked. She connected her mind to the transmission, but it wouldn't shift. The revs were frozen in place in the high twenty thousands, but she sensed no movement in the drive shaft.

All this prompted a silent, slow-motion scream. The longer she wailed, the more her voice came back. She flexed her fingers as hard as they'd go through the syrupy air. With each tiny movement, a small amount of color returned, though she couldn't be sure if she was breaking out of the spell—or into it.

"Nilah, is that you?" grunted Cyril. She'd almost forgotten about the Hambley driver next to her. All the oranges and yellows on his jumpsuit and helmet stood out like blazing bonfires, and she wondered if that's why he could move. But his car was the same gray as everything else, and he struggled, unsuccessfully, to unbuckle. Was Nilah on the cusp of the magic's effects?

"What..." she forced herself to say, but pushing the air out was too much.

532

"Oh god, we're caught in her spell!"

Whose spell, you git? "Stay...calm..."

She couldn't reassure him, and just trying to breathe was taxing enough. If someone was fixing the race, there'd be hell to pay. Sure, everyone had spells, but only a fool would dare cast one into a PGRF speedway to cheat. A cadre of wizards stood at the ready for just such an event, and any second, the dispersers would come online and knock this whole spiderweb down.

In the frozen world, an inky blob moved at the end of the tunnel. A creature came crawling along the ceiling, its black mass of tattered fabric writhing like tentacles as it skittered across the tiles. It moved easily from one perch to the next, silently capering overhead before dropping down in front of the two frozen cars.

Cyril screamed. She couldn't blame him.

The creature stood upright, and Nilah realized that it was human. Its hood swept away, revealing a brass mask with a cut-away that exposed thin, angry lips on a sallow chin. Metachroic lenses peppered the exterior of the mask, and Nilah instantly recognized their purpose—to see in all directions. Mechanists had always talked about creating such a device, but no one had ever been able to move for very long while wearing one; it was too disorienting.

The creature put one slender boot on Cyril's car, then another as it inexorably clambered up the car's body. It stopped in front of Cyril and tapped the helmet on his trembling head with a long, metallic finger.

Where are the bloody dispersers?

Cyril's terrified voice huffed over the radio. "Mother, please..."

Mother? Cyril's mother? No; Nilah had met Missus Clowe at the previous year's winner's party. She was a dull woman, like her loser son. Nilah took a closer look at the wrinkled sneer poking out from under the mask.

Her voice was a slithering rasp. "Where did you get that map, Cyril?"

"Please. I wasn't trying to double-cross anyone. I just thought I could make a little money on the side."

Mother crouched and ran her metal-encased fingers around the back of his helmet. "There is no 'on the side,' Cyril. We are everywhere. Even when you think you are untouchable, we can pluck you from this universe."

Nilah strained harder against her arcane chains, pulling more color into her body, desperate to get free. She was accustomed to being able to outrun anything, to absolute speed. Panic set in.

"You need me to finish this race!" he protested.

"We don't *need* anything from you. You were lucky enough to be chosen, and there will always be others. Tell me where you got the map."

"You're just going to kill me if I tell you."

Nilah's eyes narrowed, and she forced herself to focus in spite of her crawling fear. Kill him? What the devil was Cyril into?

Mother's metal fingers clacked, tightening across his helmet. "It's of very little consequence to me. I've been told to kill you if you won't talk. That was my only order. If you tell me, it's my discretion whether you live or die."

Cyril whimpered. "Boots...er...Elizabeth Elsworth. I was looking for...I wanted to know what you were doing, and she...she knew something. She said she could find the *Harrow*."

Nilah's gaze shifted to Mother, the racer's eye movements sluggish and sleepy despite her terror. *Elizabeth Elsworth?* Where had Nilah heard that name before? She had the faintest feeling that it'd come from the Link, maybe a show or a news piece. Movement in the periphery interrupted her thoughts.

The ghastly woman swept an arm back, fabric tatters falling away to reveal an armored exoskeleton encrusted with servo-motors and glowing sigils. Mother brought her fist down across Cyril's helmet, crushing it inward with a sickening crack.

Nilah would've begun hyperventilating, if she could breathe. This couldn't be happening. Even with the best military-grade suits, there was no way this woman could've broken Cyril's helmet with a mere fist. His protective gear could withstand a direct impact at three hundred kilometers per hour. Nilah couldn't see what was left of his head, but blood oozed between the cracked plastic like the yolk of an egg.

Just stay still. Maybe you can fade into the background. Maybe you can—

"And now for you," said Mother, stepping onto the fibron body of Nilah's car. Of course she had spotted Nilah moving in that helmet of hers. "I think my spell didn't completely affect you, did it? It's so difficult with these fast-moving targets."

Mother's armored boots rested at the edge of Nilah's cockpit, and mechanical, prehensile toes wrapped around the lip of the car. Nilah forced her neck to crane upward through frozen time to look at Mother's many eyes.

"Dear lamb, I am so sorry you saw that. I hate to be so harsh," she sighed, placing her bloody palm against Nilah's silver helmet, "but this is for the best. Even if you got away, you'd have nowhere to run. We own everything."

Please, please, please, dispersers... Nilah's eyes widened. She wasn't going to die like this. Not like Cyril. *Think. Think.*

"I want you to relax, my sweet. The journos are going to tell a beautiful story of your heroic crash with that fool." She gestured to Cyril as she said this. "You'll be remembered as the champion that could've been."

Dispersers scramble spells with arcane power. They feed into the glyph until it's over capacity. Nilah spread her magic over the car, looking for anything she could use to fire a pulse of magic: the power unit—drive shaft locked, the energy recovery system—too weak, her ejection cylinder—lockbolts unresponsive...then she remembered the Arclight Booster. She reached into it with her psychic connection, finding the arcane linkages foggy and dim. Something about the way this spell shut down movement even muddled her mechanist's art. She latched on to the booster, knowing the effect would be unpredictable, but it was Nilah's only chance. She tripped the magical switch to fire the system.

Nothing. Mother wrapped her steely hands around Nilah's helmet.

"I should twist instead of smash, shouldn't I?" whispered the old woman. "Pretty girls should have pretty corpses."

Nilah connected the breaker again, and the slow puff of arcane plumes sighed from the Arclight. It didn't want to start in this magical haze, but it was her only plan. She gave the switch one last snap.

The push of magical flame tore at the gray, hazy shroud over the world, pulling it away. An array of coruscating starbursts surged through the surface, and Nilah was momentarily blinded as everything returned to normal. The return of momentum flung Mother from the car, and Nilah was slammed back into her seat.

Faster and faster her car went, until Nilah wasn't even sure the tires were touching the road. Mother's spell twisted around the Arclight's, intermingling, destabilizing, twisting space and time in ways Nilah never could've predicted. It was dangerous to mix unknown magics—and often deadly.

She recognized this effect, though—it was the same as when she passed through a jump gate. She was teleporting.

A flash of light and she became weightless. At least she could breathe again.

She locked onto the sight of a large, windowless building, but there was something wrong with it. It shouldn't have been upside down as it was, nor should it have been spinning like that. Her car was in free fall. Then she slammed into a wall, her survival shell enveloping her as she blew through wreckage like a cannonball.

Her stomach churned with each flip, but this was far from her first crash. She relaxed and let her shell come to a halt, wedged in a half-blasted wall. Her fuel system exploded, spraying elemental energies in all directions. Fire, ice, and gusts of catalyzed gasses swirled outside the racer's shell.

The suppressor fired, and Nilah's bound limbs came free. A harsh, acrid mist filled the air as the phantoplasm caking Nilah's body melted into the magic-numbing indolence gasses. Gale-force winds and white-hot flames snuffed in the blink of an eye. The sense of her surrounding energies faded away, a sudden silence in her mind.

Her disconnection from magic was always the worst part about a crash. The indolence system was only temporary, but there was always the fear: that she'd become one of those dull-fingered wretches. She screwed her eyes shut and shook her head, willing her mechanist's magic back.

It appeared on the periphery as a pinhole of light—a tiny, bright sensation in a sea of gray. She willed it wider, bringing more light and warmth into her body until she overflowed with her own magic. Relief covered her like a hot blanket, and her shoulders fell.

But what had just murdered Cyril? Mother had smashed his head open without so much as a second thought. And Mother would know exactly who she was—Nilah's name was painted on every surface of the Lang Hyper 8. What if she came back?

The damaged floor gave way, and she flailed through the darkness, bouncing down what had to be a mountain of cardboard boxes. She came to a stop and opened her eyes to look around.

She'd landed in a warehouse somewhere she didn't recognize. Nilah knew every inch of the Galica Speedway—she'd been coming to PGRF races there since she was a little girl, and this warehouse didn't mesh with any of her memories. She pulled off her helmet and listened for sirens, for the banshee wail of race cars, for the roar of the crowd, but all she could hear was silence.

if you enjoyed
FORTUNA

look out for

ADRIFT

by

Rob Boffard

"An edge-of-the-seat epic of survival and adventure in deep space."
—*Gareth L. Powell, BSFA Award–winning author*

*Sigma Station. The ultimate luxury hotel, in the
far reaches of space.*

*For one small group, a tour of the Horsehead Nebula is meant to
be a short but stunning highlight in the trip of a lifetime.*

*But when a mysterious ship destroys Sigma Station and everyone
on it, suddenly their tourist shuttle is stranded.*

extras

*They have no weapons. No food. No water. No one
back home knows they're alive.*

And the mysterious ship is hunting them.

CHAPTER 1

Rainmaker's heads-up display is a nightmare.

The alerts are coming faster than she can dismiss them. Lock indicators. Proximity warnings. Fuel signals. Created by her neurochip, appearing directly in front of her.

The world outside her fighter's cockpit is alive, torn with streaking missiles and twisting ships. In the distance, a nuke detonates against a frigate, a baby sun tearing its way into life. The Horsehead Nebula glitters behind it.

Rainmaker twists her ship away from the heatwave, making it dance with precise, controlled thoughts. As she does so, she gets a full view of the battle: a thousand Frontier Scorpion fighters, flipping and turning and destroying each other in an arena bordered by the hulking frigates.

The Colony forces thought they could hold the area around Sigma Orionis—they thought they could take control of the jump gate and shut down all movement into this sector. They didn't bank on an early victory at Proxima freeing up a third of the Frontier Navy, and now they're backed into a corner, fighting like hell to stay alive.

Maybe this'll be the battle that does it. Maybe this is the one that finally stops the Colonies for good.

Rainmaker's path has taken her away from the main thrust of the battle, out towards the edge of the sector. Her targeting systems find a lone enemy: a black Colony fighter, streaking towards her. She's about to fire when she stops, cutting off the thought.

Something's not right.

"Control, this is Rainmaker." Despite the chaos, her voice is calm. "I have locked on incoming. Why's he alone? Over."

The reply is clipped and urgent. "Rainmaker, this is Frontier Control: evade, evade, evade. *Do not engage.* You have multiple bogies closing in on your six. They're trying to lock the door on you, over."

Rainmaker doesn't bother to respond. Her radar systems were damaged earlier in the fight, and she has to rely on Control for the bandits she can't see. She breaks her lock, twisting her craft away as more warnings bloom on her console. "Twin, Blackbird, anybody. I've got multiples inbound, need a pickup, over."

The sarcastic voice of one of her wingmen comes over the comms. "Can't handle 'em yourself? I'm disappointed."

"Not a good time, Omen," she replies, burning her thrusters. "Can you help me or not? Over."

"Negative. Got three customers to deal with over here. Get in line."

A second, older voice comes over her comms. "Rainmaker, this is Blackbird. What's your twenty? Over."

Her neurochip recognises the words, both flashing up the info on her display and automatically sending it to Blackbird's. "Quadrant thirty-one," she says anyway, speaking through gritted teeth.

"Roger," says Blackbird. "I got 'em. Just sit tight. I'll handle it for y—. Shit, I'm hit! I—"

"Eric!" Rainmaker shouts Blackbird's real name, her voice so loud it distorts the channel. But he's already gone. An impactor streaks past her, close enough for her to see the launch burns on its surface.

"Control, Rainmaker," she says. "Confirm Blackbird's position, I've lost contact!"

Control doesn't reply. Why would they? They're fighting a thousand fires at once, advising hundreds of Scorpion fighters. Forget the callsigns that command makes them use: Blackbird is a number to them, and so is she, and unless she does something right now, she's going to join him.

She twists her ship, forcing the two chasing Colony fighters to face her head-on. They're a bigger threat than the lone one ahead. Now, they're coming in from her eleven and one o'clock, curving towards her, already opening fire. She guns the ship, aiming for the tiny space in the middle, racing to make the gap before their impactors close her out.

"Thread the needle," she whispers. "Come on, thread the needle, thr—"

Everything freezes.

The battle falls silent.

And a blinking-red error box appears above one of the missiles.

"Oh. Um." Hannah Elliott's voice cuts through the silence. "Sorry, ladies and gentlemen. One second."

The box goes away—only to reappear a split second later, like a fly buzzing back to the place it was swatted. This time, the simulation gives a muted *ding*, as if annoyed that Hannah can't grasp the point.

She rips the slim goggles from her head. She's not used to them—she forgot to put her lens in after she woke up, which meant she had to rely on the VR room's antiquated backup system. A strand of her long red hair catches on the strap, and she has to yank it loose, looking down at the ancient console in front of her.

"Sorry, ladies and gentlemen," she says again. "Won't be a minute."

Her worried face is reflected on the dark screen, her freckles making her look even younger than she is. She uses her finger this time, stabbing at the box's confirm button on the small access terminal on the desk. It comes back with a friend, a second, identical error box superimposed over the first. Beyond it, an impactor sits frozen in Rainmaker's viewport.

"Sorry." *Stop saying sorry.* She tries again, still failing to bring up the main menu. "It's my first day."

Stony silence. The twenty tourists in the darkened room before her are strapped into reclining motion seats with frayed belts. Most have their eyes closed, their personal lenses still displaying the frozen sim. A few are blinking, looking faintly annoyed. One of them, an older man with a salt-and-pepper beard, catches Hannah's eye with a scowl.

She looks down, back at the error boxes. She can barely make out the writing on them—the VR's depth of field has made the letters as tiny as the ones on the bottom line of an eye chart.

She should reset the sim. But how? Does that mean it will start from scratch? Can she fast-forward? The supervisor who showed it to her that morning was trying to wrangle about fifteen new tour guides, and the instructions she gave amounted to watching the volume levels and making sure none of the tourists threw up when Rainmaker turned too hard.

Hannah gives the screen an experimental tap, and breathes a sigh of relief when a menu pops up: a list of files. There. Now she just has to—

But which one is it? The supervisor turned the sim on, and Hannah doesn't know which file she used. Their names are meaningless.

She taps the first one. Bouncy music explodes from the room's speakers, loud enough to make a couple of the tourists jump. She pulls the goggles back on, to be greeted by an animated, space-suited lizard firing lasers at a huge, tentacled alien. A booming voice echoes across the music. "Adventurers! Enter the world of Reptar as he saves the galaxy from—"

Hannah stops Reptar saving the galaxy. In the silence that follows, she can feel her cheeks turning red.

She gives the screen a final, helpless look, and leaps to her feet. She'll figure this out. Somehow. They wouldn't have given her this job if they didn't think she could deal with the unexpected.

"OK!" She claps her hands together. "Sorry for the mix-up. I think there's a bit of a glitch in the old sim there."

Her laugh gets precisely zero reaction. Swallowing, she soldiers on.

"So, as you saw, that was the Battle of Sigma Orionis, which took place fifteen years ago, which would be…" She thinks hard. "2157, in the space around the hotel we're now in. Hopefully our historical sim gave you a good idea of the conditions our pilots faced—it was taken directly from one of their neurochip feeds.

"Coincidentally, the battle took place almost exactly a hundred years after we first managed to send a probe through a wormhole, which, as you…which fuelled the Great Expansion, and led to the permanent, long-range gates, like the one you came in on."

"We know," says the man with the salt-and-pepper beard. He reminds Hannah of a particularly grumpy high school teacher she once had. "It was in the intro you played us."

"Right." Hannah nods, like he's made an excellent point. She'd forgotten about the damn intro video, her jump-lag from the day before fuzzing her memory. All she can remember is a voiceover that was way, way too perky for someone discussing a battle as brutal as Sigma Orionis.

She decides to keep going. "So, the...the Colonies lost that particular fight, but the war actually kept going for five years after the Frontier captured the space around Sigma."

They know this already, too. Why is she telling them? Heat creeps up her cheeks, a sensation she does her best to ignore.

"Anyway, if you've got any questions about the early days of the Expansion, while we were still constructing the jump gates, then I'm your girl. I actually did my dissertation on—"

Movement, behind her. She turns to see one of the other tour guides, a big dude with a tribal tattoo poking out of the collar of his red company shirt.

"Oh, thank God," Hannah hisses at him. "Do you know how to fix the sim?"

He ignores her. "OK, folks," he says to the room, smooth and loud. "That concludes our VR demonstration. Hope you enjoyed it, and if you have any questions, I'll be happy to answer them while our next group of guests are getting set up."

Before Hannah can say anything, he turns to her, his smile melting away. "Your sim slot was over five minutes ago. Get out of here."

He bends down, and with an effortless series of commands, resets the simulator. As the tourists file out, the bearded man glances at her, shaking his head.

Hannah digs in her back pocket, her face still hot and prickly. "Sorry. The sim's really good, and I got kind of wrapped up in it, so..." She says the words with a smile, which fades as the other guide continues to ignore her.

She doesn't even know what she's doing—the sim wasn't good. It was creepy. Learning about a battle was one thing—actually being there, watching people get blown to pieces...

Sighing, she pulls her crumpled tab out of her pocket and unfolds it. Her schedule is faithfully written out on it, copied off her lens—a habit she picked up when she was a kid, after her mom's lens glitched and they missed a swimming trial. "Can you tell me how to get to the dock?"

The other guide glances at the outdated tab, his mouth forming a moue of distaste. "There should be a map on your lens."

"Haven't synced it to the station yet." She's a little too embarrassed to tell him that it's still in its solution above the tiny sink in her quarters, and she forgot to go back for it before her shift started.

She would give a kidney to go back now, and not just for the lens. Her staff cabin might be small enough for her to touch all four walls at once without stretching, but it has a bed in it. With *sheets*. They might be scratchy and thin and smell of bleach, but the thought of pulling them over her head and drifting off is intoxicating.

The next group is pushing inside the VR room, clustered in twos and threes, eyeing the somewhat threadbare motion seats. The guide has already forgotten Hannah, striding towards the incoming tourists, booming a welcome.

"Thanks for your help," Hannah mutters, as she slips out of the room.

The dock. She was there yesterday, wasn't she? Coming off the intake shuttle. How hard could it be to find a second time? She turns right out of the VR room, heading for where she thinks the main station atrium is. According to her tab, she isn't late, but she picks up her pace all the same.

The wide, gently curved walkway is bordered by a floor-to-ceiling window taller than the house Hannah grew up in. The space is packed with more tourists. Most of them are clustered at the apex, admiring the view dominated by the Horsehead Nebula.

Hannah barely caught a glimpse when they arrived last night, which was filled with safety briefings and room assignments and roster changes and staff canteen conversations that were way too loud. She had sat at a table to one side, both hoping that someone would come and talk to her, and hoping they wouldn't.

In the end, with something like relief, she'd managed to slink off for a few hours of disturbed sleep.

The station she's on used to be plain old Sigma XV—a big, boring, industrial mining outpost that the Colony and the Frontier fought over during the war. They still did mining here—helium-3, mostly, for fusion reactors—but it was now also known as the Sigma Hotel and Luxury Resort.

It always amazed Hannah just how quickly it had all happened. It felt like the second the war ended, the tour operators were lobbying the Frontier Senate for franchise rights. Now, Sigma held ten thousand tourists, who streamed in through the big jump gate from a dozen different worlds and moons, excited to finally be able to travel, hoping for a glimpse of the Neb.

Like the war never happened. Like there weren't a hundred different small conflicts and breakaway factions still dotted across both Frontier *and* Colonies. The aftershocks of war, making themselves known.

Not that Sigma Station was the only one in on the action. It was happening everywhere—apparently there was even a tour company out Phobos way that took people inside a wrecked Colony frigate which hadn't been hauled back for salvage yet.

As much as Hannah feels uncomfortable with the idea of setting up a hotel here, so soon after the fighting, she needs this job. It's the only one her useless history degree would get her, and at least it means that she doesn't have to sit at the table at her parents' house on Titan, listening to her sister talk about how fast her company is growing.

The walkway she's on takes a sharp right, away from the windows, opening up into an airy plaza. The space is enormous, climbing up ten whole levels. A glittering light fixture the size of a truck hangs from the ceiling, and in the centre of the floor there's a large fountain, fake marble cherubs and dragons spouting water streams that criss-cross in midair.

The plaza is packed with more tourists, milling around the fountain or chatting on benches or meandering in and out of the shops and restaurants that line the edges. Hannah has to slow down, sorry-ing and excuse-me-ing her way through.

The wash of sensations almost overwhelms her, and she can't help thinking about the sheets again. White. Cool. Light enough to slide under and—

No. Come on. Be professional.

Does she go left from here, or is it on the other side of the fountain? Recalling the station map she looked at while they were jumping is like trying to decipher something in Sanskrit. Then she sees a sign above one of the paths leading off the plaza. *Ship Dock B.* That's the one.

Three minutes later, she's there. The dock is small, a spartan mustering area with four gangways leading out from the station to the airlock berths. There aren't many people around, although there are still a few sitting on benches. One of them, a little girl, is asleep: curled up with her hands tucked between shoulder and cheek, legs pulled up to her chest. Her mom—or the person Hannah thinks is her mom—sits next to her, blinking at something on her lens.

There are four tour ships visible through the glass, brightly lit against the inky black. Hannah's been on plenty of tours, and she still can't help thinking that every ship she's ever been on is ugly as hell. She's seen these ones before: they look like flattened, upside-down elephant droppings, a bulbous protrusion sticking out over each of the cockpits.

Hannah jams her hand in her jeans pocket for the tab. She wrote the ship's name for the shift in tiny capitals next to the start time: RED PANDA. Her gaze flicks between the four ships, but it takes her a second to find the right one. The name is printed on the side in big, stencilled letters, with a numbered designation in smaller script underneath.

She looks from the *Panda* to its gangway. Another guide is making his way onto it. He's wearing the same red shirt as her, and he has the most fantastic hair: a spiked purple mohawk at least a foot high.

Her tab still in hand, she springs onto the gangway. "Hey!" she says, forcing a confidence she doesn't feel into her voice. "I'm on for this one. Anything I need to know?"

Mohawk guy glances over his shoulder, an expression of bored contempt on his face. He keeps walking, his thick black boots booming on the metal plating.

"Um. Hi?" Hannah catches up to him. "I think this one's mine?"

She tries to slip past him, but he puts up a meaty hand, blocking her path. "Nice try, rook," he says, that bored look still on his face. "You're late. Shift's mine."

"What are you talking about?" She swipes a finger across her tab, hunting for the little clock.

"Don't you have a lens?"

This time it takes Hannah a lot more effort to stay calm. "There," she says, pointing at her schedule. "I'm not late. I'm supposed to be on at eleven, and it's..." she finds the clock in the corner of her tab. "Eleven-o-two."

"My *lens* says eleven-o-six. Anyway, you're still late. I get the shift."

"What? No. Are you serious?"

He ignores her, resuming his walk towards the airlock. As he does, Hannah remembers the words from the handbook the company sent her before she left Titan: *Guides who are late for their shift will lose it. Please try not to be late!!!*

He can't do this. He can't. But who are the crew chiefs going to believe? The new girl? She'll lose a shift on her first day, which means she's already in the red, which means that maybe they don't keep her past her probation. A free shuttle ride back to Titan, and we wish you all the best in your future endeavours.

Anger replaces panic. This might not be her dream job, but it's work, and at the very least it means she's going *somewhere* with her life. She can already see the faces of her parents when she tells them she lost her job, and that is not going to happen. Not ever.

"Is that hair growing out of your ears, too?" she says, more furious than she's been in a long time. "I said I'm *here*. It's *my shift*."

He turns to look at her, dumbfounded. "What did you just say?"

Hannah opens her mouth to return fire, but nothing comes out.

Her mom and dad would know. Callista definitely would. Her older sister would understand exactly how to smooth things over, make this asshole see things her way. Then again, there's no way either her parents or Callie would ever have taken a job like this, so they wouldn't be in this situation. They're not here now, and they can't help her.

"It's all right, Donnie," says a voice.

Hannah and Mohawk guy—Donnie—turn to see the supervisor walking up. She's a young woman, barely older than Hannah, with a neat bob of black hair and a pristine red shirt. Hannah remembers meeting her last night, for about two seconds, but she's totally blanking on her name. Her gaze automatically goes to the woman's breast pocket, and she's relieved to see a badge: *Atsuke*.

"Come on, boss," Donnie says. "She was late." He glances at Hannah, and the expression on his face clearly says that he's just getting started.

"I seem to remember you being late on *your* first day." Atsuke's voice is pleasant and even, like a newsreader's.

"*And*," Donnie says, as if Atsuke hadn't spoken. "She was talking bakwas about my hawk. Mad disrespectful. I've been here a lot longer than she has, and I don't see why—"

"Well, to be fair, Donnie, your hair *is* pretty stupid. Not to mention against regs. I've told you that, like, ten times."

Donnie stares at her, shoulders tight. In response, Atsuke raises a perfectly shaped eyebrow.

He lets out a disgusted sigh, then shoves past them. "You got lucky, rook," he mutters, as he passes Hannah.

Her chest is tight, like she's just run a marathon, and she exhales hard. "Thank you *so* much," she says to Atsuke. "I'm really sorry I was late—I thought I had enough time to—"

"Hey." Atsuke puts a hand on her shoulder. "Take a breath. It's fine."

Hannah manages a weak smile. Later, she is going to buy Atsuke a drink. Multiple drinks.

"It's an easy one today," Atsuke says. "Eight passengers. Barely a third of capacity. Little bit about the station, talk about the war, the treaty, what we got, what the Colonies got, the role Sigma played in everything, get them gawking at the Neb…twenty minutes, in and out. Square?"

She looks down at Hannah's tab, then glances up with a raised eyebrow.

"My lens is glitching," Hannah says.

"Right." This time, Atsuke looks a little less sure. She reaches in her shirt pocket, and hands Hannah a tiny clip-on mic. "Here. Links to the ship automatically. You can pretty much just start talking. And listen: just be cool. Go do this one, and then there'll be a coffee waiting for you when you get back."

Forget the drink. She should take out another loan, buy Atsuke shares in the touring company. "I will. I mean, yeah. You got it."

Atsuke gestures to the airlock at the far end of the gangway. "Get going. And if Volkova gives you any shit, just ignore her. Have fun."

Hannah wants to ask who Volkova is, but Atsuke is already heading back, and Hannah doesn't dare follow. She turns, and marches as fast she can towards the *Red Panda*'s airlock.